the elm stone saga

haunted

morgansen

Haunted

Published by Ouroborus Book Services
www.ouroborusbooks.com

Cover design by Sabrina RG Raven
www.sabrinargraven.com

In adoring memory of Missie, who chose me.
2001-2019

Also by Shayla Morgansen

The Elm Stone Saga
Chosen (2014)
Scarred (2015)
Unbidden (2016)

prologue

It should have been a straightforward surgery. She was good –
very good. It helped to be a sorcerer and Healer of great ability,
of course, but so too was she simply an excellent surgeon. A
hard worker at medical school. A devoted professional since
her internship here at the Royal London. A steady hand and
keen eye. Years and years of experience.

'Heart rate's up,' Miranda stated calmly, hands buried in
the open chest of her patient. He was undergoing a standard
coronary artery bypass and everything was progressing
perfectly normally. 'What do we do?'

Her intern, Josie, was assisting for the first time, and
glanced back at the beeping monitor to read the numbers on
the display. She bit her lip nervously, alarmed by the noise; to
Miranda, experienced surgeon and high priestess of the
world's largest magical nation, it was all perfectly minor and
perfectly manageable. Distantly, beyond this operating theatre
full of nurses, doctors and anaesthetists, her mind was
connected to the telepathic circle of consciousnesses that were
her twelve superhuman colleagues. Sorcerers like herself, they
were the best of any that could be found, anywhere in the
White Elm nation – Seers of the future, Displacers who could
teleport with incredible accuracy, scriers of actual events past
and present, Telepaths, and other Healers like Miranda. When
they had a problem, it was worth panicking about, but an
elevated heart rate, here, now, could so easily be managed.

Far away and deliberately tuned out from their frenzied

discussion, the way a radio could be tuned in and out of a channel, Miranda knew that the council *did* have a problem, but her hands were in a man's chest, holding his heart, prepared to stop it and reroute his bloodstream through a series of machines so she could operate on it safely. There was nothing she could gain for anyone by listening to the council. She couldn't help. She could only stay focused on what she was doing. This was important work, too.

Josie pulled herself together. She knew this. Miranda knew she did.

'Uh, we need to give him–'

She didn't hear the rest.

Miranda had experienced loss before, seen death, touched it, held it, but from across the world, Anouk's death ripped at her and she gasped, shock radiating through her. Like a physical injury, tearing with pain, a sudden emptiness opened up in her mind where her telepathic colleague and friend had been just a second earlier. And it was like she reached into the chasm after her but closed her grip on only cold and nothing. She squeezed her eyes shut and winced against the sudden tumult of horrified voices in her head.

NO!

Anouk! Who else was with her?

Renatus and Aristea! I can't hear him. Can anyone else hear him? He's not responding to me. Is he alright?

Renatus? Report in!

Qu'est-il arrivé ? What has happened?!

'Dr Rhode?!'

She ignored the voices in the room with her as she tried to blink away the tears of disbelief that had sprung unbidden to her eyes and reached clumsily with her mind for the collective of voices in her head. The council. From all over the planet, they reacted as one, crying out for their friend and demanding answers.

What happened?! she asked the circle, and heard her usually calm, steady mental voice convey itself shakily into the chaotic telepathic conversation. At first no one responded to her. *How did this happen?*

They were in Prague, Lady Miranda, one of her senior councillors, Qasim, reported stiffly. *We have lost Anouk and possibly some civilians. There was an explosive event. Magnus Moira seem to have been involved. We can't contact Renatus. They were there with her.*

They? Miranda asked bleakly, opening her eyes and staring blankly into the red of her patient's incision, at the worried hands grasping and steadying her wrists. But she already knew the answer. Young scrier Renatus was capable of taking care of himself, and she would have said the same of Russian Telepath, Anouk, but Renatus's apprentice, Aristea, was an untested element in an already unpredictable scenario. She wasn't even old enough to be a junior member of the White Elm.

And they'd now misplaced her somewhere in central Europe amongst members of the enemy in the middle of an 'explosive event', whatever that was meant to be, that had killed at least one highly competent White Elm agent. The teenager could be dead.

Anouk *was* dead.

'Dr Rhode, are you alright?'

Josie's concerned voice got through the mental voices and Miranda looked up and around the operating theatre. All eyes were wide and worried and on her. She became aware of the thick, slow progression of time, the blur of her familiar staff's faces, the gluey echo of nearby sounds, and the floaty, ungrounded sensation of her whole body. The numbness. The fact that she had forgotten that her hands were on a patient's heart muscle.

The fact that those hands were *shaking*.

Shock. She'd seen it enough to be able to diagnose herself. Forcibly she grounded her attention back into her own body, in this time, in this place, shutting her eyes tightly again. She could not perform this surgery. She needed to get out of here.

'I, uh... Migraine,' she claimed unevenly. She swallowed; her throat was dry. *Anouk...* 'I think I have a migraine. Can someone...?'

Dr Bellucci nodded and stepped up to carefully take the heart from her, and she slid her wobbly hands from the chest and backed away. Her gloves and the sleeves of her robe were grimy with blood. Was Anouk's death bloody? No doubt soon someone would find the body and project the gruesome images to the rest of the council. Miranda was almost sick at the thought of her friend, just alive and well *minutes before*, as a 'body'.

She kept waiting for the black hole in her mind to fill and for Anouk's dry voice to jump in and explain she was only cut out by some dark blocking spell. She kept waiting.

Has anyone got eyes on the situation? I can't get to them!
I'm nearby. All I can hear is screaming! What's going on?
What just happened?!

Miranda staggered to the door and shouldered through to the sinks. She peeled off her gloves as quickly as they would come off and tore the operating gown over her head. She tossed everything into the bin in the corner and went to work scrubbing her hands under the tap, focusing on her breathing. In, out, get a grip.

Anouk was gone. Ten years on the White Elm council against the wishes of most of the people she knew, and now she had paid for her service with the ultimate cost. Miranda couldn't begin to consider the massive consequences this particular loss would mean for the council's political position, not right now; instead she watched the water pour over her hands, grounding herself back in the present moment.

Anouk, dead.

Renatus, missing in action.

Aristea, at risk.

Councillors, in a panic.

Lord Gawain, her co-leader? She could hear his voice among the others, trying to get things organised, trying to work out what was going on. He could use her help. She had already failed the patient but Dr Bellucci would see to it that he got the proper care. She had nothing else scheduled. No one would question it if she disappeared now after claiming a migraine.

She turned off the faucet and called for the attention of one of her magical colleagues, one of those better at Displacement than she was. In this state of shock, teleportation became an even less exact science. The reply was unexpected.

Miranda! Help, I need you!

Renatus? He was alive, at least, though she'd never heard his mental voice so strained and distressed. Was he hurt, too? Aristea? How was she going to get to them? She would have to risk an inaccurate Displacement.

Now, Miranda! Please!

The young councillor went suddenly from being a loud voice in her head to being a strong and obvious presence downstairs. He'd come to her. He'd *never* come to her, asked anything of her, wanted anything from her, arrogantly self-sufficient as he was. This fact, and the stress of his plea, cut through the numbness and she burst from the antechamber with her heart in her throat. He was *there*, in Prague – did he have Anouk's body? Had she survived? No – only a death felt like a death. But perhaps she could be revived? Was it just her heart that had stopped? A stilled heart could sometimes be restarted… But after so many minutes… Miranda didn't dare to hope. She just ran.

Miranda!!

The commotion in the foyer was obvious long before she saw it. Doctors and nurses ran either to or from it. She saw Lucia, a paediatric nurse just arrived for her shift, peering worriedly through the door. The door held open, the frantic shouting was perfectly audible.

'Someone get him under control. Did anyone see where he came from?'

'Just listen to me, I need to find Dr Miranda Rhode. I know she's here. I need–'

'Sir, just let us–'

'*No!* I need Dr Rhode. *Miranda! Help!*'

'Miranda,' Lucia called tersely when she spotted the surgeon hurrying towards her, 'there's some guy demanding to see you–'

'Is he hurt?' Miranda asked, voice as clipped and calm as ever, the shakiness of a minute before disguised behind professionalism. The nurse shook her head slowly, glancing back into the foyer uneasily and standing back for her.

'Don't think so.' Lucia held the door open for her. 'There's blood all over him but I think it's the girl's.'

Miranda never froze up at work but today was a special case, and the scene that greeted her was not one she could have prepared herself for. Renatus and Aristea belonged in Lady Miranda's life – the foyer of London's Royal Hospital was Dr Rhode's. Yet here in that foyer stood Renatus, white and stricken, with Aristea's motionless form cradled protectively in his arms and blood dripping all over the floor as he kept her out of reach of worried doctors. She'd never seen him like he was now.

The most powerful sorcerer known to the White Elm, all of twenty-two and with only a loose concept of restraint at the best of times, in a state of absolute panic and tensed ready to explode with enough magic to tear a hole through the floor and walls of the hospital if it helped get him the attention he wanted. The air around him wavered like the haze of heat. The whole room tingled with the inevitable.

'Just help us!' he shouted, backing away from the hospital staff like a caged animal. Staff and security not trying to approach him were speaking hurriedly into phones and drawing other patients away from the drama. 'She needs Dr Rhode *right now.*'

His wildly seeking gaze found her just as she started forward again. His relief was almost tangible, as was the immediate drop in magical energy building in the room. He exhaled and stumbled toward her, shouldering past frightened doctors.

'Miranda…'

For all his shouting to get her here, Renatus now seemed lost for words as he brought his apprentice closer for her to inspect. She felt her stomach clench at the sight of the girl and understood why he had not waited for help to arrive onsite.

6

Aristea's pretty features were totally obscured by blood, pumping steadily from a deep, jagged gash along the left side of her face. Cuts could be closed, but eyes could not be regrown if punctured. Was her eye still there? The position of the cut made it seem very unlikely, and the volume of blood and displaced tissue made it impossible to know for sure.

She raised a tentative hand over the injury and yanked it away when a spark of crackly black energy ran the length of the cut. She sensed the stain of Lisandro's magic, his specific signature as a Crafter. She shuddered, feeling cold. How had the dangerous renegade her whole council had been unable to find for almost a year managed to get *this close* to Aristea? Was her former colleague and brother responsible for Anouk as well?

'Renatus, what happened?' It was hardly relevant now, but the question was automatic. She remembered the presence of a dozen ordinary citizens, none of whom knew magic existed, all of them watching cautiously. She shifted to obstruct their view as another ominous shock of black lightning ran up and down the cut like electrified stitches. 'Actually, don't answer that. It was a hunting accident.'

'In London?' Lucia asked sceptically. Miranda nodded brusquely, thinking fast.

Someone, a patient across the foyer, pointed and raised his voice. 'What's that on her face?'

No time to think. Miranda waved the other staff away before they could get a good enough look to answer, gathering her wits in spite of the numbness in her senses and the chaotic activity in her head.

'I need an operating theatre immediately,' she said, pushing Renatus to get him walking back in the direction she'd come. 'I need... I need...'

She faltered as she considered who to bring in with her. Most of her usual team were privy to or accustomed to her random acts of medical miracles, but they were all either in theatre with the bypass patient or off work this afternoon. The rest of the hospital's doctors were excellent but *not* sorcerers,

7

and might object to working with her if she openly confessed to practising witchcraft and heading a powerful grand coven.

Miranda glanced again at the injured girl. She didn't need doctors. Only magic could pull that spell out of her wound.

'Emmanuelle and Teresa,' Renatus finished for her, vaguely, tightening his grip on his apprentice when someone came forth to take her. He turned away to block the other doctor, and was facing Miranda again. He was tall and looked down at her, but he looked *so* young in this moment. Had he just watched Anouk die? Then seen *this* happen to his apprentice, the girl he'd chosen out of dozens of potentials, who shared his unique history and who trusted him even when nobody else would? Miranda quickly brushed the emergency doctor away, insisting everything was okay, she had it under control, and got Renatus walking again, overhearing his murmur of, 'I already called them,' even through the loud noise of the foyer and the loud voices in her head.

He's not here. Where is he?

Can anyone see him?

What's going on with Glen?

As if to confirm Renatus's claim, once they passed through the doors and into the main passage towards the operating theatres, a storeroom door up ahead of them slammed open and a blonde sorceress in her mid-twenties wearing a green velvet dress fell or stumbled out. A few of the staff accompanying Miranda and Renatus hesitated at the unexpected appearance.

'Get us a gurney,' Emmanuelle Saint Clair snapped when she saw Renatus carrying the teenager. '*Vite*! Quick!'

Demands made in French in a central London hospital and exciting strangers appearing from nowhere holding bleeding girls with lightning on their faces would not go unnoticed, but an information clean-up would have to be carried out later. There was no time to contain the probable magic rumours now.

What's going on? Lord Gawain asked in her mind. *Is Renatus with you? Are they okay?*

They're here; it's not good. But I've got this under control, Miranda confirmed grimly, all she was willing to promise. *What about Prague? Anouk?*

I'll worry about all of that.

A gurney appeared and Renatus lowered Aristea onto it hesitantly.

'Is she going to be alright?' he asked, clearly frightened. He had to be pulled away; he was unwilling to release his apprentice into their care. The doctors took over with clear relief. The gurney sped things up and they raced past a bleak-faced Emmanuelle. Miranda hurried to be at the patient's side. She wasn't conscious – probably for the best – but the blood on her palms indicated that she'd been very aware of her injury when it first occurred, probably clutching at her face in pain. How had this happened?

'She'll live,' Miranda said when Renatus kept pace with her and leaned closely over her shoulder, 'but beyond that, I can't tell you yet.'

A nurse, who had followed them from the foyer, just trying to do his job, asked Renatus what the patient's name was and what had happened to her. Judging by his tone, it was not the first time he'd asked. Miranda knew how frustrating it was trying to get information out of a traumatised family member but this was the first time she'd been sitting on that side of the fence, too. She'd not even heard the nurse's voice over her own noisy and terrified thoughts until now.

'There's so much blood,' Renatus commented unevenly. He was obviously working very hard to keep himself together, and Miranda had privately thought for some time that Renatus suffered from a strong aversion to blood. Usually the picture of detachment, in this moment he was as shattered as any ordinary person ought to be. They turned a corner into the next hall. 'Is this normal?'

Miranda shot him a look.

'Nothing about this is normal.'

Normal was day-to-day governance – council deaths, wounded teens, shell-shocked human weapons and magic in her hospital fell considerably outside the realm. Virtually borderless, the magical community Miranda's council governed extended across the world, and any threat of Lisandro's was their responsibility to address. Mostly the former councillor was underground, untraceable; then suddenly he was everywhere. Oneida was even now securing a crime scene connected to the former councillor, a dead mutineer nailed to a tree. Now this? It couldn't be coincidence.

Has anyone seen Glen? Jadon's voice asked again. *I'm just getting a weird noise. Can't anyone else hear that?*

No.

No, I can't hear anything.

I'll check in on him.

Aristea's head tipped to the side as the gurney was raced through the hospital and her blood began to stain a widening patch on the pale bedclothes. Renatus, keeping pace, groaned and covered his mouth with the clean back of his wrist, looking like he might be sick. Miranda grasped the girl's wrist and, noting the erratic pulse, tuned straight into her nervous system. A cursory examination told her what she'd already suspected – the teenager was unconscious, in a state of shock, bleeding profusely. There were several torn veins and arteries. Fragments of a very nasty, raw spell were wedged into her flesh like splinters. The body was reacting as it normally would, inflaming the area, sending platelets to clot the tear and white blood cells to fight any entering pathogens. Sadly all of the body's efforts were a waste at this point, because everything it sent to fix the injury was just pumped straight out.

They arrived at the doors of the operating room and Miranda paused to catch Renatus as the gurney went on without them. His tight, worried eyes widened as he realised he was to be parted from his apprentice, even briefly.

'No, Miranda–'

'Renatus, you need to get it together,' she told him,

calmly but firmly. Aristea disappeared inside the theatre with the other medical staff. For just a moment, Miranda and Renatus were relatively alone – they mightn't get another such chance. 'Tell me what happened to her. Lisandro?'

'I need to–'

'Renatus,' Miranda snapped, trying to focus him. His attention was beyond her, following the girl he could no longer see. 'You aren't going inside my *sterile operating environment* looking like *that*.' She pointedly glanced over him, and he seemed to notice the blood on his own hands for the first time. If possible, he paled further, and she worried he might faint. She waved quickly in his face to recapture his attention. 'You can see her again in a moment. You'll scrub in, like everybody else. Tell me what we're dealing with. How did this happen to her? Was it Lisandro?'

He was so lost, but he nodded quickly, trying to gather to himself the words she needed from him.

'She saw him before I did, and she ran... She wouldn't stop, she wouldn't let me stop her,' he explained hurriedly. 'I tried. We couldn't Displace. Otherwise I... He hit her with...' He gestured after her helplessly with his bloody hand. 'I don't know what it was. We're wasting time.'

'Qasim says there are bodies everywhere,' Emmanuelle muttered after deflecting the nurse, texting hurriedly on her phone. 'I know a medical examiner, one of ours. She can help them. Where were Aristea's wards?' She looked up expectantly. Renatus turned to her with blank, empty eyes.

'She let them down,' he murmured miserably. Aristea's wards instructor stared at him.

'She *what*? You *let 'er* into that situation without *wards*?! Why–'

'I told her, I swear.' Renatus looked like he didn't know what else to say. 'Obviously, I told her. She was shielded – she shielded everyone – and then, I don't know, she dropped them. This is all my fault,' he concluded aloud, pulling away and stalking a few paces down the hall, pressing his sticky hand to his face in distress and leaving a feral smear of blood before he

11

could realise what he was doing.

He was right, they were wasting time. Miranda grabbed his arm as he paced back past her, staring with dread at his hands.

'Can you help us heal her?'

The expression on his face when he looked immediately to Emmanuelle was nothing short of broken. She gathered there was a huge story there she'd never heard, but now wasn't the time. Emmanuelle cleared her throat.

'No, 'e can't,' she said flatly, offering no explanation. Miranda looked up at the ceiling and counted to three.

'Renatus, you're no good to anyone like this,' she said irritably, not caring if she sounded insensitive. What was the point of a superpower like Renatus if he was shedding magic everywhere indiscriminately instead of concentrating it on a task as significant as this one? 'Get a hold of yourself. There's raw magic in your apprentice's flesh. We,' she indicated Emmanuelle with a nod of her head, 'can close the wound but *you* need to pull that spell out.'

He was so white. He swallowed. Visibly pulled himself together. 'Whatever you need.' He rubbed a hand on his sleeve, wiping blood away so vigorously he pulled the sleeve up, revealing the tattoo he shared with his apprentice, half-hidden under a grimy layer of her blood. Emmanuelle, one of the few people he could reasonably call a friend, stopped him.

'You can wash your 'ands,' she said, starting to lead him into the OR's antechamber where the troughs and sanitiser were waiting. She paused, expression faltering. 'Anouk...?'

Renatus shook his head and pulled away, sweeping between them to go inside the theatre. Emmanuelle glanced at Miranda, and the priestess saw that her junior councillor was every bit as destroyed by the confirmation as Miranda and Renatus were.

Inside was a circus. A whole motley crew of emergency doctors and nurses who had followed the excitement from the foyer was dutifully scrubbing in, preparing to do their part to help this poor girl. Emmanuelle weathered the disconcerted looks of hospital professionals eyeing her velvet dress and caught her leader's eye. No one here was going to be able to help.

All at once, five pagers went off, and every non-witch in the room checked their urgent messages.

'It's the emergency room... Oh, god,' Dr Chande murmured, glancing up at Miranda. 'Have you got this under control? A school bus just crashed!'

'They'll need all hands down there,' Miranda agreed seriously, ushering the whole team away. 'Dr Saint Clair and I can handle things here.'

They milled out in a rush, the doors swinging in their wake, Renatus and Emmanuelle watching them go with looks of alarm. An illusion, but not their doing. Miranda suddenly became aware of a fourth and fifth White Elm presence in the hall. A mere second later, the door opened once more.

Miranda opened her mouth to protest.

'Don't argue,' Teresa said immediately, staggering under the weight of the older man she was supporting. Glen?! Miranda and Emmanuelle abandoned the sinks to help. Renatus looked up from his hands as water washed his apprentice's blood down the drain. 'You have two patients, you need me.' The Welsh Telepath was rigid all over and visibly seizing, his eyelids fluttering and jaw locked. 'Jadon thought something was wrong with him and he was right. I found him on his front lawn, like this.'

'You should not 'ave come, but we're not arguing,' Emmanuelle promised, backing through the doors to get Glen into the theatre where they could lay him down in sight of their other patient. His fair hair stuck to the sweat on his forehead; his thoughts were shut down. She looked up at Miranda, who'd known him much longer. 'Does 'e 'ave a 'istory?'

'Of seizures? No, I don't think so.' Miranda checked him over. No other injury, but the timing couldn't be ignored. Emmanuelle dealt more frequently than she did in healing chronic illness and disorders of the body, and she arranged Glen now with care and expertise. 'Have you got this?' She waited for the French Healer to nod, settling her hands on his

13

temples and shutting her eyes, then stood, gesturing for Teresa. 'You're with me, if you're sure you're up to it.'

'I felt Anouk go,' Teresa said, accented English uncharacteristically flat and toneless. The council's best Illusionist, she was on indefinite leave while she recovered from trauma. 'In this state I think I can handle some blood.'

Miranda tried not to let the pang in her heart distract her from what she needed to do. *Anouk...* She went to the teenager's side. Another jolt of the black spell zipped up and down the open wound.

'My biggest concern is whether the eye is intact,' Miranda told her Romanian assistant, whose step faltered only slightly when she laid eyes on the job they faced. The surgeon tilted the lamp overhead so it was directly aimed at the injury site. Now Miranda could see in sharp relief the torn skin of Aristea's cheek, eyelid and temple, the exposed fatty flesh of her cheek muscle, a little of the orbital bone... She refused to let her gaze slide to the unharmed right side of the face, unwilling to see the normal half and have to recall that this opened-up half used to look like that. Aristea had been blessed with symmetry, but that was unlikely to remain true after this surgery.

She carefully lifted the damaged eyelid, trying not to disturb the injury further. The eye was bloodshot and the surface of the cornea was rough, like it was peeling. There was minor scarring in the retina, too. But the eye was indeed intact and present. One had to take the time to accept small miracles.

'What's this?' Teresa asked anxiously, gently wiping blood from the girl's nearest hand. Miranda leaned over the prone body to look, and from the floor, Emmanuelle paid attention, Glen relaxing in her lap.

There was actually nothing to see, even under the blood. The skin was unaffected, but Teresa highlighted the arteries underneath for the three of them to see. Glowing, webbed across the palm and down the wrist, halfway to the elbow, blood vessels appeared cracked and, somehow, *burned*. Both younger Healers looked up at Miranda for an explanation.

'Burnout,' she realised quietly. 'Too much magic.

Renatus,' she called back through the doors. He appeared, looking, if possible, even paler than before. 'What did she try to channel?'

'A ward,' he said, staying back at the doors and staring at his apprentice. 'As big as a city square.'

The sorceresses looked at one another again, eyebrows raised. That was a big spell, and certainly explained the wear on the hand that had channelled the energy to create it.

It couldn't be healed with magic, but would recover in time on its own.

'Could that be why she fainted?' Teresa asked the older sorcerers.

'She didn't faint,' Renatus corrected. 'I...' They all heard him swallow guiltily. 'I couldn't listen to the screaming.'

The work for the Healers was intuitive and wordless. Miranda slipped into a trance and slowed Aristea's heart rate down as much as she dared. From the moment she touched the patient, each heartbeat was followed by a pause longer than the one before. As Miranda's senses probed the jagged cut, she could feel the decreased flow of plasma and the sluggish behaviour of the blood's many busy components. This was an ideal state, stealing time for Miranda to extend her own awareness into the body, repairing tissues, arteries and tiny blood vessels in the face that had been torn apart by the blast. It also kept as much blood as possible *inside* the patient, preventing it from being pumped out too fast by a panicked but well-meaning heart.

Teresa was as good as her word and did not seem put off, raising a hand above the wound, glowing fingertips twitching like she was playing an invisible piano. The council's Illusionist had a sensitivity for energy that gave her the ability to produce mirages as convincing as life, and she probed the spell embedded inside Aristea's skin to its deepest reaches, forcing it all into the visible spectrum. The lightning that had only flared briefly before now began to solidify in full view.

The magic didn't want to be seen and certainly didn't want to come out. It sparked dangerously. Unable to handle magic so harsh, Teresa worked as best as she could around it, but when she got too close, the spell shot forks of warning at her hand.

'He made it himself,' she commented quietly, so as not to disturb Miranda's work. 'I have never seen such a spell. Ow,' she hissed, whipping her hand away when the offending magic struck out at her again, this time missing her by millimetres, its heat briefly burning her fingers.

Renatus had been staring uncomprehendingly at the barely-breathing girl, but now glanced up. Dark magic was his thing. He strode over quickly, passing Glen and Emmanuelle, focus redirected. He brought his cupped hands down over the cut in Aristea's face. The spell blackened and sparked and shot at him, too, but he acted impervious to the effects. If it hurt him, he didn't show it.

The spell went a bit crazy, spitting and sparking, fighting for life as the determined sorcerer's hands began to glow, much brighter than Teresa's had. He tensed, fingers tightening around a bundle of energy they couldn't see, and began to lift, arms straining like he was tugging on something very heavy.

'What is it?' Miranda asked softly, sensing the change as the magic was pulled slowly from the tissue she was working on. Renatus shook his head.

'Deliberate,' was all he said in response, and his tone was acid.

Emmanuelle left the recovering Glen to take over Miranda's trance, keeping Aristea alive on a heart rate that was too slow for natural survival. Miranda felt no concern for the apprentice in this regard; she knew that Emmanuelle was diverting oxygenated blood to the brain and vital organs and prioritising the evacuation of carbon dioxide from those critical areas. The altered state made it easy for Renatus and Teresa to unpick the spell from Aristea's ruined flesh and for Renatus to slowly, painstakingly, pull it free altogether from the wound. He backed away with a handful of black magic and the three Healers started the task of reconnecting the two sides of the cut and encouraging the body to reproduce the cells necessary to fill the gap left in between.

Then there was just the eye.

Just one damaged eye between this procedure in *this* moment and the chaos that would ensue once she left this moment behind. Anouk. Glen. The White Elm. The witnesses to magic in the foyer. Prague. Lisandro.

Miranda took a beat and looked down at her hands, bloody once again.

For now, in this moment, they were steady.

This moment was the only one she had any semblance of control over. She went to work.

chapter one

The world came back to me, or rather, I came back to *it*, in blurry stages. First there was the noise, a steady dripping of liquid somewhere nearby. A tap, a leak? The next stage was emotion – around me, in the air, lying across me like a blanket, the weight of yucky feelings. It took me a groggy while to identify them, they were so mixed. Some blend of grief, confusion, anger... guilt. Disbelief. The dripping I could have ignored, but the feelings were more persistent.

Awareness began to return to me, but wakefulness did not. I struggled against the overwhelming power of my own unconsciousness. I tried to move. I tried to open my eyes. Couldn't. I started to feel the pale, sluggish beginnings of panic. Was I paralysed? What had happened to me? My breathing sped up.

Complex movement patterns like sitting up seemed out of the question so I moved my attention to my fingers. They were harder to isolate than they should have been, and I didn't know for sure whether they did what I wanted when I willed them to wiggle.

I was helpless. I tried again to sit up, or to roll over, anything, focusing every ounce of energy I had on throwing myself to the side.

There was a loud clatter of things falling onto a hard floor, and the sudden pitch of voices, the words tumbling over one another in my ears, making little sense.

'... waking up...'

'… is typical… mess. She's got no control…'

'… more sedative?'

I didn't recognise the muddle of accented tones but heard them getting closer, felt the accompanying concern that came with them, and my dim panic skyrocketed. I jerked to the other side, hoping to roll away and onto my feet.

My body didn't move. Something on my other side smashed like glass. The noise terrified me, and above me, I heard something pop. A splash of liquid burst on the floor. A door slammed.

'… trying to move… out as magic…'

'… in pain? Is…'

'… not…'

'Can't you do something?'

I stopped my attempts at struggle. I knew that voice. I felt a firm hand close over mine and hold it tightly, warmly. My escalating fear plateaued, at least enough that when the voice spoke again, I heard it and understood it.

'Aristea,' it said, 'it's alright. It's over. You're safe. You're safe…'

And my awareness dipped away once again into unconsciousness.

I suppose I slept. When the world started to come back to me, some of the blank grogginess had gone away. The yucky feelings of other people still lingered.

What had happened to me? I remembered the familiar voice speaking to me.

It's over.

My body was mine again. I could feel it. Fingers that twitched when I tried to move them. Toes that tightened and stretched back out on command. Throat that ached with dryness when I breathed down it. I swallowed; it didn't help much. I was parched.

Where was I? The drip was back. I heard other noises, not as close. Soft whirring of machines, footsteps echoing in hallways. There was an uncomfortable antiseptic scent to the air around me. A hospital? The generic feel of the blanket

19

covering me suddenly became obvious, as did the halfway-upright position of the bed I was lying on. What was I doing in a hospital?

I tried to open my eyes to look around. They did not open. I frowned, scrunched the lids a little to check for sensation, and stopped immediately with a sharp intake of breath. It *hurt*. And I still couldn't see.

A flash of memory struck me like a backhand – a beautiful city scene in a state of panic – and then the image jumped to another, and then another, jumbled up and incoherent but still distressing, and then I couldn't make it stop. Prague – magical activists, half of them only my age – music, the boom box exploding beside me – men in cloaks – a bomb made of fear, floating above the street – running – shouting – the ward – looking back, the choke of denial in my throat to see my shield would not extend far enough to save him–

'Renatus,' I mumbled fearfully, my dry voice cracking on his name, and I tried to sit up but hands caught my shoulders and pushed me firmly back into bed.

'I'm here,' he said, and I immediately stopped straining against his hold, flooded with trust even though he brought with him an aura of distress. I remembered him dropping to the ground in Prague and rolling under the edge of my ward just before it struck the ground. Safe. Right? I tried to look at him but my eyes still would not open. 'Everything's alright. You're in Lady Miranda's hospital. Here.' Something cool touched my lips and I flinched. 'Drink.' I did, taking water in tiny sips while he held the back of my head to keep me steady. 'You're going to be fine.'

Hard to believe when he was emanating such sadness and guilt. He didn't even believe his own words. His emotions made me feel sick. What had happened to us?

'Are...' I swallowed when my dry throat struggled with speech. 'Are you hurt?'

'No,' he assured me quietly. 'I wasn't hurt at all. Thanks to you.'

In my mind I could easily picture him, tall and lean with dark hair that touched his shoulders, and it frustrated me that I couldn't *see* him. I raised a clumsy hand to my eyes and felt with my fingertips the gauze padding and tape strapped across the top half of my face. Renatus's hand gently took mine and pulled it away. I heard the cup set down on a nearby surface.

'Don't touch that,' he instructed softly, in a voice that told me what his face looked like, even though I couldn't see it. Since I'd become his apprentice in magic a couple of months ago, bound my life and mind with his, we had both experienced a boost to our power and a steady melding of identity. He was in my mind and I was in his. I knew him better than I had ever known anyone else. 'Leave it for the Healers. I think Teresa is coming back shortly.'

His words were logical but his voice betrayed how upset he was.

'Am I... Am I blind?' I asked bluntly, voice strengthening. 'Is that why you're upset?'

Immediately I knew I was being selfish. I was not the centre of Renatus's universe. He was an important person, powerful and prominent in both the political sphere of the White Elm's goings-on and the magical underworld he so hated. My grievances were not the only reason he could be upset.

'You're... I don't think you're blind.'

'Then what aren't you telling me?'

There was a loaded silence and in it, I realised I was missing something massive. I thought back, trying to remember what had happened following the high point of relief when Renatus had gotten under the ward safely.

The flash, the searing pain; before that, Lisandro, standing at the other end of the street; before that...

My stomach twisted painfully. As it all came back.

'Just relax,' Renatus tried to insist, and I felt his hands on my shoulders again, this time helping me into an upright position, but I weakly shoved him away, grabbing at the gauze on my eyes when tears of horror stung at eyes I couldn't see through.

'I-I locked her out,' I stammered, feeling sick. The dark only escalated the awfulness of it all. My fingernails picked hurriedly at the tape holding down the padding. 'She... Is she...? I didn't...'

I didn't mean for her to die.

Because that's what happened. I didn't really need to ask. I remembered now the pair of hands that slammed against the solid glass wall of my giant protective energetic dome just as it sealed against the ground. I remembered the crackle of the evil magic washing over my domed safety zone and the dull heavy thud of my history teacher's body hitting the pavement when that magic shot through her. I remembered the blank emptiness of hollow understanding, because it was what I felt now.

I asked anyway.

'Did Anouk... Is she... dead?'

The answer was all around me in the sorrow and shock and anger and guilt surrounding Renatus, evident in the thickness of his prolonged silence. He was steeped with it, so saturated with negativity that my weakened energy field soaked in what he shed. I had never been strong at managing my own emotions, let alone juggling them with those of other people – one of the pitfalls of being an Empath as well as a sorcerer. I'd seen people die before, but those deaths were well outside of my control.

Anouk's, though. That should not have happened.

'Yes.' So flat, so clinical, just a statement of fact belying the truth – that we'd watched one of Renatus's colleagues die right in front of us. Maybe not a friend, but someone he trusted, respected and worked with very closely.

'Are you sure?' I asked, throat tight with the effort not to sob. I squeezed my eyes shut against the threat of tears but the flash of pain in the dark stung so harshly that I immediately went back to picking at the medical blindfold taped to my face. 'Did you go back, after...?'

After you had to chase me down through a Czech street because I lost all sense and ran after the man who scares me more than anything else in the world, like there was anything a stupid teenage witch could do that *you* couldn't do better? After I crossed a major ethical line in exploiting our ability to visit one another's minds by shutting down your thoughts about stopping me before you could even have them?

After I cast a ward that saved you and me but not Anouk?

Maybe, just maybe, I was mistaken. Maybe she'd survived the blast.

'No, I didn't go back to check,' Renatus admitted, trying again, half-heartedly, to brush my hands away from my work. 'I already knew, and I... had to get you here.'

And Lisandro, I gathered, had gotten away, using Renatus's incompetent apprentice once again as the perfect distractor.

'There were others,' I stated hoarsely, remembering other bodies alongside hers, other people I'd accidentally locked out. 'Three, four? Why don't I remember?!' What kind of person doesn't notice how many people she shut out to die? 'I did this, I let them all die—'

'You saved *seventy-two lives,* including mine,' Renatus started to say, but I interrupted wildly, 'It wasn't enough!'

'Not *enough*?!' Renatus demanded, and his pained tone distracted me from my escalating emotions. 'Seventy-two – did you not hear me? The only other White Elm who can claim heroics of that magnitude are the Healers, across whole careers. You did more than enough. You *paid* more than enough.' His hand clasped the left side of my face, over my ear, and my frantically picking fingers went still. 'You could have been killed, seventy-two times over. You shouldn't have *been* there – this is *my* fault.'

The true reason for the guilt. He felt responsible, for Anouk, for me. His immense shame fell on my self-pity like a wet blanket and gave me a moment to recompose myself.

'It's... It's not your fault,' I managed quietly. He always thought it was his fault, and his guilt was always too much for his body to contain.

'I was overconfident, and now five people are dead. Anouk is dead. You were almost killed. I'm excluded from the scene investigation in Prague.'

So that's why he was here instead of out doing something useful with his repertoire of talents. He was the most powerful member of the White Elm, and the one who should be leading the hunt for Lisandro. Sitting him at my bedside was a waste of resources, but as soon as I thought this, I understood why he'd been sidelined. He and I were *there*, part of the tragic series of events. The scene itself had to be investigated by others before we could be involved. I'd watched enough police procedural television with my sister to know that, but traditional sorcerer Renatus had never watched a TV in his life.

'I can't imagine anyone blames you,' I said finally. He'd stood back-to-back with Anouk and taken on those attackers; *I* had dropped a ward in front of her and trapped her in the street to die. I swallowed, loathing myself. This was *my* fault.

He overheard my thoughts. 'No one blames you either. You did more than enough – everyone's talking about it. *You* couldn't have done anything else.'

I pressed my lips together so I wouldn't tell him he was wrong. I *could* have done more. Anouk was just a couple of paces behind Renatus. The pair of them were rounding up the last of the endangered bystanders while I led the majority out of the square, but none of us were far enough away to be safe when that bomb went off. I cast a ward, a huge dome, and when I looked, I saw it wouldn't be big enough to encase Renatus. I panicked – I strained – I made it bigger. Why hadn't I seen her, Anouk, and pushed harder, expanded the spell further, and saved her, too? *How* had I not seen her?! She was familiar; an image of her came immediately to mind from this morning.

When she wasn't dead. Because of me.

My stomach lurched.

'I think I'm going to be sick,' I muttered, just as my fingernails got underneath the tape and tugged. 'Get this off me.' The strips stung as they peeled away from my skin, and Renatus murmured a helpless curse under his breath and I felt his fingers join mine in lifting the tape and padding away. He was much more gentle, but slower. 'Get it off, get it off...'

'It's off,' he responded, half-annoyed, more like his usual self, as the last strip of tape came unstuck and he lifted the pad away. Light brightened the unseen world beyond my closed eyelids. I tried to blink; only one eye opened properly, and it was bleary and out of focus. Tears, I realised. I was crying. Horrible mixed feelings welled up inside Renatus at the sight of whatever was underneath the bandage, and I swallowed a painful sob, confused and upset. 'Do you need a bucket or something?' he asked.

'No.' I swallowed a few times, trying to get control, still trying to blink, though it hurt. 'Do you?'

'Why would I need to be sick?'

I blinked slowly, and the right eye cleared up. I could see him. He was sickly pale and frightened-looking. I must be a mess. He was afraid of blood.

'How bad is it?' I asked softly. He was coming into focus, no longer just a dark silhouette. Definitely Renatus. The other eye was sluggish and gunky and did not want to open. It felt swollen. 'Don't lie to me. I'll know.'

He couldn't look at me. I tried to feel my face with clumsy, tired fingertips before he could stop me. He didn't need to. I touched my cheek and unresponsive eyelid and it was tacky, wet and blindingly *sore*, sending a flash of white heat through my darkened vision like the one that had put me here. My hand whipped away.

'Renatus, tell me!' I ordered, frustrated into snappiness. 'Why can't you look at me?!'

'Because it's my fault!'

'What's going on?' a new, vaguely familiar voice asked as her presence entered the edge of my awareness from my left. 'Renatus? Why is the wound undressed?'

I tried to place the thick, rich accent and soft, uncertain cadence. Not...? 'Teresa?' I said, turning my head to try to see the door she entered through. She approached from my left, invisible through my thick wet lashes and heavy eyelid.

'That's right,' she soothed as she came into blurry view. I

didn't recognise her as quickly as I had Renatus, though she was on the White Elm council with him and was once one of my teachers at the school running out of Renatus's house. She'd been absent from council business for the last few months as she recovered from her time spent as a prisoner of war in one of Lisandro's hideouts.

Right now, though I couldn't get a clear look at her through my gunky eye, she seemed to be in a much better state than the last time I'd seen her, and indeed, a much better state than me, but did I imagine that haunted look in her blurred eyes?

The hand she laid on my hair was gentle and caring.

'He won't tell me what's wrong with me,' I accused, gesturing at Renatus. I hissed with pain as I felt the sharp tug on my skin of the needle I hadn't realised – hadn't been able to *see* – was taped into my wrist, feeding a drip. Blindly I clutched the wrist to my chest, becoming aware of a general ache in the whole left arm. It was easier to feel angry than to feel sad, I noted.

'I can do that, if I may examine you,' Teresa said in her soft voice, always sounding a little unsure. I remembered her shaky classroom voice now. 'Your condition may have changed since I was here earlier.' I slowly nodded once. How long was I out? Teresa frowned over me at Renatus. 'I heard Lady Miranda tell you–'

'She wanted it off,' he said with a shrug she couldn't argue with, and since he could hear my inner wonderings, added to me, 'Just a few hours.'

A few hours. I had absolutely no sense of time in here, the white lights and the lack of windows and the overwhelming recent memories that were too big and too horrible to be so recent as just this morning.

'Marcy Pretoria,' I recalled suddenly, thinking of the friend-of-a-friend former student I'd seen in Prague. 'Is she...?'

'Not one of the deceased. Assume alive and well,' Renatus advised.

'You look much better,' the young Healer commented,

26

sitting on the edge of my hospital bed while she tenderly touched my cheek, my brow, all around my left eye. 'Stop – don't force the eye open. I'm trying to look. No explosions this time?' I shifted my legs over so she would have more room, and vaguely remembered the sensation of not being able to move them at all.

'Explosions?' I asked, feeling sick again at the thought of the huge silvery spell hanging above Lennon Wall, swelling with our fears until it exploded in a shockwave of the blackest magic. Teresa, though, gestured at the room I was in with a significant tilt of her head, and even Renatus looked around as though remembering. I followed his gaze.

A line of cabinets on the side wall were utterly broken, doors wrenched off their hinges. A mop stood in the corner, and beside it a bucket full of broken glass, mangled plastics and slashed tubing. The television screen opposite me had a big crack down the middle. What sort of hospital was this?

'This is all you, *păpușă*,' Teresa told me in her lovely rounded Romanian accent, reaching for something outside my range of vision and dabbing at my face with something wet. 'A reaction to sedation. You woke up before the drug wore off.'

'You couldn't move,' Renatus explained, his accent just like mine, melodic and thick, 'and when you panicked, you must have lashed out.'

Energetically? I kept my sore eye shut and looked around with my good eye, incredulous. The room was small and otherwise clean.

'Why was I brought here?' I asked. The older sorcerers looked uncertainly at each other across my lap. 'I mean, what is *this*?' I pointed at my eye with my left hand but again felt the painful tug of that drip. 'What did he do to a me?'

Renatus got up and stalked away, out of my sight but not out of the room. A cloud of remorse and anger trailed after him. I pressed my lips together, weathering his reaction. Lisandro was our enemy but he was also Renatus's godfather. To see me in such a state, attacked outright by the man *he* was responsible for catching, hurt him more than I could bear. I shouldn't have run. I shouldn't have been so bloody stupid. This, too, was my fault.

'You're very lucky,' Teresa answered, eyeing Renatus momentarily. She turned back to me with a bright smile that was mostly forced. 'It was a spell. Raw magic. We got it all out. So far you have no signs of infection and the swelling is minimal.' She tried to smile at Renatus. 'This could have been much worse.'

Silence. *Seething*. Teresa tried to smile at me again to minimise my worry, but she couldn't feel what Renatus emanated.

'Ignore him; he got a fright from the state you were in,' she encouraged. She gently pulled on my lower lid with one fingertip, and I could *see*, somewhat, through the sore eye. 'Your eye was very badly damaged when you arrived but your central vision should be completely restored. Lady Miranda and Renatus, and Emmanuelle, you should have seen them. They,' she said, pausing as she used another fingertip to carefully lift the upper lid, giving me some more blurry vision, 'are incredible.'

'Like *you* aren't.' I winced as she prodded at the corner of my eyelid. 'But… Can't you tell me–'

'Renatus tells me it's your birthday,' she said brightly, changing the topic quickly. Her words almost did the trick of distracting me. 'Did you get any cards? Presents?'

'*Teresa*,' I said firmly, losing patience even though I quite liked her and my natural politeness insisted I didn't have the relationship with her to be able to be pushy or rude. 'What aren't you saying?' I turned to Renatus, glaring at him. Frowning hurt my face. He would not meet my eyes. 'You said… You said I *paid* for what happened this morning. What did you mean? Renatus? *Just look at me!*'

He finally did. I didn't know what I expected him to say but this wasn't it.

'You're scarred.'

chapter two

They wouldn't give me a mirror, and despite a bond between our minds, Renatus was blocking me from accessing his thoughts. We could do that sometimes, maintain our privacy and wall off particular areas of memory or awareness, just like we were learning how to draw one another into specific areas of the mind, too. It was this two-way ability that had allowed me once before to *see* through his eyes, and for Renatus to cast spells with my brain circuits on multiple occasions.

It was this same ability that had allowed me to keep a life-shattering secret from him for *months* now.

'I *promise*,' Teresa insisted, looking me straight in the eyes, all sincerity, in a way Renatus was still not able to do, 'this is not as bad as he thinks. You can look when the swelling goes down – you'll get a fright otherwise. But yes.' She forced a small, sad smile. 'You will have a scar here, beside your eye. We did our best.'

I swallowed again, confused. 'I thought sorcerers didn't scar?'

'From normal injury, no, we don't,' she explained cautiously. 'But you didn't just fall over, did you? You're lucky to have the eye.'

Scarred. Obviously a facial scar was not something I had wanted, but I understood what she was saying. From Renatus's reaction, I must have been in quite the state when I arrived. I thought of the rippled scar that ran down his back, the one only Emmanuelle and I had seen, and the shame he

29

associated with that mark – dating all the way back to the day his whole family, similarly to mine, was wiped out in a single deliberate event.

Teresa yawned, and I couldn't help catching on. I saw the tiredness in her face and realised it was not from lack of sleep.

'You healed me,' I said, not bothering to phrase it as a question. 'Why are you so tired? I thought healing borrowed energy from the patient?'

She patted my wrist and it tingled. I didn't understand why.

'You didn't have enough for the three of us. Four of us,' she amended, looking over her shoulder at Renatus. Who, I knew, was absolutely incapable of healing anyone, a very odd trait unique to him among all sorcerers and possibly the reason for his own scars. 'You spent all your energy in Prague. Do... do you remember?'

The confusing and horrifying events in Prague this morning flashed through my mind again. A crowd of young sorcerers rallying for democracy had seemed innocent enough when I'd stupidly walked into the middle of it and let myself get caught up in the excitement, but then the men in hooded, crimson cloaks had surrounded us. Renatus's attempts to Displace us out of there had failed when we'd realised, too late, that there was no escape. A trap, and we'd walked straight into it. Lisandro's trap. He'd been there, at the end, after Anouk... I'd felt him, and then seen him, watching the street from the other end, and it made *no sense*. Clearly he'd orchestrated the attack – a grinning Irish sorcerer had taken responsibility on behalf of Magnus Moira, Lisandro's followers, while the silvery orb of magic hanging above the square had swelled with each surge of fear in the crowd – but *why*? I'd seen him a week before at a party where his goal was to garner public support for his political and ideological agenda. Terrorism was generally not a winning strategy.

Not that it seemed to have stopped him today. Gingerly I touched my fingertip to my eyebrow, lifting the lid the same way Teresa just had. I hadn't just fallen over and hurt myself.

I'd left myself open. I was a liability. This was all my fault. I felt like crying.

'She's talking about the ward.'

I turned toward Renatus's soft voice, sniffing back my misery. His didn't help *at all*, but hearing him sound sad steeled me unexpectedly. Renatus didn't do sad well, and my sadness was exacerbating his sadness which was feeding directly back into *my* sadness. He stood with his arms folded across the front of his black jacket, which I now saw was deeply stained. Blood. Mine, I had to assume. He was still avoiding looking at me.

'You made it too big,' he explained. 'It drained you. You could have died.'

I shook my head, rejecting not his words but the guilt and subliminal frightened anger they were laden with. What he wasn't saying.

You shouldn't have risked it.

I swallowed. 'Should I have let seventy-two people die instead?'

'No,' he said pointedly. I wished my eyes were both working properly so I could roll them.

'No,' I repeated. 'Just you?' I waited for a reaction, but he was quiet, and I felt annoyed with his refusal to look at me. Such a hypocrite. The spell I'd cast to save all our lives was nothing more than he would have done in my position. My arm tingled uncomfortably at the memory, and I looked down at it. There was no visible damage but I remembered the burning, in my nerves, in my blood... 'You can quit feeling guilty about surviving,' I told him flatly, knowing even before he flinched that it was touching a truth that went deeper than just today's events. 'It wasn't your decision to make.'

'I'm grateful to be alive.' He swallowed, too, and when he spoke again, his voice was much firmer. 'If we're dishing out hard lessons, *you* can quit blaming yourself for what happened to Anouk.' I felt no pity from him when I flinched as well. Sometimes being so intimately hooked into one another's thoughts was a downer. 'There is *no way* you are responsible.

The fault is with the spellcaster, and the designer.'

'Lisandro,' I murmured, wincing when I touched the outer corner of my eye and the explosion of nerves made me automatically try to blink, hurting even more. The pain did the same trick as before, making me bold and angry, chasing away the sad and raw. Probably not a good coping behaviour pattern to establish. I turned my head to look away from Renatus so I couldn't see his expression when I asked, 'Did he get away because of me? Because you decided to look after me?'

Renatus wasn't like the other twelve White Elm. Growing up in a now-renounced and now-dead family of dark sorcerers, his knowledge of illegal magic was unparalleled on the council, and like Lisandro before him, he held the chair of Dark Keeper, charged with learning and practicing the magic their enemies wouldn't expect them to dare use. Finding, facing and ultimately defeating the traitorous former councillor was Renatus's literal job, but if I was right, this was not the first time he had let his target slip away in order to protect me.

I was a liability, the very worst thing. How had I ever convinced myself I could one day do the thing needed to save Renatus from his fate?

I didn't need to see his expression to know it was stormy. I felt it before he spoke.

'Decided?' he spat back, more harshly than I had expected, and I realised I could feel him in my head. He was listening to my thoughts. I clamped down on them before he could hear anything else. 'He was gone before I got to you, and you were bleeding *everywhere*. It wasn't a decision.'

The only thing I knew of that Renatus hated more than Lisandro was blood. I should shut up and be grateful.

'Sorry,' I mumbled. An awkward silence followed; I could feel Teresa's discomfort. She barely knew us, sharing only a short working relationship with Renatus and an even shorter teacher-student relationship with me, both of which had been on pause for months. She didn't know *us*, as a bonded pair – her kidnapping had initiated the sequence of events that had led to the council approving me to start my apprenticeship, so she'd never seen us bicker and fume at each other.

If she had, she'd know this wasn't unusual.

'Don't apologise,' Renatus said eventually, relenting. In my thoughts, I heard his: *Save it for when you do something worth being sorry for.* 'There's enough to worry about. You're in hospital, Anouk's gone, Glen's out–'

'What do you mean? What happened to Glen?' I asked worriedly. He wasn't with us in Prague. Both Renatus and Teresa became uneasy at the mention of the council's most established Telepath.

'We still don't know,' Teresa admitted. 'When Anouk... Everyone else started to talk in my head, and he went quiet. I went to check and I found him on the ground.'

'He had a severe seizure,' Renatus filled in when I immediately assumed the worst. 'Emmanuelle drew him out of it but she said it was like his brain was on fire. He still hasn't woken up. His mind is totally shut down.'

I looked down at my hands. So much in just a few hours.

'And this happened...?'

'At the same moment we lost Anouk,' he confirmed. 'They were about as linked as you and I. We don't think it's a coincidence.'

One well-placed attack and Lisandro had the council in shambles, their forces halved.

'I don't like it,' Teresa admitted to Renatus, tugging her long skirt over her knees modestly with hands lost in the sleeves of her loose, too-big blazer. She was smaller than I was, I realised for the first time, and older than me by so little that in another set of circumstances, we might have been friends, yet as circumstances stood, she was a White Elm councillor and I was a kid by comparison. 'So many eyes, very important eyes, on Prague. I must wonder what Lisandro achieved today.'

In the heavy pause that followed, I turned my head enough that I could see Renatus too through my one working eye. Trying to focus in the stark lighting of the hospital room was starting to make my head achy.

'I don't follow,' he said finally, his hands on his hips. I saw him deliberately drop them, realising it looked defensive and seeing Teresa's standard look of uncertainty intensify. When I'd first met Renatus he'd given off a distinct attitude of not caring what other people thought of him, but the better I'd gotten to know him the more I'd seen that wasn't true. Either that, or he was changing. I knew *I* had changed in the same short space of time.

Teresa still looked a little afraid of Renatus so she shifted on the edge of my bed to face me instead, digging in her jacket pocket.

'Do you like magic?' she asked, presenting me with a hand of face-down playing cards. 'Of course you do,' she corrected herself with a wry smile. 'Aren't we sorcerers?' Not understanding the sharp conversation change but enjoying the novelty distraction, I reached out, but missed her hand by an embarrassing degree. I felt an unanticipated blush heat my cheeks, then a little spark of panic when it happened again on my second attempt. 'It's okay, try again.'

You're lacking depth perception, Renatus explained, talking directly to my mind as we had learned to do after being bonded. *It's just because that left eye is shut. It isn't permanent.*

On my third go I took a card and replaced it, keeping the suit and number to myself. Teresa began to shuffle, small hands deft and dextrous, watching only what she was doing.

'When I was rescued,' she said slowly, surprising us with her very personal topic choice, 'all White Elm eyes were on me and *not* on the house, and so Aubrey was able to take those boys. When Lisandro approached the Lake boy's mother in Michigan, he demanded the council's attention and Jackson infiltrated Emmanuelle's apartment, looking for the ring.' She gestured for my hand and began to lay the cards down in my palm, one by one, face-up. 'Every time we see him, this is a diversion. Today he killed a councillor. We were all looking. And Valero, and Avalon. But where was Aubrey? Where was Jackson?' She placed the last card in my hand and met my eye again. 'Where is your card?'

It had not been among the pile. I had watched every card go down. I waited expectantly, intrigued by her skill. My repertoire with real magic was expanding to include shields, teleportation, conversing with other minds and remote viewing of past and present events, but I could be as impressed by card tricks as the next ordinary person.

But her words disturbed me, even as I tried to stay emotionally distracted by the cards.

'You think... he let that happen in Prague today... to Anouk... while he did something else?'

'Or for some purpose, maybe.' Teresa shrugged uncomfortably and took back the little pile of cards, only half a deck or less, glancing very briefly at Renatus as he took a step closer, frowning down at his boots. His thoughts were swirling again.

'That sounds like his style,' he admitted. 'Misdirection and theatrics. But a public attack in a major city and the execution of a White Elm official...' He sighed. 'I don't know why I'm so surprised.'

We sat silently stewing on that for a bit, realising the immensity of Teresa's suggestion. Four years earlier, Lisandro had summoned a storm out of nowhere to cover his tracks in murdering almost my entire family. Four years before that, he'd done the same to Renatus's family, leaving the then-fifteen-year-old completely alone in the world, the last of his line, and some time years even before *that*, he'd cast what we assumed was his first storm when he murdered the Hawke family, orphaning their little daughter. Teresa was right in her card trick analogy – Lisandro had a preference for *big* acts of magic or spectacle, so big that nobody even knew what they were really looking at.

'What about where you were before?' I asked, remembering suddenly what Renatus was doing when I'd scried the vision that had sent us too willingly into Prague like the stupid sheep Lisandro no doubt believed we were. 'The mutineer?'

About two weeks ago, he and I had chased and pinned down a bearded Scotsman with three missing fingers in a forest. The man was the first lead we'd had back to Lisandro's known compound in Belarus, which the Scot had narrowly escaped, but he'd been unwilling to accept our help, and this morning Qasim, the White Elm's official Scrier, had found him dead and nailed to a tree.

'I did think the same thing,' Renatus agreed. 'When I left, Elijah and Qasim were to stay to ensure the body or scene wasn't tampered with, but they had to come to our aid in Prague. Oneida's been there since and she says there's been no action.'

'Lisandro was already finished with him,' I said, covering my good eye with the heel of my hand and rubbing it, hoping to rub the ache out of it. 'He left him there for you.' Public, gruesome, a disgusting demonstration of what he thought of disobedience and disloyalty. Because Lisandro was a psychopath who thought it was appropriate to leave dead people nailed to trees for his godson to find.

Renatus exhaled slowly, privately agreeing.

'If not that, then there's something else we're missing,' he said. 'Something we can't afford to miss.' He paused, obviously thinking, scrying, racking all his mental resources for answers, but he came up short. 'I don't even know where to start looking.'

'I will start by finding something to redress this wound,' Teresa said, pushing herself off my bed. 'Do not touch the eye.'

Her words were intended as a firm instruction but her voice was too soft and sweet to sound like anything stronger than a suggestion. Luckily for her, it all hurt too much for me to consider defying the suggestion, and I nodded vaguely as the door clicked shut behind her.

I was left alone with my master.

'Don't say it,' Renatus said instantly, stalking to the door as well. 'Don't apologise, don't say it wasn't my fault, don't say it'll work itself out. Just tell me what I can do for you. You must be hungry. What can I get you?'

I swallowed all the things he'd told me not to say and instead told him, 'Anything. Whatever's hot.'

He nodded, still unable to look at me properly, and swung out the door to find a staff member. I sensed his deep gratitude for the excuse to leave.

I didn't know what to do with his gratitude. I felt hollow, senseless. Over and over again in my head, the Russian's hands slammed into the wall of my ward and the crackling black evil of the magical bomb slammed into her, and she went down, and the people she went back to save fell with her. Gone. Such a useless waste.

And it didn't matter what anyone said. I hadn't pulled the trigger but I'd basically held the door shut on those people.

chapter three

Terror... shrieking, sobbing, yelling in different languages... All of it distant, streets away, inside a bubble of magic no one else could see...

'Come on!' Qasim's voice, beside him, holding his elbow in case they needed to go in an instant. *The sights and sounds weren't so distant for the Scrier, and it was from his mind the visions streamed. But though Elijah took calculated leaps through space, they only deflected, coming out in alleys and café kitchens and apartments that bordered the exclusion zone.*

'I can't get in!' He stretched his mind in each direction, squeezing, probing for a weak spot that he could exploit and split to get through. There was nothing. It was impenetrable. And their people were right in the centre, beacons to his finely tuned sense of location. *'We need to go on foot.'*

The square was still and quiet now but it wasn't hard to imagine how it had looked just this morning. Abandoned pens and cans of spray paint lay scattered near the bright and bold Lennon Wall where tourists had been etching their names and poetry, and not far away, a few broken bottles and mobile phones lying around a car showed where a group of young activists had been interrupted in the middle of a light-hearted political rally.

An unexpected setback. They burst from the kitchen and raced through the café, where people ate placidly, completely unaware of the horrors unfolding just a block away. On the street outside, a tourist group following a local. A collision, Elijah and Qasim apologising hurriedly in English not knowing if it was understood, disentangling themselves from the crowd of arms and backpacks and camera straps and flags. Flags? Seriously? All the while, voices in their heads, but none louder than Anouk, briskly requesting backup.

'We have to come on foot so we're at least a minute way,' Elijah apologised aloud, squeezing between strangers, putting on a burst of speed after Qasim. All the while his mind reached, and prodded, hoping for a gap…

Elijah hadn't witnessed the Czech street in its dynamic, summer morning glory. He hadn't seen it as things disintegrated, either. He'd arrived to a crowd of tearful and confused civilians and a nightmarish trail of dead bodies all the way down the length of the street back to the Wall.

The first thing he noticed was the snap of a spell breaking – the unnatural constraint on the Fabric, preventing anyone from teleporting in or out of that physical space. Then they were in, and it was horrific.

Like most horrific experiences, Elijah saw and processed it all in stark, sharply detailed flashes, none of it timestamped or considered in relation to anything else going on. It was just that: horrific. Sunshine on a vibrant graffitied medieval street littered with prone, robed figures. Terrified cries and raised voices and different levels, people crouched down sobbing over expired bodies while others stood on their toes to see over the heads of others.

'Secure the scene and get straight back to me,' Qasim directed tensely as he ran ahead.

Just one minute too late to do anything about any of it. The magic flowing in his veins and his place on a super-powered council of sorcerers didn't change the facts.

The early afternoon sun beat down on the scene. On arrival, things had been frantic and busy – awkward, multilingual negotiations between local law enforcement, tourists and White Elm investigators, the race to secure the area, the counselling and interviewing of witnesses – but now the initial panic had dulled and the obvious work had been done, and Elijah was not alone in taking pause to simply survey the mess.

How any measure could possibly fix this was beyond the scope of his imagination at this point.

It was worse than just a group of rogue sorcerers having attacked a street full of people in broad daylight and killing seventeen of them, a politically nightmarish combination of their own dozen mysterious men, two mortal tourists, two underage magical citizens and one peacekeeper shared between the White Elm and an independent magical nation. It was worse than the world's biggest magical government being proven ineffectual against a foe. Oh, no. Things could always get worse, and Elijah could already see how it would.

Two men walked by him, deep in impossible conversation, one speaking serious Czech, one serious Russian, communication enabled because the Russian was a sorcerer and a Telepath. They pointed to bodies and gestured down the street to indicate probable paths of each victim, and the Czech police officer nodded in agreement with the Telepath, conveniently having forgotten that he did not know this man and should not be discussing the crime scene with him.

Every one of the local law enforcement officers were accompanied by one of Valero's investigators, their flexible and highly trained minds hooked into the unsuspecting consciousness of a mortal trying to do his job. Influencing them. Keeping them calm. Pulling information out of them to inform their own investigation.

Completely abhorred and illegal under White Elm law and practice.

'This makes me sick,' Qasim muttered, coming over to stand with Elijah at the Wall, the brightness behind them a stark contrast to the scene before them. 'We shouldn't be working with them.'

Elijah shrugged a shoulder uneasily, privately agreeing but not willing to say so aloud with so many sensitive ears. The ratio of Telepaths probably negated his efforts, though. He didn't need to voice an opinion to have it known.

'We don't have a choice,' he replied. 'Anouk was on their council, too.'

Was. Past tense. It was surreal. They both looked up the length of the street to the unremarkable spot where, hours ago, their colleague and sister in magic had lost her life. A white blanket that should have made her anonymous lay across her prone, distant shape, but each sorcerer onsite knew which blanket covered Anouk of Valero.

'Did you find anything?' Qasim asked, clearing his throat and avoiding the moment when he'd have to acknowledge the loss. Elijah shook his head.

'The stretch on the Fabric was released when Lisandro left,' he reported. It was easier to focus on facts than the truth: that their friend was dead. 'He was keeping it taut so none of us could get into this area except on foot, then I'm guessing he had to leave in a hurry. I found the spot where he Displaced from but as usual–'

'He covered his tracks,' Qasim guessed flatly. Elijah tried not to feel as incompetent as he did. Teleportation was an extremely challenging magical skill and few could do it at all; even fewer could manage it at his level. Sensing the sinkhole in the Fabric of space where their former brother had split the air and slipped away to somewhere else, Elijah had tried to follow the wormhole to its destination and had hit the same blocked exit he always did with this particular quarry. Lisandro was too careful – he knew the White Elm inside and out, knew Elijah's capabilities, and never made a move he knew they could match.

'Some of the others weren't so cautious,' Elijah said. Men in crimson hooded cloaks made up the majority of the dead. Who they were was still a matter of confusion, although a few of the White Elm nationals in the crowd of witnesses said they'd identified themselves as Magnus Moira, followers of Lisandro, before they'd made their vicious attack. 'Most of them Displaced straight here from hotel rooms and apartments around the city. I've got Jadon chasing up any information on who they were. One hotel let him into the room and he said it's totally empty, not even a suitcase or passport to confirm the name they're booked under.'

'Naturally.' Qasim scrubbed at his face tiredly with one rough hand. A senior councillor, he was in charge of managing the crisis here at ground zero while Lord Gawain handled the stuff behind closed doors – media management, police, mortal politicians, anyone who required an actual sit-down meeting to trade information with – and Lady Miranda treated and debriefed the mortal witnesses with Emmanuelle before their release to the Czech hospital system. They'd been quite late to that party, though, stuck back in London treating Renatus's apprentice.

'She went that way,' a boy of around Aristea's age said, stepping out of the crowd and pointing in the direction of the bodies leading back to the Wall. He looked shaken and distressed. 'She said 'it's him'. Her White Elm partner followed her. I heard her scream…'

'Who?' Elijah demanded, but Qasim murmured, 'Aristea,' and with a final wretched glance at Anouk he moved off at a jog.

Having seen the fresh blood and black blast marked on the wall where the girl was struck, Elijah knew that the choice to dedicate two of three Healers to her immediate treatment was necessary. He was still waiting to learn what had happened to neutralise Glen and was trying not to worry too much about what he couldn't control.

In any case, the pressure of the explosion scene was taking its toll on Qasim, and Elijah was glad to not be in his position.

'Alright,' Qasim said finally. 'Find out which of these policemen took the photographs of the deceased and get hold of them. Once Susannah gets back, check in with her. Release the pictures to the mortal media *only* if she says it'll get us answers. Otherwise give them to…' Anouk. Anouk was the Archivist. No longer. 'Give them to Oneida and she'll file them– What?' Elijah must have glanced aside when he sensed the cross-national Displacement, such manipulations of space catching his hyperawareness of the Fabric. Qasim frowned. 'Who is it now?'

'Not sure. Coming in from–'

'Oh, no.' The Scrier scowled and pointed to the end of the

42

street, shaking his head, and Elijah turned to watch the well-dressed old man step smoothly out of thin air. None of the remaining mortal police had enough control of their own minds to react appropriately to the weirdness of this phenomenon. 'No. Scratch all that; I'll get the pictures. You deal with him. I've had enough of these people.'

Qasim stormed off, leaving Elijah to reluctantly raise a hand of wary greeting to the newcomer. To label this man as one of *these people* was a little unfair, since he was the first of his particular nation to arrive on the scene, but Elijah understood Qasim's standpoint. This was White Elm territory, a White Elm criminal investigation and White Elm jurisdiction. There was an arguable place for Valero. Avalon had not been invited to weigh in, yet here they were.

'Gabriel Winter,' the unusual-looking sorcerer said, extending a hand when Elijah got close enough. It wasn't a typical gesture in the magical world, especially not in more traditional nations like Avalon, but Mr Winter had crossed over into the modern mortal world where it was not only acceptable but expected, and he'd come prepared. His hands were gloved. They shook hands; Winter was the sort to clasp his second hand over Elijah's. 'I'm terribly sorry for your loss here today. A sister. May she be at peace.'

'Thank you,' Elijah offered, because it was polite, letting the emotion of the man's words roll off his rock-solid aura like water off a duck. There was no room for feeling while there was so much business still to attend to. 'I'm–'

'I know who you are. Elijah. You're the White Elm and you don't want another government here – I understand.' Gabriel Winter smiled thinly and released Elijah's hand. He had looked old from a distance, but it was the hair: completely white. His face was unlined, only in his late thirties or early forties, eyes sharp under dark brows. 'Quite the mess. The Steward and his council have sent me as a delegate, a mediator, and as kin. The Steward honours his alliances with both the White Elm and Valero. He offers my services. Use me as necessary; an extra pair of hands.' The man bowed, shockingly white hair reflecting summer sun. 'Naturally, I am also here to make a report back to my people – the Steward invokes the terms of Avalon's agreement with the White Elm on transparency of issues that may pose threats to Avalon's safety, and I don't want to waste your time today with paperwork proving that this constitutes – so I will not be going anywhere. Might as well put me to use.'

Elijah supressed a sigh and gestured around the Prague street. 'Doing what, Mr Winter?' Trust Avalon to stick its nose in right when it was least wanted, especially in the guise of being helpful.

'I'm a detective,' the man persisted. 'You're undermanned. Tell me what needs to be done.'

A detective seemed an awfully modern occupation for a sorcerer from the second-most backward traditionalist magical society in the world, yet he looked the part, light blazer and tie and all. The familiar voices in Elijah's head took special interest in the newcomer, as did the Valeroan tracers analysing the scene through the mortal brains they'd hijacked. No one in the White Elm's circle of minds particularly wanted Gabriel Winter involved, but Lord Gawain confirmed what Elijah had already suspected.

I know him. It'll be more effort to get rid of him. Put him to work, and deal with the consequences later.

'Fine.' Avalon would get access to this investigation eventually, and in truth, Winter was probably right in that these events had the potential to impact on their secluded society. 'We need to know who the attackers were. Ours, yours, theirs.' He nodded in the direction of the Valeroans. It was unlikely but possible that those involved weren't even White Elm nationals. 'Most likely dissidents of ours but we need to be sure. They Skipped in from hotel rooms across the city.'

'How do you know?' Detective Winter's sharp eyes flickered over Elijah's aura, shifting in focus to take in the markers that indicated which class of sorcerer he belonged to. 'Oh. My mistake.' Elijah was a Displacer, a jumper through space. 'No passports, no identification in their rooms? On the bodies?'

'One of my people is investigating the rooms now. Nothing yet.'

Winter nodded, businesslike. He looked down the street.

'Can I have a look?' he asked, waiting for Elijah to understand, swallow his emotional backlash and start leading the way to the dead. 'You don't need to be with me if it's too painful.'

'We don't need to uncover Anouk,' Elijah replied shortly. Another foreign official wandering about, a law unto himself, without supervision? Not likely. 'Most of the bodies are in perfect condition and, according to our only councillor to survive the event, they dropped dead on impact with the shockwave. It must have been quick.'

'A small mercy,' Winter agreed. He nodded toward the witnesses finally being released by Qasim, streaming with relief out of the area, only for the mortals to be stopped by three Valeroans for further questioning. Hopefully debriefed sufficiently, unlike the few who'd already managed to sneak off. 'Merciful more weren't killed. Your people must have acted admirably.'

Elijah nodded tightly, not able to think of a reasonable answer to that. Of course his people had acted admirably. They were the White Elm, the best the world of sorcery had to offer as leadership material. Anouk and Renatus, the two in question, weren't even White Elm born, joining the council and the nation as young adults to strengthen its diverse ranks with their talents and powers. But Anouk was still dead.

Gabriel Winter had incredible tact. When they reached the bodies, he politely asked which was Anouk, and avoided her motionless shape. He knelt and lifted the blanket of the nearest lost life.

'By Arthur,' he murmured, a saying Elijah normally found funny of Avalonians, but today nothing much was funny. The detective, who actually did not look particularly Avalonian, stared for a long time at the dead man in the crimson cloak. Elijah glanced, hating the way the skin had started to whiten with cold and the eyes had gone glassy and clouded. Anouk, he knew, just a short distance away, looked like that, under her blanket.

The detective peeled the blanket further back, revealing the stranger's uninjured body. Sneakers peeked from under the hem of the cloak. Normal attire beneath the horror costume. Winter waved his hand once over the body to pick up any final traces of magical energy; Valero's people had already done this, Qasim had already done this, and there would be little left to tap into by now.

'What happened here?' Winter asked, sounding stunned. 'I know – it's what you're here to ascertain. But it was a spell, wasn't it? An explosive spell.'

'The witnesses called it a silver ball, like a disco ball. Renatus said his apprentice noticed it feeding from the fear of the crowd.'

'That's something you don't hear every day. Renatus with an apprentice.' Winter smiled humourlessly, digging a small device from his pocket. It looked like a pen, but had a pointed crystal at each end and its shaft was polished brass. He began drawing symbols in the air above the corpse, eliciting sparks of faded energy from nothing. Elijah watched the antiquated magic without much interest, unsurprised that Gabriel knew of Renatus, both coming from traditional schools of magical thinking. 'I didn't think your people encouraged that anymore.'

Apprenticeships in magic had gone a little to the wayside in modern White Elm society. Surveying the field of white blankets, Elijah considered the dead innocents, the four civilians in the wrong place at the wrong time, who'd died beside Anouk. He considered the dozen or so politically conscious young sorcerers who'd survived and whose light-hearted street party-turned-rally had formed the centrepiece for this incident. If more of them had had formal training in magic as apprentices, Renatus and Anouk mightn't have been defending a whole crowd on their own. They would have had help.

Fears of things like this had spurred the White Elm into forming their Academy, where Renatus had found Aristea, but despite the leaps and bounds their current students were making, the tragedy in Prague made it feel about a generation too late.

'He's a little young by your standards, isn't he?' Winter continued, probing lightly. Elijah shrugged unhelpfully. He had plenty of opinions on Renatus's unconventional relationship with Aristea but they weren't worth voicing. This, today, would have been so much worse without the girl connected to the variously stable Dark Keeper. 'Even by Avalon's. Hmm. You were right about it being quick.' Detective Winter changed the subject smoothly. He covered the body and moved to the next one, pulling back the blanket. 'Heart and all brain activity stopped instantly. There would have been no pain, no awareness. This was potent magic.'

Elijah was surprised. 'You got that off the body? They've already been scanned.'

'I'm not *that* good.' Winter's mouth made another smile shape but it was reluctant. 'There's nothing on the body, not even residual electrical energy, which should still be present. Conspicuous by its absence. I've seen this before.'

'Where?'

'In books.'

Magic is all around us, and those sensitive to it can read it by degrees. The especially sensitive, such as high-level sorcerers like Elijah and Gabriel, were able to detect the energetic disturbance generated by someone expressing a falsehood. It manifested as a little flicker, the giveaway.

So they learned to speak cautiously. A lie was only a lie if you knew and believed it to be so; a half-truth or an allusion did not register as falsehoods and did not cause the tell-tale flicker. *In books* did not flicker in the air between Elijah and Gabriel Winter, but something in Avalon's representative's voice made him think maybe it should have. Avalon were much less barbaric and raw than Valero, but their liberal views on the spectrum of magic was more aligned with the Russian splinter community than with White Elm's rather unadventurous doctrine.

For his personal part, Elijah sat pretty impartially amongst all this and considered now that it was for the best that he, rather than a hardliner like Qasim, was liaising with Winter. Avalon definitely *did* have books in their Grand Library with content such as how to make magic like what happened here today, and more than likely, they'd done some experimenting. Qasim and Lord Gawain would condemn them, quietly shaking their heads, acknowledging that this was why they could only be allies with these independents, never expect a complete unification. The White Elm couldn't condone dark magic being played with.

Look what it had done today.

But those same hardliners on the council would turn a blind eye to Renatus, and Lisandro before him, studying, training, soaking in all the dark magic he could get his hands on, in preparation for things like this. They maintained the secret position on the council, the one person in their worldwide nation above the law on this matter.

Bureaucracy is hypocrisy. It's a system, don't question it, especially when you're part of it.

'Anything you can tell us about it?' Elijah asked the detective. 'We're calling it a fear bomb, for lack of a better word.'

'I don't remember if it has a name,' Winter admitted. 'Most spells are named at creation but this one escapes me. Your label serves perfectly, and the apprentice is correct. The design is that fear generated in the vicinity of the spell provides fuel for its expansion and acceleration, and when the spell becomes saturated with fear, it explodes with all that energy in a powerful wave. It interrupts the electrical signals in the brain, effectively switching the body off. I didn't think the spell would be put into practice, especially in your world.'

Elijah shrugged again. He felt like he'd be doing that a lot more before the day was over.

'I didn't think Avalon believed in electricity, so it's

surprises all around today.'

Gabriel Winter was patient and did not bite. He was oddly empathetic, perhaps sensing that this was not Elijah's usual kindly, gentle state of being and the ordeal of the past hours had affected more than just the victims.

'You're going after Lisandro for this?'

'The attackers were wearing his cult's uniform,' Elijah stated. 'He put Renatus's apprentice in hospital and one of our councillors is dead. Yeah, we're looking for Lisandro. Why, have you seen him?'

'Not lately,' the detective said carefully. 'He's been in contact with the Steward, wanting to build an alliance, but we've got our alliance with the Elm to consider so it didn't go anywhere. It just seems odd,' he mused, 'that a man just beginning to build his empire and forge political connections, so obviously at odds with a major power like yourselves, would imperil his reputation and throw it all to the winds like this. There's no coming back from this fall. Are you *certain* the attackers were connected to him? I know they're in the cloaks,' Winter acknowledged generously, nodding at the body at their feet while Elijah simply stared at him. 'But are we certain there aren't other groups who identify with the same attire?'

'They *identified* with Magnus Moira before they set their bomb off,' Elijah said flatly, not interested in this stupid, bureaucratic tug-of-war between truths as every party chose a stance on the issue. Facts were facts. 'Renatus heard it, and several of the mortal civilians and White Elm nationals among the witnesses confirmed this.'

'But–'

'He was here.'

It was Winter's turn to be surprised. 'You're sure?'

'Ask Renatus, or any one of our Healers, who've just finished picking his magic out of our apprentice's face. He nearly took her eye out.'

'I will.' Detective Winter moved to a third body and uncovered it. Odd, ugly bruising mottled the exposed throat and collarbone of the crimson-robed young man, and his glasses were askew. 'Looks familiar. Renatus's work?'

Probably. 'My team's response with force to an act of terrorism isn't what's under investigation here.'

Avalon nodded once, graciously, judgement reserved for now. Doubtless, the marks of vicious duelling magic like this were a common enough sight in their isolated medieval island society during their big tournaments. If it looked familiar, there was every chance Renatus learned that very spell during his brief internment there as a teenager.

'Have you seen enough of the bodies to be able to help me now?' Elijah asked curtly. 'The most use you can be to me is if you can somehow track where these men came from before they arrived in their hotels. They didn't Displace into the rooms; they would have walked, driven, taken planes. One was Irish. That's all I know so far. Does that fall within your skillset, Detective?'

Winter tucked the blanket gently back around the third blast victim and stood, looking around with his eyes narrowed against the overhead sun.

'How did Renatus survive?' he asked as if he hadn't heard Elijah. The councillor rolled his own eyes, annoyed. He didn't have time for this.

'His usual brand of luck and talent. His apprentice is good with wards.'

'Hmm.' The white-haired detective found the Lennon Wall with his sharp gaze. He was silent for a beat too long, and Elijah was about to excuse himself when he spoke again, softer this time. 'I can't imagine how you're going to explain this to your mortals, Elijah.'

The New Zealander blinked, taken aback by the comment, and looked around with the outsider. At first glance, it looked like a typical police scene, which was apt, because despite all attempts to contain things, footage had naturally been taken and smuggled out and had already found its way to national and international media, where it was being reported that an explosion had rocked central Prague and killed several people. A news helicopter had been over a few times and it would have seen seventeen blanketed bodies but no obvious structural damage to the street or its buildings, which was no doubt stimulating the rush of curious journalists gathering at the fringes of the cordoned-off scene.

The media was easy enough to influence, and most eyewitnesses would accept more logical explanations offered. Disbelief was a powerful protective force that sorcerers had relied upon for many centuries now and public displays of magic like today's would be dismissed by many. But never all.

Luckily the mortal world had words for those people, *crackpot* and *lunatic* among them.

'Yes, I'll track down the identities of your crimson-cloaked John Does,' Winter said suddenly, cracking a more genuine smile. 'It certainly does suit my skillset, and the Steward wishes me to be of any assistance you require, in honour of our treaty. I'm at your service. But once I'm done,' he made sure to mention, 'I'll be wanting to speak with this apprentice of Renatus's.'

'You'll need to talk to him about that,' Elijah replied staunchly, 'and I don't like your chances.'

Winter's smile didn't falter, even as he nodded once in respectful deference, though it did widen just enough to be called sly. As he raised his head he indicated with his chin toward the square's exit. 'Oh, look. Our mutual friends have kindly taken care of your problem for you.'

Elijah spun when he heard Qasim's angry shout, and saw the Scrier striding furiously toward a trio of Valeroans standing together near the gathered civilians. The lucky ones who weren't killed by the explosion were filing on past, grasping each other's hands in relief and chattering anxiously amongst themselves. The shortest Valeroan raised a self-righteous, placating hand to Qasim as the Saudi sorcerer approached, and would have been throttled if Elijah hadn't swiftly split the distance to step between them from fifty paces away.

'It's for the best for us all,' the Telepath soothed as the witnesses dissipated and Elijah caught Qasim's tense arm

51

warningly. They did *not* need an altercation with their most volatile and wounded ally today on top of everything else. 'It's for the best for them, too.'

'Our Healers don't agree,' Qasim snarled, 'or they would have recommended it. You just further violated the victims, you smug Russian bastards.'

But there was nothing to be done, and Qasim angrily wrenched away from Elijah so he could pace to a safe distance where he couldn't strangle one of Anouk's kinsmen. They all watched as the last of the remaining witnesses drifted out of the square, blinking in disorientation.

Memory alteration was a fundamental transgression against another person under White Elm Telepathy ethics. To Valero, it was a matter of practicality.

'If we could do the same to ourselves and forget this whole day, we would,' the shortest sorcerer said simply. 'When Glen asks for the same, send him to us.' He blinked uncertainly when Elijah lowered his gaze, unable to keep his probing mind to himself. 'What is wrong with Glen?'

chapter four

I didn't remember falling asleep, but several times that afternoon I woke up from druggy dozes. In between, I mostly sat in silence in my bed, weighed down with heavy, miserable thoughts, while Renatus either sat in his chair or paced the room, dark and broody and plagued with guilt. He pulsed with the usual caged-animal energy that infected him when he was locked out of the action.

One time, I woke up and he wasn't there. I blinked my one functioning eye groggily.

'Renatus?'

'No.'

I whipped around to focus on the person curled in the chair and felt my heart leap to see my very best friend, Hiroko Sasaki.

'Wh... what are you doing here?' I asked, disbelief fading into delight when she offered me a shaky smile. I weakly yanked at the blankets binding me to the bed and swung my legs over the edge, facing her properly.

'It's visiting hours,' she replied lightly. I felt the disconnect between her tone and her real feelings, her gaze clinging to the patchwork of medical tape and padding on my face. She was sick with worry, but she gestured to the folded pile on her lap. 'Emmanuelle asked me to choose clothes for you. She said you were here. I asked if I could come.'

Hiroko was the first person I met the day my sister dropped me off at Renatus's ancestral home in Northern

Ireland. Through a fluke of birth order we'd ended up as roommates and despite thick accents that should have made communication difficult, we'd bonded very quickly over a shared sense of humour and shared values. Hiroko was one of the nicest and most thoughtful people I had ever known, and I was so incredibly grateful for her right now.

'Thank you,' I said, meaning it. 'You didn't have to. Did they… did they tell you what happened?'

She shook her head, silky dark hair brushing her shoulders. 'Not much. I saw Renatus, arguing with someone I don't know. Emmanuelle is with him. He said you took a hit. He… seems upset.'

I reached lightly for Renatus, his presence joined with magic to mine no matter where we were, and I found his energy signature at the other end of this ward. Hiroko was right; he was in a sour mood. It was easy to feel his moods in place of my own, and I had to work against it.

'It was an upsetting day,' I confirmed, swinging my legs experimentally. Considering my only injury had been to my eye and cheek, the rest of me felt pretty shot. I kept my eyes on my feet as I added, hollowly, 'Some people died.'

'Emmanuelle told me. She said Anouk was killed, and you were badly hurt.' She pulled her legs closer to her chest, uncomfortable, eyeing my bloody clothes, my hidden face. 'I thought I would feel better after I saw you.'

'But you don't,' I guessed. She smiled woefully and shook her head.

'Not really. You look… No wonder Renatus is worried. But how do you feel?'

'Below average.'

I hopped down and instantly whistled in pain, the catheter in my left arm tugging brutally when I pulled too far away from my drip. Angrily I tore the tape holding it to my skin and pulled the needlepoint from my flesh and threw it onto the bed. Unbalanced slightly by my impaired vision, I grabbed at the side table to keep myself from falling on my face.

A water glass placed down… 'We're not discussing this in here…'

'Are you alright?'

Hiroko had jumped up and caught my hands, stabilising me, the psychic impression left on the table surface fading from my mind as quickly as it had struck.

'Just a reminder that my mental barriers are down.' I was good with wards, and concentrated on building a series of invisible energetic layers around myself, shields against Telepaths, shields against magic being thrown at me, shields against impressions. Many that I'd tapped into over the past few months had really shaken me with their frightening, impassioned insights into past events.

'Impressions?' Hiroko asked sympathetically. A Displacer like Elijah, she didn't have the same issue; for me, a scrier, this was an occupational hazard, and as I grew into my gifts I was finding the impressions were also often very helpful, but right now, with one working eye and lots of other problems, I did not need them. Hiroko released me, attention also on my eyes. She nodded at the bandages uncertainly. 'What is under it? Is it... very bad?'

I tentatively raised my hand to the left side of my face and unexpectedly, behind her, the door was wrenched open. I let my hand drop and took an unsteady step backwards, feeling caught out.

The feeling was soon substantiated.

'What are you doing out of bed?' Emmanuelle demanded, dropping her bag on Hiroko's chair as she swept over. 'And *who* changed your bandage?'

I knew she was barely older than Teresa, but the French Healer did not *suggest* when she spoke. As usual, it did not cross my mind to argue. She helped me back onto the bed I could only half-see, and settled beside me just as Teresa had. Hiroko hovered at her shoulder.

'I took it off. Teresa had to put a new one on.'

'Hmm.' It was clear Emmanuelle was unimpressed with her colleague's bandaging skills, and without asking she began unwrapping it from my head. 'Well, she is not a doctor, I suppose. 'ow do you feel?'

I was quite certain Emmanuelle was no doctor either, but I refrained from asking.

'Tired,' I said honestly. She nodded as she unravelled, and I considered that she felt the same. Her long blonde hair was uncharacteristically tied up in a messy ponytail, and her pretty face was drawn. 'Groggy. My eye hurts whenever I blink or move my face too much. And my arm hurts.'

'Hmm,' she said again, taking my chin in her many-ringed hand so she could better see the padding over the left eye. 'You are also awake, which is an improvement on the last time I saw you.' She smiled, softly conveying her affection for me, and I smiled back even though the pull on my facial muscles made my eye twinge. 'You scared us.'

'So I heard.' I kept still while she unpicked the tape Teresa had liberally laced across my cheek and forehead to keep the sterile padding in place. I didn't miss the startled look on Hiroko's face when our Academy supervisor dumped discarded tape and bandage in her arms. 'Where's Renatus?'

'Doing what 'e does best, arguing. There's a delegate from the colony in Avalon 'ere. Things between those two are... 'eated.'

'Avalon is real?' Hiroko asked in surprise.

'What are they arguing about?' I asked. I knew Renatus had spent some time as a teenager living in Avalon, though he never talked about it and, given that the stint immediately followed the murders of his parents and sister, I didn't think it was a positive experience.

Emmanuelle smiled wryly. 'You, of course. What else? Hold still,' she ordered when I twitched. I tried to do as she said. Had the council made a ruling already? Had they deemed me at fault for what happened to Anouk and those other people? Or was it something else, something to do with Lisandro, something Renatus didn't think I could handle if I overheard?

I should be grateful for his foresight and his protectiveness. I was freshly eighteen but in our world twenty was the first age of adulthood, preparation for the traditional initiation at twenty-one, and I'd proven today that I was *not* the competent young woman I imagined a White Elm apprentice ought to be. Still, Renatus treating me like a kid he needed to look out for grated on a newly emerging node of my identity – the part that acknowledged that I *was* a kid that needed looking after, and despite outward appearances, so was he. I was his responsibility, but he was mine, and a terrible, unknowable fate awaited him if I didn't find some way to redirect him.

I was trying not to think about it around powerful sorcerers like the White Elm's members, since it was a secret only I and one other knew about, and the only solution I'd yet come up with was both unfeasible and likely to be very unpopular.

Emmanuelle peeled the last of the padding from my face and Hiroko, out of my line of sight, couldn't hide the wave of horror that rushed through her.

'What? How bad?' I tried to turn to read her face; Emmanuelle held me still, looking only at her. Whenever she looked at me injured, I got the impression she saw something deeper than my skin.

'Hiroko, contain yourself around the Empath,' she instructed. 'Get me something to clean it with. This, I am not 'appy with,' she added irritably, gesturing at my face as Hiroko rushed to the nearby sink. I frowned, quickly relaxing my expression when it hurt.

'Why?' I asked nervously, thinking I should be glad I couldn't see if that was her assessment even after scolding Hiroko. 'Teresa said everybody was happy with it.'

'If you 'ave seen Renatus you know that isn't true,' Emmanuelle dismissed. Forever brutally honest. Hiroko silently came back with a plastic bowl, and with a soft wet cloth, Emmanuelle set to work clearing whatever gunk had accumulated on my wound. It stung briefly but then her fingertips brushed my skin, too warm. Healing. 'You scared 'im the most. On that note,' she mentioned, annoyed again, lifting her fingertips away from my face, 'he said *this* 'appened because you dropped your wards.' She punctuated the emphasis with a light tap to the site of my injury, which stung disproportionately and made me pull away. 'What were you thinking? Did you run out of energy?'

I shook my head, unwilling to think back over the events of this morning but not really able to think of much else anyway.

'No, I... I lost sight of Lisandro, and... I couldn't sense him through the wards. So–'

'Lisandro?' Hiroko repeated, ill-feeling creeping into her aura, into mine. 'He attacked you? For what?'

My face must have looked bad, because she'd never reacted like this before when I'd told her about previous misdeeds of the council enemy. When he'd burned me; when he'd tried to strike me dead with lightning. The difference, I suppose, between being told and seeing the reality.

'For almost catching 'im, I gather,' Emmanuelle replied, not sensitive enough to notice her words did nothing to help Hiroko's dread. 'It might be your job but that's why you *use wards*.'

Didn't I know it. Some wards, like the big one I used in Prague, were short-term things thrown up as shields against specific threats. They went away as soon as they served their purpose, or when they were broken by a force too strong for them to hold up against. Others, like the type Emmanuelle was referring to, were more permanent structures, layers of mental magic over people or places to serve ongoing protection.

Hiroko swallowed nervously. 'I am going to practise wards every day. Is that...?' She nodded at my face as Emmanuelle began packing new cottony padding over the wound, taping it down quickly and expertly. 'Will it go away?'

The Healer's piercing blue x-ray focus dropped from me briefly. Remorse.

'No,' I answered for her. 'Not fully.'

'It could 'ave been much worse,' she admitted. 'Ideally there would be no scar, especially on your face, but...'

'Beggars can't be choosers,' I guessed quietly.

'*Non,*' she agreed reluctantly. 'As you say. It is a small cost, in the grander scheme.'

'What if she comes back to the school?' Hiroko asked, suddenly inspired. 'Will it make a difference?'

I snorted. 'Why would it?' But Emmanuelle nodded seriously.

'It will 'elp. All the magic,' she explained to me. 'So many magical people making so much magic every day. It makes you stronger.'

'Magic breeds magic,' Hiroko agreed. 'This is why the White Elm brought us together to study, not only day school. We make one another stronger over time.'

It had never occurred to me as the reasoning behind the boarding school-style approach.

'Renatus doesn't want 'er to go back yet,' Emmanuelle told Hiroko. My friend seemed to understand.

'He is worried others will fear her?'

I laughed; the resultant expression stretched and tightened the skin around my eyes, and it stung. 'Ow. Fear me?'

Emmanuelle placed the last strip of tape down tightly and withdrew. It had taken her half as long as it took Teresa earlier, and felt twice as secure. She looked me straight in my remaining eye.

'And so they should,' she said seriously, sobering me. 'After only one season studying magic, your power rivals that of adult sorcerers casting the most sophisticated of spells. Avalon says it would 'ave killed you all. You survived. Seventy-two other people survived. They would all be dead without you. I wish I'd seen it. Your ward,' she filled in quickly, when I stared blankly. 'The whole street?'

Aside from Renatus, Emmanuelle was my favourite White Elm councillor – roughly the same age, I supposed she stood in as a super-powered version of my older sister. At the Academy, where I studied magic with other underage sorcerers in the hopes of becoming White Elm ourselves one day, Emmanuelle was my instructor in wards and shielding spells. She was also the White Elm's official Healer, and she was kickass and bold, and I aspired to be just like her.

She would never have failed as completely as I did today, but I didn't dare voice my feelings of self-blame with her. The closest thing Renatus had to a best friend, she reminded me at times of my sister, but my gentle-natured Angela could never command the sort of intimidation Emmanuelle did, and even headstrong Renatus avoided confrontation with her.

'Don't look so miserable.' From my blind spot, Hiroko took my wrist, her fingers covering the elegant black tattoo on my wrist that matched Renatus's, marking us as master and apprentice. She felt more comfortable now that my face was covered again. 'It is your birthday. We brought you something.'

Emmanuelle reached for her bag and offered me what was inside.

'Where did you get that?' I asked, sitting forward. Really it was a rhetorical question, since the pink-wrapped gift was mine and I'd stashed it safely in my shared bedroom at Morrissey House just a few hours ago. I looked gratefully to Hiroko, knowing it was her doing. She smiled.

'Hiroko said you would want this, and…' Emmanuelle kept digging in her bag until she found her cell phone. 'This.'

Oh, Hiroko, you intuitive angel. I smiled, accepting the phone and hugging the present to myself. The gift was from my big sister, and the phone was to call her as per Angela's request in her card. The generations of high-level magic steeping Renatus's house disrupted many magical and electrical signals, rendering electronic devices like phones or televisions useless. I hadn't used a phone in months. Mostly I'd been too busy to mind.

'Thank you,' I said, opening the flip phone and running my thumb over the keys. A brief impression struck me – *Emmanuelle, upset and angry, arguing in passionate French with the caller* – and I tried not to flinch and let on. I needed gloves.

'We will leave you,' Hiroko said diplomatically as Emmanuelle got up to leave. I shook my head.

'You don't have to,' I insisted. 'My sister wants to hear me open my present, and…'

I blushed. It sounded dumb, the whole thing, but it was our first family occasion apart. Opening birthday presents surrounded by the rest of the household was one of those cheesy but warm rituals my family had upheld throughout my childhood, one that Angela had wanted to simulate as closely as possible today with this call.

In a very short space of time, Emmanuelle and Hiroko had become like family, but that was too weird to say aloud. Hiroko didn't need to be told. She settled against the side of my bed, the very best of best friends.

'I need to speak with Renatus,' Emmanuelle dismissed herself. 'Talk as long as you need, the battery is fully charged.'

'But what…' I began hesitantly, turning my head all the way to be able to see her walk to the door. 'Uh, what do I tell my sister about today?'

If I said I was in hospital on my eighteenth birthday after watching a White Elm councillor die and finding myself on the receiving end of a vicious act of magic in a foreign country neither of us had previously visited when as far as she knew, I was restricted to the safety of Renatus's house on our home soil, she would *flip out*. I would be unenrolled from the Academy and grounded for the rest of my life. At least. I'd only seen my sister in protective overdrive mode once before, and the resultant blow-up between Ange and our aunt had almost splintered what was left of our family.

'Everything or nothing, it is your decision,' Emmanuelle answered apologetically. She hung in the doorway for a moment, hesitant. 'Please, do not blame yourself for today. Enough others will try.'

She left. Hiroko and I exchanged spooked looks. Weird words.

'Are you sure you would like me to stay?' she asked finally. I quickly dialled from memory and handed her the phone.

'Completely. Angela will love you.'

Hiroko used her superior eyesight to set it to

speakerphone, and each ring rattled inside my ear, loud against the new silence in the room.

'Aye, hello?'

Inside my tight, constricted chest, my heart leapt to hear that voice for the first time in months. I'd forgotten how long it had been since I'd actually *spoken* to my only surviving sibling. We wrote, but I hadn't seen her since March. It was now July.

'Ange, it's me,' I said, pushing some of my dark hair off my face self-consciously even though she couldn't see me. 'I got your note.'

'Aristea!' My sister's voice was bright and excited, a direct contrast to the atmosphere of the place I was in. I shared a tentative smile with Hiroko. 'I wasn't sure I was going to hear from you. Happy birthday!'

'Thanks. I'm here with my friend Hiroko. We're on speaker.'

'Hello Angela,' Hiroko spoke up, leaning forward to be heard. I listened as two of my favourite people warmly introduced themselves, having heard so much about the other, and I felt content for the first time in hours. I could picture Ange exactly. I imagined her standing in the corner of a crowded café sipping her tea, phone pressed hard to her ear. Golden blonde hair swept up tidily in the same high ponytail as ever, collared shirt crisp and pressed, her smile playing at the edges of her eyes like mine did. I'd never noticed before it started hurting every single time I smiled. My mental picture of her swam a little and I realised I wasn't imagining at all. I was scrying her, truly viewing her in real-time, but it was tiring me out, so I released my hold on the image.

'You're *eighteen*,' Angela gushed. 'I can hardly believe it. Do you have time to talk? Tell me everything about your day so far.'

I fidgeted with the ends of my hair and considered what to tell her. Prague, Anouk, the hospital? As far as she knew, she'd packed me off reluctantly four months ago to live with the White Elm council to compete against my peers for a chance at an apprenticeship in advanced magic. She knew I'd received the honour, knew my master was Renatus, but she'd never met him, and I'd deliberately omitted most of what our work had involved. I was happy for her to think I was tamely attending school every day, and for her to *not* think I was also teleporting around the world chasing dark sorcerers, consorting with shady underworld figures for information and on occasion, finding myself drastically injured.

Like today.

'I...' The lie only hitched for a moment, and though sorcerers could read untruths around them from the tell-tale energetic flicker, it didn't work over the phone. 'I've... not done much, really.' Hiroko stared at me and I swallowed the guilt of lying to my sister. After our parents and brother were killed in what we thought was a freak accident almost four years ago, we had been one another's everything. 'It's been one of those lazy birthdays.'

'Are you sure?' Hiroko asked, a layered question. 'I think you have a busy day.'

I shook my head silently at her, pleading without words. Over the phone, unable to do a thing to help? This wasn't how I wanted Angela to find out.

'I suppose it has been,' I agreed, and I proceeded to detail a happy and carefree day modelled on the hours before I left Morrissey House with Anouk – the opening of presents from our aunt, reading the handmade comic book put together by my five beautiful friends, and chilling in the summer sun. I told her about the magical snowglobe Hiroko made, with leaves and stones and things, the latest in her line of funky little spells. I left out the gift from Renatus, a pair of sai and the promise of lessons, thinking that Angela wouldn't appreciate that as much as I did.

Hiroko was quiet, trying not to be judgemental, except when Angela complimented her spellcasting.

'Thank you,' she said immediately, genuinely pleased, and I could tell she also genuinely liked my sister even just from this first conversation. 'I like to try new magic.'

'I'd love to see that snowglobe one day. Thanks for joining us to open Aristea's present.'

'I just had to wait until I saw Emmanuelle,' I said, which was mostly true. I handed the phone back to Hiroko to free up my hands for unwrapping, which as everyone knows is serious two-handed business. 'Okay, I'm ready.'

Angela hadn't mentioned Prague, and she didn't sound concerned. Presumably news of what had happened this morning had not struck the mortal news channels, or at least, my sister hadn't yet heard about it. I wondered how long that would last.

'Do you have any idea how hard it was to choose something for you this year?' Angela asked incredulously as I started unpicking the tape. 'I wanted to get you something you'd actually use, but I barely know what your life looks like there.'

My fault. 'I know I'll like whatever you picked out for me.'

'Are you opening it? I can't hear the paper.'

'She is being very slow,' Hiroko reported.

'Calm down, I'm still at the tape,' I protested. I tore the paper away from the shoebox within and tugged off the lid, Hiroko narrating for Angela as I went. Inside the shoebox were the two items I had heard rattling around when I shook it this morning. I reached in and missed both, knocking my fingers on the cardboard at the bottom before I got a grasp.

'Okay, so that one isn't something useful,' Ange said hastily when Hiroko told her which one I'd picked out first, an ornately carved wooden box. 'It was just cool.'

'It's pretty,' I agreed, finding and then running my fingernail along the seam to open it. It did not budge. I felt around the back for the hinge, but the back was smooth. I turned the whole thing over in my hands, seeking a latch or something else to explain why it wouldn't open. 'I can't...'

'A puzzle box,' Hiroko realised, taking it with interest for a closer look and balancing the phone on my knee. Angela agreed.

'There's a secret panel on the side, and when you slide it, it unlocks the next bit. The lass at the shop showed me, naturally I've forgotten the rest of the steps, but after your letter a few weeks ago telling me about your scrying lessons? I thought you might have fun with it.'

'It's meant to be my birthday,' I whined playfully, watching Hiroko press on the smooth wooden sides, unable to find anything that would give. 'No one said there would be a test.' In my scrying lessons at school we'd been learning to look inside things like this, combination locks and the like, to fine-tune our focus when viewing what wasn't visible to our eyes. It warmed me that Angela had taken note of what I wrote in our letters, especially since I necessarily left so much detail out. 'It's really cool. Thank you.'

She responded but I missed it, distracted by the door opening. Annoyed, because it wasn't something I could see without physically turning my whole upper body, I frowned – which *hurt* – and thought an irritable *Go away* in the direction of the door.

It was Lord Gawain, leader of most of the magical world. He was an older man, grandfatherly-aged, with grey-white hair and a short, tidy beard. When not dressed ceremonially for magical business, he always wore a suit, and today was no exception. I gathered he was some sort of lawyer in non-witch society, but what that involved was utterly beyond my understanding or, to be honest, my interest. Still, he was the most influential and socially important person in my world, and I swallowed, internally cringing at my impulsive thought projection. Had he heard me? Renatus stepped in after his mentor, glancing at me. *He* had heard, evidently.

'You okay?' my sister prompted, sounding like she was repeating herself. I forced my attention back to her.

'Uh, yeah, sorry,' I said quickly, meeting Hiroko's meaningful gaze, feeling her disapproval of the intrusion. Right? It was rude. 'Paper cut. Ouch.' I extended my senses out toward Lord Gawain and Renatus but both were guarded, and I was too tired to probe. I figured my take-as-much-time-as-you-need phone call was being encouraged to end. 'Uh, Ange? I think the battery's running low on this thing.'

I hated lying to her, especially in order to cut our first proper contact in *months* so short, and she made me feel even worse by buying it immediately, even apologising – a bad habit I'd picked up from her.

'Okay, quickly, open the other one,' she urged. 'I want to know what you think.'

'She is picking it up now,' Hiroko promised, then covered the phone's mouthpiece and addressed the two men by the door. 'Can you please let her finish this call? Alone?'

Far from the timid thing people assumed, Hiroko Sasaki did not waver, facing off with the two most powerful men she'd ever met. Lord Gawain had the grace to look apologetic, but his Welsh-accented voice was reluctantly firm as he answered, 'No, I'm afraid not. We're sorry. Please finish quickly.'

I wasn't the world's biggest fangirl of Lord Gawain, either as a person or as a leader, but I mostly kept those thoughts to myself, since Renatus didn't share them and he maybe qualified in my place. Not today, apparently. He met my eyes briefly, then dropped them. Simmering with resentment.

He'd lost whatever argument Emmanuelle had referred to.

I determinedly turned away from them both, not understanding, feeling vulnerable and uncomfortable. Hiroko withdrew her hand and told Angela I was opening the second gift. She sounded convincingly normal. For me.

This box was thinner, smaller and lighter. Leathery-feeling, like the ones from jewellers. I got the paper away but then struggled to open this one, too, frustrated tears and tiredness blurring my vision.

'Another puzzle box?' I tried to joke, giving up and closing my eyes when my sister laughed. I missed her laugh. I wished I was with her right now, doing this for real. I wished this entire day hadn't happened.

I opened my eyes. Eye. I was sitting on the same hospital bed wearing my bloodied clothes from this morning and I had torn pink wrapping paper scattered over my lap.

Hiroko took the box.

'Thanks,' I murmured as she cracked the box open and presented it to me to see first. A sparkle instantly grabbed my attention and I leaned forward, the phone slipping and needing to be caught. 'Oh, Ange – *thanks*.'

'Do you like it?' she asked anxiously, though I couldn't imagine why as I reached for the source of the sparkle. A thick silver bangle lay on the cushioning of the box. Set into its classic, simple design was a chunky pink-red faceted stone, which was scattering the yucky, harsh hospital light into tiny sparkles.

'No, I've never liked pretty things, silly,' I said sarcastically, turning the bracelet over in my hand to admire it properly with Hiroko. I hated to think what it had cost my sister, who worked as a receptionist to afford our little house when she should have been doing something much more satisfying and incredible with her life. 'Of course I love it, it's stunning.'

'It's beautiful,' Hiroko agreed. 'Where did you get it?'

Angela launched into the story of shopping with her good friend Sian but I overheard Lord Gawain clearing his throat and saw Renatus's warning look at him. What was going on?

'Hey, Ange,' I interrupted, feeling just awful, 'I'm, uh, I think you're about to cut out. I… I keep, you know, hearing the beeping.' I winced, certain it was lamest attempt ever to end a conversation. Luckily my sister was wonderful and too tolerant of me, because she apologised again and hurriedly wished me a happy birthday again.

'Let's organise calls like this more often,' Angela suggested hopefully. 'If Emmanuelle doesn't mind you using her phone. Or let me know when you've got time free, and I'll come and visit.'

It did sound like a good idea, and I hoped I would remember to do that, though my track record with letter-writing hadn't been stellar.

'That will be nice,' Hiroko said. 'We can show you around.'

'Yeah. Listen, Angela, thank you, for my presents.' I clutched the bangle in my fist, adoring it already. 'You're the best. I…' I swallowed painfully. 'I miss you.'

'I miss–'

Angela's voice cut out abruptly, and in Hiroko's hand, the screen had gone blank, dead, despite having been on *full battery* when I made the call just a few minutes ago. Gone.

I jumped as the door opened loudly, the noise and the barrage of new emotions breaking my sad thoughts.

'That is my personal property,' Emmanuelle said furiously as she stormed back in, accompanied by three unfamiliar men. I turned myself enough to see them as Renatus, driven by distrust, moved to put himself between them and me.

'You said five minutes,' one newcomer said in a smooth, Welsh-ish-but-not accent. His hair was white. 'I gave her five minutes.'

'What's going on?' I asked Renatus warily as Hiroko drew back.

'Bureaucracy,' he answered. 'Meet our allies, Avalon and Valero.'

chapter five

Representatives of the White Elm's two most intriguing alliances stood in my hospital room, and I should have been fascinated to meet them, but I felt inexplicably sick.

'Please, Renatus, be charitable,' the white-haired stranger said lightly. I twisted, straining my neck, trying to see the speaker properly. 'It's perfectly reasonable–'

'Who interrupted my phone call?' I demanded, surely sounding far from reasonable, but I was half-blind and bad vibes were emanating from the side of the room I couldn't comfortably see. 'What do you want?'

'It's an interrogation,' Renatus said bluntly, sweeping the pink paper off my lap and scrunching it forcefully. He balled it up into a dense sphere. 'And that was Avalon.'

'An interrogation?' Feeling vulnerable just sitting there in the hospital bed facing away from my visitors, I again swung my legs over the edge to hop down. I saw Emmanuelle hovering, wanting to rush over and help, but Hiroko and Renatus were either side of me and did not offer a hand or attempt to steady me. I appreciated it, this chance to appear something other than needy and weak in front of these people I already did not like.

'An interview,' the white-haired man corrected. 'You must know your master's tendency toward the dramatic by now.'

Lord Gawain looked incredibly uncomfortable.

'Aristea,' he said, 'these people need to talk to you. Emmanuelle?'

He glanced meaningfully at his Healer. Unhappy about it, she jerked her head at Hiroko. She was being made to take her home. My friend understood, but paused, touching my arm questioningly. I very much wanted her to stay, and Emmanuelle too, but suspected this was one of those pick-your-battles occasions.

'Thanks for visiting,' I said, hoping to convey I'd be alright. She wasn't convinced, but nodded, casting a dark look at my interviewers.

'I can take myself,' Hiroko told Emmanuelle as she went with her to the door, but they went out into the hall, and I didn't see who Displaced who. I took a slow breath. Provided Renatus stayed, I'd be fine.

'This is Detective Gabriel Winter, who is here representing the Isle of Avalon.'

Lord Gawain gestured at the white-haired man, whose face, I saw now, was much less lined than I expected for hair so far past grey. Gabriel Winter smiled politely, maybe encouragingly, and stepped forward with his hand outstretched, murmuring about it being an honour, but the tiniest, nearly imperceptible movement of Renatus stilled him. He dropped his hand, widened his smile, and bowed his head, sliding back to where he'd started.

'And on behalf of Valero, the city keeper Demyan Vasiliev, and guardian Viktor Rodchenko.'

The Russians did not attempt to shake my hand or move toward me. Heavyset, mean-looking with his small eyes and thick black hair extending down into a wild beard, wearing some weird brown tunic and leather-wrapped boots, Vasiliev didn't even nod, but Rodchenko did. He was the younger of the two, his strong, sun-hardened face clean-shaven and his oddly-dressed body built and imposing. I wondered what he was the guardian of. The pair looked terrifying, almost savage, beside the sleek detective from Avalon.

'This, of course,' Lord Gawain finished his introductions quickly, 'is Aristea Byrne, apprentice to Renatus. She's not long woken from emergency surgery, as we told you outside.

Aristea,' he said now, addressing me with a voice steeped in both gentleness and warning, a nuanced tone I did not like at all, 'Councilman Vasiliev is one of the leaders of Valero. He worked for many years with Anouk to run and uphold their great city.'

The name felt like a kick in the chest, and I slumped back a little against the hospital bed for support as I looked anxiously to Renatus. *Am I in trouble?*

He'd said it wasn't my fault and I wasn't to blame, but here were her countrymen, clearly unhappy, in my hospital room against Renatus's wishes, and he usually got his way unless something out of his hands swung over his head. This was one of those things. I was going to be arrested, and he couldn't stop it. No wonder he wasn't sharing his thoughts with me.

In the moment of panic that followed, I questioned how far I could get if I attempted a Displacement out of the room and started running…

'No,' he answered me aloud, his effort to be calm much more soothing than his leader's. 'They're investigating Anouk's death for an inquest. She was their citizen, so it's their right and responsibility. You are a witness. These are normal proceedings.' *Or so I'm supposed to tell you.*

Yet he was telling me otherwise. *What do they really want?*

They want what they say, he assured me, touching the hand I couldn't see and taking the bracelet from my fingers. *They want to know what happened this morning to Anouk. But they're also looking for someone to blame—*

'We waste time,' Mr Vasiliev said, words obscured in his thick accent, unaccustomed to the shapes of English. 'We have not time.'

'For what?' I asked, nervously rubbing my wrists. Would there be handcuffs?

'I told you what she'll say,' Renatus said from my blind side, and into my head as Detective Winter tried to explain, largely ignored, he added, *Valero wants open access to your memory of this morning.*

'No,' I said bluntly, without even considering it. I had no intention of letting anyone, least of all a total stranger, into my mind. It felt like the most intimate act, an act of such vulnerability and trust I couldn't imagine offering another person. Even Renatus, melded as he was to the edge of my consciousness and by now a second voice in my head, was not perfectly free to roam my every private thought, nor was I free to poke through every thought of his. Boundaries, people. 'No one is going through my head.'

'That's absolutely your right,' Avalon's representation agreed slickly, addressing me. He looked straight at me, pretending like half of my face wasn't covered, like I wasn't dressed in blood. 'I can't tell you what a pleasure it is to meet you, Miss Byrne, and I wish it were under more fortunate circumstances. What an honour to meet today's hero.' He smiled. I felt like I was meant to smile back but I couldn't. 'It's your right to withhold your own mind, but Valero is interested in your account of what happened in Prague. Renatus has given his already.'

His words were reasonable and spoken respectfully, and yet... I distinctly *did not like him*. I balked at the idea of recounting this morning's events to these strangers, but I swallowed, trying to be reasonable, too.

'What's Avalon's interest?' I asked. The white-haired detective arched one fine eyebrow into his unlined forehead. He smiled. I was unsure what to read from that smile, as he was careful to withhold his emotions from me.

'The Steward of Avalon sent Detective Winter to assist in our joint investigation with Valero,' Lord Gawain said, trying to sound patient but clouded by a firmness fuelled by his discomfort with this situation. He glanced guiltily at Renatus and I knew his guilt had nothing to do with me at all. Renatus was the one annoyed about the intrusion into my recovery – Lord Gawain had been forced to do one of his least favourite things and pull rank on his favourite subordinate. Time and time again I'd noted the White Elm's leader's reluctance to order Renatus around the way he did his other councillors.

Political dramas were apparently where he drew his line. 'He's here to ensure impartiality. This is a tragic day for both the White Elm and Valero.'

Emotions are troublesome things. Luckily, looking at Winter, it appeared he wasn't particularly affected by them, so his task wouldn't be too hard. The Valeroans, however, were tense, barely holding back the negativity that soaked them through. Constrained like this – more for their own sanity and saving of face than for my benefit, I was sure – it was impossible to know exactly what they were feeling, but it seemed plausible that among the yuckier things like anger and impatience with me, there would be some degree of grief.

I tried to soften. I nodded my compliance.

'My associate, a scrier from Avalon, has already independently confirmed Renatus's story down to all but one detail,' Detective Winter said smoothly. 'You don't need to talk about Anouk. I'm sure it's painful. We'd like to hear about Lisandro.'

It shouldn't have been such a big deal, just a normal, expected part of proceedings – they do this in crime shows, after all, interview miserable witnesses – but his words, though calm and reasonable, brought up a new hurt.

'I…' I glanced at Renatus, uncertain. He met my eye and nodded subtly, prompting me to continue if I could. I turned back to Mr Vasiliev, who was closed off by comparison, cold. I swallowed. 'What do you mean? What I saw?'

'That's right,' Winter agreed. 'Renatus said the former White Elm councillor Lisandro was present at the scene. No other witness can corroborate this, and Avalon's scrier did not see him. Did you?'

'Aye. Yes. After… the bomb, the shockwave, all the black…' *Two hands slamming into magic as solid as glass.* I blinked away the waking nightmare, terrified of the consequences. Valero ran the biggest magical prison in the world, a legendary place of torture and madness from which no one came back. What if they deemed me responsible? I swallowed the fear. 'After, when I dropped the ward, I felt him. I looked up and I saw him at the end of the street.'

'And how did you know it was him? Lisandro?'

I stared. 'Because I've seen him before. I know what he looks like.'

'But you went there expecting to see him,' the detective pointed out reasonably. 'Could that have influenced your perception?'

'I didn't *imagine* him,' I insisted. 'He was there, he was responsible for all of this.'

'Perhaps. Could he have been an illusion? A trick to your eye?' Winter pushed. He looked between Lord Gawain and Renatus for support as the door reopened. 'It would explain why our scrier couldn't see him at the scene.'

'As would the correct execution of a ward,' Emmanuelle said, shutting herself in, Hiroko safely delivered home. 'We told you, Aristea is an Empath. An illusion feels no emotion – there must 'ave been a man. It would take more than a ward to keep 'er from detecting a presence, even one nobody can see.'

Winter bowed his head to her in acknowledgement of her point and turned back to me.

'Another special gift. This ability to *feel* a man's proximity by feeling what he feels... Can you tell us, what was Lisandro feeling when you noticed him? Just your observations, not coloured by the opinions you've inherited from your master,' Winter said, quite kindly. I looked to him, dislike burning inside me.

'I have my own opinions,' I stated firmly. He smiled again, wider than before, and he turned to Lord Gawain.

'Two of a kind? Lucky you.'

'Lisandro,' the guardian Rodchenko reminded me abruptly. 'What was it you felt of him?'

I felt the cool of metal at my fingertips and closed my hand over my new bracelet as Renatus gave it back to me, distinctly yet subtly different. Oddly... alive. I slipped it onto my wrist, playing with it, admiring the pinkish red stone that shimmered even in the harsh hospital light. I realised the gemstone was energised, pumped full of power from the short time he'd held it, and now that it was on my skin I could tap into it like a reservoir. I straightened, emboldened knowing it was there if I needed it, and looked up. Emmanuelle was still by the door, arms folded, between Valero and Avalon. Lord Gawain was still in the corner of the small room, waiting. And Renatus was still in my blind spot, which should make me feel anxious, except that his being there meant no one else could approach me from that side.

'Lisandro felt… satisfied,' I managed finally, remembering. 'Sadness. He felt… it was a waste.'

'*Is* a waste,' Vasiliev agreed seriously, and I bit the inside of my lips, feeling slashed down again. Winter nodded soberly.

'Did you feel this also in the vision you scried of him, before you left for Prague?'

'Not the same. I mean, I felt *stuff*. He felt confident,' I explained.

'Fascinating,' Winter noted. 'To *feel* when you scry. Does this always happen? When you scry Lisandro?'

'I hardly ever see Lisandro. None of us do. When we get a glimpse, we assume he lets his guard down on purpose. That's what he's done in the past.'

'Like laying a trap?'

'Don't put words in her mouth,' Renatus warned irritably. 'Yes, like a trap, but we weighed the risks.'

'Aristea's testimony,' Lord Gawain reminded him, putting his hands on his hips wearily. Everyone looked back to me.

'Yes, like a trap,' I repeated dutifully. 'But Renatus and Qasim *and* Anouk weighed up the risks and decided they couldn't afford not to go and spring it. Twenty or thirty lives were in the balance.'

'More, it turned out. How lucky you were so close to the action when it happened. You were in the midst of this rally, yes?' Detective Winter asked pleasantly. 'Surveying?'

'I wanted to talk to the people, convince them to leave before any trouble started,' I said, unsettled by his cheery voice. The detective nodded like this was understandable.

'And this is what you were told to do?' he asked, still smiling. I refused to answer. No. It wasn't what I was told to do. He seemed to have already known that, perhaps from Renatus's testimony, because he didn't wait or push for my response. 'Have you been formally processed for insubordination under the White Elm previously, Apprentice Byrne?'

I flinched, feeling startled by the unexpected title as much as the suggestion. Processed for insubordination? As in... charged?

'No, she hasn't,' Renatus snapped in my defence, 'and I haven't complained of it, so mind your–'

'What a surprise,' Avalon's representation cut through his words dryly. He continued questioning me. 'So you were in the wrong place and in your failure to guard your master's position, you did not see the Irishman and his accomplices arrive. Go on.'

I stared at the white-haired detective with my one blurring eye, realisation growing as I moved my attention to the Russians. Renatus had called this an interrogation. He and Emmanuelle had both insisted I'd done nothing wrong, but they weren't the ones who got to decide.

I squared my shoulders and stepped forward, away from the hospital bed I'd been leaning against. My suddenness must have come across threatening, because those on the other side of the room shifted back very slightly in response.

'I did see his accomplices arrive,' I retorted. 'Twelve men in crimson cloaks with long knives boxed us in and killed a boy not much older than me. Slit his throat and dropped him to bleed out on the road in front of us all. Isn't that what you should be worrying about?'

The detective blinked. 'This is simply due process, Miss Byrne. We will explore the rest at the inquest. The men in cloaks – Renatus and Anouk engaged them in conflict, yes?'

Mr Vasiliev growled something in Russian, apparently offended by the implication that his fallen friend might be at fault, and Winter bowed his head apologetically.

'Let me rephrase. Who struck first?'

'The guy who shot the stereo. The ringleader who commanded all the rest. None of the others wanted to be there, not really. They felt...'

'They felt what?' Renatus asked, not being able to sense what I did on that street. I struggled.

'I don't know, like they were as horrified as we were. Listen,' I said in frustration to the council allies, seeing that I was getting nowhere. 'These people were Lisandro's followers. The Irish ringleader guy cast the fear bomb–'

'Your Empathy enabled you to detect the connection between the spell and the fear it was inspiring in the crowd,' Winter interrupted yet again. I nodded stiffly. 'Another impressive skill of yours.'

'One that saved a lot of lives,' Lord Gawain spoke up. I felt grateful for him for once. He looked around at his allies. 'I'd like you to wrap this up. She's looking tired.'

'Of course,' Detective Winter agreed smoothly. 'Miss Byrne, did it not occur to you or your White Elm companions to attempt to disable the bomb spell?'

Mr Vasiliev answered snidely in Russian before I could speak, and Viktor Rodchenko translated immediately, 'Obviously not, or they would have attempted. Also,' he added, apparently speaking for himself now, 'Anouk would know better than to engage a foreign spell in that situation.'

The three had come into the hospital room like a wall, three parts of one antagonistic entity, but it was becoming clearer that Valero and Avalon were far from one and the same, and their reasons for being here were different, too.

'Of course,' Winter said again, eager to keep everyone on-side. 'My understanding is that Anouk was a highly trained sorceress, a sister both Valero and the Elm could be proud of. Likewise, Renatus's knowledge of spellwork is remarkable. If more could have been done, I'm sure between them they would have considered it.'

Suck-up, I thought, trying not to project my assessment.

You have no idea, Renatus confirmed.

'Miss Byrne,' the Avalonian detective redirected, 'how did you know the attackers were associates of Lisandro? They self-identified?'

'Yes, twice,' I answered coldly. I paused, remembering. 'The leader did. The others didn't say anything at all but they were following the Irishman's orders, wearing Lisandro's signature uniform.'

'But the Irishman's weapon also killed them all,' the detective countered, 'which doesn't seem to support the theory that Lisandro was involved, since he's currently garnering public support. Killing his followers wouldn't make sense.'

'None of it makes sense,' I responded. 'It doesn't make sense that he would attack at all. It doesn't make sense that he would *be there*, but he was.'

'Or so you perceived.'

'So we *both* perceived,' Renatus said irritably, and I raised my eyebrows even though it hurt my injured eye and cheek. 'I have the curse I pulled out of her still in a jar, if you really need proof the bastard was there.'

'I didn't shoot *myself* in the face, Detective,' I added.

'Of course not.' Again he bowed his head, deferent, but I didn't trust it. 'Renatus, I would appreciate seeing that spell after we leave here, and offer any assistance you require in your assessment of it.'

'Your ward,' Vasiliev said gruffly, artfully ending that discussion before Renatus could respond rudely but bringing us uncomfortably to the part of the morning I least wanted to talk about. 'Anouk was not under it when the bomb exploded.'

That was the most succinct and unemotive way to explain what happened, and did nothing to depict the real horror. 'No.'

'Why?' Viktor Rodchenko asked. His voice was steady but his grief slipped through the cracks he didn't know had opened up in him when he uttered the question. I withdrew again, reaching behind me for the edge of the hospital bed, pulling away from the fresh hurt that spilled into the room. It was deep and bright and almost alive with his shock.

'She's important to you,' I murmured, realising where I'd felt pain this deep before – from Renatus, reflecting on his dead sister, though his hurt was old and bitterly unaddressed. 'Not just kin.'

Viktor Rodchenko the guardian from Valero looked the same age as Anouk, though he looked more hardened than she had, skin rough with sun exposure and minimal care. He lifted his chin, attempting to pull back on the spilled feelings already permeating my skin, soaking into me, feeding my own grief and guilt.

'Anouk Kashnikova was my friend from childhood,' he confirmed flatly, squashing whatever resolve I still had to stay objective and removed from all this. 'Tell me. Why is she dead?'

Why? Why is she dead? I didn't even know that was her surname, I hardly knew anything about her and now it was too late to ask. The only thing I *did* know right now was the answer to Viktor's question. I drew a shuddery breath, feeling immensely fragile, and closed my eyes.

'Because my ward...' Wasn't big enough. Don't cry. 'Because I...' Wasn't thinking of her, I was worried about someone else.

'Because a bomb went off, and she was hit,' Renatus said staunchly. 'This line of questioning is unreasonable.'

'I agree,' Lord Gawain sighed. 'Sirs, I need you to–'

Emmanuelle strode impatiently over to take my hand, and I felt her warmth.

'She could not 'ave done more,' she said angrily, holding my aching arm out. I opened my one uncovered eye and choked – my arm lit up with eerie, stark black veins that were not there before. I blinked. No, not veins, *cracks*, under my skin, thick at my palm and becoming sparser all the way past my elbow.

Demyan Vasiliev stepped closer to me, shifting past Gabriel Winter and Lord Gawain to peer at my arm as the magical fractures began to fade from sight. His eyes lifted to my one, and I blinked away the threat of tears.

'This ward took all your strength,' he noted. 'If you made

bigger, perhaps it would fail, and all would be dead. You saved many. The many outweigh the few. Rodchenko?'

His companion did not come over, but nodded stiffly. 'Anouk would have chosen the same, if the situation were reversed.' He bit his lower lip lightly, the first physical indication of a nervousness or uncertainty in his otherwise uptight façade. 'You saw her death?' I couldn't speak, my lips pressed closed to keep his sadness and mine inside, so I nodded. 'It was...' He cleared his throat and recomposed himself. 'It was honourable, you believe?'

Like my heart could take any more. I didn't know what to say. Was instant senseless death in a foreign city street an honourable death? It was fast. It looked painless.

Immediately I felt Anouk's childhood friend forcibly yank back on his emotions and work harder to get them under his control. 'That is enough for me,' he said. He shared a glance with Vasiliev, businesslike. He addressed the councilman in fast Russian, who responded in kind, and then he conveyed to the rest of us, almost reluctantly, 'We are finished here, for now, and we are reassured that Renatus and Aristea of the White Elm did not deliberately allow or manifest Anouk's death today.'

It sounded like a *not guilty* verdict off a television crime drama, a greyish half-win unworthy of celebration.

'Emmanuelle?' Lord Gawain gestured to Viktor with a tilt of his head. 'Will you please escort Mr Rodchenko to Glen? Emmanuelle has been treating him but we are grateful for Valero's offer,' he said to Vasiliev.

With a final supportive squeeze of the hand, my supervisor left with the Russian guard, and I remained in the dark as to Glen's situation as the Valeroan councilman began talking again.

'Valero will continue investigate cooperative with White Elm,' Mr Vasiliev told Lord Gawain. His voice was thick with accent and warning. 'We will uphold accords and make any help for our friend Glen. Together we will find these *ublyudki*. But also, Valero understands Avalon will investigate. We hold inquest in five days. Get to the truth.' He held Lord Gawain's eye for a moment too long to be considered friendly, and both men eventually bowed their heads in respect and acknowledgement. 'We hold funeral in Valero. We will be honoured for White Elm to attend.'

The white-haired representative of Avalon smiled another of his wide, supposedly sincere smiles at Renatus and me.

'I really am very sorry for your suffering today, and I intend no harm or disrespect,' he claimed calmly. 'It was a delight to meet you, Miss Byrne. I'm sure we'll be seeing more of each other, and I look forward to getting to know better the young sorceress whose magic saved seventy-two lives.'

I was sure his words were honest, but I couldn't think of anything to say except that the feeling of delight wasn't mutual or some variation of the same, so I made myself say the least offensive thing that came to mind. 'Okay.'

Did Winter's smile get wider?

'Of course. Renatus.' He nodded once more, intense gaze shifting to my master, who didn't respond, and finally, finally, he got out. Lord Gawain held the door for him, casting an apologetic look back at Renatus that wasn't immediately accepted. My master flicked his hand after them; the door snapped shut against the high priest's grip.

When they were gone, when it was just Renatus and I, that's when I started to cry.

Seventy-two lives. It sounded like a lot. It sounded heroic, enough.

But it wasn't enough.

Because though I had other things to cry about, Renatus didn't know what I knew – that his destiny was to kill Lisandro one day, and to take his place as the White Elm's enemy, unless I could stop it. Today I'd proven two terrible truths to myself: I was no match for Lisandro, and seventy-two saved lives did not fill the hole of losing one.

It wasn't enough.

chapter six

It wasn't enough. Nothing could ever *be* enough to make up for *this*.

'Cassán doesn't think it's going to be enough,' Eugene Dubois voiced worriedly over the chanting of the others. His fear, a thin and skittery extra skin when he'd arrived an hour ago, was increasing in unsteady little leaps in response to every possible trigger, and had gone overboard when Moira stepped into the middle with their sacrifice. Already shaken, overwhelmed with the effort of containing his own reaction to what they were doing and having his thoughts overheard and misinterpreted, Cassán tried to shrug off the Telepath's bleeding emotions before he could absorb them, but for an Empath who'd just been broken open, this was easier said than done.

Just do your job, he thought desperately at Eugene, not trusting himself to speak as he watched the woman he would have called their ringleader finally stand, stumbling back from her choice. Moira Dawes had never looked less colourful, more *empty*. She dropped the knife and returned to her place in the circle of sorcerers, staring at her hands. It was done. It couldn't be undone. Her lips began to move to match the unsteady chant of the rest.

One chanter, the lowest voice, stopped, and the melody continued but notably lifted, getting even eerier. 'Why not?' Mánus Morrissey asked, staring across the circle of ten at

Cassán with wide violet eyes. 'Why won't it be enough?'

The scrier was wealthy, powerful, confident, aloof, but had never seemed as young or unsure as he did in this firelit moment. Feelings of regret and revulsion radiated from him, feelings that Cassán didn't have the strength left to deflect because they matched his own. *What have we done?*

'That's not...' Cassán Ó Gráidaigh shook his head, his tongue slow and thick, ignoring his instructions like it wasn't his. His whole body felt like it wasn't his. Were those really his hands, weaving dutifully in the air before him, shaping magic automatically, intuitively, with moves he'd practiced a thousand times before tonight, *knowing* he wouldn't be able to remember them once they got this ritual started? Were those really his legs, shaking with the effort of holding him upright? Were those really his feet, planted on the compacted earth of the field they'd chosen, dressed in shoes that were presentable before he wore them here and got them soaked in blood?

Certainly that was his stomach, twisting and heaving, but he'd had the foresight not to eat today. He kept his eyes away from the centre of the circle and raised his hands high. Inhale, two, three...

There. He started on the next sequence of motions, reaching for the golden shimmer of Fate hanging reluctantly over their tragic crime. A trap, sprung.

'If it's not going to work, tell us now,' Eugene demanded snappishly. His words were reflected around the circle in the spiralling uncertainty of others, in their nods. Cassán pressed his lips together, annoyed by his inability to allay their concerns without dissolving into wretched sobs. Didn't they see? It *had* to work.

But even when it did, their prize would not match the price they'd just paid.

'It's going to work,' Andrew Hawke insisted, the strength of conviction in his voice crushing the whispery worries of the coven. 'Buck up and do your jobs. It's here.'

It's here. Cassán could feel the spike in apprehension, almost a sense of relief, from the others in the circle at those words, but that was because they didn't understand what *it* was. Not really. They knew it was Fate, the immense golden force that held past, present and future together, the golden thread of the very Fabric of space, the golden substance of human relationships, the golden light that was the magic they channelled as sorcerers. They knew because he'd told them. But they didn't *know* the way Cassán and Moira, as Crafters, or Andrew, as a Seer, *knew*. Fate was the whole natural order of the universe, and Cassán, former academic turned rebel, had written a spell to subvert it. If anything, *anything*, went wrong, the consequences could be quite catastrophic.

Cassán didn't want to think about things going wrong. He'd been careful, a surgeon in his precision; been over the spell a hundred times, line by line. There was no room for error.

And with a dead body still spilling blood at the centre of their circle and the horror and guilt shared equally among the ten participants in the ritual, there was no *excuse* for error. The price had been paid. To fail now was unforgiveable. A waste. A crime.

The chant solidified as all the voices returned to their unintelligible murmurs. The words were irrelevant – this was old magic, blood magic, and words held different power to different practitioners. It was just a tool for channelling their magic into the circle, which Cassán's spell drew on to cage the transcendent force he'd caught above them. Fate would never have allowed itself to be summoned to a ritual as unnatural as this one, so they'd had to trick it.

It was a risky spell.

The intangible bars of the spell locked around the golden force and in almost animal-like rage, Fate flushed downward into their circle as a thin golden wind, wild and strong. Cassán felt its shove against his side as it whirled about, looking for a gap in his spellwork. He grabbed the hands of those either side of him, as practised, closing his eyes against the bright gold of Fate's touch – for the briefest moment, he saw into its infinite knowledge. *A baby wrapped in pink, a storm, Morrissey's estate, a dark cave.* But as soon as the wind ripped through him and buffeted the next man, the images were gone, lost to his memory, known only while in contact with Fate itself.

His eyes were shut but his attention still drifted to the life lost in the middle of their circle. What fate had they stolen from their victim?

No backing out now.

Time for the final stage of the spell. Cassán gripped the hands of his unwitting neighbours tightly, opening his eyes to watch the others do the same as they too were slammed by the pale golden wind. His friends, if he could really call them that considering how little he liked the four of them most of the time, were interspersed with strangers, the new coven members they'd conscripted for this ritual. The final hands clasped, closing the circuit Cassán had built into the spell, and a blast of energy tore around their circle of bodies, electrifying them with the potential of their unity.

The golden wind of Fate spun faster, whipping Cassán's dark blonde hair across his face and slapping him with unknowable futures he couldn't hold onto – *an initiation, shells, a wedding, two weddings, a scar* – as he concentrated on this final step. The fear and awe of his coven mates flooded him but he didn't have the energy to fight it, not in light of his own immense sense of guilt and betrayal for what he was doing. As if taking an innocent life wasn't enough, as if tricking five people into participating in a spell that would kill them wasn't enough, here he was, meticulously unpicking his own connection to Fate. He'd dedicated his life to learning about it, understanding it, sharing its wonders with others through his books, books the White Elm had tried to bury despite their peaceful, academic content. Now, caging it like an animal, using what he'd learned of it against it, he felt like a traitor. Was it sentient? He'd come to think of it as if it were. Did it truly feel the betrayal and anger he imagined he saw in its behaviour?

Mánus, Eugene and Andrew weren't Crafters, so they couldn't manipulate magic on this fundamental level the way Cassán and Moira could. They couldn't see its code, its makeup, and reorganise it.

Moira shook her long, dark hair back and Cassán felt her take over her part of the spell with her mind, fighting the fury of Fate as she unwrote herself from its plan, unwriting the images and visions it slammed them with. Futures they might never get now. The concept of such emancipation was both exhilarating and terrifying. To live forever without Fate? They'd all agreed, and there was no going back from what they'd already done. Cassán activated the pre-written spellwork concerning his other three friends, watching as they sensed his magic beginning to act on them and caught on, actively channelling their power into the complex spells to allow them to complete their sequence.

'How much longer?' Kitty Wiley – Cassán had tried so hard not to learn their names, he really had – asked loudly, frightened and overwhelmed by the flashes of her own stolen future as Fate lashed about in its magical cage. He tightened his hold on her hand, hoping to convey a false sense of comfort. She was an anchor. His anchor. The spell's success hinged on her participation, hers and the participation of the other four coven newcomers. Without them, this next part would kill the five *real* participants.

And then what would be the point of all this?

'Hold on,' Cassán encouraged, ignoring the brief golden flashes – *hazel eyes, blue eyes, hazel eyes, hazel eyes*. 'It's nearly over. Don't let go.'

Across the circle, Mánus caught his eye. Both Irish, though from very different traditions, the Morrissey heir was the only one in the coven Cassán would have honestly called a friend. Wordlessly, their shared guilt spanned between them. This was wrong, so wrong, but backing out now would benefit nobody. The spell was too delicate, too tightly wrought to undo at this critical point, with Fate itself thrashing in their midst like an injured beast. It would turn on them and consume them all for their reckless arrogance.

They deserved it.

'What if it doesn't work?' Eugene asked, unable to hold

his fears back. His anchor, Helen, to his left, glanced at him anxiously, then let her gaze drift down to her own left hand, where she was joined to Mánus. She'd been fascinated by the mysterious Irishman ever since they'd met her in that Salem café, much to Moira's ongoing disgust, and seeing his hand in hers seemed to strengthen her resolve.

'It will,' she determined firmly, closing her eyes and lifting her chin. Expecting immortality. Expecting a lifetime of power, as they'd promised her.

She wasn't to know it was a plan for five and she wasn't one of them.

The winds of Fate swirled fiercer as the last threads of their beings came unravelling from its divine tapestry, sweeping dust up from the ground and threatening to send them sprawling with its force. They held onto each other, digging heels into the dirt to stay upright, even as a spark of sourceless golden electricity flickered once, twice in the air over their horrific sacrifice. Kitty shrieked as the lightning struck the ground before her; terror flashed through her but she didn't, couldn't let go, and Cassán felt her grip constrict even further, beginning to hurt his hand.

'Cassán...?' she called over the howl of the wind, over the crackle of the storm building inside their circle, her fear flowing freely from her hand to his. His barriers to this kind of thing were totally gone – she was afraid and it was his fault, she was about to die and he would know her confused terror, along with the other four anchors. Like he had the little life they'd already taken this night.

It was only the beginning of an appropriate price for his crimes.

'I'm sorry,' he called back, feeling tears sting the corners of his eyes. The five unpicked their final stitch all at once and the unnatural storm exploded outward at them in a blaze of bright gold. A side-effect long anticipated, the final layer of spellwork kicked in, channelling the captured force of Fate five ways. Straight into the anchors.

It wasn't horrible at first. Pillars of golden light streamed into the five sorcerers, Kitty Wiley and her brother Frankie and Jim Bennett and Samuel Godfrey and Helen Flanagan, and for a long, silent moment, they were glorious. Their fear was gone, replaced with awe and peace to be filled with Fate in its purest form. Their hands, held tight in the grip of the five friends, went warm, soft. Cassán looked again at Mánus, relieved. The less suffering endured by the anchors, the better.

But Fate is also power and no mortal conductor is intended to channel so much. The gold filled the anchors and flowed along the chain into their neighbour, their lives and bodies linked to one of the five with complex spellwork woven weeks ago. Insurance. Power filtered into Cassán from Kitty at a stable, manageable rate through her hand, but quickly overwhelmed her, filling her toward capacity. Her palm went hot, blisteringly hot, and he felt tears of his own spill down his cheeks as her awe turned to confusion and fear and realisation and desperation.

On his other side, Kitty's brother Frankie was burning hot, too, shouting incoherently in agony and trying to wrench his hands out from Cassán and Moira's. Neither relinquished their grip, no one did, even as the hands they held began to blacken dangerously, even as black cracks of disaster began snaking their way up Kitty and Frankie and Helen and Jim and Samuel's arms and necks.

Jim went first, in a fiery blaze almost too shocking to describe. The black cracks spread and widened, lacing his skin as the magic forced inside him battled to get out and found no adequate release except the controlled flow into the next sorcerer. Like a resistor in a circuit overwhelmed by an unanticipated surge, Jim all at once burnt out.

It was a saying among sorcerers – to 'burn out', to channel more magic than your specific capacity could handle and to die as a result – but this was the first time Cassán saw it happen, and discovered that unlike many sayings, this one was entirely literal. Jim burned from the inside out, erupting into flames with a scream that tore the night. Moira and Mánus visibly flinched and wrenched away, but a sharp, indistinct yell from Andrew opposite them made them maintain their grip, even as the hand they held burned, even as their own hands blistered from the contact, ensuring the last of the magic flowed from Jim to Mánus.

'Oh goddess,' Eugene gasped, staring. Radiating with horror. 'I can hear them. I can hear them...'

'Hold!' Andrew shouted, and everyone did.

The Wiley siblings went at about the same time, twin pillars of glowing fractured black engulfed in burning agony. Cassán's hands roasted, skin peeling, flesh sizzling, and he was sure he screamed but he didn't hear it over theirs, and whatever he felt inside was drowned in their overwhelming deaths. Kitty's in particular, the power refined through her burnt-out body flowing directly into him through their burning hands, dragging her unspeakable terror with it.

Exactly as he deserved.

Jim's flames were dying down now, his voice finished, his body almost spent, and the gold streaming into him paled and thinned and finally ceased as he began to collapse, a grotesque raw puppet with his strings cut. He crumpled to the ground and his hand slid from Mánus's, which the Irishman raised to survey with wide eyes. His skin was ruined, melted with the intensity of the transfer, revealing the ugly tendons and bloody meat beneath.

Kitty and Frankie fell at Cassán's sides, leaving his hands shaking and paralysed, stinging in a way that was too painful to call stinging, hanging where they'd been. But he felt inside him the power Kitty's sacrifice had given him, a glowing dangerous thing that wasn't there before. Half the prize they'd paid this terrible price for.

'Something's wrong,' Eugene insisted, looking fearfully between the anchors still clasping his hands. Samuel and Helen were still bright with the last of the golden wind flooding their bodies, their arms and necks and faces blackening with horrific lightning-like fault lines but their physicalities not yet overwhelmed. They were the most powerful of the five conscripts they'd charmed and lured into their coven. They had the greatest capacities – they would take the longest to burn out. But Eugene wasn't listening to the reason in Cassán's thoughts, or that of anyone else's. 'What's wrong with these two?'

'Nothing,' Moira hissed between her teeth, her ruined hands remaining claw-like in place as Cassán's did. 'Shut up and wait for it.'

'Y-Your hands,' Eugene stuttered, staring across at her. His gaze shifted to the others, all of whom had burns to at least one hand.

'Don't move,' Andrew warned, but the words might as well have not been spoken, because even a spell as expertly crafted as this one was only as strong as the resolve of its participants and Fate wasn't out yet. Samuel lit up next, buffering the intense energy being funnelled into Andrew. Eugene cried out, ripping his hand away from the burning man before anyone could stop him, staring in dread at his scalded palm.

Cassán felt the collective panic of his friends and raised his immobile hands automatically, already weaving magic around Andrew and Samuel, closing their circuit to negate the effects of Eugene letting go. It didn't take much – the anchors were bound to their ships, so to speak, not to the circle, and Samuel had already been drained almost entirely into Andrew before catching alight.

'My hand,' Eugene mumbled, beginning to shake loose Helen's grip despite the shouts of the rest of the circle to stop. She was the last of the anchors, her head tipped back as golden magic poured into her like liquid light, skin cracked black like a hellish porcelain doll, and her grip was a vice. Any second now, she would burst into flames too, unless the Telepath broke his connection to her–

'Don't–'

'Eugene–'

He shook her off and the light funnelling into her split in two, a pair of spotlights parting ways to follow two leads across a stage otherwise darkened for dramatic effect. The carefully coded sequence of magic Cassán had built fell apart. He felt the circuit trip and surge back on itself, too fast for him to do anything about it. The last of Fate's magic broke free of its trappings and thrust itself equally at both anchor and intended recipient, blinding in its fury with them. Mánus shouted in shock as the energy from Eugene and Helen's aborted exchange backfired through Helen into his hand, and he dropped hers quickly. Spontaneous golden lightning zipped up and down the cracks in her skin and sparked out at Mánus and Eugene as everyone else shielded their faces against the brightness with scalded hands.

It was exactly as Cassán had worked so hard to avoid – breaking Fate. There was no knowing what would happen because no one had ever been foolhardy enough to think they could undermine it like this.

Well, what had they expected? They'd circumvented the traditional convention of inviting Fate to preside over the ritual, summoning it instead through the ultimate affront – the untimely death of a little boy, a tiny innocent thing taken from the street by the deceptively charming smile of Moira Dawes and now lost forever.

They deserved whatever they got.

The brightness flashed once more, undeniably angry with them, and a sonic explosion of golden light blasted outward from Eugene or Helen or Mánus or maybe all three. Cassán took the impact straight to the chest, briefly in touch once more with the beautiful golden insights of Fate – *Moira's eyes in a different face, gravestones, a wristwatch, Anthea brushing a little girl's curly dark hair, then a similar picture, only she wasn't Anthea and the child was different* – before he landed, sprawling, in the grass several yards back, all the wind knocked from him.

There was a second of deathly silence. Cassán stared up at the clear night sky, at the indifferent stars, the same indifferent stars shining down on all the better people of the world, trying to get his breath back. His emotions and those of anyone else who'd survived were all jumbled inside him, inseparable. The circle was broken, the spell was in tatters.

People were dead. What had he done?

'We survived,' someone nearby noted. Andrew, with his Scottish accent.

'Did we?'

'How can we tell if it worked?' Moira asked from further back. No one had an answer, not even know-it-all Andrew.

Someone began to moan unintelligibly. Rolling over uncomfortably onto his elbows, Cassán looked back at the sparse patch of land they'd chosen for their spell. Mánus was struggling to his feet and hurrying to Eugene's side. The older American, whose tolerance for pain was apparently lower than the rest of theirs, was kneeling in the dirt, staring at his hands, which were…

'No,' Cassán breathed, refusing to believe his eyes. The moon was dark tonight, the stars hardly bright enough to be reliable, and their fires had all but gone out in that blast. His own hands were too sore to put any weight on so he fought his way upright with his knees and elbows, and stumbled to their fallen friend. Moira knocked into him on his way over, linking her arm through his in lieu of catching him with her hand. He was surprised by how heavily she leaned on him for support in her roiling shock, self-sufficient Moira whose reckless, indulgent idealism had started them all on this insane endeavour in the first place.

'But we paid the price,' she was muttering, raising her other hand vaguely and casting a light spell accidentally. She and Cassán both paused, taken aback by the washed-out, sourceless light that suddenly illuminated the gross scene that had been bad enough in the dark. Taken aback by her automatic show of magic. 'Well, my magic's not gone.'

That had been a concern of Cassán's, too – what would be the point of eternal life without his connection to magic?

'Don't touch him,' Andrew ordered from further back, jogging over with a pronounced limp. The Scottish Seer looked pale in the haunted light cast by Moira's spell, but just as irritable as he'd been all night, given the stress of it all. 'Mánus–'

'Shut it, Hawke,' Mánus snapped, his better hand of the two already on Eugene's forearm, sticky blood flowing over his fingers. Pitiful jolts of gold still sparked from the Telepath's skin at Mánus and back again, evidently causing him some discomfort, but the scrier kept his hand in place. Trying to heal him.

Trying to close the gaping, bloody wound at the end of Eugene's wrist where his right hand used to be. Moira deflated against Cassán's side while he looked about, surveying the mess they'd made tonight. Kitty and Frankie Wiley were smoking, burnt-out corpses, side by side – a whole family line ended. Samuel Godfrey and Jim Bennett were the same, black and used, lying alone. Helen Flanagan hadn't caught alight but she was unrecognisable all the same, white white skin taut and dry, cracked in deep black crevices. Her chapped lips trembled with unsteady breaths into undoubtedly burnt lungs, chest rising shallowly, fiery red hair soaking in the pool of blood that had only just begun to congeal.

And the little schoolboy, whose mother called him Bunny, lying in the middle of it all, blood spilled all over the scene of their horrific crime, while everyone else's attention was with Eugene.

He hadn't eaten today for this very reason, but Cassán had not anticipated the true awfulness of what he would see that night. Now, faced with it, even with an empty stomach, he shrugged Moira off and turned away, insides flipping. He fell to his knees and retched, coming up dry until he vomited bile, and then retching and retching until he was truly empty.

As if there was any doubt.

When he got control of himself, at least partially, he lifted a shaking arm to wipe his mouth on his sleeve. His face was streaked with tears. He looked at his stiff, raw hands. Was his magic intact, like Moira's and Mánus's? Self-healing was a talent afforded to all sorcerers, except those who dabbled in darker arts and committed soul-scarring acts like murder. He exhaled slowly. Not much point in trying, then. Behind him, his friends were arguing in blurry, bitter voices. He felt the flicker of magic behind him, heard the angry shout in response.

'What is it?' he asked wearily, forcing himself again to his feet and returning to them. He felt exhausted but figured it was probably to do with the nausea. Rituals that drew on Fate usually left the participants it acted upon, like initiations, feeling like they'd been hit by a train. Logic, with a liberal dash of hope, dictated that his strength would return with sleep.

'Don't fight,' Moira begged the others as Cassán came to stand beside her.

'What do you think you're doing?' Mánus was demanding of Andrew, waving his unburnt hand, the only remaining usable hand in the whole coven. The pair stood over Eugene, who was sobbing openly over the bloody stump of his wrist. Despite Mánus's short-lived effort to heal him, it looked no better.

'Don't you see what's happening?' Andrew shot back. He cradled his ruined hands against his chest, wincing, apparently having just used one to lash out at his friend and knock him back from Eugene. 'You can't heal him. None of us can heal *anyone* until the stain of this ritual washes off.'

'Where's the harm in trying?' Mánus gestured at Eugene as the Telepath began rocking back and forth in shock, mumbling on repeat, 'My hand… My hand…' and then turned to the side to guiltily notice Helen. 'God…'

'Don't you go trying to save her, too,' Andrew admonished when the scrier immediately dropped down beside her, ignoring him. But Cassán could sense the not-rightness around Eugene, around the tendrils of collapsed spellwork still lying across him like twisted scaffolding. Some were still active. He glanced at Moira while Andrew and Mánus argued and knew that she saw it, too.

Part of the transfer was still working, *for* Eugene, *from* Mánus.

'You have to stop,' Moira interrupted, her voice finding its usual confident steel, the steel they'd followed all the way from a fake book club meeting in her basement three years ago to this crime scene tonight. 'You have to stop everything.

You're draining power into Eugene.'

That made Mánus finally stop trying to heal Helen, and Cassán tread carefully between him and the sobbing Eugene, feeling the air for leftover magical bonds with clumsy, stinging hands. He tried not to notice the squelch of his shoes in all the blood.

He really didn't like Moira, didn't like the younger sorcerer's dangerous arrogance or her persuasive charm or her questionable morality, but she was an incredible Crafter, and he had trusted her skill all these years since throwing his lot in with her and the others. When he caught hold of the active magical strand and began to deactivate it, he felt her mind join his, working quickly to unwrite the offending magic that was posing an unanticipated threat to Mánus.

He could always trust that she would act to defend Mánus, hopelessly smitten as she was.

The spell finally fell apart and Andrew stepped forward to loop his elbows under Eugene's arms.

'He's safe to touch now,' he said gruffly, pulling him upright. 'I worry he's taken more than energy from you, Morrissey.'

'You *worry*,' Cassán repeated, uneasy. Andrew Hawke was a great Seer. He didn't *worry* about anything because he always *knew* what was upcoming.

It was why they'd carried out this ritual. Because he'd Seen it. He'd Seen them tear themselves from Fate's grasps and thus achieve empowered immortality. The ultimate experiment, the ultimate test of their knowledge. Had it worked?

'I think so,' Mánus replied automatically, brushing his dark hair back from his face with his unbloodied wrist. 'I feel different.'

Cassán cocked his head curiously. He hadn't asked that aloud, and Mánus was no Telepath.

'We're all different,' Moira voiced. She was watching Andrew and Eugene. 'Look.'

There was nothing different to see, minus the burns, the

twisted ankle and the missing hand. The physical world was painful to behold. But a change of focus, a shift in perception, and Cassán saw it. He brought his friends' auras into focus, coloured fields of energy emanating from the physical body.

They were unrecognisable. Eugene's was diminished, Andrew's bigger, swollen perhaps with the power they'd drained from Fate at that last stage of their spell, which had been the desired result. They would be stronger in their spellwork going forth, able to manage big spells with less risk.

But what made them chiefly different was not their new size, but their new features. Deep black spots, like sinkholes in the colourful mix, had appeared all over their auric fields. Energy swirled around them like clouds around mountains or water around rocks. Cassán had never seen anything like it in all his years of self-driven study.

It made him very, very worried. They'd thought they were tearing themselves from Fate; here it seemed was evidence that Fate had in fact torn itself from them.

'Your spell... took my hand...' Eugene stuttered accusingly at Cassán, white-faced, and Andrew hoisted him up higher to get a better grip.

'I'll take him to a Healer,' he said. 'You lot, do the same with those hands. Meet tomorrow at mine.'

He Displaced away with Eugene before anyone could disagree or make any suggestions. Cassán looked down at his hands, the guilt washing back.

'Your spell was flawless, and you know it,' Moira countered instantly. She wandered away from the Irishmen as Mánus again knelt beside Helen, whose gasps were becoming thinner, more desperate. 'You couldn't have known he would mess up.'

'Hawke should have.' Mánus went to lay his hand on Helen's shoulder but, emanating helplessness, paused, and looked around. 'We should never have done this.'

'A bit late for a conscience now, darling,' Moira replied, her swagger returning. She stooped to pick up her knife from beside the dead boy and began to wipe it clean on the child's shirt. Cassán couldn't watch her cold indifference. He moved to kneel opposite Mánus, preferring his swirls of hopeless remorse and the confused fear of Helen as she waited to die. She blinked unseeing white eyes with chapped lids, reaching shakily for help from the handsome stranger she'd trusted enough to follow here.

'We'll get her to a hospital,' he said softly, extending useless hands to his friend, ready to be directed on how best to lift her. Mánus slid his good hand behind her head, raising it enough for Cassán to get his forearm beneath it. 'Mortal doctors won't detect the trace of our spell and they'll have half a dozen of them working on her at once. We'll say we were electrocuted. A fuse blew.'

Mánus nodded and began to hastily gather up Helen's legs but Moira scoffed.

'And if they save her? What will *she* say?' She came back over while the two men slowed and looked at each other. 'Let her go. What the spell's done to her skin? Her insides look like that, too.' She held out the knife. 'Make it quick.'

For a long moment no one moved. Cassán looked once more at Helen and knew Moira was right. No hospital team could salvage this. But no way was he touching that knife after what she'd used it for.

'Me either,' Mánus said, again answering Cassán's unspoken thoughts. 'I don't need to relive that.'

Moira looked embarrassed to have forgotten the tendency of scriers to tap into intense impressions left on objects. 'Sorry.' She slid the knife into her belt as if it belonged there, and stalked away. 'Do it, and I'll take care of the rest.'

Cassán didn't know what that meant and didn't strictly want to know, especially once she began chanting, lifting her shaky hands to the sky and summoning something *big*. He concentrated on the dying redhead in his arms. This shouldn't have happened to her, this extended agony.

'I don't want...' Mánus shook his head, unable to finish. Neither did Cassán. But Moira was right.

'Here,' Cassán murmured, touching his fingertips to

Helen's sticky, cracked cheek. He hadn't used this technique on anyone out of pity before, always out of selfish motives like knocking out security guards at museums he was trying to break into and heiresses he'd charmed into letting him into their priceless treasuries. Helen's consciousness drained away without any more than a light pull, shutting off her fear as she slipped into sleep. Peace. Without her conscious mind fighting for survival, the body soon gave up, and the shallow gasps ceased.

'That's a good piece of spellwork,' Mánus mumbled gratefully. 'I'll remember that one.'

A strong gust of wet, cold wind lashed past them, and they looked up. The clear sky had gone murky with thick, swiftly gathering cloud, and Moira, hands raised in exaltedness as she directed it, stood at the centre of all the destruction like she owned it. She had a flair for this dramatic kind of magic – evidently her exhaustion was wearing off – but weather magic was top-shelf illegal under White Elm law and more likely than other spellwork to draw their attention.

Other than, of course, murder, which he knew was a bright magical signpost. He'd done what he could to build diversions into the spellwork to cover their acts tonight, but an unnatural storm might bring eyes looking earlier than he'd anticipated.

'Moira–'

'Trust me, Cassán,' she called back at him as he stood, opening her arms wide and encouraging the clouds to open, too. On cue, cold rain began to fall. It dampened, and then saturated, Cassán's hair. It stung his hands. It landed with a repulsive sizzle on still-cooling burnt-out bodies. It landed on a little boy whose life had been cut too short, diluting the blood and washing it into the ground.

Her storm lasted a few minutes, and Cassán stood there and let the water run over him. He didn't flinch as Moira directed lightning strikes all over the field, not even when the thunderclaps followed split seconds later. If she thought this was cleansing, she was deluded, but that wasn't a surprise.

He'd known. He'd known all of this, and he'd gone ahead anyway.

Weak.

The clouds blew and rained themselves out and the rainfall began to steady, control shifting back to natural wind currents and pressures. Moira turned back, manic excitement brightening bronze-brown eyes.

'Our traces are gone. These five look like they burnt out trying to perform a spell too big for them. We were never here.' She raised her face to the rain. 'Long live Magnus Moira.'

She stepped back and disappeared, Displaced, leaving them alone in the rain.

With their regrets.

'Long live Magnus Moira,' Cassán repeated hollowly. They'd not had a coven name before just a few weeks ago, when he'd jokingly moved a letter on a handwritten sign advertising for new members and accidentally named the group. And now this.

'Some legacy,' Mánus muttered, finally lowering Helen's body to the rain-soaked ground and getting up to survey the disaster with Cassán, who couldn't have agreed more.

chapter seven

Protective spells Renatus had written around Morrissey Estate prevented anyone from dreaming there, and it seemed that whenever I was not under the influence of those spells, like when he took them down to rewrite them stronger, or when I slept elsewhere, the same kind of dreams found me. Well, not dreams.

I was scrying.

The dreams, or visions, were indistinct and hard to remember, but I woke from them incredibly disturbed, certain I'd been witness to very alarming past events. The main focal point for each vision seemed to be the reason for my emotional attachment to these past moments – Cassán Ó Gráidaigh, my maternal grandfather long dead. I'd never met him, and my mother hadn't remembered him, either, yet dark moments from his life in the 1950s and 1960s were reaching out to me. Insight into his time left me uneasy and I was cautiously glad to remember so little of them.

Renatus was called back out to duty in the days that followed so I saw him less, and when I did, I was both relieved and upset to see him looking calmer, more objective each time. I hated seeing him like he was after Prague, but as he worked through the case and joined the others in damage control, I sensed him pushing his trauma further and further beneath the surface. It was his way to cope like this, ignoring grief and burying himself in work, but for the first time we were grieving together and his coping strategies were very alienating for me.

I knew I was central to his struggle, me with my patch over my eye reminding him of his powerlessness that morning, so it didn't surprise me that he avoided me now that my initial neediness had passed.

Understanding didn't stop my imagination whiling away its time backfilling alternative motivations for his distance, all of which could be summed up as my fault. Talking about it would no doubt have been healing for both of us, but I practiced the same cold stoicism that he presented. Healthy.

'I can bring you that pendant if it'll help you sleep,' Renatus offered when he came to see me on the Tuesday morning. I'd shared what I recalled of the latest vision, but it was choppy, making no sense except for feelings of foreboding. I shook my head, thinking of the black pendant he'd loaned me before. It blocked scrying.

'Thanks, but I won't need it at your place,' I said confidently. 'You're taking me home.'

'For sure,' he replied, and did not move from his seat. Worth a try.

'The non-magical media seems appeased with the cover story,' I mentioned. I gestured with the remote control at the television in my new hospital room, since I'd trashed the other. There was nothing much on to interest me at any time of the day after so many months living television-free, especially with my blurry and limited depth perception, but the noise and moving colours helped dull my thinking whenever I woke up. Almost having my face taken off by the White Elm's number one enemy had given me new perspective on the big secret I wasn't supposed to know, and my irresponsible, ill-conceived plan to prevent it, not to mention my deep, conflicted shame whenever I thought on it. Shouldn't I be grieving Anouk and worrying about the other families who'd lost someone on Saturday?

I didn't want Renatus seeing any of that in my head.

'It surprises me more that there's a non-magical explanation,' he answered, watching the screen with curious interest. I knew he'd never owned a TV and probably had only a passing understanding of what it was for. 'A gas explosion? Knowing something like that could still have happened without our interference is worrying.' The reporter's face was replaced with footage from the day of policemen standing around together in pairs, talking intensely, and Renatus frowned. 'Turn it off.'

I did as he instructed and dropped the remote back beside me on the bed.

'Can I get this thing off yet?' I asked, picking at the edges of my fresh eye dressing. I still wasn't allowed to see myself but could feel with my fingers that the swelling had gone down significantly, my face feeling relatively symmetrical again. 'I've made the executive decision I'm coming home today.'

'I noticed, but I'm not your doctor,' he replied vaguely, sitting back in his visitor's chair and glancing at me without really looking at me. He'd mastered that since Saturday. I regarded him as he looked away.

Half a year ago, I hadn't even known he existed, and now he was part of the furniture of my life. I knew I'd scared him when he'd thought he might lose me, but what he didn't know was that I'd been quietly dealing with that same fear for weeks now. Susannah, one of the White Elm's more authoritative Seers, had told me Fate's devastating plan for him, and I couldn't unhear it or tell him, no matter how desperately I wished I could. In some quiet moments, like this one, it was hard to imagine Renatus – loyal, compassionate, noble – as anyone's enemy. He was too strong and too good to fall like she'd foretold.

But I knew him better, and I knew his darker side was already apparent in other moments. Moments of instability, moments of rage.

His goodness was worth preserving, not just because he'd be a terrifying force to have on the other side, but I'd only come up with one way to save him. Remove the catalyst – Lisandro's execution. Do it myself.

Though it looked like an unlikely path at this point. I looked down at my arm and concentrated on channelling a miniscule amount of energy through it to generate a shapeless, insubstantial ward between my fingers. It shimmered briefly but my gaze was on my forearm, where the black cracks Emmanuelle had shown the interrogators had darkened once again under my skin.

Renatus paused and his eyes flickered up to watch what I was doing. 'They said that should heal, given enough time. Fade to nothing.'

'But they're not sure,' I intuited. Renatus's gaze met mine only briefly before angling expertly away.

'It's an educated guess, since there are few medical examples of burnt-out flesh like yours on living patients to study the healing process. Most sorcerers who experience burn-out... burn out. Completely.'

Lovely. I covered my arm with the edge of the thin hospital blanket so I didn't have to watch the fissures slowly fade. 'How's Glen?'

Renatus sighed and flattened his hands on the arms of his chair.

'Not his best. I really don't know too much about it. We've had to send him to Valero for rehabilitation–'

'Magical *rehab*?' I repeated, taken aback by this news. 'I thought it was a seizure?'

'I told you, I don't know,' Renatus said, raising his hands helplessly. 'I can't find him in my mind. He's completely shut himself off from the rest of us, and Emmanuelle says he's unrecognisable energetically, non-verbal...' He shrugged against the backrest of his chair. Uncomfortable. 'The Valeroans say they'll find out more as he recovers, but it seems that when Anouk died, it took something from Glen, too. I... we don't know what the long-term effects could be. In the meantime... Lady Miranda says it presents as brain damage.'

I exhaled slowly, swinging my legs back and forth to give myself something to focus on. Glen was one of my teachers, like most of the council. He was fatherly, patient. The kind of person you'd hope to get as a driving instructor. Now he was in rehab with a broken mind because I'd failed to widen my ward enough to save his best friend.

'What... What else is happening?' I asked, fidgeting with the catheter still taped into the back of my hand. I tugged it out, cringing at the pain. Anything to distract me from thoughts of Glen. I jumped down. 'Tell me while we walk. I need to get out of here.'

'It doesn't get much better. Avalon's hosting the inquest in two days, Lisandro hasn't surfaced, Valero has crossed a dozen ethical lines that we'll be the ones hung for, and Jadon's compiled all the names of the men who attacked us in Prague. All the families Qasim and Rodchenko have contacted have been shocked and outraged by the suggestion that their sons and husbands are Magnus Moira. Not that I expected them to be forthcoming about it or even necessarily aware.'

I spun the bangle from my sister, hearing it chink lightly against the watch my brother gave me. Part of me wanted to demand, wouldn't they know? How could they miss something like that? But I had come to understand that it wasn't so simple. Angela had no idea of my part in this simmering civil war. The entire White Elm council had failed to notice that three of their brothers had turned their loyalties from their initial oaths. Renatus had lived in ignorance of his godfather's role in his parents' and sister's deaths for *years*. You could be intimately close to someone and not know their deepest intentions or capabilities.

Likewise, you could be deeply self-aware, like Renatus, and not know your *own* capabilities. I cleared my throat, not wanting to get caught thinking about this, and grabbed my puzzle box.

'Come on,' I instructed authoritatively, heading for the door. 'Jailbreak me. Let's go.'

Renatus sighed, brimming with reluctance, but he did get to his feet. 'Emmanuelle won't like it.'

'You could take her in a fight,' I assured him, opening the door. He met my eye finally.

'Alright. *I* don't like it. You should be here, healing.'

'Emmanuelle said I might heal faster surrounded by

other sorcerers,' I quipped, and he sighed again. I counted it as a win when he waved a hand at the door; it closed beside me.

'Are we walking?' he asked rhetorically, gesturing me over. He took my elbow and pulled me with him when he started forward. But with one step, I felt the pressure of the air around me change, the Fabric stretched and split, and our next step was onto soft grass.

The moors. Wind caught up our hair and sunlight made us squint. I turned until I was facing Morrissey House, a beautifully preserved centuries-old four-storey structure atop the next hill, completely surrounded by a high stone fence and protected by generations of magic. I inhaled the fresh air deeply, relieved to be out of that hospital, however my healers felt about it.

Renatus headed for the gates, and I hurried to keep up.

'The detective from Avalon,' I broached, sensing Renatus's immediate distaste for the topic. 'He's still around?'

'Yes, but staying out of my way, thankfully.'

'You've been busy too, I gather?'

He nodded and we both went wide to dodge a ditch.

'Trying to find Lisandro,' he agreed. I was a few paces away but I was sure he knew my smile faltered and fell away at the mention.

Lisandro was as confusing as my dreams, his motives unclear, his actions extreme. He led a semi-political movement against the White Elm for reasons he wouldn't divulge, sent spies into the council to steal from them, kidnapped junior councillors and students to manipulate his former brothers and sisters, and had now twice seriously injured me to keep Renatus from following him.

Renatus hated him like nothing else in his whole life. I hated him, too, but I was also righteously terrified of the man's cunning and ability.

It wouldn't stop me, though, I was determined.

'Either no one's seen him or no one's talking,' Renatus continued with a tired shrug as I fell back into step with him. 'Shanahan, Raymond, Quinn, even Declan.' Here he rolled his eyes at the mention of his least favourite roguish relative. 'I'm not sure most of them would even tell me if they *had* seen him, but Declan doesn't have any good reason to lie. And he seemed *surprised*, which never happens.'

'Knowing Lisandro killed his own followers and a bunch of innocent people, including a White Elm councillor–' I still wasn't saying her name out loud if I could help it '–would have to be enough to break any new loyalties he's forged with them, surely?'

'I'm not certain they believed me,' Renatus responded, clearly troubled from his failed interaction with the underworld kings of fringe White Elm society. 'Declan, yes, I think so, but the others... They mightn't have even heard me out if I hadn't spent the time rebuilding things with them last week at the masquerade. But even still, there's no clear motive, nothing but our word that he was even there, at least in their eyes.'

We crossed the dirt road and I stared at Renatus incredulously. 'Nothing but our word? What about the spell you dug out of me? What about my arm? Will they try to deny that I almost killed myself trying to make that ward?'

'Oh, they believe it happened,' he said. 'News travels fast. Everyone's heard about the White Elm's new apprentice whose ward covered a city square. Robert Quinn asked again after your hand for his son. He's got big plans for you two,' he added, his almost imperceptible teasing an attempt to lighten the mood. 'What's up for debate, apparently, is whether Lisandro was involved.'

'Of course he was involved.'

'*I* know that,' Renatus replied impatiently, stopping outside the gate, 'but we can't prove it. You could have overdone yourself on any old spell. Anyone could have struck you. No one else saw him. That's what the investigation's for, why we're putting up with Winter and Valero.'

'But I didn't do this to myself,' I insisted, raising my hand to my face before he could stop me and yanking at the tape holding the medical padding to my eye. I inhaled sharply at the immediate sting of the tape ripping clear, ignoring Renatus's terse noise of discouragement. The cover came away and I blinked rapidly against the light, my lashes still feeling gunky and my eyelid tender.

'Why did you do that?' Renatus asked me tiredly as I rolled the tape up in my palm. Gently I touched my cheek and brow with the cotton pad, drying the skin. No blood. The crease of the eye was still sensitive so I probed clear of what I assumed was the actual wound, not quite healed over. Strange that there was no scab that I could determine.

'How does it look?' I asked Renatus. He was glaring at my shoulder, determinedly not looking at my face.

'How do you think?' he shot back. He snatched the puzzle box from my other hand, presumably to be helpful. 'You can be the one to explain to Emmanuelle why it's uncovered when she catches up.'

'I mean, you can barely look at me. Is it because it looks gross and it makes you feel sick, or because it looks like I was hit with magic?' I waited; he didn't reply, but I knew it was both. 'It's different from a normal cut, isn't it? How?'

'Put the bandage back,' he muttered disdainfully. Eyes still averted. I tapped my foot, chewing my lip, thinking. I felt bad for pushing him into discussing things he didn't like but what was the alternative with stubborn people?

'Tell me what it looks like,' I said, 'or I'll go inside and find a mirror.'

I gave him three beats of moody silence before reaching out for the gate. He grabbed it roughly, holding it closed. His mind was still at a distance from mine but I felt his lowkey anger and frustration as he raised his eyes and finally looked straight at me.

'It looks like a fresh scar,' he said flatly. 'Pinkish, red, shiny, as thick and long as your finger, straight through the edge of your eye. It's impossible to miss. And it doesn't look any different from anyone else's cuts or scars...'

My senses melded into his as his honest depiction drew my mind in, and in a new layer of sight over my perception of the real world, another vision faded in, a vision of a familiar girl with long brown hair hanging over the shoulders of her jacket, her olivey skin dry… and an impossible jagged mark, exactly as Renatus described, cushioned by blue bruising, from her eyebrow down through her eyelid, *my* puffy eyelid, to curve at my cheekbone. Through my master's eyes I stared in unsettled dismay at my visage, utterly weirded out to be looking at myself, and unable to quite believe that that mark wasn't just make-up. Renatus's voice shifted from auditory to telepathic and I heard the rest of his sentence skip my ears completely: *…except that you're a sorcerer, and you shouldn't have one. Only two kinds of people in our world have scars, and I didn't want you associated with either of them.*

I blinked and lost my view – his view – of myself, my senses returning to my own body. But the startling impression of my marred face haunted me like the shadowy afterimage of a camera flare.

'Oh,' I said. It was both worse and better than I'd imagined, but its permanency now hit home.

'We told you not to look,' he reminded me, though his anger gentled at my dismay. 'It's still a bit swollen. It won't always look this red, Lady Miranda has assured me. And I can teach you how to hide it with magic. Illusions are common cover-ups.'

He'd said I was scarred. He meant it. He dropped his gaze from me again, twisting his fingers carelessly to generate a tissue from nowhere. He held it out.

'This is the problem, isn't it?' I asked, taking it. 'That people will see me differently?'

Pause. 'Yes.'

'But you don't,' I said, more to assure myself than to confirm anything I didn't already know. He softened.

'I don't.'

'Alright, so what does it matter?' I queried as I dabbed at my eye some more, telling myself that his was the only opinion in the magical world that affected me. He still hesitated, though I was certain he heard my thoughts, and maybe didn't

108

believe them, even as I tried to.

'They're going to think…' Renatus rubbed the back of his neck, uncomfortable. But I waited him out. He redirected. 'Healing is tied to morality, somehow. I don't understand it exactly, I'm not sure anyone does, but when someone uses magic for harming others, selfish reasons, it blocks that ability. It's why we say dark sorcerers can't heal. It's why they scar.' He looked at his own hand, rubbing his thumb into the palm, painful memories clouding his mind in the moments before he could clear them away. 'It's why I don't advertise my own difficulties in that area.'

In the short time I'd known him, Renatus's moral code had been called into question more than once, even resulting in a formal trial by the White Elm to determine whether he was the killer and dark sorcerer some had accused him of being. Even I had been convinced, and we had worked our way through it, but he was an easy target for such suspicions, with his shady past, his bad egg family, his abrupt and quiet manner, his secluded mansion, his dark attire and, yes, his mostly undiscussed inability to heal either himself or others.

'People will think I'm one of the bad guys?' I deduced. He shrugged slightly.

'Possibly. Or maybe they'll see you as a victim of black magic, which isn't any better.'

'Well, that's what I am,' I countered. He pulled open the gate. He did not need a key.

'That is not all you are,' he said, handing back my puzzle box, 'and you didn't need a signpost like that across your face to beg the question of what you did to earn it.'

Renatus held the gate open for me and I stepped through. He followed and immediately froze, feeling something I could not. He looked skyward.

'What is it?' I asked, pausing on the path. I looked up, too, though the sunlight hurt my sore eye. Renatus raised a hand and traced a line in the air with a finger. Above us, briefly, a web of shimmery threads lit up against the blue and white of the sky – the house's wards and other spells that kept us safe inside the fence.

'The spellwork's loose,' he said, though I didn't have a strong enough grasp on crafting to know what that meant. He pulled the iron gate shut behind him with a clang. 'Someone has tried to break in.'

chapter eight

As worrisome and impressive a pronouncement that was, any associated anxiety quickly burnt up. Tending to the loosened spellwork involved a lot of Renatus standing around in silence and concentrating on magic I couldn't see. Inside his head, I put together that select threads of the protective web over us had been sort of *unpicked*, compromising the strength of the dome by allowing tiny gaps. He could find no trace of *who* had done it, which was apparently a concern of its own.

'There should be a trace,' he kept saying, annoyed, as he started fixing it up, 'but in truth, it's probably Lisandro, taking advantage of me not being at the house much these last few days.'

And he called his godfather a name I wouldn't be prepared to repeat.

'Why would he need you out of the house?' I asked.

'Because the house would alert me if this was happening while I was here,' Renatus answered simply, and I nodded as if this were a sensible response. He lit up another set of threads over our heads, still working, and I looked away to the house. Magical alerts aside, it looked multitudes more interesting.

'I'll see you inside,' I said, thinking I'd chance a short Skip before he could remember he didn't want anyone seeing me scarred like this. I found the Fabric, and stretched my senses toward the house. I located the familiar energy of my favourite Displacer and focused on going *to* her.

Renatus noticed. 'You shouldn't try something like that

so soon after burnout–'

I think he stepped in front of me, but my attention was arrested by a flash of unwanted memory: *burning, tingling in my arm, the ward streaking for the ground, Renatus rolling underneath… Touchdown, two hands…* In a panic I threw out my own hands, either to push the vision away or to grab the ghost out of that moment, I don't know, but all I caught was Renatus offguard. I shoved him back and he grabbed my wrist as he stumbled, pulling me with him. Black grasped at us both, and my foot was falling, falling…

'It's Aristea!'

My shoes hit solid floor and Renatus let me go, stumbling back and regaining his balance. The high-ceilinged dining hall was occupied by a long carved wooden table that looked like it had been constructed inside the very room, since it was too big to have been brought in through the doors. Another good-sized table and a buffet bar were installed off to the side, clearly later additions. More than a dozen young people were sitting at the main table, eating, or at least had been. They were all frozen mid-bite, their attention captured by the Academy's most controversial student and her master, the council's most controversial member, suddenly appearing dramatically in the middle of the room.

I don't know why, it's not as though we were known for subtlety or anything.

'God, I'm sorry!' I said immediately, looking straight at Renatus and feeling sick with the realisation of what I'd done without meaning to. I'd Displaced us both, less than a hundred metres but still taking us through the void between, where an inexperienced sorcerer could easily get lost. Renatus had once killed a man by sending him into that blackness. And now I'd almost done the same to him. To us both. 'I didn't mean–'

'I know,' he interrupted, and though he was unsettled I could tell he wasn't angry. He looked around at our little audience and switched to mental dialogue. *Trauma affects magic like it does the body and mind – unpredictably, deeply. We'll keep working on controlling the visions.* Aloud he said, 'I was actually exactly where I wanted to be, but thanks for the lift.'

A light joke, in case I still thought he was upset.

'I can take you back,' I offered, and he waved a hand dismissively as he turned to leave the room.

'I'll pass. I can walk.' *You should try the same for a while.* No Displacement. I didn't need to be told twice. I couldn't believe I'd just shoved him through a hole in space without even realising.

There was a swollen silence. I fidgeted with my puzzle box, unsure. I knew little of what had happened here in the days since I walked casually out of a conversation to go and visit Renatus and had never come back. Jumping in here didn't feel so thought-out now.

If I was self-conscious standing there alone, I wasn't to be left there long. Arms flung around my neck and shoulders and I was pulled into a big twin hug by Kendra and Sophia Prescott.

'You're here!'

'You're okay!'

'I'm here,' I agreed weakly, surprising myself with how good it felt to hug them back. 'I'm okay.'

'They told us you were in hospital,' Sophia admitted worriedly, squeezing me tighter. The mildly painful squeeze brought me back to myself. 'They said Lady Miranda had to treat you for an injury.'

'In the line of duty,' Kendra added, her voice muffled by my shoulder. 'They made you sound like some kind of war hero. Hiroko said it was bad.'

'She said it looked...' The Canadian witches pulled away and two pairs of shiny, apprehensive green eyes looked back at me, appraising my altered face. 'Oh...'

I averted my gaze, understanding now Renatus's concerns about perceptions of my injury. We were standing in the middle of the most popular common area of the house, with what looked like more than half of the student population present. I noted with discomfort the waves of curiosity and interest that floated to me, perfectly matched to the open staring of my classmates. I suppose I couldn't blame them. I was a regular spectacle here; if it were somebody else, I'd probably join in the staring.

In trying to avoid eye contact with most everybody, I found myself looking past the twins at Hiroko. Her arms were crossed, her smile guarded; her discomfort with my appearance resembled my master's, down to the complex blend of pity and unfounded guilt, though she likewise tried valiantly to keep it to herself. All the same, she was the person I was most happy to see. Normalcy. Study sessions, walks around the grounds, opening presents over the phone with my sister – with Hiroko I was still that girl Angela dropped off at the gate all those months ago, just another student, just another girl. She opened her mouth to speak, to say something reassuring and probably profound like she always did because she was my best friend, when a hand landed genially on her shoulder.

'*Oh* is right,' the other Displacer said dryly. 'Did you escape or something? They said you wouldn't be out 'til the end of the week. You look like shit.'

I couldn't help but smile and nod reluctantly at Addison James, towering beside Hiroko. He winced as Kendra leaned away from me to punch him in the arm in warning.

'Thanks, Addison. You know, smiling hurts,' I told him, gesturing at my left eye. My hand disappeared quickly from my peripheral vision. Distracted, I turned to look at it. It was still there, of course, attached to the end of my arm, but when I waved it a second time, experimentally, I found that I saw much less out of the corner of that eye than usual.

'What's wrong?' Addison asked, waving his own hand in front of me. 'Can you still see out of it?'

'Add–' Kendra started resignedly.

'I can see, but...' I watched Addison's hands come together in the middle and begin to part, slowly moving toward the edges of my field of vision. His right hand vanished; his left kept moving. My stomach turned over. 'I think...'

'I think you should say no to the next knife fight.'

'I'm sure she doesn't want to discuss it, here in front of everyone,' Sophia interrupted him pointedly. She smiled more warmly at me. 'It doesn't look that bad.'

'It could be temporary,' Addison added quickly, a disclaimer.

'No, it's okay. I know it does. The bandage just came off five minutes ago and I saw it for the first time. It was pretty shocking,' I admitted. I hesitated, playing with the puzzle box to keep myself from experimenting further with my reduced vision, wondering what else to say. 'But you're right, I don't want to talk about it.'

'And that's fine,' Kendra insisted. I nodded, reassuring myself.

'Aye, yeah, it's fine. It's okay.' I looked around at the four of them, four of my favourite people, and briefly felt something I hadn't felt in some time. 'God, it's good to be back. I missed you.'

I stepped between the twins and stepped straight into Hiroko's hug. We weren't huggy friends, typically, but this occasion definitely called for it. As soon as her arms closed over my shoulders, I felt tears sting at my eyes, not because I was sad. Just… grateful. I swallowed.

'Thanks for coming to see me the other day.'

'I could have come again,' she said at the moment when the hug should have ended. I held on. 'There was no rush to come back too soon.'

Too soon. She meant that, no linguistic slip of the tongue.

'The hospital was driving me insane,' I complained, sniffing back tears. 'The bandage, too.'

But I knew she was right. I'd watched people die, I'd lost most of my birthday to emergency surgery, I'd been interrogated by White Elm allies, and as always, Lisandro hadn't been caught to be held accountable for his part in it all. In the last five minutes I'd learned that my scar was a marker for dark sorcery and might have permanently affected my vision.

It was too soon to be back, but when would it not be?

'We're glad to have you back, whether you're meant to be here or not,' Kendra insisted determinedly, stroking my unwashed hair like flattening some flyaways might make me look less tragic. Her eyes alit upon my wound and she nudged her sister. 'This will heal, won't it, Soph?'

Sophia's emotions betrayed her as much less confident, her senses as a Healer already gently probing my injury, but she forced a smile and petted my arm affectionately. 'Most of it.'

Most, but not all, a bit like *most* of the people in Prague saved, but not all.

Two hands slam into the transparent wall of an impenetrable ward…

I flinched, grateful for Hiroko's extended embrace. What had the White Elm told the other students? Other than Hiroko, what did they know about Anouk, about Prague?

Wondering, Anouk had told me before she died, was as good as an invitation to Telepaths, and while none of my friends were genuine Telepaths like Anouk, Renatus had unnatural powers in that department. He overheard, from wherever he'd gotten to.

They know, he said. *Lord Gawain gave them the basics – Anouk, the attack, Lisandro's probable involvement – and he sent Susannah and Teresa to speak to the families, except yours.*

It was rare to have a situation arise where I could say whatever I wanted to my friends, as normally I was sworn to secrecy. For once, it was like they had top-level clearance and I was free to talk about my experiences. But I couldn't. I swallowed, feeling unstable, and shrugged, wordless.

It didn't seem to matter. The twins joined the cuddle, each leaning their heads against mine, enclosing Hiroko and me in their affection, and Addison, with his long lanky limbs, threw his arms around all four of us. Home.

'Are you hungry for something more than hospital food?' Hiroko asked as she released me, jerking her head at the buffet table behind us, her grown-out asymmetric bob swaying. 'Or do you want to go somewhere else?'

116

'Yeah, where the whole school isn't staring at you,' Kendra said brightly, loud enough for a lot of people to hear, blush and turn back to their meals. She picked up a red hardcover book from the table where she'd been sitting.

'Half the school anyway,' I agreed, ready to follow them away from the remaining stares, but Sophia looked back at me grimly.

'No. This is everyone.'

Less than twenty faces. In March, we'd started with about forty attendees.

'Everyone?' I repeated, momentarily surprised but then realisation dawning. 'People have left?'

'Nine so far,' Kendra confirmed. 'Lord Gawain spoke to us on Saturday night about… well, you. And he said we could go home if we wanted and he'd get in touch with our parents. Suki and Isao's grandparents turned up and took them home an hour later, and then it was just one after another. Heath went this morning.' She looked down at the book she carried, trying to hide her expression, but I felt her disappointment to have her new boyfriend whisked away so suddenly. I kept scanning the table, looking for one face in particular.

'Where's–'

'Iseult is gone too,' Hiroko informed me apologetically, and my freshly fortified nerves shook again at this unexpected news. I had just wanted to get back here to relative normality, to be with my friends, but some of those friends were no longer to be found here. Renatus had neglected to mention this to me on his visits. 'She and her parents spent a long time in a meeting with Qasim yesterday. She found us later and said she will be back. She said she will be, uh, at a distance.' She paused, looking for the right word. 'A distant student? What did she say?'

Addison helped out. 'She arranged to continue studying with the White Elm but as a distance-education student. Lien Hua is going to do the same.'

'Yes!' Hiroko clicked her fingers, grateful for the language assistance. 'She will no longer live on the estate but will come for lessons on some days. So we will see her again.'

Not long after I first arrived here, Lisandro had made an attempt to discredit the White Elm, and seven families had pulled their children out of the Academy. Back then it was no one I was close with, though I knew the Prescotts liked Marcy Pretoria, but the brilliant and not unintimidating Iseult Taylor was someone I'd genuinely miss. At least I'd see her again.

'Some of the shared rooms are totally empty,' Kendra confided as we squeezed through the door three-wide. 'All of Willow's roommates left and now she's got the whole room to herself.'

'Our room is the one exception,' Hiroko said coolly, leading the way. 'Our roommates will not leave. Sterling is sleepwalking again, but she is always back at morning.' Things had initially been friendly between us and the two girls we bunked with at Morrissey House, but a fatal misunderstanding had derailed us and made for an awkward couple of months in silence. 'I am glad you are back.'

'Oh, I'm so sorry.' I felt immediately guilty, realising what I hadn't even considered in all these days of lying in bed thinking of my own problems and wallowing in self-pity – while I was sleeping there, Hiroko was stuck in our room with the cattiest girl I'd ever known and her impressionable underling, ignored and alone.

Hiroko waved a hand dismissively. 'Do not be sorry. You were at the hospital.'

'You forget,' Addison reminded me slyly, 'our Hiroko can hold her own.'

I looked back at him, trailing behind us, feeling incredibly out of the loop. Weirdly, I couldn't see him. I twisted further until he came into view.

'What do you mean? What did I miss?' I faced Hiroko expectantly. 'What did you do?'

'It was *excellent*,' Kendra exclaimed, wringing on my hand as we started up the main staircase of the house. Opposite the staircase was the main entrance, and beyond that, I could sense Renatus, still working on the spellwork hanging over the property. Part of me knew I should be out there with him, helping him solve whatever mystery he was dealing with, and normally I would, but right now, I just couldn't. I didn't want to be a White Elm apprentice right now.

Tomorrow, or the next day, I would have to face all that came with it – Anouk, Prague, Angela knowing nothing about my life, Emmanuelle's fury at my removed bandage, Renatus's awful fate. And I would. But not in this minute.

So instead I listened to my friends describe a lunchtime scenario in which Hiroko put our nastiest roommate in her place for some characteristically ignorant comment she'd made about the withdrawn students, and immersed myself in the breathless laughter of the Prescotts and their third wheel Addison as they re-enacted the scene, while Hiroko shook her head and insisted it wasn't that funny.

'Oh,' Kendra redirected through her giggles, remembering the book she held. She pressed it into my hands. 'That's for you.'

'Another birthday present?' I joked, shifting my puzzle box in my fingers to turn the book over. *Butterfly Swords and Sai: An Introduction*. The Seer shrugged.

'Tian gave it to me. He said… Well, now I know it's for you. I assume it makes sense?'

I knew very little about how Seers' abilities worked, but yes, this made sense. I let Hiroko and Addison take the book in interest and open it where I could see as they flicked through the pages. Diagrams of footwork patterns, grips, combinations, all based around a paired weapon I'd been given a few days earlier.

Renatus had said he'd arrange for Tian, a martial arts and weapons specialist, to give me lessons. It seemed it would begin with theory.

Hiroko was right that our roommates hadn't gone anywhere. She and I were curled up on our beds later, freshly showered, dressed warmly in pyjamas and sai out with the book I couldn't read – my eye covered with tape and padding once again, courtesy of an abrupt interruption halfway up the stairs by a most displeased Emmanuelle – when Sterling Adams and Xanthe Giannopoulos returned from dinner. I glanced over at them when the door opened. Sterling, the shorter of the two, paused when she saw me, looking spooked. For half a second I thought she was about to say something, but Xanthe came in behind her, pushing her between her shoulders to keep her moving. Xanthe was the one I couldn't work out, and it was she who ignored me completely, going to "their" side of the room and beginning to dig through her drawers.

'What does Khalida think?' she asked over her shoulder, re-establishing the protocols of our shared existence. Sterling only hesitated a couple of seconds before answering as if Hiroko and I did not exist in the same space.

'She said Bella always gets her way, so probably not,' she said, tugging her key free of the lock. Hiroko and I turned back to each other and continued our conversation, too, as if there really was a glass wall running down the centre of the room between my bed and Sterling's.

And so life resumed in the snow globe of Morrissey House, hours blending into a night of deep rest and then a day of leisure with my friends, the White Elm presence at the house minimal, classes postponed. And I might have believed it would all be as I felt on that first night, that it was okay, that I was okay, except that as I'd learned in a very harsh lesson on my first day of adulthood, things can change very quickly from okay to very far from it.

chapter nine

If the scar was less prominent today, as Lady Miranda claimed in an encouraging aside over a hasty lunch at the estate, Renatus couldn't tell. He'd noticed she was determinedly not wearing the bandage, which had pissed off Emmanuelle but only made Lady Miranda shrug.

'There's some vision loss that I don't think is coming back,' she said gently. 'The covering isn't going to make a difference, and it's probably best that she gets accustomed to her new blind spots.'

Great. Blind spots. Renatus cast his fork down onto his plate moodily, startling a handful of students eating at the main table. He ignored their reaction. Miranda's was harder to ignore.

'How much?' he asked, trying to manage his temper with the situation – yet another situation he seemed to have zero control over. 'How much vision loss?'

Like the scarring wasn't enough of a punishment to both Aristea and, more selfishly, himself.

'We knew when you brought her to the hospital that there was damage to the eye itself. The cornea was stripped off, and we healed that completely, but there seems to have been some retinal scarring.' Lady Miranda shrugged again, grim and apologetic, concentrating on her meal. 'The effect is similar to looking directly at the sun or an eclipse, except only in the corner of the eye where the impact occurred. It's hard to say,' she added, coming around to answering his question, perhaps taking note of his tense fists on the tabletop or his angry glare at the distant wall. He tried again to relax and give off less aggressive body language. 'I think the outer quarter is gone. A third at worst; a fifth at best. I'm sorry.'

'You have no need to apologise,' Renatus said automatically, deliberately opening his clenched hands and flattening them on the table in an attempt to dismantle his appearance of hostility. 'You did everything and more. I know.'

The high priestess surprised him by resting a hand over one of his, the only time he could remember her ever initiating physical contact with him. It was not quite proper in the magical world to seek out touch like this, especially when there was any risk of harm. A sorcerer can do a lot of damage in a moment of contact, and Renatus had always been an outsider to the council, suspected of dubious intentions and known to possess the knowledge of how to exploit something as careless as a touch. Needless to say, nobody ever really went out of their way to touch him. Even now, meeting his eyes, Lady Miranda looked briefly surprised by her own boldness, but did not remove her hand straightaway like he expected.

'You did everything you could, too,' the older sorcerer reminded him. She seemed to be speaking directly to the wall of denial and self-loathing he found between himself and the rest of the world since Saturday. 'This wasn't your fault.'

A matter of opinion, and not one Renatus agreed with. He pushed his plate away and stretched out his awareness from the dining hall to the rest of the estate. He found his apprentice out on the lawn with her friends, playing a board game. Her mind wasn't closed off but she was definitely ignoring him, the same way he'd been ignoring her for the most part, not eager for the inevitable reminders of his failings. Her scarred young face. Her troubled mind. Her *vision loss*. Because he was a poor excuse for a responsible adult.

'Let's hope our allies see it your way,' he said finally, taking back his hand, uncomfortable with Lady Miranda's too-willing forgiveness. 'We don't need more enemies at this rate.'

She nodded, frowning in thought, taking a last bite of her lunch.

'You said there was a breakdown in the warding over this estate?'

'Some unravelling, yes. I can't explain it. Other than Lisandro, maybe Jackson, I don't know who would have the skill to dismantle that much magic in such a short time. It must have been last night.'

Openly opposed to the council for almost a year now, Renatus couldn't guess why they'd waited until now, but motive or not, it had to be them. Someone who knew that the entire place was sensitive to his bloodline. Doors opened at his whim. Permanent wormholes had been built into the Fabric of the house, functional for him alone. While he'd been spending his days chasing up leads and his nights guarding that London hospital room, someone must have known it was the perfect time to strike – that he wouldn't be around for the house's magic to notify of a breach, however slight.

'Hmm.' Miranda played with her knife, drawing patterns in the sauce on her plate as Renatus finished off his drink. 'But you've got it under control?'

'I do.' One thing, at least.

'We won't keep you away for long today in case they try again,' she decided, arranging her cutlery for the household staff and standing in unison with Renatus. 'Would you like a minute? I can meet you there.'

She was referring to Aristea, not knowing if the girl was up to coming. When he'd touched her mind this morning and reminded her of the inquest, she claimed she was. He had his doubts, especially after Tuesday's minor Displacement misadventure, but proving her wrong required a deeper delve into her mind, which *he* didn't feel up to.

He walked the Healer to the front doors, and outside, Lady Miranda gave him a final encouraging smile before Displacing the distance to the gates at the bottom of the sloping green hill. The cluster of teenagers lounging on a picnic blanket on the sunlit lawn with a Monopoly board were within sight and must have noticed his appearance, because the other four looked expectantly at Aristea. He was no Empath but her mood was clearly telegraphed in the way she stood reluctantly and threw her paper money down in the middle of the board, forfeiting. Addison James and one of the Prescott twins scrabbled with one another for a share of Aristea's forsaken funds as the apprentice dismissed herself from the group with a wave and crossed the lawn to meet Renatus.

'You could have told me no,' he said when she got close enough and fell into step beside him. He turned with her, deliberately not letting his gaze rake over the left side of her face. 'I would have made an excuse for you.'

Her friends were casting worried, caring looks at her retreating back. He appreciated that she had them and the stability they provided, and he appreciated that, when families had started turning up at the gates again for their children, these four hadn't been among the first to go. He'd moved Mr Sasaki, the Prescotts and the Jameses to the top of Susannah and Teresa's list the minute he'd heard the sickening news that Aristea's main competitor at the Academy, her friend Iseult Taylor, was being summoned home. Emmanuelle's phone had gotten a workout as Renatus ensured that these three families had every reason to believe their children were safe and happy, each walked out into the moors to make their calls without the electromagnetic interference of all the wards. He was still concerned about what Emmanuelle had said of the tone of the conversation between Hiroko and her father, but Aristea's favourite friend had not said anything to Emmanuelle, and no one had turned up for her. So far so good. He didn't think, despite a brave face, that his apprentice could take such a loss at the moment.

'I said I'd come,' Aristea answered, kicking a stone as she passed it. 'It'd be pretty low of me – no, what was your word? Atrocious – to make you go there on your own.'

He shot her a querying glance, having not said anything so manipulative when he'd asked her. Her eyes avoided his the same as he'd been avoiding hers, staring blankly at the far-off gate, and her expression gave away little except that she'd intended the comment lightly. Understanding her was always as easy as stepping into her mind, and he was annoyed with his own childish reluctance to do so. Who was the adult here, exactly? He scratched the back of his neck needlessly, embarrassed, and hesitantly opened the door between his mind and hers.

He was immediately rewarded with an explanation. Her surface thoughts were of a recent memory, the interaction they'd shared on their way to a high society masquerade party hosted by magical underworld kings. He'd claimed it would be atrocious of her to make him go alone, and she'd remembered the comment with both amusement and fondness.

He felt a rush of affection for her then, followed by immense guilt for what he'd put her through even in the week since that stupid party, followed by a swift emotional shutdown when he recalled how deeply she felt anything projected by those around her.

The glance he sensed from her made it unclear whether she appreciated the shutdown. Perhaps she perceived it as more of a shut*out*.

'Yes, well, it would be quite atrocious of you,' he agreed, attempting to maintain the light mood between them and forge ahead with reconnecting with her. He'd lived a very isolated life since being orphaned at fifteen, and hadn't acknowledged how lonely that had been until he'd been bonded with Aristea and been able to make the comparison. They'd hit a stride in their relationship after the first time he'd almost lost her to Lisandro, realising how much he'd grown to both care for her and depend on her, but this latest horror felt like it was doing the opposite. He was the adult. He should be the one to make sure it didn't happen. 'I don't want to go any more than you do.'

'I don't think you're half as scared of being found guilty as I am.'

'No, because we're not.' Not of that. 'But you don't hate

125

Winter half as much as I do.' And their destination was the place he'd first met the detective.

'You couldn't ask them to choose a different location?' Aristea asked as they neared the gate. Renatus tensed his shoulders in something of an uncomfortable shrug.

'I could have asked,' he admitted, 'and looked weak. Petty.'

Aristea offered him a sympathetic look and Renatus made sure to raise his head to accept it, even if it meant he had to face the still-red mark on her other cheek. He *should* have to face it. It was his fault. He should have to live with the guilt, the fear of one day having to explain the scar to her family – people he was increasingly nervous about ever meeting. But more than any of that, he should be the one with the mark broadcasting a connection to dark magic. Not his apprentice. If only he'd been quicker to realise Lisandro was there, he could have been the one leading the way around that corner. If only he'd been quicker with his spellwork, he could have slowed her down and saved her from this.

'For what it's worth, I wouldn't have let them call you weak and petty,' she said as they paused at the gate and he pressed his fingers to the wrought iron. Everyone onsite had a key to unlock it but like the doors of the house, the gate's magic was directly connected to his blood – through some very gruesome magic cast by his ancestors – and it opened for him instantly. He caught the swinging gate as Aristea slipped through the gap and made sure to close it properly behind them. Whoever had tried the house's defences was going to have to work a lot harder than they already had, and if he was going to leave the property, even in the capable hands of Susannah and Teresa, he sure as hell wasn't going to leave the front gate open.

'It might have been worth asking, then, just to see what you'd do to stop them,' he replied, running his hands over the gate and his most precise attention along with them, feeling for chinks in the energetic armour of the place. He, and Emmanuelle once she'd arrived to chide Aristea for leaving hospital, had worked extensively on these spells and he was quite sure they'd made them solid, but it was worth checking again once the spellwork settled.

Aristea smiled briefly, and Renatus stepped away from the gate, appeased. Even with the scar along the side of her face, it relieved him to see her smiling, to feel like their friendship wasn't as scarred as they were. He followed her away from the fence line, out of the field of interference generated by the house's copious magic.

'This inquest,' Aristea mentioned as they reached the other side of the dirt road that led up to the estate from the "main" country road that brought the occasional driver out this way. 'You said it's in Germany?'

'That's right. Are you volunteering to Displace us there?'

She recoiled at the comment, and he held out his hand for her, amused. She accepted, and he concentrated on a place he'd been only once before but remembered very well, opening a controlled wormhole between their location and south-west Germany. He pulled her closer and stepped through the tear he made, bringing her with him through the black abyss in between, and then they were striding out of Northern Ireland and into a forest clearing, one time zone away and a good five degrees warmer.

'Thanks.' Aristea let him go and turned in a circle, taking in the fairytale beauty of the fabled Schwarzwald. 'I wouldn't have blamed you for shoving me through, to be honest.'

'Then it'd be you calling me petty.' Renatus straightened his jacket and turned to his right, where a well-preserved sixteenth century half-timbered house had been erected to take the place of the twelfth century stone watchtower that existed now only as rubble beside it. Clearing the worn stones away in the elapsed centuries since the tower's collapse was eternally out of the question. Even as scattered rocks the broken tower served as a powerful monument to the hardest-won magical alliance of all time.

Evidently elected as lookouts, Emmanuelle and Tian paced the perimeter of the clearing, mirrored on the other side by Viktor Rodchenko and another Valero guardian. Emmanuelle looked pointedly at her favourite student, disapproving of her uncovered face, but said nothing of it as she passed them.

'You're two minutes early,' she said instead, 'but I think they started without you.'

Unsurprising, considering the meet was being held on the less-than-neutral ground of Avalon soil. 'Winter?'

'I get the impression 'e doesn't like you,' the Healer noted, continuing her round.

'Wonder why,' he muttered in her wake.

Aristea stepped up beside him, assessing the heavily warded, beautiful building with her usual mix of pessimism and imagination. 'Looks like the gingerbread house, and I'm about as excited to go inside it, too.'

'This is where those stories originated from,' Renatus responded vaguely, trying not to reminisce on his last visit here, as a freshly orphaned boy with his godfather. 'The predecessors to the White Elm operated here, as did those they hunted. Witches working blood magic, shapeshifting, stealing scores of children, giving the rest of us a bad name.'

'No, I meant I feel like we're about to be eaten alive,' Aristea explained grimly. Renatus tried not to wince at the fairytale reference that in this context hit a little close to home.

'I believe chicken bones are a good defence,' he suggested, starting forward reluctantly.

'Aye, but ovens are better,' she countered, and when he glanced aside at her, her playful smirk was almost enough to distract him from the scar. Almost.

Aristea's spirited confidence lasted as far as the building's front step, and then the worried thoughts she'd been holding back and keeping to herself rose to the surface and even drifted into Renatus's mind. This had happened a bit at the beginning, when their minds were first broken open and fused together, their thoughts and memories spilled between the two brains with minimal organisation. It had taken only days for things to settle, but in recent weeks, Renatus had noticed that whenever the pair was in-sync, in thoughts, in purpose, they began to fuse in other ways. See through one another's eyes. Use one another's powers. On Saturday Aristea had even *unthought* his actions before he could enact them, rendering him helpless to prevent her from running at Lisandro unwarded.

I should have made the ward bigger. I should have seen her. They're going to find me guilty.

Overhearing her concerns was a much more passive experience when they were in-sync, too, and now her chief worries swirled into his head. They were almost as clear as his own, her thoughts and worries increasingly influential, and he knew the same was occurring in reverse. Aristea was growing sullen, dark, reckless, while he felt more cautious and idealistic since he met her. He didn't know what the longer-term consequences were for either of their identities.

That's not what this is about, he reminded her, reaching the door of the building and knocking hard. A series of antiquated clicking noises began on the other side, and he stood back, trying to remember whether this had happened last time he was here. *It's supposed to be about getting all the evidence on the table and ensuring all sides are on the same page. But, as always: wards up.*

'Renatus,' she said suddenly, anxiously, as she automatically fortified the energy around herself. 'In Prague – I'm sorry–'

'Don't.'

'No, it was my fault–'

'Don't,' he repeated firmly, uncomfortable with apologies at the best of times but even more so when the situation was clearly *his* fault. 'Don't even think it.'

'But *you* were just thinking it. If they find us guilty,' she pushed on hurriedly, touching his sleeve when he tried to dismiss her words with an irritated wave of his hand, 'I'll tell them what I did to you, I'll tell them, I won't let them–'

'Aristea.' Renatus twisted his arm out of her light grip to grab her wrist, jolting her slightly. No one was going to ask unless she drew attention, and if she did, it was a line of questioning neither of them needed. It was a crime to do what she did, manipulating someone else's thoughts; but only if one of them sold her out, and it wasn't going to be him. 'Shut up.'

The ominous clicking ended with a particularly loud clang, and the door swung open. With a dubious look at his apprentice, Renatus released her and pushed inside with her at his heels.

A tight argument seemed to be simmering.

'Who else could it have been?'

'That's hardly evidence–'

'Fashionably late, Renatus?'

He ignored Winter's jibe and quickly took in his surroundings as everyone went tensely quiet. The lodge was, as he recalled, a two-storey, open-plan space with high ceilings, exposed timber beams, and gorgeous frosted windows even in the height of summer. A huge, ancient round table of carved stone took up the middle of the room, with almost thirty wooden chairs arranged around it. By the looks of it they were the same uncomfortable things that had been here when Lisandro brought him to meet the Avalonians. This time, though, most were filled, and filled entirely with familiar faces. Lord Gawain glanced up at him with an apologetic, knowing smile. He, too, had been here the last time, albeit reluctantly, beholden to Lisandro's plans for the Morrissey child as the legal guardian.

When Aristea was through, Renatus caught the door and closed it, noting with interest the complex clockwork-like locking mechanism that laced the entirety of the back. Had he seen this last time, and not paid it any mind? As soon as he pushed it shut, the components began clicking once again, all the cogs and chains working together to latch the entrance firmly. In the land of cuckoo clocks, it shouldn't be such a surprising feature.

'Welcome, Aristea Byrne, to Avalon's mainland outpost,' Gabriel Winter said with what was intended to sound like warmth from what was not intended to look like the head of the table but most certainly was, in the chair framed by the ornate fireplace behind it. He gestured around at the six White Elm and the five Valero councilmen already gathered. 'Join us.'

It was certainly promising, three nations sitting interspersed instead of on opposite sides of the circular table, but the absence of Anouk, the glue between these uneasy allies for the past ten years, smoothing out the best decade of their working history, was notable.

Behind Renatus, Aristea shrank back, reacting to something on her Empathic level.

There's a lot of tension, she told him before he could ask. *It makes me queasy.*

'No need to be shy,' Winter encouraged. 'Come, sit... Oh, my dear,' he interrupted himself sadly when the pair started forward, stilling Aristea and turning the attention of everyone at the table to her scarred and quickly reddening face. 'Renatus, you should have said. We would have understood.'

Damn it, he shouldn't have asked her along. She wasn't ready, and he should have known she would get this reaction, the same reaction she was going to get from now on, and protected her from it.

'Don't,' she muttered, hearing his thoughts. To Avalon's representative, she said, louder, 'I'm not *dear*, and I don't need Renatus to make excuses for me.'

Good girl. Renatus looked back at the room, quietly proud to see eyes dropping back to the evidence strewn on the tabletop. Lev Zarubin, one of the more prominent of Valero's city keepers, grunted in approval and laid his hands on the table before him. Renatus felt the attention of the room shift from Aristea to the Russian's hands as though by suction.

'Indeed you don't,' he agreed, flexing heavily scarred fingers and confidently providing no explanation to those at the table still eyeing the girl warily. Aristea's shoulders lifted, bolstered to see someone in authority with scars. 'Young Byrne, do you know where you are?'

'Renatus told me this is like a kind of embassy,' she said aloud, clearing her throat and pushing herself forward in his shadow. Winter smiled at her as Renatus led the way around the table to the only remaining pair of chairs side-by-side.

'That is one way of putting it. Avalon's treaty with the White Elm requires irregular and sometimes spontaneous meetings between our leadership, and sometimes involve other parties who must be appropriately vetted before they can be allowed into the very tightly controlled borders of Avalon. So we use this location as a sort of halfway house.'

'That *is* one way of putting it,' Renatus agreed, careful to sound casual rather than spiteful. He slid into the first seat and Aristea sat beside him with a quick glance at her other neighbour, Qasim. The Scrier. Renatus knew his apprentice admired, feared and clashed with nobody less in this entire room, but also that his older colleague was someone she trusted immensely, so he hoped her scrying teacher made her feel more secure.

He himself was seated directly opposite the person who made him feel most safe here. Lord Gawain caught his eye across the table and nodded almost imperceptibly, a gesture of support. He knew what this place really was to Renatus – a railway station with only one train scheduled, only one destination, and, if not for Lord Gawain's interference, no return trip.

But he'd also believed Renatus was strong enough to pretend to be past all that, or he wouldn't have agreed to this location. Renatus sat a little straighter, determined to prove his mentor's belief in him correct, and coolly met Winter's look of smug pleasure.

'How would *you* choose to put it, Renatus?' Detective Winter asked, unable to help himself from poking the wound he knew he'd find if he prodded hard enough. 'I'm interested.'

You're really not. But Renatus kept his thoughts close, aware that he was surrounded by Valeroan Telepaths. He shrugged delicately.

'I'm not sure. Cottage, maybe?' He looked around the main room of the house. 'Aristea thought it looked like the gingerbread house.'

Winter's eyes narrowed by the slightest degree, choosing to take offence to that dig, though that was reflective more of his arrogant determination to self-identify as Avalonian than of any real insult made. A few others at the table looked up in curiosity to see where this went, reminding Renatus disappointingly of the students back at his own house, and Winter opened his mouth to reply, probably just as bitingly.

'As fun as Renatus can be to antagonise, can we redirect our attention to the case?' Qasim asked shortly, effectively cutting Winter off. The detective had to force an apologetic, graceful smile as Councilman Demyan Vasiliev nodded in shared irritation with Qasim. Lev Zarubin elegantly stood to be at the same level at Winter.

'*Da. Khorosho skazano*, Scrier,' he said, acknowledging his people's agreement with the sentiment. 'We have business today. Before we continue, let us more formally begin. Valero thanks Avalon for their impartial and unconditional assistance in this investigation at this most tragic time for both Valero and White Elm,' he nodded his head in almost a bow to Lord Gawain, who responded in kind, 'and for hosting us here to examine the evidence on neutral territory.'

Winter likewise bowed. 'Our pleasure. Our alliances with both Valero and the White Elm nations...'

Renatus reclined in his seat, resisting the urge to roll his eyes at Aristea and wondering when he lost his endurance for these kinds of plodding political dances. He knew she had none, and assumed it was another by-product of the bond.

But the dance ended more quickly than he expected.

'The evidence collected and analysed by Valero, the White Elm and Detective Winter requires much more interrogation to gain a full picture of what happened on Saturday in Czechia,' Councilman Zarubin said, placing his mangled hands firmly and deliberately on the table before him. 'Specifically, Valero has two main interests – identifying the attackers in Prague, and verifying the source of blame.'

He shared an expressionless glance with other Valeroans around the table. Seeing Aristea raise her hand to her temple to massage away the pain caused by her sudden frown, Renatus sat forward, starting to feel wary.

Councilman Vasiliev sat forward, too.

'We will see evidence of Lisandro's involvement,' he said, 'or blame is with the White Elm.'

That simple with them. Black and white. And he didn't look at the council in general. He looked at Renatus and Aristea.

Renatus worked not to react. Beside him, Aristea's thoughts were jumping to terrified conclusions, her many paranoias seemingly proven correct before falling strangely silent, and across the table, Lord Gawain slowly got to his feet.

He was an old man now, almost seventy, his hair gone white and his skin gone loose, but rarely did Renatus see him that way. Most times, Renatus saw a leader, quietly confident, unshakable, the calm side of the strong and unassuming man who had found Renatus first after his parents and sister had been killed and had believed in him ever since.

Today Renatus saw both the leader and the old man.

'Let us open proceedings, then.'

chapter ten

I think I forgot how to breathe, even though it was exactly what I'd been waiting to hear. Here was the moment. Time for me to face the consequences. A cell in Valero's infamous prison, or perhaps just exile or something.

'First order of business: the validity of claims that Lisandro was either at fault or present,' someone, probably Winter, stated, and I heard discussion begin. Testimonies being read out. Statements being dissected. I processed it like I was underwater, far away and not truly present. The first responders to the scene – Elijah, Qasim, someone from Valero whose name I couldn't say – reiterated points from their accounts, and Renatus had to tell the table again that he'd seen Lisandro. I was asked to share my memory of the event, something I thought would be harrowing, but I delivered it in monotone, numbly, waiting for someone to leap up and pronounce me guilty. It didn't happen, probably only because I left out what I'd done to Renatus's mind, and soon I was sitting down again.

'And this memory has been verified?' Winter asked, jotting something down on the paper in front of him. He looked up at me when I couldn't answer. 'It hasn't been changed?'

'No.' His question made me think. 'Well. I wouldn't know if it had, would I?' The idea that memories could be overwritten was equal parts fascinating and disturbing.

'I've verified it,' Renatus spoke for me. 'The White Elm

135

doesn't condone memory alteration except in very particular circumstances so there's no need to question its authenticity.'

'Right,' Winter said as though humouring him. 'Aristea Byrne saw Lisandro but this has only been confirmed by Renatus. Any further evidence to review?'

I only heard bits.

Elijah, in frustration: 'There *is* a second Displacement well in the alley where Aristea went down.' The New Zealander was one of the calmest, most upbeat members of the White Elm. I rarely saw him out of sorts. 'But it's blocked, and I can't verify who used it.'

A tracer from Valero, unhelpfully: 'The explosion that killed the supporters, the spell, it does not bear any connection to any source outside of the square. We can match it only to the Irish ringleader Renatus identified as its caster.'

Renatus, producing a glass jar containing a floating black knot of electricity: 'We removed this from my apprentice's skin after she was attacked.'

I brought my attention back to the proceedings, leaning forward to get a better look at the thing in the jar. It zipped and jolted against the glass, suspended and trapped. The Valeroan who remained standing, Zarubin, whose hands were scars and nothing more, glanced aside at one of his fellow city keepers, who stood silently and went to the door. No explanation.

'But finish the story, Renatus,' Detective Winter prompted. 'Neither you, nor anyone else, not myself nor any of Valero's esteemed tracers, has been able to determine *conclusively* that this spell – though undoubtedly vicious – originated with your godfather.'

My attention was back. Across the table, I saw Lord Gawain's eyes flicker to Renatus with a spark of concern that no one else would feel. Renatus took a beat, seething at the unnecessary poke but outwardly keeping calm.

'That's right,' he confirmed finally. The guy at the door set the clockwork locks turning. 'It doesn't bear any energtic signature tracing back to him. But it's his design. He's the one who taught it to me.'

He opened his clenched fist on the tabletop and black lightning sparked between his fingers, making several people lean away automatically. Lord Gawain watched warily as Renatus ended the spell, demonstration made, and looked cautiously around the table at the reactions of others. I often wondered why Lord Gawain had chosen Renatus for the position he had when he was so conflicted about it, other than the obvious reason that the last Morrissey was clearly made for it, certainly more so than anyone else on the council. His experience with illegal magic through his family made him uniquely qualified to study it, his disposition and quick thinking made him the perfect modern warrior, but I knew he was a particular favourite of Lord Gawain's. When things went wrong, Renatus was on the front line; when suspicions were aroused, Renatus was the one with the cursed object or dangerous spell at hand.

'Still not conclusive,' Winter said simply, 'but we can take it into account.'

Beside me in my hindered peripheral vision, Qasim coughed an incredulous laugh, muttering a foreign curse under his breath. Oneida, the newest initiate to the council and newly appointed Scribe, was hurriedly recording the proceedings, her pen flying across the loose pages before her. Winter leaned across on the pretense of reading what she wrote.

'Thus far in support of the White Elm's claim of Lisandro's responsibility, we have established that *someone* was present to Displace away after Apprentice Byrne was attacked, and that the spell used against her was *written* by Lisandro, but not necessarily cast by him. Against...' He shrugged delicately, indicating how much longer that list was. I wanted to throw something at him – even with the room's emotions blocked off from me, Renatus's dislike for the Avalonian detective still permeated my attitude. 'Well, most significantly, there is no energetic trace of the man, and no one – not your Scrier, not ours – can confirm what Renatus and his apprentice claim to have seen.' He looked up at the door as the clockworks finished clicking and it opened. 'Do we have a witness?'

Two unfamiliar Valero guards came in with a blindfolded young man between them. He wasn't bound, but what I could see of his face looked nervous as he was wordlessly led around the table.

This was basically how I expected today was going to end for me, blindfolded and doomed.

'*Co se děje? Kam mě to vedete?*' he asked worriedly, reaching up uncertainly for the blindfold but not touching it as he walked unsteadily between his guides. The rich, full-bodied language was evident even in such a short utterance – I'd only very recently heard it for the first time. I lowered my defences warily, shifting the focus of my eyes until I could see his aura. The newcomer was a sorcerer, too, I could tell, but in the glare of the other bright and expansive and overlapping energies, I was going to need to reach out to get a proper reading on him.

'Why the blindfold?' Lord Gawain asked condescendingly as the guards found their blindfolded friend a seat and all but pushed him down into it. The youth turned his sightless head toward the voice.

'Who's there?' he asked, detecting English and switching. 'Can I take this off now?'

'Yes,' Lady Miranda answered immediately, but, 'No,' Detective Winter overrode her crisply, attracting the young man's attention. He added, 'You're in a safehouse. I'm sure this was explained to you.'

'An explanation does not negate his rights,' Lady Miranda said coldly, holding Winter's stare firmly without getting to her feet. Often, in her role as High Priestess, she left the leading to Lord Gawain, preferring to say little. But I admired her immensely, a woman of action rather than words, not to mention one of the women who'd saved me just a few days ago with her incredible gift of healing.

I had extended my own senses toward the newcomer. The instant my awareness touched his, a flash of unwanted memory struck me – *medieval city, screaming, burning in my arm,*

138

crimson cloaks, two hands slamming into the glass of my ward – and I flinched away, taken back to that moment more powerfully than any of the preceding discussion.

'Jaroslav?' I asked, recognising all at once the Czech boy who was there beside me when the Irishman cast the fear bomb, when I stopped to throw out that ward, when Anouk died on the wrong side of it. I'd first seen him standing atop a car, inciting the youth rally to drink, dance and think peace, before it all went wrong.

My voice gave him pause. Unable to place me, he swiftly tugged the blindfold down despite Winter's protests.

'Aristea.' He looked relieved to see a face he knew. His eyes darted from me to Renatus, recognising him from that day, and became less certain as he looked further around the table at the strangers gathered there, watching him with various expressions of interest and concern. He looked back to me. 'I wondered what had happened to you.' He noticed my scar and sat back, rendered unsure. 'You look… uh, alive. I'm glad.'

I refrained from touching the left side of my face self-consciously and made myself smile.

'Thanks.'

Lord Gawain looked to Renatus questioningly, and Renatus explained out loud for the rest of the table's benefit.

'He was in Prague, with the youth rally Anouk and I were there to break up,' he said. 'One of the instigators. He helped us to organise the locals caught up in the confusion.'

'What is he doing *here*?' Qasim asked coldly, glaring at one stoic Valeroan city keeper after another expectantly. 'Valero should be able to tell us what each witness saw.' He turned his commanding glare on Vasiliev. 'Your people had their noxious little hooks in the witnesses within hours of the attack, tampering with their minds – which is one of our highest offences, let it be reminded.'

I didn't need the reminder. I twisted my hands in my lap. But the Russians were at a loss, I could tell.

'He's here to give evidence,' Winter replied, smiling at

the newcomer, who was still looking anxiously around the table. 'Valero kindly collected him for me. Our scrier places this young man as the closest surviving person to Renatus and his apprentice at the moment they claim to have seen Lisandro.' He smiled wider. I hated him. 'If anyone else was to see him, it would have been this witness.'

'Jaroslav, what were you told about coming here today?' Lady Miranda asked cautiously, leaning forward to catch his gaze and offer him a reassuring smile. 'Are you here by your own will?'

'You're Lady Miranda,' he guessed, looking a little awed. He looked again around the table at all the faces he didn't know, pausing on Elijah, who'd interviewed him, stopping when his eyes caught mine. When I'd first met him he was smiling, bright and loud under a summer sun. He wasn't smiling now. He looked haunted. Someone else I'd failed to protect – though he'd been safe inside my ward, he'd still been witness to the same horrors. The deaths. The fear bomb. Now, abducted to be part of an awkward international court hearing. 'I... I am. What I saw... I never imagined magic being used that way, and I want to help. I was hoping, if I helped you, you might give me some time to discuss some of our group's views on–'

'Yes, yes, later,' Winter dismissed, whipping a colour photograph out of thin air and slapping it down on the table in front of the Czech sorcerer. 'Can you please tell this table of esteemed colleagues whether you saw this man anywhere in *Velkopřevorské náměstí* on Saturday before, during or after the attack?'

Jaroslav sat forward to look, untangling the blindfold from his neck idly. Slowly he shook his head, and looked up at me.

'No. I didn't see him. Who is he?' He waited a beat but then added, 'It's Lisandro, isn't it? It's who you were chasing. I heard you,' he explained quickly when glances were exchanged around the table. I felt their interest in the witness's intuition, and I nodded a confirmation.

'But you didn't see him,' Winter checked.

'No, but he could have been there,' Jaroslav admitted. 'It was chaotic, and the men in red said they were Magnus Moira supporters.' He looked to Lady Miranda. 'I don't know why they were there. Our movement doesn't support–'

'The supporters are all conveniently dead, and none of the witnesses can recall seeing Lisandro at the other end of *Velkopřevorské náměstí,*' Winter interrupted, writing again on his notepad. 'On the question of Lisandro's presence and fault, after reviewing all available evidence, we remain inconclusive. All parties to continue investigation. Move to continue into second order of business?'

'Seconded,' Zarubin agreed flatly. 'The attackers.'

The White Elm was displeased with the swift end to that line of investigation, but every Valeroan sat straighter, fuelled by their emotional investment in finding not whose idea the attack was, but who pulled the trigger. I got a weird shiver at the change in topic; I couldn't say why. The disagreement was brief but intense. Lord Gawain had spent enough long years of his life in courtrooms to know how to argue, but this nonsense seemed to be wearing him thin. Jaroslav was watching me, bewildered by these erratic proceedings. I offered him a weak smile. Beside me, it felt like Renatus was ready to pull his hair out.

'Fine,' he announced finally, silencing the table. 'Fine. We'll move on, not that there's much point. They self-identified. I heard them. Is that up for debate?'

'I'm sure Renatus is just as good at hearing as he is at everything else,' Detective Winter said coolly, and beside me I felt the flicker of my master's annoyance, though his face betrayed nothing; he didn't even glance. One of the other representatives from Valero spoke up.

'We know already what Renatus heard. In our work with Glen, he has many times revisited the final minutes of his connection with Anouk Kashnikova. She heard this announcement also.'

The mention of their mutual fallen comrade and her

traumatised surviving other half quietened everyone at the table momentarily. I fidgeted in my lap, picking at my flaking nail polish. Every time her name came up, I waited for the declaration of my own guilt. They kept missing their chance.

'We wish to have their identities made available to us,' Zarubin said simply. 'We want to know the names of her killers.'

'I can help with that,' Jadon, the youngest White Elm councillor, spoke up. Younger even than Renatus, the American Telepath had been sitting between Oneida and another representative of Valero with his head in his hand, running his fingers over his very short brown hair tiredly. His other hand was playing with the edge of the manila folder in front of him. He reluctantly sat up and sifted through the papers inside the folder. 'But… it's not good news.' He met Renatus's gaze across the table. 'The guys in the red cloaks that attacked you – White Elm citizens.'

'You told me this,' Lord Gawain said calmly, not seeing the problem. My stomach twisted a little at Jadon's words, which seemed the precursor to something worse he was preparing to tell us, but Renatus let the words slide right off him.

'We knew they would be. That's who Lisandro conscripts.'

I exhaled slowly. Of course this would be true. Colonies like Valero and Avalon, and smaller independents like Oneida's village in the western USA, were harder to penetrate and more likely to be dedicated to their way of life, whereas the White Elm encompassed the majority of magic users, many of whom hardly identified with the nation to which they officially belonged. Shady and subversive characters like Renatus's distant cousin Declan O'Malley were technically White Elm citizens as much as I was.

'Right, that's what I said when Viktor and I started cropping up their names,' Jadon agreed, tucking all the documents back inside the folder. 'We went and spoke to their families and none had any clear Magnus Moira connections.

Most were adamant we were wrong. Which, again, we expected to hear.' He closed the folder and held it up; Renatus extended his hand for it, and because it was more than a metre out of reach, he flicked his fingers and the folder flew to his hand. He grasped it and opened it in one fluid motion. I leaned closer to see what he was reading. It looked like a transcript, or a record of a meeting. 'In fact, they're all from the same Finnish coven, and extremely pro-council, which just confuses things further.'

'*Pro*-council?' Renatus repeated, flicking through the pages. I glanced at him, feeling uncomfortable with this. 'We were attacked by…? I know this name.' He stopped on the fourth page and pointed. 'I've seen a few of these names…'

'Where, Renatus?' Winter asked pointedly, and I knew immediately that he knew.

'They're…' My master turned another page, starting to feel agitated, though he didn't look it. 'They write in sometimes to the council's newsletter.'

In peacetimes, resources like Renatus were a waste, and he'd been put to work as a secretary of sorts, reading and answering mail sent to the White Elm. Now he had plenty of other tasks to keep him busy.

'You're looking at the minutes to their last meeting, translated into English because I can't read Finnish,' Jadon went on. 'They're a fundamentalist pro-White Elm organisation. Not surprising that they've written in to you before. There are more of them, about forty all up. They talk a lot about how best to undermine Lisandro's Magnus Moira movement and two have been arrested for harassment, released without charge, of a woman they claim, at least privately, to be associated with Magnus Moira. Nothing about that in the police report, as far as Viktor was able to tell.' He looked uncomfortable; I couldn't tell specifically why. 'Anyway, in their last meeting…'

I read quickly, still shaky. What was Jadon saying? Ignoring where Renatus was up to, knowing he could simply read through me if he needed to keep up, I flipped through the pages, scanning. My eyes caught on *Prague* on the seventh page of motions, seconding, and other boring meeting conventions.

'*Youth rally in July, Prague, Czech Republic. Raised by Miro,*' I read aloud for the benefit of those at the table who hadn't been made privy to this yet. '*Gathering of young political activists to discuss and promote peace and political stability. No solid alignment. Potential for action? Miro to investigate.*'

'Should… Should I be here for this?' Jaroslav asked awkwardly, glancing uneasily back at his guards. Everyone ignored him. I allowed Qasim to take the pages. This was not going the way I expected. This was… all wrong. Not just the total omission of dealing with my own crimes, but something else. This new evidence. I felt deeply about its wrongness, with a certainty I couldn't explain.

'Miro Järvinen was one of the deceased found at the scene,' Jadon spoke. 'The rest of the coven, when I met with them, were absolutely mortified to hear he was involved. It was never the wider group's intention, they said, to engage in destructive activism.' Jadon raised a helpless hand in a sort of shrug. 'There can be extremists in any following, I guess.'

'How did they even know about the rally?' Qasim asked irritably as he read. 'We didn't know until I scried it. This meeting was a *month* in advance.'

The table went silent with a lack of answers. Jaroslav looked around again.

'Maybe they read us,' he suggested. He became centre of attention.

'*Read* you?'

'My blog. Marcy's, too, and a few others. They…' He trailed off at the blank looks some of the table were giving him. I jumped in.

'Digital journaling. What about your blog?'

'I study political sciences and I write about politics and policy in magic,' he said. He looked just to me and tried to explain. 'A few of us do, and people all over read it, follow us, you know. Then we have forums for discussing our views, and the rally on Saturday was meant to be the first time we met for real.' He swallowed, visibly upset by how it had deteriorated. 'Marcy and I both shared the date on our blog back at the start of June, and between us we probably have eleven thousand readers. The post I made on Saturday already has more than two thousand views. These people, the attackers, if they're political...' He shrugged, distressed now by the realisation of the trap he'd unwittingly helped set for us, for his friends, for all those non-witches. 'They could have read it there.' He looked down at the blindfold in his hands. 'I'm sorry. I wouldn't have posted anything online if I'd imagined–'

'Don't blame yourself,' Qasim interrupted brusquely. 'Anticipating acts of terror is not your responsibility. You have every right to assume the best in people.'

My focus was on something else Jaroslav had said.

'What post from Saturday?' I asked. He hesitated.

'I went straight home and wrote it straightaway,' he confessed, glancing uneasily at Lady Miranda and Lord Gawain. 'Before I could forget a single detail: the bomb, the silver ball in the sky, another explosion. And you. A shield that saves everybody.'

My stomach dropped a few centimetres. 'Not everybody.'

'I thought everyone should know,' he said sincerely, looking from me to Renatus. 'The White Elm saved us. My followers range from anti-council to neutral but there's a lot of ignorance, too. Some of it, arguably, the White Elm's fault. But now no one can say the council doesn't do anything for us. It's been my most popular post ever.' He looked around again, worried. 'If I wasn't meant to post it and you're going to kill me in a ditch somewhere...'

'You took a photo of me,' I reminded him, and he hesitated again.

'Knowing now who some of my readers are, I think it's best I take that down.'

I leaned forward, shocked. 'You shared my photo online and *two thousand* people know who I am? I'm meant to be a secret.'

'In my defence,' he said quickly, raising his hands, 'Marcy had already talked about you extensively. But I'll take it down, I swear.'

'Alright, back to the proceedings, please,' Lord Gawain said tiredly. I sat back, staring at the exposed beams of the ceiling, overwhelmed. Two thousand views? How many sorcerers were there in the blogosphere? Was that a lot? 'The attackers have been revealed as supporters of *ours*, so why did they identify as followers of Lisandro, and why did they attack our councillors?'

'They were fundamentalists. They knew his Magnus Moira movement would never recover from such tragic association,' Zarubin suggested, accepting a handful of the pages when offered to him. His eyes drifted up to Lord Gawain's. 'Valero will *assume* the White Elm had no direct part in this.'

'We *appreciate* the benefit of your doubt,' Lady Miranda replied with the same coolness.

'Valero is suggesting that these rogue supporters were acting in the White Elm's perceived interest and portrayed themselves as Magnus Moira members in an attempt to further sully Lisandro's image?' Winter clarified with the daintiest of feigned frowns. God, I hated him.

'Far from proving any one truth,' Qasim countered, reaching across me for the rest of the folder, still reading, 'this documentation supports the probability of infiltration. Members we found at the scene are the names beside the more provocative, controversial motions and topics in this transcript.' He lowered the paper to look around the table. 'Lisandro is not stupid. He would know that whoever he sent to do this would be heavily scrutinised. So he planted his men as a cell inside a pro-council group, knowing this would come out. Knowing we would have to answer to Valero when this came out.'

'Or,' Winter began, only to be steamrolled by Renatus's firm voice.

'And that's why the spell killed them,' he guessed. 'No

one for us to interrogate.'

Logically, this made much more sense, yet I couldn't shake the deep certainty within me that Renatus was wrong, too.

'This is a line of investigation the White Elm will support,' Lord Gawain said. 'What does Valero say?'

Everyone looked to Zarubin; I looked to Winter. The pale-haired detective was still smiling thinly, but I saw the flash of cunning contempt in his eye for Renatus. I didn't understand it. I understood why Renatus would hate the detective, one of the men who'd stood in this very room and painted a picture of their home, of their freedoms and opportunities, while they eyed him up and assessed whether they wanted him. He never talked about what happened there, except to admit that the scars that laced his back came from that time in his youth, but even still, I couldn't imagine what fifteen-year-old, angst-ridden Renatus could have done to so offend Winter.

Lev Zarubin appeared to be considering Qasim and Renatus's counter. 'It seems plausible.'

'Well, which is it?' Detective Winter sounded annoyed. 'Were they White Elms pretending to be Magnus Moira, or Magnus Moira pretending to be White Elm pretending to be Magnus Moira?'

It came out like a tongue-twister or a riddle and it might have been funny except it wasn't, because they were wrong.

'Neither,' I spoke up. Renatus looked down at me in surprise. I hadn't even thought about speaking, it had just come out. 'There's another explanation.'

'Oh?' Winter invited, faking his indulgent warmth again. I shook my head slowly, wishing I hadn't spoken, but as I looked up at Renatus, I knew with such certainty that I couldn't have *not* spoken.

'Can I go?' Jaroslav asked again, thinking he'd spotted an opening to be heard, but once again he was largely ignored.

'What have we missed?' Zarubin asked. My feeling of certainty was joined by a strong rush of frustration. I raked my hair back from my face, further annoyed when my left hand disappeared into my peripheral before my right.

'I don't know!' I said again. 'I just... I just *know*. I know that *this*,' I took the stapled transcript back from Qasim and tossed it irritably onto the table, 'this is all a distraction. We're being played. I don't know how I know. I can't explain. I know how it sounds. I just...'

'You just know,' Detective Winter finished for me, his smile more of a sneer. Bastard. Whose side was he on here? Neutral party, pfft. 'You just know *what*, exactly? I imagine that there's *a lot* you know. Things from Saturday you haven't told us, no?' His eyes glittered – he knew. I swallowed.

'I...' I couldn't lie; not in this room of energetic lie-detectors. 'I told you everything I saw. I don't know why I'm so sure about this.'

'Aristea is not under investigation,' Renatus reminded his rival staunchly, standing slowly, protectively. Nearby, Vasiliev nodded, surprising me.

'Valero agrees. We wish to hear the girl.'

'Is this why you refused a memory check?' Winter pushed, like the others hadn't spoken. Beneath the stone table, I clutched the sides of my seat, the edges of my inner secrets curling like burning paper, determined not to betray anything in my face or my surface thoughts. 'Because you know something you don't want to share? How–'

'Detective!' In a flare of temper that made me flinch, I felt rather than saw Qasim stand beside me in my blind spot, joining the other big powers in the room on their feet. 'Another *word* out of you and it won't matter whose house this is, you'll be out on your arse.' He worked to control his angry voice and I worked to turn my neck far enough to see him properly. 'Aristea, at the hospital, did you dream?' I nodded. 'About what?'

'About...' I was empty again, the frustration burned up. 'About Prague, mostly. And once, I scried something from the past.' Something awful I couldn't call back to mind.

'In your visions of Prague, what do you see? Is it the same every time?'

I frowned, tenderly rubbing the new skin beside my sore eye when it twinged. Renatus exhaled in annoyance.

'What does this–'

'Shut it, you,' Qasim snapped at him. 'You're next. Aristea? Yes, the same each time?'

'It's just a playback,' I said quietly. 'The men closing in on us, and Anouk's hands… on the outside of the shield…' I blinked, dimly surprised to find I was close to tears. 'Over and over.'

'But no storm.' Qasim waited for me to wipe my eyes and look up at him again in uncertainty, slowly shaking my head again, realising. No storm. Following the deaths of my parents and brother in what I thought was a tragic storm, I dreamed of the event every single night. Since finding out that the storm was not an accident, but a tool of the extravagant Lisandro to commit murder without being caught, the dreams had ceased. Qasim lifted his gaze to Renatus. 'And you?'

My master felt immediately vulnerable, I could tell even without looking at him. His fear of his own traumatic dreams of a deadly storm had prompted him to coat the entirety of Morrissey Estate in magic that prevented him from having to dream at all.

'When I fell asleep at the hospital… No storm, just Prague. Just Anouk.'

'Then we have missed something.' Qasim closed the folder in front of him with finality. He addressed the whole table. 'You may know already that when scriers are present at a fateful moment but secrets remain buried, Fate uses regular dreams to prompt them to revisit their memories. Both Renatus and Aristea are highly intuitive scriers. This has happened to them before. If Aristea says we are wrong in our theories about the attackers, then she is right.' He tossed the folder to the centre of the table. It slid a few centimetres along the smooth stone and came to a stop out of everyone's reach. Qasim sat down, calm again. 'I believe her.'

It took a moment. I bit the inside of my lips, feeling a warmth encroach on my inner vacuum. Qasim was my scrying teacher, the meanest man around and also a talent to be reckoned with – to have him on my side felt like getting to put my metaphorical foot down and winning an argument. Authoritative and next in line for Lord Gawain's job, I had previously reflected that he would be good at it, as blunt and action-ready as Gawain was careful and tactful. I let my eyes drift over the others in the room. The White Elm leaders said nothing – they gave Qasim a lot of leeway, a bit like Lord Gawain did for Renatus – and their allies seemed unsettled by the council's collective mind having apparently been made up. Valeroan Telepaths shared uneasy glances and tilted their heads toward each other, listening, nodding unconsciously. Gabriel Winter looked around, seeing his support in the room fall away, and Vasiliev sat forward in his seat.

'We keep looking,' he agreed gruffly. 'We find truth.'

Lord Gawain looked relieved. 'Thankyou, Councilman. We will find the truth together.'

'Valero is not yet convinced that the White Elm is faultless in this incident,' Zarubin quipped firmly before anyone could get the idea that all was well. 'The onus is on your council to prove this when we next meet. Until then, our alliance's future is frozen.' He stood in complete synchronicity with the rest of the Valeroans. 'This meeting is ended. Guardian Rodchenko and I will be in communication with updates of Glen's rehabilitation.'

'That's it?!' I demanded, finally getting to my feet as well when I saw the Valeroan procession depart from their seats around the table and start for the door. My words must have spoken for the thoughts of several White Elms because no one shushed me. 'You're leaving? Nothing's been sorted out, no decisions made. All we have is more problems.'

'This is politics,' Mr Vasiliev responded, more kindly than I expected. He and the other Russians kept walking even as I continued.

'But… All you did was argue about the wrong stuff. You blamed them,' I waved vaguely, irritably, at the White Elm leaders opposite me, 'when they weren't even there. What about me?'

'What about *me*?' Jaroslav countered, standing and trying to get the attention of the two guards who brought him here. 'Aren't you taking me back?'

'Don't ignore us,' I snapped at the retreating Russian backs. Renatus touched my shoulder, trying to make me back down. The Valeroans set the door unlocking itself, and Lev Zarubin paused to lay his scarred hands on the back of the empty chair beside Jadon.

'You expected blame for the deaths in Prague,' he said bluntly, and I closed my mouth, struck. 'You want blame and punishment to match your own guilt. Perhaps Avalon is right, that you did more that you are not telling us. Questionable things, in the heat of the moment. But this is the nature of battle. You saved many. Your master. This boy.'

'My ward–' I began, desperately, pushing Renatus's insistent hand off my shoulder, ignoring his voice in my head telling me to be quiet. He and I were both cut off by Zarubin's calm, sharp voice.

'Aristea Byrne, you are scarred,' he reminded me. Behind him, the door opened and his fellows filed out. 'Others can see that now, but your real burden will be to live with the scars unseen. No,' he corrected, when I ran a self-conscious hand up my left arm, thinking of the black cracks under my skin. 'That will heal, with time. Other hurts are not so easily escaped. I am sorry. We have no blame for you. You must find your atonement elsewhere. Boy,' he added when Jaroslav tried again to ask what was going to happen to him, 'you are a White Elm citizen. I am sure your government can help you get home.'

He nodded his acknowledgement to Winter, Lord Gawain and Lady Miranda, shared a final loaded look with Renatus, and left. In the silence that followed, I remained standing, feeling lost. *We have no blame for you*. No prison, no price to pay at all, at least not from Valero. I don't know why this didn't make me feel better. Was it, as Zarubin had suggested, that I *wanted* to be punished and held responsible for what had happened? That was sick, right? I didn't want to

151

be taken from Renatus or to lose my position as a White Elm apprentice; I didn't want to disappoint and devastate my family with the news that I was a criminal. Confused, I slowly sat down. What was wrong with me?

'That went well,' Lord Gawain sighed, sitting down as well and putting his hand to his forehead as though to address a fresh migraine. Not that I could blame him. 'Thanks for your support, Gabriel.'

He wasn't normally snarky and even now, the sarcasm was only subtle, but the Avalonian detective had the grace to look abashed. Which he certainly was not.

'Business, Gawain, you understand,' he replied. He packed up his notepad. Jaroslav got to his feet awkwardly.

'Uh…'

'I'll take you home,' Elijah offered, 'and we can talk about your group's objectives. I think we need to chat about what of today is appropriate to share in your blog, anyway.'

'Yeah.' Jaroslav glanced apologetically at me. 'Good idea.'

He left with Elijah, and I let my head fall into my hands. Great. Another *two thousand* people who thought I was some kind of hero, when I'd never felt like more of a fraud.

chapter eleven

There were many "best" things about Hiroko Sasaki. Her warmth. Her surprising humour. Her sense of loyalty. After Renatus returned me to the estate and promptly continued inspecting invisible magic in the air, along the fence, wherever, I went straight back to my shared room and fell heavily onto my bed. It was halfway through the afternoon, and everyone else was about the house and the estate, enjoying the summery day and the unexpected free time with the council still tied up with this investigation, but I just wanted to be alone with my dark and jumbled thoughts.

One of the best things about Hiroko was that I could be alone even when she was there.

She must have seen me come back, because I wasn't lying there more than five minutes, staring at the ceiling with the emptiness inside me swelling out like a black hole that would surely absorb this room, when the door cracked open.

'I'm not very fun to be around right now,' I warned as she stepped inside emanating mild concern. I turned my head to watch her push the door closed behind her, swinging her key on its chain.

'When are you ever?' she asked, casting a light, teasing smile down at me as she sat on my bed, nudging me over with her hip. I made room and she settled back, resting her head affectionately on my shoulder. Her face was in my blind spot so I didn't see her expression as I nodded reluctantly.

'That's fair,' I admitted, picking some more of my flaking black nail polish off onto my stomach. Since I started on it at the round table, I'd almost totally cleared one thumb of paint. 'Who won Monopoly?'

'Does anyone ever *win* Monopoly?' Hiroko wondered. 'I have never played it to the end. Addison bankrupted Sophia with a hotel on Mayfair, then the twins got into a fight over the rules and we ended things before they could disown each other. I think Kendra had the most money. Is that how you win?'

I had to think. 'I don't actually know, either. My brother and sister used to team up at the start and the game would always end when Aidan turned on Angela and things got bitter. We never made it past that.'

I couldn't see her face but I heard her smile in her next exhalation, not quite a laugh. I smiled, too. With my sister, it was easy to smile sadly and reminisce about the funny, competitive and fiercely protective brother we'd lost with our loving parents, but outside of our family, the loss was never something discussed. It was awkward, and uncomfortable, and just best left alone. Then I'd come here, to the first place beyond my home where I felt like I belonged in any meaningful sense, and found Hiroko, who'd lost her mother in a car accident when she was small. And I'd found that I could talk to her. She knew what it was to miss someone and still smile. In sadness, she said, memories could fade, or turn sour. I had seen this in the way Renatus dealt with his past, with no one around to relive those memories with. Fionnuala, his childhood nanny who was still on staff in the household, and Lord Gawain, who clearly adored him, too, had indulged him in this regard, allowing him to stubbornly suffer in silence rather than forcing him through it, and he was not any better off for their charity.

The silence I fell into with Hiroko knew nothing of suffering, and for long minutes I smiled blithely at the thin cracks in the ceiling of the old house, feeling more settled and less empty than I had all day.

'What about you?' she asked after a while.

'Hmm?' I saw her hand take the back of mine, stopping

my unconscious picking, and turn it over to show the black tattoo on the inside of my wrist. I knew it was there, it was a part of me now, but seeing it reminded me of things I'd been happy to forget for a few minutes, and I started to feel wary. 'What do you mean?'

'How do *you* win? Every time you leave this house with Renatus, it takes something from you. You return hurt, afraid, sad, or burdened with a new secret. Today, you did not want to go. Did you tell this to Renatus?'

I kept my gaze firmly on my tattoo. 'I didn't need to. He knew. He told me I could stay behind if I wanted.'

'Because he knew it would be yet another unpleasant experience. Like every time you go anywhere with him. A party, a, uh...' She searched for the English word. 'A task, no, mission, or a visit to an exotic city, always, you lose something. Still, you went today. Emmanuelle said you should still be at the hospital–'

'I was going crazy at that place,' I argued. I felt her shrug against my shoulder, dismissing my attempt to veer away from the uncomfortable truth of her main point.

'And I am happy you came back, but what will you prove? Renatus already chose you. He trusts you will take his place one day. He also knows you were badly injured and you are still recovering. He cares about you. Talk to him about it.'

'It's the job,' I insisted, shrugging as well, careful not to dislodge her head. Hiroko sighed, apparently not getting through to me.

'This job,' she tapped the marking on my wrist, 'is costing you. But this is not paper Monopoly money. This is your happiness, your safety. Is this price fair?'

No. 'I don't set the price.'

'Do you think Renatus is happy for you to pay this price?' Hiroko pushed. 'What about your sister? You have to lie to her,' she reminded me of the phone call. 'The people who love you will not like to see this. You cannot win this way. You can only lose.'

I was not having the best day. Her words brought those

tears back to my eyes, stinging the still-healing wound beside my eye when I tried to squeeze the lids closed. I tried not to think about what had already been lost in my time as Renatus's apprentice, least of all Anouk, and what was still on the line: the White Elm's alliances with Valero and Avalon, the threat of Lisandro's Magnus Moira movement, the lives of the four boys Aubrey stole right from this very house, including Hiroko's sweetheart Garrett. Before his abduction, I used to tell Hiroko everything I heard from the White Elm, then that had hit her hard. She was tough, and had handled it like a pro, but every time I learned something new that shook me, as much as I wanted to share it with her, I had measured up how miserable the news had made me and decided that making her life that much worse was not worthwhile. So secrets had grown between us, and I knew she knew, though she never brought it up. Now she took my hand in hers, letting my wrist fall to the side so the tattoo was no longer visible, and when she continued speaking, her voice was gentler.

'The burns, the truth about your family, now your eye,' she reminded me. 'Every class you've missed because you were too tired. Months without your family. Even Sterling and Xanthe. This is what you have paid to be his apprentice.'

I swallowed and it hurt. 'Do you think I should have said no?'

'No, not at the beginning. But now, sometimes, yes. I think you shouldn't push yourself so hard. Renatus doesn't ask it of you. It's okay to say no.'

I heard the logic in her words and knew she was right. Anytime I wanted, I could back off from this job with Renatus – he always gave me an out, a chance to say no thanks without letting him down. I could decline any mission, refuse any investigation, avoid any training session, the same way I could skip any scheduled class with any other councillor. And he would never be disappointed.

But.

I knew something he didn't. I knew something almost *nobody* knew. Any missed training session was a missed chance to upskill, to become better. Any investigation I wasn't part of was any number of unexplored contacts and lost opportunities to widen my own network and understanding of Renatus's world. Any mission I didn't go on with him had the potential to spiral into another Prague. Up until recently, I knew I'd been little more than a burden on my master in the field, but if I agreed with Valero on anything, it was that I had saved Renatus on Saturday. Maybe he'd have cast his own ward, but he'd be dead now without my Empathic perception of the Irishman's weapon. I was only just starting to reach my potential, not only as a White Elm apprentice, but as his friend and partner. I was becoming someone who could stand beside him and have his back the way he had mine.

I was becoming someone who could save him from his own fate.

'Aristea?' Hiroko squeezed my hand, concerned, and I realised I was crying.

'One day,' I managed, my throat feeling thick, holding her hand tightly, 'something terrible is going to happen. Don't ask me how I know, I just do. Something's going to happen to him and I'm the only one who might be able to stop it. So I can't price-match what it's costing me – whatever it takes.' I rubbed the tears off my face, glad it was just her. 'I can't let this happen to him, Hiroko. I can't slow down or back off the job until I'm good enough, strong enough, to... do this *thing*. To help him. I know you think it isn't my responsibility–'

'Our friends are always our responsibility,' she interrupted. 'That's why we are having this conversation.' I nodded, warmed by her words, so grateful for her. I inhaled slowly, trying to get a grip on myself, but all I had a grip on was her, and she was trying to be reasonable with the information she had at her disposal. I wished I could tell her more but it wasn't fair to burden her with it. She was quiet for a while, then shifted so she was staring at the ceiling, too. 'At that point, when you are strong enough to do *this thing*,' she said finally, slowly, 'will you still be the same girl he calls his apprentice and I call my friend?'

That wasn't something that I had properly asked of myself, and I turned my head to look at her, surprised and worried that I couldn't immediately answer. She kept her gaze on the ceiling above us, resolute while she waited for me to respond. The truth was, I didn't know. Everything that had happened since I came here had done its part in changing me, little by little. I could tell myself it was just growth, that all my peers had experienced the same, but the bond with Renatus was affecting me more all the time. In hurtling down this path to save Renatus's soul, could I be compromising my own?

I couldn't know. I just knew I couldn't *not* take the risk.

My other friends, to their credit, were likewise patient and understanding with me as I reacclimatised to living at the school as though my world hadn't been turned inside out yet again. At breakfast the next morning, their usual playful antics served as a comforting reminder that a big part of my life was here as a commonplace magic student at Renatus's house, and it was nowhere near as complicated or responsibility-laden as my life as his apprentice. I never had to worry about Kendra and Hiroko's alliance breaking down over the death of Addison, or about Sophia destroying herself under the weight of revenge.

'Do you know when classes are starting again?' Kendra asked me as she scraped the last of her scrambled eggs onto her fork. Beside her, her twin looked up briefly from the origami swan she and Hiroko were trying to construct – it should have been sad to see Hiroko learning the papercraft artform Garrett had taught himself in his attempts to impress her before he'd gone missing, but Hiroko had a way of shining sunshine on sad things – to wait for my answer. I shrugged and looked up from Tian's book.

'No. Do you?'

'No, but you're our insider source,' she reminded me, licking her fork clean. 'I thought Renatus might have told you.'

'He hasn't said anything about it,' I said, neglecting to mention that he hadn't said much of anything since we got back from Germany. He wasn't sure how to deal with downer me; avoidance was his typical strategy. He would be there when I sought him out.

'They've probably got heaps on their plate without worrying about our lessons,' Sophia said, glancing up at me for confirmation, then snatching up her fork to fend off her sister's when it encroached on her unfinished meal. 'Heaps on their plate that they're *saving for later*.'

'It's going to go cold,' Kendra complained, trying again for Sophia's mushrooms. Soph flicked Ken's fork and looked back at me, determinedly ignoring her twin.

'Once they start classes back, Iseult and Lien Hua will start coming back for day lessons,' she explained, keeping Kendra's fork pinned down with hers. 'Hopefully, unless they've changed their minds. I didn't even get an address from either of them before they left so we can't write to them.'

'It is strange without Iseult here,' Hiroko agreed, going back to her napkin swan. Addison leaned across the table and with his long arm reached out the pen he was holding to scribble a messy eye on the head of her paper bird.

'I mean for now I miss having Iseult around, but once classes start up again I'll probably be glad not to have my arse kicked in every single subject by the same chick,' he confessed while Hiroko indulgently held the origami still for him. He grinned up at her as he drew. 'Then I just need to think of some way to get you kicked out and I'll be top of Elijah's class.'

I frowned, ignoring the twinge more easily today, thinking of all the students withdrawn and missing, many of whom were Displacers in the small top class with Hiroko and Addison.

'Wouldn't that make you the only–'

'The *top of the class*,' Addison confirmed proudly. 'The number of competitors is irrelevant.'

'If enough people pull out of the Academy, what's that going to do to the classes?' I wondered aloud. 'Only two of you left in level three Displacement…'

'Addison needs to rethink his takeover plan,' Hiroko said patiently, waiting for him to finish adding to her swan before

159

completing the final fold, fluffing it up and arranging it on the tabletop for us all to see. It had a smiley face on the side of its head. 'Lien Hua and Iseult will be attending for Displacement classes. So he will be back at the bottom.'

She shot him a cheekily triumphant smile as the twins briefly let up on their fork war to laugh at Addison. The most easy-going guy I'd known since my brother, nothing fazed him, least of all being made the butt of a joke, and he sat back in his seat like he was accepting defeat, always smiling.

'No punches pulled with you, hey Sasaki? We can't all be as talented and humble as you,' he simpered playfully, extending a hand out to the side. He opened his fist; the happy-faced napkin swan unfurled crunchily from his palm. We all looked quickly back to the centre of the table but of course the bird was no longer there. 'Or as good at getting the last word as me.'

Our collective laughter attracted attention from our fellow breakfasters, but I'd already grown reaccustomed to filtering their notice of me to the very back of my awareness. This was why I didn't sense the approaching presence of Fionnuala, Renatus's head of staff and favourite person, as she sidled up at my elbow.

'Mail for you, Miss Aristea,' she said pleasantly, surprising me. I turned, still laughing, and saw the string-tied envelope she held out. I tried to swallow my laughter quickly to apologise for not noticing her, but she reached out a soft hand and laid it on my cheek, silencing me. 'Don't apologise, my dear. It's so good to see you smiling.' Her warm, sparkling eyes scanned my face quickly, clinging to the new wound beside my eye. She nodded once in approval, the first person to look at me like that since my Healers at the hospital. 'It's good to see you *alive*. They did an excellent job.'

'They did, didn't they,' I agreed, though I hadn't seen what it looked like before Lady Miranda, Emmanuelle and Teresa took care of me. I could only imagine. I'd seen the blood on my clothes, on Renatus's, and I could remember the pain and his reaction. The housekeeper dropped her hand, smiling at me with the same adoration she usually reserved for Renatus.

'And so did you,' she reminded me, seeming not to notice that her words were enough to make my own smile finally slip away under the weight of yet another unfair congratulation. 'Thank you. For what you did.'

There was no need for elaboration. What I *did*, among plenty of other things I shouldn't have, was save her boy. It should have been an easy thank you to accept, because it was something even I could believe I had done, but in this moment, after my conversation with Hiroko the day before, it only reminded me that I had not yet, in fact, managed this feat. His life had been preserved but Renatus was not saved, not yet. The grey-haired woman smiled extra warmly, the lines around her eyes softening with graciousness and love, and she pushed the letter into my hand before she left me to my friends.

'Celebrity status, much?' Kendra commented when we were alone again. 'I wish I'd seen this heroic ward of yours.'

'It wasn't that impressive,' I insisted weakly, turning my attention to the letter in my hands and hoping no one could see the discomfort in my face. The envelope was a thick sort of brown paper, bound with string and sealed with wax. It had been stamped but I didn't recognise the crest.

'You make it hard for anyone else to achieve fame, living in your shadow,' Addison explained in a long-suffering voice. 'Phase two of takeover plan, after I get rid of Hiroko and become star student: find some way to get rid of Aristea and overthrow her celebrity rule. Although,' he said generously, leaning forward to put the swan back where he'd teleported it from, 'you'll probably manage that in time without much help from me.'

'Addison!' Sophia scolded, giving up on defending her plate from her sister to toss her fork at him. Kendra took the opportunity to swap the plates and dig into what Sophia hadn't eaten while Addison protested the attack and the fork tumbled to the ground.

'What?! Like she doesn't know that drama follows her everywhere.'

'Doesn't mean you *point it out.*'

'Doesn't mean you *throw your fork,*' he shot back, but her frown didn't relent. He turned to me charitably. 'I'm sorry for pointing out your generally dramatic circumstances. I don't actually want you to get yourself kicked out. Obviously.'

'I know.' I nearly had the string untied from my letter. It had no return address, and my name on the front was written in a precise, unfamiliar hand. Not Angela. Not my aunt. I couldn't think of anyone else who would write to me. 'You're not wrong.'

'Yeah, see? She knows. She's the resident bad girl. Underage ink, constant drama. Rock chick,' he added to me in an aside, nodding seriously at Sophia, 'control your rabid fans.'

Another good-natured argument broke out between the three, helped along by the occasional sly remark from Hiroko, as I finally got the envelope open. I shook out the contents into my hand.

Open French doors with lace curtains billowing luxuriously, caught in the breeze… a plush armchair at a white desk… a dainty hand with perfect nails scribes the "y" of "Aristea Byrne" on elegant stationery… tossing blonde hair, the girl stretches out and looks–

I inhaled sharply and dropped everything I was holding. The sounds of the dining hall returned to me and I glanced quickly around. No one had noticed my momentary lapse of attention. Teagan Shanahan – I knew the girl in this vision, though I'd never seen her unmasked – had *looked at me*. I didn't know how, or whether it was even truly the case, because I was, after all, known for overreacting and a vivid imagination. I mean, the vision was an impression, a moment in time captured as energy left imprinted on the paper she'd been touching at the time, and I'd tapped into that. But those big eyes had seemed to know I was there, from exactly what downward angle I was viewing her from. Which was impossible for her to have known at the time of writing this card. She must have just happened to look up at that very moment the impression had captured, and I must have imagined the knowing smirk on her face.

Forcing my breathing pattern back to something like normal, I picked the notecard and envelope up off Tian's book, feeling foolish. The half sheet of pretty, pinkish paper was the only thing the envelope contained, and its handwriting matched Teagan's etching in the vision.

Dear Miss Aristea Byrne,

It was delightful to meet you at my engagement party last week. Now that we are to be family, I would be pleased for the chance to get to know you better. You are most cordially invited to tea at Shanahan Manor at your convenience.

I hope we can be friends.

Yours sincerely,
Miss Teagan Shanahan

P.S. I heard about your actions in Prague. Everyone is very impressed.

I put the letter down on the tabletop, biting the inside of my lip thoughtfully. News did travel fast, not that it surprised me that the shady Shanahans had heard what even internet bloggers knew about. At the overwhelmingly ostentatious Shanahan-Raymond engagement party the weekend before Prague, I'd been introduced to the bride-to-be, Teagan, who couldn't have been older than me, if that. I'd been interested to learn that she was a blood relative of Renatus on his late mother's side, and even more interested to discover that her family were the trade experts at making people disappear. Her older, missing-a-decade-presumed-dead sister Keely had run away as a teenager, but I was fairly certain I'd met her, twice. Lisandro's new wife Nastassja had attacked me in the forest and cornered me at Teagan's party for a very insightful and entirely unwelcomed chat, and had fled before Teagan could recognise her. Not that attending her little sister's party was likely to end any other way.

So, while Teagan's family was immensely interesting to me, befriending Teagan came with the downside of having to spend time with Teagan, who'd presented as a pretentious, spoilt airhead requiring constant attention and entertainment from those around her. Admittedly it was her party, and all the girls I'd seen attending to her like a little princess were her friends who probably hadn't minded for the day, but wow, it had been intense. Teagan had that in common with Renatus. Either way, it wasn't something she had in common with me – I could think of very little that she and I had in common, truth be told.

I tucked the note back inside the envelope. I had no interest in playing dollhouse to Renatus's bratty cousin and no need for the added drama of such a friend. Addison was right. I had plenty all my own.

'Who is it from?' Hiroko asked, distracting the antics of our friends momentarily. She nodded at the envelope under my hand. I smiled, finding yesterday's emptiness further away today, and real feelings starting to return to that space.

'Fan mail,' I joked. 'From my rabid fans. Apparently the whole world knows I was in Prague.'

chapter twelve

The whole world did not know that Aristea Byrne was in Prague.

Angela Byrne didn't know. She didn't know a thing about what her sister was up to at any hour of any day, though Aristea's occasional letter suggested a wondrous, rich learning journey complete with great new friends and a guaranteed government job at the end of her apprenticeship, and right now, she didn't know where her keys had gone.

'Shit,' Angela muttered, dumping her hangbag on the roof of her car to dig through it. Purse, phone, lipstick, business cards, office keys on their lanyard… She squinted in the late afternoon summer sun, still high in the sky, her fingers brushing all manner of junk she'd thrown in at some point or another, but had to concede defeat. The car keys were not in here.

Angela tried the car door vainly and of course it did not budge, because like always she'd ritualistically checked every door before walking away from it this morning.

'Seriously?' she demanded, yanking fruitlessly once more on the driver side door and leaning down to peer into the window. 'You'd think there'd be a spell for this kind of thing…'

You'd think there would be *some* upside to having magical blood. When their parents and brother were alive, the sisters used to practise some magic, but for Angela it had been a long time since she'd performed anything that reminded her she was a sorceress. If not for Aristea's weirdly clean and quiet bedroom at the end of the hall, the only clue, Angela would find it easy to forget that their family was more than the unassuming Protestants they'd posed as for generations untold. It just didn't feel real.

Aristea had never let Angela forget, the little dreamer to Angela's realist. Aspirations of learning how to scry, a frivolous casual job at a New Age and crystal shop, that fragile cotton-wrapped soul so prone to emotional overload in the presence of others that she couldn't be sent to a normal high school – there was never any question of Aristea being a witch. Of course she would fit right in at that place. Of course someone would notice how special she was.

Meanwhile Angela was glaring at the very *down* lock inside the car, feeling incredibly unmagical. If the comparison were with anybody else, she might have felt envious, but Aristea was everything. There was no room for envy in a love like Angela's for her surviving sibling.

'You alright?'

Angela's imagination was the thing her sister's was modelled on, intensely vivid, though darker, less wild. Unsheltered. It knew. To others, it looked like paranoia. Maybe it was. She turned, every nerve alert behind her automatic smile, expecting a murderer that was never there, and met the friendly concern of a familiar face. Daniel the delivery man had always been cute, dropping into the optometry office every few weeks with a box of new glasses for Angela to sign for and a dishevelled mop of hair. He was always nice enough for the ninety seconds she interacted with him, and nice enough to look at, but he'd never seemed to show any interest in her until this week when, after she signed his clipboard, he'd initiated conversation. With eye contact. And a smile. Warning signs she was an expert in detecting.

He was smiling at her now, and he was standing in front of the store beside her office, a box under his arm. Her clinic had just closed but some of the other stores on the street kept longer hours.

As much an expert at deflecting as she was at detecting male attention, Angela smiled back reassuringly to cover up how loudly her inner monologue was screaming *go away* because being upfront about how little you wanted a man's attention wasn't socially acceptable, or so society said.

'Oh, hi, Dan,' she called back, raising her hand in a small wave. 'Aye, yeah, I'm fine, thanks. Have a good afternoon.'

She grabbed her office key back out, hoisted her bag back over her shoulder and returned to the clinic, internally stamping down on the worried little alarms that had started ringing in the corners of her brain. *Trapped! Alone! No way out!* They were stupid, overreactive in their panic, but they served their purpose, she supposed, of keeping her safe.

She let herself back into the office, controlling her breathing with conscious effort. She was safe in here. Surely the keys had just slipped out of her bag or been left on a counter or something. Everything could be solved with a minute of clear thinking.

'It's Angela, isn't it?'

Go away, go away. She looked up from the reception drawer to see Dan the delivery guy loitering uncertainly in the doorway. Boxing her in. Blocking her exit. Not deliberately, of course, she knew as she smiled quickly to counteract her leaping pulse. He was checking on her, a normal, friendly, fellow citizenly thing to do. She said it to herself twice more, willing herself to listen to logic.

'Something wrong with your car?' he asked with a concerned frown. Because he was a nice guy. But Angela's instincts warned against showing weakness.

'Car's fine. Thanks.' She smiled again, pretending to look again in the drawer in the hopes that she would appear competent and he would leave.

'Lock your keys inside it, did ye?' He took a step into the office and she felt her hands, which had been busily pushing things around in the drawer, falter. He sounded sympathetic. Like a perfectly nice person, much like the vast majority of men she encountered and brushed off, but there was no way of being sure, and she'd learned wariness from her mistakes.

She'd also learned her brittle coldness. She looked up at Dan once more, this time with a more clearly forced smile, and prepared to tell him, oh so politely, to get the hell out.

Weirdly, the words didn't come. He was standing awkwardly just inside the door, hands deep in his pockets while he waited to be told to get the hell out. His lack of confidence disarmed her a little, made her feel less threatened. Or something.

'Yes,' she admitted unexpectedly, surprising herself. *Never* admit to being helpless. 'Uh, I mean, no. I can't find the key anywhere. But it has to be...' She gestured vaguely around the office. 'I'm sure I'll find it.'

'Can't you do a spell, or somethin'? To unlock it?'

Angela stopped what she was doing to stare at him. 'Excuse me?'

'You're a sorceress, yeah?' he prompted, smiling a little shyly. 'I've never been able to do much magic meself. But ye – well, I'm just assuming.'

Angela was lost for words. Her initial fear of Daniel hadn't gone away, but when she reached for it as fuel for her usual frigid retort, it was subdued, intangible – she was finding it hard to remember why she'd ever wanted him to go away. She shook her head once, trying to clear the fog. Facts, Angela. Fact one: no man gets near you. Ever. Fact two: he's talking about magic. In your office, the least inspiring and magical place in the hemisphere, at least. The idea that she was a witch by blood, that one part of her world was governed by sorcerers and that her little sister was an apprentice studying at their magic school was one thing; the idea that *she* was capable of anything worthy of calling "a spell" was laughable. And anyway, how did he know any of that? Unless.

'You too?'

'I never noticed before,' Dan said, nodding at something above and beside Angela's head like he was impressed. 'Crazy, this thing with your sister. Can't believe I've been dropping in here all this time and never knew.'

She couldn't have explained why she was feeling so calm and relaxed in his presence when she was simply never calm and relaxed in the presence of men, but Angela's protective instincts ran much deeper than whatever trust Dan had inspired. Something flared inside her; the fog in her head started to peel away.

'What about my sister?' she asked warily. She stood, no longer content to sit and look up at this stranger. He fell quiet, looking surprised.

'Oh, I, uh, I saw your name tag,' he answered lamely, gesturing bashfully at her chest. She looked down at her full name. 'Put two and two together. Aristea Byrne, ye know. White Elm apprentice? No?'

'How do you know her?' Angela demanded, spiralling to insane unlikely explanations that shook the irrational calm that had cloaked her thoughts since Dan came into the office. Strange men acting interested in Angela were problematic but she was well-versed in getting rid of them. Strange men interested in her teenage sister? He continued to look taken aback.

'I... I don't. Just by name. I didn't think it was a secret. The first White Elm apprentice in thirty years.' He tried another smile. 'Ye must be proud.'

Breathe. Angela tapped her nails on the desk, counting the clicks of French tips on fake timber. Everything he'd just said made perfect sense. How many Byrne witches would there be in Coleraine? Nothing had been in the White Elm's newsletter – her aunt was keeping her usual eagle eye out for it – but there were thirteen councillors on the White Elm, all with families and contacts. It was doubtful that Aristea's apprenticeship was a secret.

'I am,' she said finally, then laughed a little, feeling foolish. She'd just totally overreacted and probably just scared off a perfectly nice man, who also happened to be one of the first sorcerers she'd met in a long time. She rubbed her forehead. 'I'm sorry, I didn't mean...'

'You're protective of her,' he filled in, smiling more

warmly, and Angela felt warmer, too, less stupid for freaking out and thinking he was some kind of serial killer. 'That's nice. She's lucky. Listen, I don't have to be anywhere. Do ye have a spare key at home?'

Instincts said to insist someone was coming to get her, to message Aunt Leanne. Instincts had never served Angela wrong before. So it came as a surprise when an unfamiliar surge of rebellious confidence pushed her to say, 'Yeah, I do. Could you give me a lift?'

The car ride made her feel like the rest of her life was the lie – the life where she was afraid of being alone with strangers, where she battled anxiety and trust issues, where she wore a mask of normality and stability because it was what her sister and family needed to see from her. Dan talked about magic like it was real, and Angela responded with the ease she usually had to fake. Dan's experience was similar to hers, or so he said – some family who were quite witchy, others who couldn't care less, and a few old family friends who practiced but a social circle mostly devoid of magic.

'So ye really don't do any magic?' he asked, amazed, as she directed him up her street. The small delivery truck rumbled as it started uphill. Angela shrugged casually, the little voice dully muttering from the back of her head that it would be better to suggest she could take care of herself, but she felt uncharacteristically safe. Like she was wrapped in a security blanket, warm and cosy and with her limbs bound to her sides. It was simultaneously reassuring and alarming, though the alarm was distant. Dan changed gears and glanced at her. 'Where did your sister learn it all, then?'

'Our uncle, I guess,' she answered, wondering vaguely why he was asking and why she cared. Aristea was no one's business. *That* thought sobered her a little, fed the protective instinct. 'I'd rather not talk about her, actually.'

'Sorry, that's fine,' Dan said immediately, following her final directions to her flat and pulling up at the driveway. 'Well, what about ye?' He turned off the ignition and looked over at her with interest. Her worries went away again. How was he doing that? 'Your uncle didn't teach you the same?'

'I'm older; he was still working as a teacher when I was that age. Then I went to university, he retired, and he started tutoring Aristea.'

Why had she said her sister's name, after she'd just decided she wasn't going to talk about her? Angela shoved open the car door, shook her head, feeling unclear. Less sure. Opposite her, Dan got out of the cab, talking again, voice easy and friendly, easy to trust.

'I didn't finish university,' he admitted, closing the door behind him. Angela trailed after him to her door, distantly aware that she should be the one leading, that she hadn't invited him in, also that she hadn't told him otherwise, either, but unable to muster the concern that would normally be making itself known by now. 'I wasn't a good fit, ye know?'

'I didn't finish either,' Angela found herself agreeing, making conversation she didn't need to make as she fished her house keys out of the bag. She should ask Daniel to wait while she fetched the car key. Where had her self-preservation instincts abandoned her? Why wasn't she more worried?

'Not for ye?'

'My parents died.' She paused with her key in the lock, that dull voice in her head knocking on a door like it was underwater. Reminding her that she didn't tell anyone this. Why wasn't she listening? Her instincts – coupled with their overpowering besties, her traumas – instructed her, in no uncertain terms, to get rid of Dan immediately. He was too persistent. He would hurt her, he would cause more damage than good, he was just like all the others.

But this new influence, maybe logic or something else previously unvoiced, reminded her that she was paranoid and ignorant. She could detect lies and he wasn't telling any.

'I'm sorry,' he said, sombrely. 'I shouldn'a asked.'

Strangers weren't allowed inside. This was her place. This was where she kept herself and her sister safe. So she didn't know why she turned the key, except that Aristea, her usual excuse for keeping eligible and interested men at a

171

distance, was not here to protect.

'They died and I came home to look after my sister. It was a long time ago.'

The inner argument was getting louder in her head as her sanctuary was pierced, as she pushed the door open and went inside with Dan on her heels. Dan, Dan who? What was his last name, the licence plate on his truck, any of the little facts she'd normally sort through in trying to make an assessment of a new person?

'Ye raised her?' he asked idly, putting her slightly at ease by hanging back at the door while she went into the flat's kitchen for the spare key. The space he allowed gave her both a sense of logical calm and a bit of clarity. She found the key in the drawer and remembered what she'd said just minutes ago in the car.

'I still don't want to talk about her,' she reminded herself, loud enough that it sounded like an answer to Dan. She'd been silly enough to bring Aristea back up into conversation. What was wrong with her? She walked back to the door, feeling the beginnings of annoyance and vulnerability, but once she was in his presence again, taken in with his friendly smile and disarmingly casual hands-in-pockets, the negativity faded. Where was it going?

He nodded at a photo frame on the shelf beside the door. 'That her?'

Angela didn't need to look. It was a picture of the sisters at their aunt's place for their first Christmas as orphans. Aristea was fourteen, still a kid; Angela was twenty, and looked the same as she did now. Hair in the same ponytail. Warm arm around her baby sister, first on the line to defend her.

No charm could undermine that.

'Why are you asking?' she asked, a little flatly. Was it impolite? She suspected so. Dan's glance of surprise confirmed it. She felt immediately guilty and went to apologise, but he smiled before she could and she felt the warm confidence fill her again.

This was unnatural. He knew magic.

'No reason,' he assured her. He gestured again at the picture. 'Ye raised her, ye said?'

The answer came unwillingly through the rebellious confidence. 'I was her guardian after our parents died, until…'

Until Saturday, when Aristea turned eighteen and Angela's legal custody expired. The day had come and gone without ceremony, without even seeing each other, although Angela was grateful for the call. Hearing Aristea's beloved voice had made Angela realise how long it had been and how much her baby sister had grown up in that time. Without her. With new friends, who sounded lovely. The clock had not stopped.

With effort she kept all that inside her mouth and didn't let it out. It was none of anyone's business. 'Why am I telling you this?'

'Nothing's wrong. Until when?'

'Something *is* wrong,' Angela insisted, fighting the fog in her head that told her everything was okay. She'd let a stranger drive her, let him into her house. She was talking about her sister against her will. She wasn't in control. 'Listen, I appreciate the lift, but I don't know you. I don't want to talk about my family.'

Dan regarded her for a second, seemingly waiting something out. All that happened in that second was a further recession of the careless, warm ambivalence she'd been operating under since she left the optometry clinic. Something *was* wrong.

Angela reached for the door to back up the forceful suggestion she was about to make when she heard a crashing sound nearby. She and Dan both froze and locked gazes. Her heart stopped for a beat inside her already tight chest.

'That was inside,' she said quietly. 'That was just up the hall.'

The two-bed flat was small and cramped, but its compact design meant that, living with her sister, it was easy to stay out of each other's space. Most rooms were not visible to one another, doors closing off the living room and the kitchen and the hall. Now, it meant that she couldn't see what had made that noise.

But she was a witch. That felt like a lie most days, but right now she felt certain of it. She stretched rarely-used senses throughout the house, feeling out other presences. Nothing she could detect.

'Did you leave a window open?' Dan asked, very softly. Angela shook her head, listening intently. There was no further sound. 'I'll go and check.'

That *trust him, let him* voice agreed, but territorial Angela took charge now.

'No,' she said forcefully. This was getting ridiculous. 'I'll go. You stay here.'

She hitched her handbag onto her shoulder and grabbed her phone out. Like it would do her any good, but going into any unknown situation without a cell phone seemed foolish in this day and age. She glanced back at Dan. He watched her innocently. She turned away and sneaked down the hall, wondering which darkened room the noise had come from. She couldn't *feel* anything or anyone, for whatever that was worth. She flicked on the hall light. The bathroom door was wide open and clearly the room was empty.

What had fallen down? What had made that noise? Something from her room, or Aristea's? Anger at the thought of someone breaking into her house and entering her baby sister's space, vacant or otherwise, made her reckless, and she pushed the door open with force. Equal parts relief and disappointment hit her simultaneously. No intruder, but no Aristea sneaking in to surprise her, either. Nothing out of place. Seashell windchimes hanging from the curtain post, mismatched books stacked in a white-washed bookshelf. Everything put away, exactly the way Angela had insisted her sister leave it.

So, the noise must have come from her own room. Angela swallowed, nervous again, and slipped back into the hall. Her room was at the end of the house, with two outward-facing walls with huge windows that a dangerous person could, supposedly, break if he wanted to get in. She forced her fears down and pushed the half-open door.

The source of the noise was immediately apparent. A lamp was on the floor, purple ceramic pieces spread across the carpet. She was glad to be wearing shoes as her feet knocked some of the shards. Angela glanced quickly around. Still, her other senses told her she was alone, and a visual check confirmed not only the room's emptiness, but also that her windows were firmly shut and locked. How, then, had this sturdy lamp managed to throw itself two metres from its usual spot on her nightstand to end up almost in the doorway?

She knelt to inspect the mess, but straightened suddenly when a tiny alarm bell went off in the back of her brain. Her door creaked; she spun around, heart leaping again, in time to watch it slam shut. How? There was no draught. She grabbed the handle and tried to turn it. There was absolutely no give. She yanked twice. Nothing. The fear and paranoia returned, and this time there was no cool, confident voice to fight it off.

'Dan!' Angela shouted. 'Daniel! My door's jammed.'

Silence was her only response, and her fears deepened. Had something happened to him? Had this mysterious intruder done something to him, too?

'Dan?'

Still, nothing. No, wait. Angela pressed her ear against the door, listening closely. Footsteps, quick ones, and the familiar, loud click of Aristea's wardrobe door opening. Someone was in Aristea's room. Dan? What would he want in there?

He was a thief, she realised suddenly, with a cold sort of fear. She'd let a burglar into her home and now he was casing her sister's room. She jabbed at her phone's touch screen with shaky hands, ready to call the police, but when she went to dial, her mind pulled a blank. A blank. On emergency.

Frustration with her helplessness slammed Angela like a fist.

'Dan, let me out!' Angela demanded, smacking the door with her free palm, certain now that this was his doing. He was a sorcerer, and despite his implication that only distant, oddball relatives of his practiced, he obviously knew exactly what he was capable of. Hence the lamp and the locked door. 'Dan!'

He didn't answer her, but she did hear his voice. Bastard, she thought venomously as she opened her phone's list of contacts. He'd tricked her into letting him inside, even tricked her into coming up the hall and walking into his trap, but this was where it ended. She scrolled down to 'E', where she knew she'd entered the emergency number. He'd underestimated her powers of paranoia. Dan was still talking, and she leaned again to the door to listen as he spoke in short, muffled sentences. She caught only a little but gathered he was on the phone.

'… normal sort of room for a kid her age… just clothes and things… trashy type of teenage fiction, that's all… expect me to find here? She doesn't even live here now… Yeah, I know, I'm still looking… got heaps of time, got the sister locked in…'

Angela's breath was shallow and slow, totally out of sync with her pulse, as she tried to digest two sets of information. Her ears fed her the bad news, that Dan was more than a common burglar. He was scoping out Aristea's room, investigating her. Was he some sort of enemy of the White Elm? Was Aristea in danger?

Meanwhile, her eyes, glued to the screen of her phone, let her know that she'd scrolled one contact too far down her list, from "Emergency" to "Emmanuelle".

Fate, surely, could work in her favour sometimes.

Angela hit "call" and waited for the line to connect. It took a while. Emmanuelle's phone was probably in France, so a delay was to be expected, and when it began to ring, Angela tried to quell the hope that rose like a phoenix in her chest. The French councillor had told her she rarely kept the phone on her, usually leaving it in her apartment. This call was likely to go unanswered.

'*Bonjour?* Hello?'

Angela couldn't hold in the nervous, relieved laugh that

escaped her, into the hand she used to cover her mouth and her phone to keep the sound from reaching Dan.

'Emmanuelle? This is Angela Byrne.' She waited for a second to let the councillor remember her, then added, 'Aristea's sister.' She tried to make herself wait for Emmanuelle to acknowledge her, but the sound of Dan's voice in the neighbouring room drove the words out of her before the other could reply. 'I'm so sorry to call you like this, but there's someone in my house, he's locked me in a room and the door won't open and he's going through Aristea's things, looking for something for someone, I can hear him talking on the phone–'

'Are you hurt?' Emmanuelle interrupted, her tone firm and authoritative. Angela shook her head.

'Uh, no,' she answered, looking over herself as if to check. 'I just feel stupid.' And scared.

'Stay exactly where you are. Do not try to engage the intruder. I will be there momentarily.' Emmanuelle paused. 'I will 'ave to 'ang up. Do not move.'

'Alright,' Angela agreed softly, hearing the click as the other woman ended the call. 'Thank you.'

She let her head fall against her door and closed her eyes, wondering what she'd just set into motion. She'd only met Emmanuelle once and had really liked her, surprised that a White Elm councillor could possess so many qualities she'd never thought to associate with the council – youth, poise, enviable confidence, unexpected normalcy. But the woman had also turned up dressed like she was heading to a medieval festival, hardly the warrior type. Had Angela just worsened the situation? Was Emmanuelle coming here out of a sense of duty, only to knock politely on the locked door and be attacked by Dan? Was he violent? His true capabilities were not known.

Angela pressed her empty hand against the door, furious – with herself for her stupidity, with the goddamned missing key, with Dan for his motives, with the universe for unfolding in this particular manner this afternoon. This should not be happening. Aristea was all there was left. And there was someone sneaking around, touching her things, reporting back to somebody else about her. Angela exhaled sharply, livid, all that foggy feel-good warmth gone. There should not be a man in her baby sister's room, for any reason. It seemed irrelevant that she wasn't there, hadn't been for months.

Tick, tick, tick... Angela's watch, given to her a decade ago by her long-dead brother Aidan, counted the seconds. She opened her eyes and stared at its face. Aidan would not have stood for this shit. Any time anyone had overstepped boundaries laid out by one of his sisters, he'd dealt to that person with his fists. Angela felt an urge to follow his lead. If only this stupid door weren't in the way. She ran her hand down its surface. It was just wood and a standard handle. There was no actual lock, so how was Dan keeping it shut? There had to be something else, something she'd missed, the magic...

Angela experienced a momentary flash of golden light, something she'd never seen before. She gasped and stepped back, her shoes crunching the ceramic beneath them. What was that? The door looked the same, but she felt like it had something to do with that gold flash, so she reached tentatively for the handle. It turned without complaint, and when she pulled, it opened as per normal. She didn't stand around pondering the mystery.

'Dan!' she snapped, shoving Aristea's door fully open. He knelt in the centre of the room, surrounded by upended drawers of clothes and elbow-deep in a box of childhood journals, kindergarten photos and birthday cards. Special things. Not his. The digging hands whipped out of the box and Dan threw himself to his feet.

'Angela,' he said quickly, smiling quickly, raising his placating hands quickly, everything quick, everything unconvincing. 'I was looking for something to get that door open–'

'Don't,' she stopped him, dismissing him with a wave of her hand that made him flinch. His lie, his first lie, flicked at her in much the same way, but she made sure not to let it show. Her brittle, authoritative façade was back. 'Why are you in my sister's things?'

He tried once more for charming. 'I told ye, I was–'

'Don't waste my time lying. I said I don't do magic, not that I can't.'

Could he tell she was bluffing? Dan regarded her again, something slipping away. He was still the same reasonably good-looking man in his late twenties, with a strong jaw line accentuated by several days of artful stubble, but the casual smile disappeared, and he wasn't half as attractive.

'Are ye threatening me?'

'I'm asking.'

The glaring face-off was interrupted by another crashing sound, this one louder than the lamp. Both Dan and Angela jumped; Angela glanced to her left down the hall as her front door slammed open. Emmanuelle the White Elm councillor strode in, and Angela stepped back automatically to press herself against the wall. Conflict was not Angela's game – amiable half-arsed agreement usually got people off her back – but it looked as though it might be Emmanuelle's.

In the room, Dan must have sensed the power level of the new arrival, because he spun suddenly, totally abandoning his search, and ran to the windows to seek an escape.

Emmanuelle glanced briefly over Angela as she passed, an appraising look that seemed to be looking deeper than just the skin, and turned into the bedroom with her lead hand already glowing with energy. She seemed to cast her first spell before she even saw where Dan was, because when he ran at the window, shoulder-first, he bounced solidly off the air several centimetres away from the glass. He stumbled and tried again as the sorceress moved fully into the doorway. When his second escape attempt failed as well, he turned back to the women, desperation clear and bright in his pale eyes.

'White Elm?' he seemed to realise, the easy confidence that had characterised him up to this point gone with his smile. He looked from Emmanuelle, who materialised a wand from nowhere, to Angela, who still hung back in the hall.

'Friends in high places,' she replied, glad to hear her

voice come out even despite her thudding pulse. How had the weird calm felt anything akin to control? *This* was control – being scared, pretending not to be and being believed. Emmanuelle took it one step further, positively exuding fearlessness. Two young women versus one man. Angela had never felt so sure of those odds.

'Who are you?' the councillor demanded, no room for nonsense. Her wand remained pointed at the intruder's chest, and her other hand glowed with an unspent spell. As with the last time Angela had met her, she was dressed like she'd fallen out of a storybook. Dan was appropriately intimidated.

'I'm… It's not what it looks like, alright?' He looked between them, trying to appeal to Angela, the lesser threat. 'I wasn't going to hurt ye.'

'Who are you?' Emmanuelle repeated. She flexed her fingers around the cool white glow. 'You don't want to test my patience after the week I've 'ad.'

'I didn't think White Elm were allowed to hurt– Dan, Dan O'Conner,' he backtracked hurriedly, taking her seriously when she advanced into the room. 'I was just looking to make some dosh, okay? I mean it, I wasn't going to hurt her.'

'He was asking about my sister,' Angela filled in, not wanting Emmanuelle to be drawn into his seeming reasonableness, though there didn't seem to be much risk of that. The French blonde looked upon the intruder with utter disdain.

'Why?' she asked him roughly. 'What do you know?'

'Nothing,' he insisted. 'Just… people are interested, okay? And… I thought the information might be worth something.' He looked again to Angela. 'I'm sorry. It was nothing personal. I wasn't trying to–'

'Don't talk to 'er,' Emmanuelle snapped. 'Worth something to who?'

'People,' Dan answered cagily, making Emmanuelle sigh in frustration.

'*Merde.*' She cocked her head to the side, like she was listening to a noise Angela didn't hear. 'Two of my colleagues just arrived.'

The late afternoon sunlight streaming through Aristea's lace curtains cast warm colour onto Dan's face but Angela still thought he paled at the words, and she didn't think she imagined his voice shake a little when he asked, 'Renatus?'

'Oh,' Emmanuelle said coolly, 'so you do know who you were crossing by coming 'ere.'

The pounding of heavy shoes caught Angela's heightened attention as two men entered the wide-open front door. Her heart clenched in momentary fear as the newcomers thundered into her home, but the leading man had a face she recognised. He slowed when he met her gaze.

'Qasim,' Emmanuelle called over her shoulder, 'I 'ave 'im.'

'Check the rest of the property, outside too,' the Scrier directed his younger companion, who moved off immediately, and he himself strode quickly down the hall toward Angela. 'Are you alright?'

Angela exhaled in relief, nodding, feeling safer than if she'd called the police. Qasim briefly clasped her shoulder. She felt no impulse to shy away, and not because she was foggy or strangely charmed. He was in his fifties, wore a gold wedding band and was her sister's teacher. She accepted the contact, unable to feel the same threat she felt from men her own age. The first White Elm she'd ever met had given a good enough impression that she'd entrusted these people with the life of her precious sister. Seeing him here, on a day that could have been much worse, reminded her to be glad that Aristea was safely in his care.

'I am now. I just feel stupid.'

'Don't,' he insisted, dropping his hand as he turned to Emmanuelle and Dan inside Aristea's bedroom. 'You couldn't have anticipated a spy.'

'No, ye got me wrong, I'm *not* a spy,' Dan claimed, beginning to sound more desperate now that he was facing two White Elm councillors.

'You told my colleague you intend to make money off information about our council's apprentice,' Qasim noted, to

Angela's surprise, since he wasn't here to hear that. He gestured back up the hallway. 'And what's the energetic mess my other colleague has found littered from your car to the entryway? A spy and a manipulator.'

'I'm a Crafter,' Dan relented uncomfortably. 'It's just a talent, influencing moods. It comes in handy.'

'We're familiar with the practice.' Emmanuelle glanced back at Qasim. 'Where the 'ell is Renatus? 'e isn't answering me.'

'Busy. But he's certainly upset,' the Scrier told Dan, who'd betrayed his fear of the name in his expression, 'and if we're still trying to get answers out of you by the time he's free, we'll be happy to pass you over.'

Dan went back to blustering about them having it all wrong and Angela, frowning, leaned forward to be heard when she murmured to Qasim, 'Why's he scared of Renatus?'

'Ye haven't met him?' Dan asked suddenly, overhearing. He stopped his nervous prattling. 'Ye'd sign her over to a man ye'd never met? Ye have no idea, do ye, what's been going on? Prague, Lisandro–'

'Is that who you're working for?' Emmanuelle cut him off. He shook his head adamantly.

'No, I told ye, I'm just looking to make some money. I'm not in this for some political agenda. But ye,' here he narrowed his eyes, 'yer lying to yer own people.'

'Alright, let's get him out of here,' Qasim said irritably as Angela turned to him questioningly. 'Take him to Lord Gawain.'

The younger councillor looked uncertain for the first time. 'But–'

'We can't wait for Renatus. You can handle it.'

'Yes, sir,' Emmanuelle muttered, closing her hand on the glow in her palm and beginning to trace quick, efficient shapes in the air with her wand. Dan's wrists drew suddenly together like they had been magically cuffed, though there was nothing visibly there.

'What is this?' he asked uncertainly, straining his arms. His wrists stayed locked together, and when Emmanuelle turned and left the room, he abruptly jerked forward as though pulled behind her on a rope. 'What *is* this?'

'Just a talent that comes in 'andy. And don't try any magic–' His hiss of pain made Emmanuelle pause in her dialogue and cast a satisfied smile at Angela as she passed. She touched Angela's hand lightly and lowered her voice. 'You did the right thing. I'll be back later to ward this place. This won't 'appen again.'

She and Qasim both hesitated then, gazes dropping down like they were listening in to a radio broadcast Angela wasn't tuned into, and they looked at each other.

'Block him,' Qasim advised, shrugging slightly at her dubious expression. 'You can handle it.'

'He won't like it,' Emmanuelle warned, but she carried on. Dan followed unwillingly in her wake, tripping over his own feet and trying to catch Angela's eye, calling back to her in an increasing volume that he wasn't a threat, that he was sorry, and whatever else. Angela's attention, though, was with the Scrier.

'Qasim, what's he talking about?' she asked, starting to feel shaken with the whole afternoon's ordeal. 'Prague? Is this about that gas explosion on the weekend?'

The man turned from watching Dan's retreating back to give Angela his full attention. Did Angela imagine the slightly pitying shine in his eye?

'You saw it on the news, I imagine? I suspected that would happen. The gas story is a cover. There was an attack.' He paused, evidently uncomfortable. Angela realised this was probably confidential. 'We have identified Lisandro as responsible, but we're still working through the evidence to explain how he did it.'

'People died,' Angela mentioned slowly, recalling the repeated newscast, connecting the impossible dots. Mundane news was not so mundane. Ordinary people wandering through her office door were not so ordinary, nor were their motives.

'Yes,' Qasim said seriously. 'We lost one of our councillors, as well as two White Elm nationals and two mortals. Others were hurt and terrorised. We are giving it our full attention.'

Angela nodded, feeling an embarrassed blush creep into her cheeks. He and Emmanuelle had been busy fighting real world-class crime when she'd called them away to help her deal with her minor problem of a persuasive guy. She felt even worse. She cleared her throat and asked her other important question, 'Why was he afraid of Renatus?'

Angela knew relatively little about her sister's master except that Aristea thought he was wonderful, according to her letters, and their aunt – who'd impulsively stormed up to the Academy and demanded to have Aristea back after a very tense phone discussion with Angela, a long and annoying story of internal family power wars – was thoroughly impressed with him after meeting him once. The White Elm had that effect, she supposed. She'd approved of both Qasim and Emmanuelle the first time she'd met them, but, on that first occasion, Emmanuelle had come here *because* she said Renatus, the man requesting to train Aristea, did not make a good first impression.

'Renatus usually makes the arrests on our council's behalf,' Qasim said patiently. 'Criminals are likely to know that. And he…' He seemed to consider his words here. 'He came from a rough start. A well-known family, not well-liked. It's a hard reputation to shake.'

Angela inhaled and counted to five, berating herself for overreacting yet again. She knew what it was to live disconnected from the person others saw when they looked at her. She tried to control the exhale too but it came out as a nervous laugh.

'I'm sorry,' she said. 'I didn't mean to… I feel so stupid for letting Dan inside the house and telling him about Aristea, and I suppose I'm just projecting…' She trailed off, turning her head to watch as Emmanuelle and Dan were met at the front door by the other young man she didn't recognise. Jeans, hoodie, sneakers, so *normal*. Magic all around her, disguised as normality. Something occurred to her once again. 'Why did he go to all this effort to dig up useless information about my sister? I didn't think anyone knew about her.'

Again, Qasim looked cautious as he picked his words.

'We thought the same, until this weekend just gone,' he said, watching her for her reaction, though she didn't know what he was looking for. 'Earlier in the year some students were withdrawn from the Academy and it seems that our trust in them was misplaced. They have shared Aristea's identity as Renatus's apprentice. It would have happened eventually,' he added, alleviating Angela's frown, 'but it would have been nice to have been released on our terms.'

'Does it put her at any risk?' Angela asked, grateful that she felt like she could expect straightforward answers from the Scrier, even though he clearly hesitated before replying this time.

'It seems that it puts *you* at risk more than it does her,' he said finally, 'but we will deal with that. This won't happen again. Emmanuelle's wards are exceptional.' He seemed done with talking, and nodded, businesslike, at the room. 'Would you like some help cleaning up?'

'No.' Angela forced a smile and clutched at her handbag. 'I can do it. Thank you. Thank you both, so much, for coming, and... I'm sorry–'

'There is nothing to apologise for,' Qasim insisted. 'Absolutely nothing. You were right to call us, and we'll deal with this intruder.' He backed out of the room. 'I'll be outside, checking for any residual spellwork. Call if you need me.'

He left, and Angela sighed loudly, dropping her bag at her feet. What an afternoon. The handbag landed against her ankle and tipped over.

The first thing to fall out was her car key.

chapter thirteen

The novelty of no classes in a tech-free, enclosed environment wore off very quickly. Kendra was intermittently mopey, missing Heath. Addison, though enthusiastic at first, eventually lost interest in trying to coach me on footwork from Tian's book, but not before I did. Hiroko, primly setting aside a letter from her father, suggested we resume our ritual of practising wards and Displacement together in empty classrooms. It had started off as a sort of playful peer tutoring, our strengths happening to match the other's chief magical weakness, but despite being surprisingly effective for us both, I valued the sessions more for the part they'd played in my bonding with Hiroko. I could be my useless awkward self in our practises and know she wouldn't laugh or judge me. So I definitely hesitated when our other friends overheard and Kendra asked if they could come, too.

'I'd love to learn how to make wards like you do,' she added hopefully. She smiled at Hiroko. 'And something tells me you're less stuck-up about your Displacement skills than *some*.'

Addison rolled his eyes dramatically while I confirmed, 'Hiroko's a very good teacher.'

'So are you,' Hiroko insisted. 'Everyone here should be working on their wards after what happened to you in Prague. And we all have skills the others could benefit from studying more,' she added, nodding meaningfully at the twins.

She was right. A Healer and a Seer, two talents I lacked

but which would enhance my skillset significantly, since Renatus lacked them, too. I thought of Renatus's penchant for attracting danger, injuries he'd already sustained on the job – shouldn't I be doing more to prevent that? Imagine if I honed my ability to see these things coming, or developed my ability to heal us both when we were hurt?

'Okay,' I said finally. 'A trade.'

'Perfect,' Kendra enthused. 'Sophia can dumb down healing enough for anyone.'

'Yeah, even you,' her twin quipped as we got ourselves together. Beside her, Addison sighed and got up, too.

'Did we just consent to magic homework club?'

All rooms on the second floor counted as empty classrooms now but Hiroko and I had kind of claimed Teresa's old one. Our stock of cushions waited for us in the corner where we'd left them.

The twins and Addison filed in after us and, after looking around briefly, looked to me expectantly. Me first, apparently. I started to feel that useless awkwardness rising before we'd even started. I grabbed one of the cushions off the pile to give myself something to do.

'We, uh, we always start with wards,' I said, feeling put-upon. I didn't feel self-conscious about working with just Hiroko but the other three were classmates I'd never done much magic in front of. They nodded, reserving any cheeky or teasing comments for now, waiting for directions. Apparently genuinely interested in whatever I could teach them.

'We defend ourselves,' Hiroko explained, clapping her hands once at me to signal that I should toss the cushion I held. She caught it and in one fluid movement pegged it at Sophia, who squealed and shied away. The soft projectile bounded off her side. 'Too slow.'

'Try me, try me,' Addison dared Hiroko, stepping away from the Prescotts to give her a clearer shot. She smirked, knowing he'd just Displace.

'Aristea will correct our technique,' she continued, hefting the next cushion I tossed her. She glanced at me for confirmation while I reached for a third. 'What kind of ward did you use in Prague? We will practise this.'

Two hands slamming into a solid glass wall...

My attention faltered and my throw was clumsy; I knew immediately that they'd all noticed my involuntary reaction as the pillow fell pathetically short.

'Um, yeah.' I turned away to snatch up another couple of cushions, clutching them to myself like little shields, hiding my face for a moment of reprieve. The guilt and grief chased each other in circles around me, and I wanted to furiously stamp them out and shout at them that I *wasn't* useless, *wasn't* going to let that happen again, but it would have looked more than weird. I swallowed the emotion and lapsed into the same detached emptiness I'd fallen into at Avalon's embassy. I wasn't useless. Not at this. Normal expression back in place, I turned back to my friends and threw down the last few pillows. 'I used a really solid one. Nothing gets through. Not magic, not matter, not even air.'

Nothing. And no one.

Stepping away from my own emotions had benefits, such as the dismissal of my self-consciousness. I paired up my friends and got them to show me what they could already do. The cushion-throwing went down very well with the twins and Addison even though none of them were quick enough with their wards to deflect the assaults of their partners. Their enjoyment was infectious and chipped at the edges of my distant emptiness, drawing a smile to my face.

'Okay, so we suck,' Kendra complained, catching the cushion her sister tried to get in while she wasn't looking. 'Show us how it's really done.'

She lobbed the pillow at me; it was nothing to flick up a brief wall of energy between us. The cushion bounced off and landed on the floor.

'You make it look easy,' Soph said enviously as she went to pick it up. I shrugged apologetically – for me, it was.

'There are a few tricks to it,' I admitted, repeating the energetic process, slower, for their benefit. I channelled the magic down my arm and extended my hand this time so they could see me directing it. I focused the energy and made the ward materialise in front of me as a shimmery circle of solid magic. 'One is to know exactly where in space you want it, which is why I normally point my hand in the direction of whatever's coming. Emmanuelle probably tells you that, too, though? The other is to be economical. If you keep it small and only up for as long as you need it, it'll be stronger, but it's also more likely to work than if you overreach.'

Like I almost did.

Addison tapped the ward I'd made with his finger, and we all heard the solid sound his fingertip made. 'It's like glass. Mine are like glass, too. Broken glass. They just fall apart.'

I picked up one of the discarded pillows and readied it; I made an energetic change to my ward and threw the cushion. We all saw the ward dissolve. 'Like that? I didn't give it enough power. There's this point where you kind of *sever* yourself from it, but I think you're doing it too early before the ward's got enough integrity. Show me again.'

It was a good lesson all around, productive for them because they got to practise an important skill and insightful for me because I got to see my friends casting wards for the first time. I usually only spent time doing magic with either Hiroko or the White Elm, and I hadn't realised how unreliable the rest of my social circle's level of self-protection was. They wouldn't have stood a chance in Prague, and that thought made me anxious.

We kept at wards until Addison and Hiroko started teleporting to avoid each other's cushions.

'You can't put it off forever,' Hiroko teased me. The twins had been working on their precision, and Sophia now tried once more.

'Put what off?' she asked, pointing her finger, and a tiny ward sparked briefly about a metre in front of her, exactly in line with the tip. She smiled in satisfaction.

'I always try to stretch out wards practise to avoid Displacement,' I admitted, balancing a cushion experimentally on a horizontal ward like a tabletop.

What's going on with your sister?

I took back the cushion slowly, letting the ward fade to nothing as Renatus's voice reverberated in my head. I hadn't heard from him since morning when he said he would be back later and had left the grounds. He'd been silent ever since. I'd figured he was somewhere shady, keeping me out of it.

I don't know, I answered, confused. He didn't even know my sister. *Why? What are you talking about?* I reached further along our connection and felt his distress, which ignited the same in me. *Renatus?*

Emmanuelle is responding to a disturbance at your home, he told me, sounding uncertain. *I thought you might have seen it.*

Seen what? I waited, my heart thudding in my ears. A disturbance? At my house? Angela, my defenceless Angela. Addison and the Prescotts might be a little rusty with their defensive technique but they were streaks ahead of my sister. *Renatus? Don't ignore me.*

He didn't respond for a very long beat, and when he did, it was less than helpful.

Qasim is going, too. It's... it's probably nothing.

Probably nothing. How convincing.

What are they saying? I asked. He didn't answer, maybe talking to his colleagues. Worry was rising quickly inside me, and each second of silence felt longer than the last. *Are you going there now?*

'You okay?'

My friends were looking at me oddly, waiting for me to snap out of my trance.

'I, uh...' I dropped the cushion on the pile on the floor and looked around, starting to feel faint and lost. Renatus wasn't responding. Something was up with my sister. And I was stuck here, playing magic with my friends like a child. I started for the door. 'I have to go...'

'Anything to get out of Displacement, huh?' Kendra asked playfully, and normally I would have smiled or indulged in her lightness but today it just annoyed me.

'I can Displace just fine,' I snapped, turning back to her with my hands out and open to my sides. I don't know whether it was the words or some subconscious defensive desire to arm up, because I impulsively initiated the energetic process I knew for Displacement without thinking. Again. Dangerous, given that my understanding of wormhole physics and the Fabric was very poor. As it was, something happened, and all of my friends took a wary step back. I felt weight in both hands and closed my fingers instinctively around whatever I'd summoned.

My sai swords. One per hand, perfectly teleported from their hiding place in my bedside drawer *to the palms of my hands*. In shock I forgot my flare of annoyance and looked to Hiroko.

'I didn't teach her that,' she told the others helplessly. She looked as shocked as I felt, and I didn't like her looking at me like that. Like I scared her. I backed away, flexing my hands on the unfamiliar hilts.

'I need to go,' I repeated, immensely sorry but without the time to fix things right now. I shoved open the door with my arm, careful with the ungainly weapons. *Weapons*. I shifted them both to the same hand, blades down, so I could run through the house without looking like an armed madman.

'Renatus,' I muttered, projecting the same words with my mind as I jogged down the stairs, 'what's going on? Where are you?' I got to the bottom of the stairs in seconds but it felt like he'd been ignoring me for half an hour. *Renatus! Tell me what's happening!*

I bolted for the front doors, blind with panic by now. He wasn't answering – why, was something wrong with him, too? Or was he dealing with whatever danger my sister was in? *My sister*. In danger. And what was I doing? I grabbed the door handle and stopped.

I made myself breathe. One, two. Plenty. Now what? *Are you coming to get me?* No answer. No bloody answer. I reached out for Renatus with my senses, feeling the auras of all those on the estate as I extended further and further out, all the way

191

to the fences, even though I knew he wasn't on the grounds. The only presences were the usuals, the house staff and the students, and the glowing-white aura of Susannah as a White Elm, but I wasn't much accustomed to viewing her as helpful or even as being particularly on my side, so it didn't occur to me to go to her.

I'm ready, come and get me, I told Renatus desperately, feeling like my words were stones dropped in a pond. Swallowed, gone. Could he even hear me?

But then I heard his voice in my head. *I don't know much. Emmanuelle's got it. I can't talk right now*, he added, sounding angry, which did nothing to resolve my frantic state. I raised my hands in the air helplessly, unseen, as I felt him block me out. I didn't know where he was. I didn't know why he was angry. I didn't know what was happening with Angela. I felt lost, stricken.

What do you mean you can't talk right now? I asked, opening the front door and letting myself out onto the steps. The sun was hanging at eye level, still deceptively warm and yellow to hide how late it was getting, and I shielded my eyes. *Renatus?* I waited. Nothing. My fear began to bubble and warp inside me. 'You can't tell me something like that and then say you can't talk!'

I slammed the door heavily. It didn't make me feel any better.

Feeling like crying or kicking something, I looked around, squinting, taking stock of my situation. My sister and Renatus and even Emmanuelle might be in trouble. I was here, useless. I had two unedged swords I had no idea how to wield, but no one needed to know that, and if my family was in danger, my place was wherever I could be of help. Not here.

I didn't have to be here. I could Displace. I got these sai out of my drawer from a whole floor away.

Suddenly determined, I took off for the gate at the bottom of the sloped lawn. Under my shirt was a key hanging on a necklace, and I had it out by the time I arrived at the gate, breathing unevenly. I needed to get back into running, like

192

Angela did in the mornings. I jammed it into the lock and got the gate open; closing it took a disproportionate amount of time and I swore angrily when the key wouldn't come out straightaway.

Come get me or I'm coming to you, I warned Renatus, hefting the weighty sai in my hand. They were heavier than I'd expected; footwork study or not, I wasn't going to be doing anything very impressive with them today.

Displacing too close to the house, I knew, would warp the teleportation, though I wasn't sure of the exact distance necessary to avoid this, and didn't know how my more advanced tutors made those judgements. I ran across the dirt road and hoped it was enough.

I pulled myself to a reluctant stop, closed my eyes and tried to settle my breathing so I could concentrate. I was a scrier. I should be able to find my own master.

Not necessarily, apparently. He didn't answer me and I got no mental image of him, wherever he was. Somewhere warded, perhaps? Not my house, because I should be able to see that.

'Fine,' I muttered. I focused instead on Angela, and after a moment got a clear picture of her standing in our hallway, *hair up in her trademark blonde-brown ponytail, dressed in her work clothes... button-up blouse, pencil skirt, the way she would dress anyway... nametag on the breast pocket... 'Qasim, I 'ave 'im in 'ere'... Emmanuelle, ahead of Angela... hands poised mid-spell... Qasim arrives... 'Are you alright?'... His hand on Angela's shoulder...*

There. Now, just to get there. Renatus wasn't coming. I shouldn't expect him to. I was a White Elm apprentice, the Dark Keeper's apprentice, and after Prague – *two hands, banging on the impenetrable glassy dome* – everyone else thought I was some hero. Time to act like one.

Despite my discomfort with it, Displacement had in fact always worked well for me in times of desperation, so I felt good about my chances when I stretched my brain to feel deliberately for the Fabric around me. I found it, weirdly light and golden like I remembered Fate from my initiation, and hurriedly twisted it.

I had no finesse, no technique – Hiroko's lessons flew uneasily through my mind only after I had already lifted my foot to step through the hole I made in the universe – and in the space in between, I felt the void tugging at me. My second foot followed, as per usual walking protocol, but my stomach bottomed out like missing a stair when my lead foot kept falling, no destination presenting itself. I didn't know much about this place between places, except I did not like it and it was cold and dark and getting stuck here was akin to being erased from my reality. Still, my foot fell; then *I* was falling, all of me, my forward momentum lost, and I could no longer see the sunlit countryside I'd been in such a hurry to depart, and my suburban street did not appear, either. Just black.

My chest arrested in panic. What had I done? Something incomprehensibly *stupid*, and no one knew so no one could help, and now I was going to be *stuck*–

I hit the ground hard, my body unprepared for a fall. Both of my hands were at my sides so my shoulder and jaw took the brunt, cheek and knees skidding across the uneven stone, making me gasp at the unexpected sting. My sai skittered away, dropped, and I squeezed my eyes closed despite the twinge in my still-healing temple.

'Ouch,' I murmured, getting my hands under me and pushing upward, tenderly at first but then more hastily as I took in my surroundings. People. Statues. Voices, motion, city smells, and a glorious medieval horizon.

Prague.

Two hands slam into the transparent solid dome...

A black wave of terror...

Crimson cloaks, closing in...

I grabbed for my sai and staggered to my feet, trying to stay out of the way of the dozens and dozens of people who were passing me. A couple paused to ask me something in Czech, and I nodded quickly, assuming they were confirming I was okay. They smiled kindly and walked on, apparently undisturbed by my sudden teleportation into their proximity.

What just happened?! I was shaking, the void still fresh on my mind but now half of my face smarting with the impact onto the old stone street. I was about a third of the way along the beautiful bridge Anouk and I had landed at when we first arrived in the city last weekend. Charles Bridge, she'd said. It spanned a wide river. I must have been thinking of Prague before I Displaced. I'd left the country, transported myself more than a thousand kilometres further than I'd intended, and I was standing in public with a pair of swords I didn't know how to use. And in the crush of people, no one had seen me appear, but they were looking at me weirdly now, seeing the weapons I held, seeing the dirty state of me. I brushed my face self-consciously; gravel stuck to my fingers with a smear of blood.

Anouk hadn't bled when she died here.

Two hands...

Green eyes still open...

I shook my head. Angela. I still wasn't there to protect her. I'd seen her with Qasim and Emmanuelle, two of the toughest people I knew, so logic said she was probably fine. A moment of focus on her – *standing with Emmanuelle... worry, irritation, shouldn't have overreacted... outside my bedroom... a stranger inside it... thick hair, good-looking, but displeased, accusatory... 'Yer lying to yer own people'... Qasim, waving dismissively... 'Alright, let's get him out of here. Take him to Lord Gawain'* – confirmed the prediction. Renatus was right. Someone had gotten into my house, maybe threatened my sister, but she was fine and they'd taken care of it.

Confusion, uncertainty... Emmanuelle, looking back at Qasim for confirmation... 'But–'...

'We can't wait for Renatus. You can handle it'... Resolve... 'Yes, sir'... Emmanuelle's glowing hand closes... the stranger's wrists draw suddenly together...

Meanwhile, I was hopelessly lost, alone and injured, not to mention feeling incredibly stupid. *I* was the one who'd overreacted, Ange. No way was I brave enough to try

Displacing anywhere else. I limped along the bridge, turning away from the stares of the tourists and locals and wincing as every step pulled on my skinned knees. Stupid, stupid. If I'd only stayed at the school, I'd be refining my Displacement skills with Hiroko and Addison instead of stuffing it up royally in the field; I would be practising Healing with Sophia rather than needing it; and maybe I'd be working on Seeing with Kendra, learning to consider the foresight I clearly lacked.

My gift for scrying, in which I'd wrongly placed my Displacement trust, had let me down, and my skill with wards had proven so far unhelpful on this venture. Well, I could think of a use, now that I was avoiding yet more concerned gazes, though I'd never done it before. Not all wards deflected physical matter or energy. Having learned today's lesson about rushing things, I worked carefully on a web of magic around me to deflect thoughts and attention. Could I bend light, make myself invisible to the eye? I wasn't game to try today.

I had no way of being certain, but as I stepped into the shadow of an imposing saintly statue, it seemed I was no longer attracting the same interest. Eyes skimmed over or past me without lingering. Maybe it was working, or maybe these people just didn't care.

The bridge was edged with a low stone wall and I gingerly hoisted myself up to sit on it, staying in the statue's shadow. A cool breeze lifted off the water and brushed my back. I lay my sai across my lap, shiny beautiful things they were, but utterly useless in my unpractised hands. Those unpractised hands were dirty and I dusted them off on my skirt before getting to the painstaking work of gently brushing gravel from my grazed cheek and knees.

With my eyes I watched people mill about, fascinated by the beauty of the Bohemian city or too busy to notice. In my head I watched as Qasim tiptoed around the topic of my involvement in the Prague tragedy with Angela. I could tell that keeping the truth from her was difficult for the honourable Scrier, and that my smart sister knew that information was being withheld. She didn't push it, and Qasim eventually made his excuses to end the conversation. I kept my focus on my sister as she went inside my bedroom and started packing it up. I felt a burn of indignation to see my things strewn about. Who the hell was that guy, and what was he doing with my stuff? Was he with Lisandro and Magnus Moira? Had my association with the council and my continuing opposition to that psychopath seeped into my sister's life and put her in the line of fire?

More importantly, where was Renatus in this scene? Powerhouse sorcerer and protector of the White Elm, dealing with this kind of thing – crime, namely, but also, I'd assumed, violations against me and my people – was kind of his job.

Cringing, I picked a tiny sharp stone out of my knee. I was a fine one to talk, failing utterly as both a sister and apprentice all in one dumb move. And scaring my friends. I looked around the beautiful city, no sign of the horrors I'd endured just days ago, a few blocks away. It had pulled itself together, and was getting on with things. That was its job.

My job was simpler than a city's. Learn magic. Get awesome. Protect Angela. Save Renatus and have his back in the meantime.

I probably wouldn't pass a performance review today.

chapter fourteen

'Stay at the house. That's one of your jobs, too.'

I had seen Renatus angry before. Plenty of times. He'd been angry with Qasim for disagreeing with him, with Lord Gawain for grounding him, with me for challenging him, with Lisandro for pretty much everything, and it was usually warranted.

He approached me now out of the crowd, shedding anger and frustration like leaves in autumn, and I didn't blame him. I'd screwed up.

'I'm sorry,' I said with a wince, shifting my position on the stone wall and making myself meet his gaze, prepared for the dressing down I knew I deserved. He shook his head in dismissal as he reached me, folding his arms as he leaned in to critically assess my face. His mind was back online with mine, unblocked, and despite the immensity of his anger I chanced a quick step into his head. I was getting quick at accessing his senses, and took a look at myself from his viewpoint. As I had suspected, the graze wasn't deep but wide and vibrantly red. I looked as demoralised as I felt.

'That hurt?' he asked, and I nodded once, deciding against trying to lie or act tough.

'Aye. Apparently I shouldn't have walked out on Hiroko's Displacement lesson.'

I pushed away the cold, too-recent memory of the void and the fall with an involuntary shiver, but Renatus saw it anyway. 'Apparently.' There was more he wanted to say, I could tell, but he prioritised and thought through his words. Because he was an adult. 'Would you like to go to your sister?'

Yes. He could take me there safely, probably right to the door. But I didn't hesitate to say, 'No.' I did *not* want her to see me like this, with fresh trivial injuries and a new scar I couldn't explain and a tattoo I hadn't mentioned yet and a pair of swords that would make her question letting me attend the Academy in the first place.

'Good,' Renatus muttered, dropping his gaze and raising a hand to scratch his eyebrow much too hard before tucking it tightly back under his other arm. 'Qasim told me to stay away.'

I frowned. 'Why?' I'd seen them waiting for him, Emmanuelle holding the trespasser for Renatus's arrival to make the arrest. Also – since when did Renatus follow Qasim's orders? Renatus was higher up the White Elm chain of command and had never displayed any hesitation in throwing that fact around.

'I think he thought I'd break something,' he confessed tightly. He paused, positively emanating fury, and I could understand Qasim's caution. I'd really pissed him off this time. He cleared his throat, trying to be mature about it. 'He said everything's fine now. Have you checked in?'

'You were right,' I admitted. 'Qasim and Emmanuelle have it under control.' I picked at my itchy knee as my blood cells raced there to deal with the minor trauma. 'Where were you?'

I tried not to sound accusing but flinched when I felt my master's anger flare again. 'Raymond's. I got away as quickly as I could. There was a Telepath there, Jones. He could tell I was talking to you – it was making negotiations awkward. I'm sorry,' he added, an unusual phrase from him and not one I expected today. 'The timing was terrible. I'm sorry I scared you like that. This is my fault.'

I eyed him uncertainly. 'You're... not mad at me?'

'No, I am,' he assured me, but he didn't sound it. 'What the hell are you doing in Prague? Just once I'd like to visit this place and not find you bleeding in it.'

'I was *trying* to get to Angela,' I explained, tenderly touching my fingertips to my chin to feel for blood. The contact stung. 'What did they want with her? It was because of me, wasn't it?'

'I imagine you were the intended target, yes. Emmanuelle should be able to tell us more once she unblocks me.'

'Why would she be blocking you?'

Nearby, Qasim stepped between two Australian tourists.

'Because he's a mess,' he said sternly, having overheard our conversation from afar the same way I'd watched on while he spoke with Angela a few minutes ago. My master unfolded his arms and moved his hands to his hips, looking away and exhaling his breath in a heavy, frustrated sigh, and I knew from this body language that his anger wasn't directed at me at all. 'If the intention was to see whether this would draw you two out, you'll confirm that theory. The suspect is already terrified of the idea of Renatus–'

'He should be. I'll kill him,' Renatus spat without hesitation, 'and he's more than a suspect, you just caught him in the act.'

'Of being in your apprentice's messy bedroom, that's all I saw. Innocent until proven guilty.'

'You're the Scrier. Proving it takes ten seconds.'

'And I cleaned my bedroom before I left,' I added, for the record. Renatus wasn't done.

'He attacked Aristea's sister.'

'And you think we should kill him for that?' Qasim challenged, an unspoken reminder that the Scrier knew of Renatus killing the man he'd thought to have attacked his own sister. I bit my lip, glancing guiltily at my master, who wisely said nothing. I could see straight into his head. And I didn't disagree. Wrathful Renatus was a terrifying creature of blackness and without remorse – what did that make me if I supported it? Especially if I knew that this vengefulness was a direct path to his own undoing?

Qasim was unimpressed with the lack of answer, translating it with ease. 'You can both relax. He strolled in her

200

front door. I don't think he even touched her.'

My breath hitched a little at the suggestion, even though Qasim was denying it, and beside me, Renatus flared up again.

'He'd better hope not. Aristea is one of us,' he asserted passionately. 'Her family is our family. A move against her family is a move against our council.'

'No,' Qasim countered irritably. 'We follow due course. Don't pretend that this reaction has anything to do with the council.' He frowned, always so superior, always full of judgement, most of it warranted. 'If the trespasser sees you like this he'll know that Angela Byrne is a tripwire to destabilising the pair of you. Is that something you want getting back to Lisandro? To anyone?'

'Where is he? I want to talk to him.'

'How nice of you to share what you *want*.' Qasim narrowed his dark eyes. 'Lord Gawain is handling the interview. You worry about getting your apprentice cleaned up.' I rolled my eyes, not caring that he could see. He straightened his tailored jacket at the waist. 'Angela is fine. Jadon's watching the house. A Crafter with the same awareness of his atmospheric control as Aubrey and Lisandro convinced her to let him inside the house. We caught him, and Emmanuelle's heading back now, setting up a proper security system over the premises so it can't happen again.'

'Thank you,' I said, trying not to sound begrudging. I was truly grateful for the Scrier's concern for my sister, especially in a situation like this when Renatus and I were unable to help her. My stomach twisted at the mention of the former White Elm brothers. 'Is that who this was? Someone connected to Lisandro, and Aubrey?'

'He claims not, but we'll check into that. His story so far is that there are people or parties who might pay for intel on the White Elm's new apprentice. Small-time opportunist, by the sounds of it, and probably one of your blogger friend's numerous readers.' Qasim cast an unhappy look around as though expecting to see Jaroslav ambling along the bridge.

'I don't understand,' Renatus burst out. He gestured back

at me. 'One of us should have seen this. How could someone get so close to Angela Byrne and *none* of us scried it?'

I hadn't considered this until now. Whenever something big happened with Lisandro, I got a vision to alert me, something to do with the way my fate was entwined with his that made all his ill deeds relevant to me, but my own sister could be vulnerable and Fate didn't feel I needed to know?

'Honestly?' Qasim leaned past Renatus to admire my sai, still across my lap. 'I don't think Angela was in any true danger. The intruder scared her because she cottoned on that she was being manipulated, whereas most wouldn't, but he doesn't seem to have had any intention of harming her.' He looked up at me. 'Are you quite sure you wouldn't rather be upfront with her?'

I was already shaking my head. 'No. What you told her is fine.'

Qasim looked frustrated. 'I don't know what you think you're avoiding by putting this off. She's going to learn the truth, all of the truths, at some point. Then what will you do?'

'Work it out then,' I snapped, and in doing so I finally reached the end of my scrying teacher's patience. He turned away and dissolved into the crowd on the bridge.

Renatus turned away, too, pacing a short distance from me where he could think. I watched him silently, feeling his thoughts race through his head, trapped in hateful cycles. His sister, my sister, me, Anouk. Anger, fear, anger, fear, the two inextricably tied. Being unable to help my family when she needed it compounded on his feelings of inadequacy around what happened in Prague to Anouk and to me, around Lisandro's escape, and now finding me here again bloody and worse for wear – it made him feel useless, like when Ana died right in front of him. Rage spilled from him without consideration, dark, twisted and consuming.

And rather than deflect it with my wards like I always did, I slowly dropped my defences, one layer at a time, cautiously, and let it in. Felt what he felt. Tried to understand, because we'd been out of sync since the last time we were in this city.

Renatus was a deeply emotional person and his capacity for negativity had overwhelmed me in the past, but with each ward peeled away a manageable tide of it soaked into me... and I found it frighteningly relatable. He *hated* this intruder for targeting my sister. He didn't know her, wouldn't be able to pick her out of this crowd if she were here right now crossing the gorgeous Charles Bridge, but if he could get his hands on this little nobody who had upended his day by upending hers, there would be no holding back.

And I... wouldn't stop him. I would help. How dare anyone threaten my family? Renatus's anger met with mine and filled me, and I felt my fists tighten on the hilts of my sai. His protectiveness of me extended to the people I loved, I saw for the first time, and what was once his personal quality had become mine, too. I'd never felt particularly protective of anyone – a baby sister, a youngest niece, an apprentice, I was always someone else's responsibility. But now I felt fury I knew I should fight, because I'd seen this already in Renatus and I'd been told where it ended for him, but I couldn't. My sudden public profile had exposed Angela today, which in turn had triggered Renatus's fierce protective streak and mine, and now I felt like hurting someone and I knew that was wrong when I was supposed to be the rational voice tempering my master's darker urges. And that made me *so angry* because here was yet another easy slope for Renatus to slide down: one provided by me, and my love for my family. How easily he would chase down his own destruction if it came bundled as revenge or loyalty.

I was a doorway to all kinds of horrific fates. But I knew it – which meant I'd know if we were going too far.

I know what I'm doing, I told myself, and the confidence in my own head brought me an unreasonable degree of calm.

Gingerly, grazes still stinging, I climbed down from my seat on the wall. The sai blades clanged together lightly in my hand, but no one around paid me any mind. The outer attention-redirecting ward seemed to be holding.

'You're a sieve,' I advised Renatus, retrieving his

attention. Immediately I felt him start to pull back on his rampant emotions, realising what effect it usually had on me. 'But it's okay.'

You're getting better at managing it, he noted, briefly checking inside my head to see that I was dealing. Aloud, he said, bitterly, 'I really do feel like breaking something.'

'I know. Maybe not here.' I cast a meaningful look at the sunny city, the busy footbridge.

'Are we going to talk about you leaving the estate without me and almost getting yourself trapped in the void?' He looked back at me over his shoulder. 'You should know I can't bring you back from there. No one can.'

I shivered again. 'I promise you, I regret it.' I rearranged the sai in my hand, letting their metal sound ring again. 'Are we going to talk about you leaving me behind this morning?'

He turned to face me, and I could sense both his confusion and his guilt.

'I didn't think you wanted to be as involved,' he said, 'which is completely fine.'

'I am involved, whether we like it or not. My eye isn't getting any better, so we don't need to pretend I'm staying at home to recover. I'm not studying, I'm not getting stronger… I don't even know how to use these.' I raised the pair of swords. 'They came after my sister today, and this,' I nodded at my knees, at the beautiful river view, 'can't happen next time. I don't want to feel useless anymore.'

He regarded me for a long time. People streamed past him, eyes lingering on him longer than they did me. He always caught attention.

'I left as soon as I could,' he said again, like he wanted me to believe him and wasn't sure I would. 'I won't let you lose her, not if there's anything at all I can do to prevent it.'

'I know that.' He never let me down, not really, and he always meant what he said. 'But she's part of this – her name's on the list you found with the ring – and this could keep happening. This guy got scared when he heard you might get involved. I want…' I swallowed, this unfamiliar anger threatening to choke me. I'd never wanted this before, as recently as ten minutes ago when I lashed out at my friends and burned under their frightened gazes, but as the words came out, I knew they'd become true. 'I want that. I want to be someone to be afraid of, someone whose sister no one would *dare* mess with, because they wouldn't want to cross me.'

'I don't want that,' he answered, unsurprisingly. I smiled apologetically; the expression hurt my face.

'I wasn't going to stay a kid forever,' I reminded him. 'I have the scar, my name is out there. Let's use it.' I watched him hesitate, heard his thousand counterarguments, and threw down my last determined card. 'She's my sister. They came to her house. Never again.'

His arguments collapsed in his own head.

'All in?' he asked, a little doubtfully. My voice was firm when I replied.

'All in. Whatever it takes.'

He came back over to me and extended a hand to take my arm gently.

'I think Teresa is the better bet for clearing up those scrapes,' he said diplomatically, since our usual port of call Emmanuelle was likely to give me a hard time and was busy with Angela anyway. Renatus walked me forward and then through the void so quickly I barely felt it, landing us in the hilly Italian street where our journey as master and apprentice had begun. We started up toward what I recalled was Teresa's house. 'Then should we see Tian about scheduling some lessons?'

The next morning when I walked into Anouk's old classroom, there was a strange mixed sense of familiarity and deep change. Renatus was there, sitting on the edge of a table as he gazed thoughtfully at the whole-wall bulletin board, a cardboard box of folders at his elbow and piles of open boxes all over the room. I joined him, leaning back against the same table to get the same view of Anouk's final project, and I felt the brush of his arm against mine as he folded his arms. His organised brain fired fast, faster than mine could ever hope to keep up with except when I was in a panic (in which case I won the race every time). The space wasn't ours, but the mission was, and without him saying so, I knew we'd just taken over this room.

We were back on track, focused again, destination nowhere particularly good.

'You took your time,' he noted. I took no offence, and knew he meant none.

'Emmanuelle caught me in the dining room. She said she called Angela this morning and everything's still fine there. She's put every kind of ward there is on my house.' I touched my chin unconsciously. 'She knew I'd been healed, and she wasn't happy. How could she know?'

'She always knows,' Renatus commiserated, and I felt a small and unexpected pang of loneliness. Renatus didn't have a lot of friends, but his connection with the Parisian Healer was new, hard-earned and visibly valuable to him. Contrarily, I had a stack of amazing friends, all of whom had been unusually quiet with me at breakfast this morning. I knew I'd scared them yesterday, and though I'd apologised to Kendra for snapping at her and she'd smiled and said to forget it, I couldn't forget, and I couldn't forget what I'd said straight after, on the bridge.

I want to be someone to be afraid of. Wasn't I already? Last night when I got back, Hiroko had listened silently to my debrief about what happened to Angela, asked if my family was alright, and then claimed a migraine and gone to bed. I'd dismissed it, my head too full of worries to consider that she was avoiding me. Was she? No way. She'd asked me to come for a walk after breakfast, but I'd had to decline, having already agreed to meet Renatus. I'd catch her afterward.

'Lord Gawain took Oneida into the Archives,' Renatus said, bringing me back to the present. I immediately thought of the very cool underground library just a stone's throw from *the* Stonehenge, storing hundreds of years of White Elm history, from old ledgers to minutes of meetings, crumpling letters to copies of police reports. 'To start her training on managing it, until Glen can show her Anouk's system. It seems Anouk was putting together a collection for us.' He leaned forward a little so I could glance between us at the box behind him, dates 1994-1997 written on the side in permanent marker. On the floor beside the desk he lightly kicked another box, which I guessed was probably the next four years of cases, since that covered our window of interest. 'Homicides investigated by the White Elm. Your request?'

I browsed over the wall with my eyes, taking in the dozens of old photographs and post-it notes joined with twine and thumbtacks. We hadn't talked about this in a while, certainly not since Prague and Anouk, but what an odd coincidence that, the very day after being drawn to the place of her death, the day after I myself had experienced the cold of the void, and the day after my own sister had been threatened, this should arrive. A final, begrudging, helping hand from the historian, putting us back on the path of looking for the man Renatus had thrown into the void when he thought he'd killed Ana Morrissey.

I'd learned over and over that there were no coincidences. We needed a direction. Fate provides.

'It was a hunch,' I explained. I gestured at the wall, which Anouk had worked on exhaustively in her last week of life. Every photo was taken from one of the open "missing persons" boxes scattered around the room. 'We didn't find your stranger but Anouk realised that all these cases you and I overlooked were actually suspected clients of Thomas Shanahan's, and somehow he made them disappear. Most of them reappeared later, working for Lisandro. She said to me that she thought it was the same deal offered to Aubrey.'

'Except he already worked for Lisandro,' Renatus pointed out. I nodded and turned to face him.

'Yes, and except that they tried to make us believe he was dead,' I reminded him. I jerked my head at the wall. 'No one went to that much trouble with these lads.'

'They knew the White Elm would look harder for Aubrey

than some of these criminals.'

'Yes,' I said again, 'but Aubrey can't be the only high-profile or recognisable person to require Shanahan's services. What if they've faked other deaths?'

Renatus's sceptical gaze drifted from my face to the box at his feet and back to the wall. I gave him a second, sensing his discomfort with the situation. I misread it.

'I know he's your uncle,' I said, more carefully. 'It can't be nice to have your family accused of something like this.'

'No, it doesn't surprise me at all, and having family in the middle of a White Elm investigation is how I grew up.' He shot me a brief look that would have included a smile if he were anyone else. 'It always seemed... grimly ironic, I suppose... that Uncle Thomas could never find Keely, considering his work. I knew it was along these lines, cleaning up people's messes for them. He taught me how to erase energy traces,' he remembered offhandedly. Just a casual afternoon at the uncle's place learning how to remove criminal evidence. My uncle home-schooled me through mandatory schooling, so tame by comparison. 'He and Lisandro had a blow-up after my parents died. It's so strange to think of them working together now, but I suppose a lot of time has passed.' He kicked the box again, a little harder this time so it slid closer to me. 'You know my case has been moved into that one, don't you? My parents, my sister.'

I hadn't considered it, but yes, he was right. Anouk and Lord Gawain had reclassified our families' deaths from accident to murder after the truth had come out, but like my own storm, I couldn't imagine that any evidence existed to make much of a file.

'A lot of time has passed,' I repeated his words, and he nodded automatically, going back to staring at the wall. My scar went through my eye; his were under his skin, traumas he would be dealing with for years still to come. 'What do you think of my hunch?'

'I think there's a lot of empty space on that wall.'

We had to tidy up the room first, put files back in the

boxes they'd come from before adding more to the equation. Several times when my fingers made contact with different files and folders, swift impressions came to me – *desperate strangers writing out detailed descriptions, Qasim accepting a photograph, Anouk smacking her hands down on a folder as she suddenly realised* – and I let them pass without comment.

I made sure to be the one to open the box on the floor, and to take out the two-page stapled document recently added to the top before I placed the box on the table for us both to reach. Renatus sat down opposite me and accepted the next folder I withdrew.

'I don't know how we're going to do this without Anouk here,' he admitted, opening his folder and closing it straightaway. 'She made these connections because she filed everything we put into the Archives. She knew which names were also on other lists – criminal watch lists, mortal police investigations, civil and financial disputes. She remembered.' He got back up, suddenly agitated, and turned to her wall again. He tapped roughly on a note she'd tacked under a bent photograph. 'See? 'Gambling debt, multiple arrests, charges of aggravated assault and burglary, Interpol watchlist'... I don't know what she knew. She *was* the Archive.'

I could feel his confidence fading and my own, by extension. Determinedly I held onto mine. 'You know heaps, especially about these people.'

He was shaking his head. 'I need what she knew. I need Glen.' He tapped the note again, slower, concepts clicking together in his brilliant brain. 'This is Glen's writing. English. He knew... because she knew.'

I tilted my head in interest, waiting for him to go fetch, but he didn't move.

'Can we *get* Glen?'

'No. They're still working on getting him to talk again. His mind is totally shut down. But he's eating, finally,' he added as though this made things less horrible. I pressed my fingers to my forehead, thinking hard. No way had Fate sent us in here this morning, set up to discover so much, and left us in the lurch. No. We were just expecting too much from it.

'You know heaps,' I said again, deciding, 'and we *have* the Archives. These names are all on lists, you said?'

'In her head,' Renatus answered dully. I shrugged, unseen behind his back.

'Well, we'll make our own lists. A list of unsolved murders and suspicious deaths. A list of sorcerers being watched by non-witch authorities. A list of people the White Elm actively tracked for crimes and suspected crimes, without eventual charge. We've got all the same information. Maybe more,' I considered, waving my fingers, thinking of the impressions we both got as scriers. Renatus was looking at me over his shoulder like I was crazy.

'That could take months,' he protested. I shrugged again.

'Do you have a better idea?' I waited; he looked like he wanted to say he did but I could see in his head that he didn't. 'We always find things out right when we need to – have you noticed that? If we go through the Archives and write up these lists, we'll have something to cross-reference. Add to that all the special access you have to some of these families–'

'They're not going to talk to me about this,' he insisted, but he had turned around to face me properly. He was thinking about it. He looked once more at Anouk's wall. 'It really could take us months.'

'You have other plans?' I asked, starting to look around for a pen. My hand closed on a pencil – *Anouk scribbling words in hasty Russian* – and Renatus dropped back down into his seat opposite me, yellowy legal pad already in hand. I was pretty sure that wasn't in here before but he had an arsenal of party tricks like nobody else you'd ever meet. Making objects appear and disappear was low-key for him. I thought of my sai yesterday and the way I'd summoned them to my hands without ever being taught how. Was this another of his abilities I'd tapped into in a moment of urgency, borrowing tricks from the recesses of his mind?

'Are you writing or am I?' he asked, holding the pad up in case I wanted it. I reached instead for the closed folder in front of him and rolled the pencil over.

'I'll read them out. Your handwriting is nicer.'

We spent the whole morning like this, like old times except not in his office. The files were fascinating and I had to remind myself to stay on the task of just announcing whether or not they were closed. Most of the suspicious deaths investigated by the White Elm, at least in this time period, were solved and prosecuted in cooperation with local, non-magical law enforcement agencies. I hadn't realised the White Elm had so many citizens in positions of power in non-witch society, out there doing good.

I also hadn't realised how creative murder could get when magic was added to the mix, though it shouldn't have surprised me, orphaned by magical climate control as I was.

'This guy's *head* was missing when they found the body, and the neck was partly cauterised,' I read aloud, grimly captivated. 'His ex-wife was with him when they found him, and she confessed to the crime, but she never said where the head had gone…'

'Can we focus?' Renatus asked rhetorically, reading another file, having lost patience with my pace. I turned the page, incredulous.

'But she never even left the room after he died. No footsteps through the blood, no movement of the body, no blood on the door handle.' I put the page down. 'How would she even do that?'

'I can think of at least two ways she might have managed it.' Of course he could. Renatus looked up from his list. 'What was her motive, does it say?'

'Uh…' I flicked back through. 'Apparently he'd come over to tell her he was taking the house. She and the kids were going to have to find somewhere else to live.'

'Hmm. Probably a legitimate death, then. I found one possibility here,' he said, turning around the document in front of him for me to see. 'Solved, but not very cleanly. A house fire, two dead, burned beyond recognition. Mr and Mrs Bishop, apparently, since it was their house. But…' He turned the pages quickly to show me what was missing. 'No blood tests and only a cursory dental analysis on *one* victim. Their business rival, Jamie McNulty, was found in possession of the fuel cannister used to light the fire, and his prints were found at the scene, so he was convicted without a confession.'

'What did the White Elm say?'

'He wasn't one of ours, but the victims were, so it looks like we had a team step in. Qasim's vision confirmed McNulty's guilt. Now, I'm not brave enough to claim he's wrong, but we've been sent false visions before, and this one wasn't corroborated with another scrier.' Renatus looked up at me. 'Jamie McNulty could have been framed by a clever spellmaster, and those bodies could have belonged to anyone. The Bishops could, theoretically, have walked away from this.'

'They could be alive right now.' I put the headless father of the year aside. 'Nice work, Sherlock.'

He went back to his list. 'Does that make you Watson?'

I paused, unable to help smiling. 'I didn't think there'd ever be a pop culture reference I could throw at you that you'd actually get. I've just got to go back a century, apparently. And yes,' I added, standing to reach into the box for the next file, 'I am definitely the Watson here. The *sensible* one.'

'I liked Holmes better.'

'Unsurprising.' I sat back down, amusing myself with a comparison of my master with the fictional detective. Moody, arrogant, much too smart for his companion to keep up with, pseudo-detective... 'Did you read the books growing up?'

But Renatus had gone still, eyes out of focus, and now he stood abruptly. He cut me out of his thoughts quickly, though not before I heard the frantic stream of *no, no, no* running through them. Aloud he said, very firmly, 'Stay here,' and started for the door.

'Renatus.' His change in demeanour rattled me, and I unsteadily got up, wishing I sounded more certain, more like the kind of apprentice he would be confident to take with him. I pried his thoughts but they would not give. I felt only his worry. 'If something's wrong...'

'No, it's not… Just stay here.'

'I said 'all in',' I reminded him, trying to follow, but he stopped at the door and caught my shoulder with an open hand. I got the briefest flash of the estate's front gate, a carryover from the contact. I glared at him; he didn't back down.

'I'm not going anywhere. It's a headmaster thing, not a you and me thing. I'll try to sort it out.'

He left, and I stayed put with effort. What headmaster duties could garner that reaction? The first time we'd really talked, Qasim had dragged me to him for breaking a very serious law – Haunting – and he'd been nothing but calm about that.

The gate. I turned to the only window in the room and raced over, dodging between disorganised classroom furniture and open boxes. Renatus could sense people coming and going from this estate.

The window wasn't directly facing the front of the house but from the edge, pressing close to the glass and angling my gaze, I could just see Fionnuala walking up the path with an unfamiliar man in a business suit. His hair was dark and his physique slight. An accountant? A banker? They stepped into my blind spot and I couldn't turn my head without knocking my nose into the glass and losing sight of them anyway. I tried to reach out my senses all the way to them, ignoring the people I brushed against in between. A sorcerer… powerful, though not more so than anyone on the council… I closed my eyes and concentrated on feeling out his aura. Displacer. And oddly familiar…

'Do you really need the window?' I turned, startled. Hiroko was in the doorway, a backpack slung over her shoulder, piece of folded paper in her hand. 'Aren't you a scrier?'

'I was just…' Actually, it hadn't occurred to me to try. But something about her stance, her energy, her blank expression, distracted me. 'Where are you going?' She dropped her eyes from mine and I had my answer long before I put the dots together. Renatus's abrupt departure and now Hiroko's weird appearance through the same doorway put me on edge. I glanced out the window, though the gate and the people were out of view. 'You mean him? Who is he?'

'My father,' she answered, managing to sound both gentle and defeated. She forced a tiny smile. 'I wished you could meet him someday, but I did not expect it like this.'

'Your father.' I must have known, but the sound of my own pulse rushing through my ears had become incredibly apparent and I couldn't hear myself think. 'What's he doing here?'

Hiroko waved the paper she held, a little lamely. 'I... I have been accepted into the university where he once studied.'

'Oh.' It's a good thing, I reminded myself over the noise in my ears. She was my friend and something good had happened to her. I went through the motions while I tried to understand. 'Congratulations.'

'Thank you.'

'Wait, when did you apply?' I asked suddenly. We'd been here since March. Some students at the Academy were still completing their mandatory schooling via distance education, receiving thick A4 envelopes – forwarded by their parents – full of coursework that they presumably attacked in their dorms, but like me, Hiroko had been done before she arrived.

Her dark eyes fell from mine.

'After Garrett left,' she admitted, referring to her almost-boyfriend who'd been tricked into defecting to Lisandro's army, we assumed, by the traitor Aubrey. His current whereabouts were unknown: his Seer mother and the parents of the other three boys taken had decided together to trust in a vision of the boys returning home and denied the White Elm the right to search for them, lest their well-meaning actions endanger this future. 'You were busy with your training. I felt that I was wasting time here. I asked my father to send me the forms. He has been worried about me, and I promised him I would leave here if I was accepted...'

214

'You wanted to leave.'

'I did. I thinked– I *thought*, what future do I have here? So I applied to study economics at the university.' She smiled a little wryly. 'It sounds dull beside what I came here for – an apprenticeship with Elijah.'

I tried to get a grip on my spiralling panic. *Focus, focus.* 'What's your father doing here, then?'

'He has come to take me home.'

Well, of course he had, though it made no sense to me in that moment. It wasn't like the magical world was falling apart at the seams and civil war was looking increasingly likely. It wasn't like being close with me was a quick path to danger. Shaken, not knowing what to say or think, I reached out clumsily for Renatus with my senses. I found him in the most obvious place, meeting Mr Sasaki at the front doors, ready to advocate for Hiroko to stay, knowing what an anchor she was to me. He had not done this for any other student; I supposed he didn't think family affairs to be any of his business.

But he'd try for me.

'You can visit me in Sapporo,' Hiroko said hopefully when I just stared at her. 'We can write letters.'

'But you won't be here,' I concluded, the inescapable crux of the truth needing to be let out to sit between us so we could deal with it. She nodded uncomfortably. But we could deal with this, we could solve it, I was sure of it. 'You don't want to go, do you? Tell him you changed your mind.'

'I do not have a sister I can simply refuse whenever I do not like her decisions,' Hiroko said quite firmly, and her words stung me more than I expected. 'This is my father. I must keep my promises. We agreed I can come here and try to win an apprenticeship–'

'If you leave, you'll lose your chance,' I said, stricken, realising I was losing her and trying to pull her back. I crossed the room to her, appealing. 'It's what you want. It's why you came here.'

'It is why I came here but no longer what I want.' She watched me approach, watched me stop in front of her, and her eyes clung to the scar down my left temple and eye. 'I am proud of you, Aristea. Your strength is inspiring. But knowing you has been a window to a life I do not want. Knowing what you give up… There is something you have that I do not, and for this reason I cannot be a White Elm apprentice.'

'What's that?'

'I do not know.' She took my hand with her empty one, and turned my wrist enough that we could both see the tattoo.

'They'd give you one,' I attempted, and we both smiled tiny smiles, catching on to one another's quirky sense of humour. She looped her pinky finger around mine and our little matching silver rings clinked together. She'd made them for us, friendship rings, forged out of magic. She was so, so talented. I tried another tack. 'You can't go, you'll miss out on so much. Garrett and Josh and the others, they're going to come back someday. Iseult visiting. The fallout from the Valero and Avalon thing. Guessing who Kendra dates next.'

'You can write it down. Write to me.' Her eyes looked a little shiny but I could feel in her demeanour that she wasn't budging. 'I will not be dead. We will still see each other and be friends. I will just be somewhere else in the world.'

'I need you here,' I tried, swallowing the lump that was forming in my throat. She shook her head and pulled me into a hug. I closed my eyes and breathed her in, hoping to draw on her warmth and affection, but the air I inhaled only flowed cold into the dark, empty cavity that was inside me. She was leaving, really leaving.

'You do not. You have Renatus. You have the others. I need to do this.' She withdrew so we could look at each other again, and I realised I was crying. My cheeks felt wet, though I hadn't felt the tears start. Her tears were dripping from her chin. 'You are my friend, but this is for me. Do you understand?'

Words swirled in my head. Yes, no, other excuses to make her stay. It was selfish, I knew. Staying here if she no longer wanted to be chosen as Elijah's apprentice really was a waste of her time. I opened my mouth to let some words out but couldn't pick which ones to say, and lost my chance.

'Hiroko?'

We both turned; the slim Japanese man I'd glimpsed through the window had arrived with Renatus, who was looking at me grimly. I hadn't even noticed their approach.

'Papa.' Hiroko wiped her face hurriedly and smiled warmly in greeting at her father. She tapped the strap of her backpack, slung over one shoulder. '*Watashi wa shuppatsu suru junbi ga dekite iru.*'

Her father nodded, thin, silvered dark hair shifting as he did so. He was in his fifties, I suspected, though his face bore few lines. About the age my dad would be if he were still alive. Mr Sasaki extended an expectant hand to his daughter and she moved automatically away from me. A good daughter. The newcomer offered me a distant smile, seeing me brush tears from my face.

'Hello,' he said, clearly not having a clue who I was, and I wanted to shout at him that I was Hiroko's friend, her *best* friend, and he should know who I was. But Hiroko herself did not introduce me, only casting a final look over her shoulder, and I kept quiet. I didn't know how far my name had spread by now, and what people were saying about me. So I forced a polite smile and answered, 'Good morning, Mr Sasaki.'

He laughed lightly, and Hiroko rushed to translate.

'It is night where we are going,' she explained. 'He has just finished work.'

'Thank you for look after my daughter,' Mr Sasaki said to Renatus, his careful cadence reminding me of how Hiroko sounded when I first met her. I hadn't noticed how much she'd improved. 'We will go now. Perhaps, we will meet again.'

Hiroko sent me a determinedly bright smile as she offered Renatus her key. 'We will.'

I didn't share her confidence. I didn't want her to leave. The compulsion to dissolve into wracking sobs didn't stop a sudden flare of spite from opening my mouth.

'Whatever you say,' I said tightly, coldly, and Hiroko's smile, her whole energy, faltered. I regretted it immediately but I couldn't move as Renatus declined the key and told her to keep it, as her father said his goodbyes to Renatus and guided her away. As she walked out. I didn't even say goodbye.

I struggled to draw my next breath.

'Aristea,' Renatus murmured with a sigh when the Sasakis were out of earshot. 'I'm sorry. I tried.'

'I...' Talking was too hard. I was going to crack. I was full of emotion – sadness and confusion and loss and self-hatred and anger and guilt, all of it yucky – and I was sure I was going to explode with it. *It isn't your fault*, I said instead, hoping the message made it through the swampy moat of ill-feeling that surrounded me. I should have said goodbye, I should have put up more of a fight, I should have made more time for her, I should have let loose and told her how hurt I was, I should have seen this coming, I should have been more supportive, I should have noticed her things packed up last night, I should have gone for that walk, I should have, I should have, I should have...

I drew a shaky breath, prepared for the moment when I would break, *finally* break, after *everything* with Anouk and Angela and Valero and Fate's plan for Renatus and now this...

But it didn't come. The mushrooming grief and misery inside me collapsed into that black empty space I'd been feeling more and more, and I felt... eerily calm. A flatline.

'I'm fine,' I claimed, voice a little raw from the crying, and the words came out as truth. All the tumult was clear. I pushed my hair back off my face and rubbed the tears from below my eyes. When my fingers came away, my vision was clear, and so, it seemed, was everything else. I gestured at the table, the files still where we'd left them. 'Can we get back to work?'

Renatus watched me with hesitant wariness as I brushed past him and returned to my seat. All my worries were gone, far away, and I felt so much more room for focus within me. He followed at a small distance, his concern touching me and flowing right through without effect, his thoughts all centred on me, all woven through with worry. An emotional shutdown

218

was far from healthy, but he didn't need anything else to worry about. I looked up at him so he could see the honesty in my face when I answered his unspoken concerns.

'This is what I want to do,' I said, holding up the next file. He glanced at it and then back at me, unsure, his thoughts still loud, fearful that I was mad with him. 'With you?' The words left me before I could do anything to withhold my surprise, but a moment's attention to the shape of his concerns told me what I should have guessed. 'No, of course not. You tried.'

'I keep letting you down,' he noted, sitting opposite me, slowly. 'I thought you'd be more upset.'

'I'm not upset,' I assured him, getting into the file. I considered whether to tell him the next bit. 'I don't feel anything.'

'I know,' he admitted, and I wondered how but he chose not to respond to that thought. 'It scares me.'

I felt an unexpected smile tug at my mouth, even as I felt Hiroko's energy move further and further away from me, down the staircase and across the front hall. As I felt her regret and hurt getting further away from me being able to fix it, as I felt her run into the energies of our friends.

'That was the idea, remember?'

Renatus caught my hand as I went to flick the page over, surprising me again. With his thumb and forefinger he found the friendship ring Hiroko had made me, and he turned it slightly. In my numb stillness I wasn't prepared for the sharp pang of loneliness that struck inside my chest, or the flash of connection I felt with my departing friend at that moment. My breath hitched and tears stung the backs of my eyes again. I ripped my hand back.

'Whatever you say,' Renatus echoed me, going back to his own file, and I sat for long minutes in silence with my hands in my lap, rhythmically turning the ring on my finger and keeping my attention on my best friend all the way to the gate, until she really was gone.

Goodbye.

chapter fifteen

'We've known all week that this would happen. We should have prepared them.'

The other Seers had made their position on the matter clear, but Tian was still feeling uncomfortable with the group's decision to withhold this intuition. The four of them were sitting on low cushions on the floor of Oneida's new flat, lights low, incense heavy in the air, smoke burning the inside of Tian's nose and making his head swim.

'They would have tried to stop it,' Lord Gawain reminded him, tiredly. He shifted on his plush seat, old knees beginning to ache, but he kept his eyes shut. 'Aristea isn't the only student to whom we have a responsibility.'

No, but she was the only student whose fundamental goodness they were concerned about compromising through their puppeteering. Both Susannah and Tian had voted against Renatus taking Aristea as his apprentice, foreseeing futures in which the girl's innate loyalty drove her to greater and darker heights to save her master's unstable and probably doomed soul. Already they could see it in action, little pushes down that path, little pushes back, and this departure of her closest friend was nothing short of a shove.

But knowledge like this was a matter of balancing ethics on cosmic scales – Lord Gawain had known the same destiny and had voted *yes*, believing the risk was worth it because Renatus was worth it. All four had known when Hiroko Sasaki decided to leave the Academy and realised the implications, but only Tian had wanted to warn Renatus. Now Aristea was devastated and the Dark Keeper was at a loss, indulging her withdrawal. Letting her stew. Letting her slip.

'Some pain is part of her path,' Oneida advised calmly, drifting her fingers through a curl of smoke. Disturbed, it dispersed, but then came back together in the shape of a broad-winged bird. A phoenix? Hawk? It was hard to tell from Tian's angle through the haze, and then was gone. 'The Sasaki girl is where we need her. We were losing her.'

'Aristea has started to frighten her,' Susannah told the other three. Lord Gawain sighed and shifted again, wincing. Renatus and the unusually dark and silent Aristea were today at Stonehenge in the Archives, picking up where Anouk left off in her search into likely conscripts of Magnus Moira. Even with Aristea's help, the young scrier had reported, he expected the task to take weeks or months. Renatus worked well with something particular to focus on, but Tian knew the council leader was also wary of keeping the increasingly volatile pair inactive for a long-term task like this. Renatus wasn't talking about it, but Aristea had left the estate for the first time unattended this week, spurred to impulsive action by a perceived threat to her sister and landing herself halfway across the continent.

With her sai. Gods only knew what she planned to do with them.

'She's starting to frighten me, too,' Lord Gawain admitted. 'I knew there would be... consequences... to bonding her with Renatus, but I thought they would go both ways. And I didn't think it would be this swift.' Eyes still closed, he, too, interrupted the rising smoke with a hand, and it slipped between his fingers, taking new shapes. People seated in rows. An audience. They were gone.

'You thought the consequences would be *good*,' Susannah corrected. She hadn't moved from her cross-legged position, her straight hair clipped neatly back from her face and hanging still as a photograph. Eyes unseeing. 'You partnered him with an Empath, knowing he was too intense for her. You didn't entertain the notion that they might only exchange their negative qualities, which is what's happening. It's just harder to tell with him, because...'

She left the words unsaid but her meaning clear in her tone. Lord Gawain cut an irritated look her way.

'Renatus keeps proving us wrong. He can do it again.'

Susannah finally broke her poised stillness to meet their leader's gaze, and after a second moved it to Tian's. They weren't Telepaths, they weren't close, but he imagined he still understood her doubt in that silent exchange. She looked back to the old Welsh Seer, and bowed her head in deference.

'Your faith is a gift greater than you might realise, Lord Gawain,' she said cryptically, and Tian glanced aside at Oneida. The newest councillor had quickly grown comfortable with these games and the complex inner politics of the White Elm, certainly seeming more comfortable with it all than Tian. Knowing different aspects of different futures, and the weight of deciding who to share that knowledge with, made Seers careful with their words, even – or perhaps especially – with one another.

The lesson of Susannah's mistake with Lisandro, trying to protect a friend and fellow councillor before his betrayal was revealed and resulting in the deaths of the Byrne family, was still fresh on all their minds.

'Perhaps we can offer the same faith to Renatus's apprentice,' Oneida suggested, still playing with the smoke idly. If the shapes she created were symbolic, they were in a language Tian could not interpret. 'I saw her potential when I first met them. We underestimate her if we say she can't handle Renatus, or her path. It doesn't *have* to end in disaster.'

Disaster for whom? Tian dropped his gaze to the weapons lying across his lap, glad there wasn't an Empath around to detect his unease. It didn't *have* to, but a majority of indicators said it would. He thought now of reckless behaviours manifesting in a previously cautious girl, and of cautious, protective behaviours appearing in Renatus.

Seers were the most common class of sorcerer and the most diverse. Fate communicated with Oneida, an independent from outside the White Elm, through smoke and skin contact. Susannah experienced trances; Lord Gawain's gift was broader than hers, but, another new magic purist, the visions manifested similarly. Tian felt Fate's insights in numerous ways, though most strongly through objects, and particularly through weapons. Meeting his fellow Seers today for group meditation – very early for him, very late for Lord Gawain – he'd brought along the three from his collection that had been speaking to him this week.

The sai said Aristea was ready to begin the training he'd promised Renatus.

The ceremonial sword, polished and curved, said it would be necessary soon, a deep sense of conflicted unease, his life at stake, and more... it also showed him when, but very oddly, the golden vision showed his hands hanging it back on his wall. And going without it.

Who was he, an instrument, to question Fate?

And there was the dagger, sharp-bladed and leather-hilted, which said it needed to be available at Morrissey House but also showed him images of bloody hands wielding it over an illegal spell. Distinct impressions of danger and loss clung to the object, questions of trust, and he knew the hands were Aristea's.

And he knew, on some level, they were soon to lose her, and he could tell nobody. He couldn't explain the certainty he had that Hiroko Sasaki's departure yesterday was tied to the destiny of all three weapons balanced on his knees, nor that it somehow connected back to Susannah's mistake with the Byrnes, nor that Aristea's fall from their grasp was imminent.

A short fall was necessary, he knew, for the best outcome for the many.

He could only hope that in its pulling of strings, Fate had shared enough of its plan with the other three council Seers that, as a team, they would have the wisdom to know when to catch her.

Deciding he'd had enough miserable reflection, Tian wrapped his hand around the sai.

'What is our verdict?' he asked, nodding at the polaroid on the coffee table. Lord Gawain looked over at the photograph of Daniel O'Conner, would-be crook and infiltrator. Having yielded little in questioning, the real O'Conner was in lock-up, being held for burglary by mortal and witch law enforcement officers at the police station closest to Aristea's home.

'Unchanged,' Oneida spoke for the group. 'There is more in motion here than we can yet see.'

'I agree,' Lord Gawain said thoughtfully. Tian stood, sheathing the two blades he'd brought with him. 'It will become clear very soon.'

Susannah reached back for the polaroid and examined it.

'Ironic that Fate should send Emmanuelle to help Angela Byrne,' she said vaguely. 'They would have been initiated together.'

Fate was indeed ironic. Through Angela, or her brother if he'd been chosen instead, Renatus would have met their sister; but instead Susannah's attempt to circumvent Fate's plan had given them Peter Chisholm, another Seer whose final acts were to betray the council but in retrospect had to be questioned, because he'd also exposed Lisandro's plan to undermine the White Elm. Lisandro's betrayal had led to the council opening the Academy, which in turn had led to Qasim finding Aristea.

'Angela Byrne will never be on this council because of me,' Susannah said now, dropping the photograph abruptly, 'yet Fate brings her name back to us.'

Oneida went back to the smoke. 'There is something in that blood.'

'Your actions prevented her from joining our council, not from influencing it,' Lord Gawain cautioned. 'It's by her goodwill that we have Aristea – a resource none of us, I think, anticipated – but if she's scared off, or given cause to mistrust us, she could just as easily take her sister back.'

'Aristea is loyal to us,' Tian insisted uneasily, images of

bloody hands crossing his mind before he could stop them. 'She chose us when her aunt came for her.'

'She chose Renatus. She's loyal to Renatus,' Susannah corrected. Tian was acutely aware that she knew something big about their fate she wasn't sharing, but he was in no position to push for it.

Nor was he sure he wanted to.

Lord Gawain nodded slowly, wearily.

'I'm starting to think there's a difference,' he agreed. 'Also, her aunt is not her sister. I'm sure Aristea will appreciate the distraction,' he redirected with a look at the sai. 'Say nothing about O'Conner, or about–'

'Anything else,' Tian finished knowingly as he bowed. Much as he might sometimes feel compelled, the caution of the other Seers was evidence enough to him that Fate wanted this withheld from the young scriers for now. It would find its own way of presenting to them.

It was late at Morrissey House, the midsummer sun finally setting, and Fate arranged for Tian's arrival to perfectly coincide with Renatus and Aristea's.

The Dark Keeper looked eager to get back inside his estate to eat, sleep, and otherwise not spend any more time reading in the dark. The girl looked underslept, her energy spiky with unhappiness, but her eyes found the sai in Tian's hand as they exchanged greetings.

'I have swords like those,' she voiced while Renatus opened the gate and they filed in. Tian nodded and stopped just inside, waiting for her.

'I know,' he said, offering them to her with both hands. She stopped abruptly and shook her head.

'Oh. No, it's okay.' She forced a smile to be polite, perhaps realising that there would be an expectation on her to learn something. Internally Tian sighed, because he'd been reluctant to agree to this in the first place, for *this* reason. More of a fitness activity to complement their many stationary learning areas, students were already instructed in basic swordplay, footwork and defensive postures for spellcasting and wand or tool use. Higher-level ones were experimenting with the use of weapons and tools to channel their magic. Aristea, despite her capabilities, was *not* one of those students.

Don't say "I told you so" yet, Renatus requested without words as he closed the gate and ran a quick hand over the iron, sensing for any changes.

Fate suggested it's time to start these lessons, Tian replied silently, *but it's been known to mislead me before*.

Make it relevant, Renatus insisted. *She'll be all yours*. Satisfied, he turned to his apprentice.

'Good night,' he said simply, an unexpected dismissal if her face was anything to go by, and cast a silent grateful look at Tian before Displacing up to the house. Aristea frowned after him.

'It looks as though you have time,' Tian noted, extending his hands further. Aristea had never been disrespectful to him before, and didn't start now, but he knew she'd been testing boundaries with her master for a while, and he saw the flash of frustration in her eyes as she reached reluctantly for the blades.

'Looks like it,' she agreed, going for the hilts, and Tian dropped his hands away, keeping the weapons from her. She blinked in surprise, and he offered them again.

'I told Renatus I would teach you how to use this weapon,' he explained. 'You will learn the *right* way. From the beginning. First lesson: handling. Try again.'

She reached again for the obvious hand grips, and Tian whipped them again from her reach. She visibly bit her tongue, keeping her instinctual flare in temper to herself.

'It's too late for a lesson,' she complained. Tian glanced at his watch.

'Is it? I woke ninety minutes ago. A lesson occurs when a lesson occurs. This lesson,' he said firmly, offering the sai a third time, 'is now. Have you read the book I left for you?'

That made Aristea pause and think. Yes, he was relieved to see in her face, she had bothered to read it, or at least start to. She repositioned herself to stand more directly opposite him, and extended both hands, palms up, ready to accept the swords. Pleased, Tian bowed and placed them in her hands. Her unbloodied fingers closed over the shafts; he held on until she mirrored his bow, and he released his grip.

'The ceremony, the ritual of swordplay must not be overlooked,' he told her. 'It reminds us to value the weapon, so we look after it. Keep it clean, store it properly, keep it from the wrong hands. It reminds us to value our skills, and to remember that with it we can inflict harm. That, we should not take lightly. We can hurt each other with these. We can hurt *ourselves*.' He took back one blade, again by the shaft, showing her how the non-confrontational grip prevented him from waving a sharpened point at either her or himself. 'Control. But until you have that, lesson two: warding.'

She was good with wards, he knew. He modelled warding the blade of his sai, and watched as she quickly copied on the other so that it could not cut or make contact with anything or anyone. He gave her back the second blade.

'Can I assume you recall the warm up exercises outlined in the book?'

She was good with wards so her interest had picqued; she was not good at focusing on repetitive actions, especially not after a day of reading, and so her interest fell again. Her eyes went flat, but she nodded and looked at his blades in her hands. Self-conscious, she shifted her grip to the hilts and stepped back from the gate to begin slow, stilted attempts at the moves. Tian watched critically, observing her loose wrists, incorrect grip, wide elbows and narrow stance but saying nothing. One thing at a time.

She dropped a blade. She blushed and stooped for it.

'I'm no good at this,' she mumbled. Tian nodded in agreement.

'No. You are just beginning. Try again.'

She didn't. 'I don't see any point.'

'In?'

'Predetermined movement patterns in a book. Doing lots of little broken-up drills.'

Qasim had complained extensively about this particular trait of hers, and Tian had seen glimpses of it, too. He smiled tightly and gestured for the sai back.

'The point,' he said patiently, stepping away from her where he could not strike her, 'is that you have a pair of these sai. I know you took them with you when your sister came under threat. I cannot promise that will not happen again. I *can* promise you will not help her by dropping your weapon.'

'I can't help her by waving swords around at nothing and reading books, either,' the girl challenged as he warmed up. Rolling his shoulders. Stepping out the necessary patterns with his feet, checking for firm ground. 'I need to learn how to *fight* with them.'

'But this is not relevant to you,' he assumed, commencing a set of simple drills. High strike, low strike, block, pivot, block. Aristea froze, attention immediately arrested. Her tired gaze clung to the left-hand blade when Tian twirled it quickly in his palm to demonstrate an inverted strike followed by a stabbing strike with the other sai. Without a pause, he started the combination again from the start, slightly slower. 'High strike, page sixty-six. Low strike, page sixty. Double-blade block, page fifty-one. Footwork, pivot, back foot, page twenty-two.' He watched Aristea's expressive eyes as the connection between the book, the exercises and their application became clear. 'Block, page fifty. Blade flip, warm-up exercise seven. Kill strike, page seventy-eight.'

He relaxed and straightened out of the final pose, looking back to the apprentice. The girl was rivetted, her thoughts hard to determine.

'Why did you move to the side?' she asked unexpectedly, glancing at the ground where he'd pivoted. 'If that was a real fight, why would you give your opponent your unprotected side?'

An astute question. Tian gestured down at his body.

'What do you see?'

She cocked her head. 'A swordmaster.'

'A small swordmaster,' Tian confirmed. 'I am unlikely to

find myself in a fight with a smaller, or weaker, opponent. Never try to match strength for strength. You are slight; I am short. Bigger opponents are strongest face-on. Face-on,' he said now, positioning himself directly opposite her, 'I give the advantage to my enemy. He will win. I must take that advantage from him. I must get inside his guard,' he explained now, pivoting as he had before, this time sidestepping into the girl's personal space so that they were side by side. 'I must stay out of his reach. I must employ my weakness, my size, as my strength. A small target is hardest to hit. A near target is hard to strike with a long reach. But for a short reach…'

Again he inverted the sword so that the pommel faced forward instead of the shaft, now a shorter weapon, the shaft running parallel to his forearm, a shield. He lightly poked Aristea's middle with the pommel, while with the stronger right hand brought the kill strike gently against her throat. Impressed, she looked down at both sai in their final positions, then backed up as Tian did the same.

Now was the moment of truth. Whether he could convince her to stick out these lessons both Renatus and Fate wanted for her.

'Excuse me,' she said, and disappeared. Displaced. Up to the house. Gone. Tian sighed, annoyed, and spun the sai back to downward position. So much for making it relevant for her.

Give her the benefit of the doubt, Renatus prompted, and Tian might have replied sharply except that the Dark Keeper's apprentice reappeared right then. Clutching her own sai. Holding them the way he had just taught her.

'You're right. I can use this,' she said, eyes gleaming with engaged interest. Tian felt an eerie brush of gold, the sense that there was more to this than Aristea was ever going to let on. 'To protect my sister, and… others.'

And others. Tian chose not to explore that.

'Alright then. We will begin.'

chapter sixteen

The first time I'd been inside the Archives, I'd been blown away by the cavernous underground space. The heavy ancient beams of wood holding up the earth ceiling. The countless rows of dusty shelving. The thousands and thousands of yellowed scrolls, water-damaged books, moth-eaten cardboard boxes of folders, files and documents. The magical entryway. The *location*, buried beneath one of the many Bronze-age barrows scattered around the Stonehenge site. So freaking cool.

Coming back in the the days after Hiroko left, a lot of the impressiveness was lost on me. Part of it was the unwelcome punch of realisation, as I took the winding steps down from its foyer into the main chamber and breathed that musty, still air, that Anouk and Glen would not be here like they were last time. Mainly, though, my indifference was carryover from Anouk's classroom the day Hiroko left.

What I said.

What I didn't say.

I rubbed my eyes and checked the oil in the lamp in the middle of our work bench. It was hard to keep track of time down here with no natural light and no electricity, just the eerie night-timey glow of oil lanterns, but today I'd woken sickeningly aware of the date, and it'd been impossible to shake all day. For almost a week now, every day, we'd come straight here from the house kitchens where we'd eat a quick breakfast and accept the lovingly packed lunch from

Fionnuala, and we hadn't been returning to the house until dark, meeting Tian for hour-long drills that wore me out just in time to lie restlessly in bed. Days had blended. Time got lost. I hadn't seen much of the sky, or any of my friends, since she left.

But today was its own day, distinct from all the rest.

I still hadn't seen Stonehenge. I kept wanting to ask Renatus to take me there for a study break, which I knew he'd do, but something stopped me every time.

The idea of seeing the summer sun and resuming real time, perhaps. I hadn't had to *deal* yet – it was like Renatus and I hadn't left that first day, when I couldn't convince her to stay. And Renatus, true to style, was not going to push me to deal.

'Done. Well, another box, anyway.' He sat back in his seat and rolled his shoulders and neck. I heard the crick of stiff vertebrae adjusting. 'Please tell me we're done for the day.'

I abandoned the lamp, which was most definitely not bright enough to work by for the periods of time that we'd been spending in here, even with some help from Renatus's magic, to cast him a brief smirk and reach for the list he had in front of him.

'Quitter.'

'Me? You haven't picked up a file in ten minutes.'

For good reason. I kept tapping into irrelevant impressions left all over the paper from past contact with White Elm hands, usually Anouk, which gave me a sick shock every time – *two hands slamming into the glass wall of a ward* – and the longer I worked, the harder it got to brush them aside.

We'd completed our list of missing persons and suspicious deaths after the second day – that was relatively easy, just a yes or no judgement – and had moved on to blacklisted sorcerers from the same time period. This was taking us much longer. There was no box of "bad guys" or "people to watch" like there were boxes of people who were dead or missing. Instead we were trawling through *years* of White Elm paperwork, starting with minutes of circle proceedings (snore) and then moving into old letters and correspondence once we ran out of those. Which we still had not. Apparently there'd been a lot more council circles than there had been murdered sorcerers.

'What time is it?' Renatus asked.

'Time to get a watch.' Reluctantly I checked my wrist. Felt my stomach drop at the sight of the clockface. 'Two twenty-six.'

I mean, I knew better than to lie to him and expect it to work, but wishing is its own kind of magic, right? Too bad my master had access to my eyes nowadays if he wanted.

'*Five* twenty-six. Nice try. Time we were done for the day.' Renatus pushed his chair back and got to his feet, ignoring my groan. 'Come on, pack it up. They won't keep letting us use this place if we leave it looking like this. We're going home, and we're going to eat something other than sandwiches for dinner. You were going to have to go back to your life sometime,' he reminded me.

I looked resentfully around at our piles of disorganised files all over the tabletop as he started stacking the folders back into the 2000-2001 box. I'd been counting on his willingness to play along, to avoid reality with me and say not a word about what I was trying not to think about, but apparently an overworked week underground had worn him thin on that front.

He couldn't feel the dark cloud of anger that had gathered around me but he could read auras and he could read me. He braced his hands on the table opposite me and considered his words before continuing.

'Listen to me,' he said carefully. 'I'm the last person who should be lecturing you on appropriate mourning periods after a loss, so I won't. But I know you're trying to keep busy and avoid thinking, and I know you haven't been sleeping. Don't,' he advised lightly when I tried to argue. 'You know I'm happy to throw myself into work with you, but you're a useless research assistant if you're too tired to focus. We're not getting anything done in this state. Agreed?'

I didn't want to agree with him, even if he was making perfect sense. I didn't want to acknowledge that I'd seen the dark circles under my eyes this morning in the mirror or that I'd been blinking away eyestrain and then a headache for more than an hour. I certainly didn't want to accept that I was being an ineffective apprentice in my avoidance of the rest of my life.

But he had an annoying habit of being right, and when I met his distinctive eyes, I felt a flicker of memory that I managed to stash away before he could overhear: he was destined to go dark side. I still didn't know what moments were the deciders, but I knew I was the only person who could intervene, and here I was dismissing his attempts at compassion and supportiveness.

'Fine.' I got up and helped him pack away our day's work. The muscles in my shoulders and back protested the new range of motion. 'We'll be back here tomorrow, yeah?'

Renatus winced. 'If that's what you want. I doubt there is any better use for our talents than poring over old documents in a dirty basement, after all.'

I winced too, dumping manila folders into the box while he went through our research for the day, committing the new names and dates to memory. He was right. This was mindlessly boring work that anybody could do, and the Archives were stale-smelling and vaguely claustrophobic, but the monotony of our routine was wonderfully numbing. Today I needed it more than ever.

I reached for another open folder to brush the pages back inside and blinked against the brief flash of leftover psychic energy from the last time someone touched it – *Anouk, arguing half-heartedly over her shoulder with Glen*. I tried to swallow it away like a well-adjusted person but before I could – *green eyes staring blankly*…

Maybe the escape from the ghosts was overdue.

'Let's just go,' I suggested, backing away from the table and making a beeline for the staircase. Renatus, artfully pretending not to be as concerned as he was, silently gathered up his lists and followed, shrugging his jacket back on.

Upstairs, reopening the magical portal door that let out into summer-sunshiny southwest English countryside, I closed my

233

sore eyes and felt the tingle of warm sunlight on my skin as I stepped outside. A late afternoon breeze; the distant drone of a highway. Reality.

'Home?' Renatus asked, tucking his folded-up lists inside his jacket. I wasn't game to Displace myself after my encounter with the void. Luckily there wasn't much Renatus couldn't do, and even less he was afraid to try. 'Or another stop first? We've got time.'

I looked back at him suspiciously, my eyes still strained from days of close reading in poor light on little rest.

'Another stop?' I repeated, tuning into his surface thoughts. I got an unexpected glimpse of Angela's tidy herb garden edging the little two-bedroom house that I used to think of as home. He'd never been there, so it was no memory – he had scried it. I swallowed a bitter taste of fear. 'Is she…?'

'No, she's fine,' Renatus assured me hastily. 'Qasim and Emmanuelle handled the interrogation and Lord Gawain laid charges and released the trespasser to the mortal authorities. Dan O'Conner. No one of consequence. They won't tell me anything more than that. But she's safe. I thought you'd like to see for yourself.'

He had to know I'd been seeing for myself constantly since O'Conner was dragged out of there, scrying the house every hour or so, new paranoias growing where once I was secure and stable. I envisioned her now, and immediately I had a view of her unlocking the front door. Golden hair up high. Work done for the day, home to an empty house, *today*, of all days. My chest tightened at the sight of her. I should be there. My sister looked normal but her life had been touched by my drama. Because someone tried to use her against me, because my photograph and my story was out there, because I was in Prague when I shouldn't have been, because Lisandro was the bane of my existence.

The anger burned in my veins.

'You should talk to her,' Renatus prompted. I was transparent. 'I can drop you there and come back and get you…'

Later, tonight, tomorrow… I heard the different options in his head, a gentle push in the direction he thought would be beneficial for me. Love and support from my most favourite person in the world. I followed her movements around the house, closing my inadequate eyes. He had to know how badly I wanted to do as he suggested.

'No,' I said finally, folding my arms and turning away so he didn't catch my eye. For *months*, I hadn't worried about my sister for more than a passing moment, until this last week when two of the three foundations on which I'd built my pseudo stability had been kicked out from under me. Hiroko was gone. Angela was targeted. 'I don't want her to see me…'

'Scarred?' Renatus finished. I frowned; the pull on my facial muscles and skin no longer twinged, and I felt like I was taking full advantage, frowning more than I used to. 'As you keep reminding me, that isn't going anywhere. Are you going to avoid her for the rest of your life?'

'No, of course not. But, right now…' I took a breath and made myself swallow the anger that rose up at his words. He wasn't the one I was mad with. 'Please, just take me home.' He waited in meaningful silence, and I exhaled heavily, torn. I dropped my arms. 'Your home. You know what I mean.'

He sighed, having tried his best, and offered his hand. 'Fine. Whatever you say.'

We didn't speak the whole walk up the path from the gate to Morrissey House and we arrived at the door to the noisy dining hall in silence. Even with so few students remaining, laughter and conversation had not quietened. It should have been a warming concept, but I felt no connection to the swelling of positive emotion in that room. Weird, because as an Empath I usually tapped into all emotions around me unless I worked hard not to.

I tried not to reflect on what that said about my current state.

Can you smell that? Renatus asked me rhetorically as we approached the dining room. The rich smells of foods both familiar and unfamiliar reached my nose and made my

235

stomach stir. I hadn't thought I was hungry; I hadn't been hungry in days, and I'd eaten listlessly the sandwiches Fionnuala had sent us off with. *Real food.*

Real food. Angela was probably making real food right now at home, a meal for one. She was a decent cook, my sister, though she wasn't always. Growing up, she burned everything, and our brother Aidan joked that it was the only thing Miss Perfect wasn't good at. I guess she showed him, in time.

I rested a hand on my stomach, less to do with my hunger and more to do with the dull ache of missing my family that had started there. I should have let Renatus take me to Coleraine. I should have run to my sister and let her shriek my name and grab me in the warmest hug in the world. I shouldn't have been so stubborn. Hadn't I learned my lesson with Hiroko?

It wasn't too late.

'Renatus–'

'Hey!' We both slowed in the doorway and looked toward the house's main staircase, which started in the entrance hall. Addison James had paused upon spotting us, and now his familiar face broke into a wide, relieved grin. He bounded down the remaining steps two at a time and jogged across the hall to reach me. 'You're still here.'

'Uh, hey,' I responded eloquently, self-consciously running a hand through my unbrushed hair, aware of the shadows under my eyes. I knew I looked perfectly pitiable.

Addison smiled quickly at Renatus – both the Academy's headmaster and only a handful of years older than even the eldest student, none of my classmates ever seemed to know how to behave around him – who nodded back in acknowledgement and said, 'I'll leave you.' Leaving me standing awkwardly with one of the few friends I had left, one of three people I'd avoided religiously since Hiroko went.

'I thought you might've left the school,' Addison explained, looking me over passively and doing an excellent job of not letting on how awful I looked. 'We haven't seen you all week.'

'I know, I've been busy,' I said hurriedly. I shrugged, feeling guilt start to permeate the complicated mix of anger and loneliness I already harboured. I'd neglected my remaining friendships, given them reason to worry, which was of course entirely my own fault, but also Lisandro's for making this world so unsafe and unpleasant that Hiroko had not wanted to be part of it anymore. I suddenly wasn't hungry. 'Trying to keep distracted. I haven't... been dealing well.'

I gestured at myself vaguely. Addison nodded sympathetically.

'Neither have we,' he confessed, though he looked perfectly fresh and well-rested. I tried to banish that uncharitable thought – not everyone dealt with missing people by working and failing to sleep. 'A few of the classes started back up, and it's weird not having you or Hiroko in them.'

My chest tightened unexpectedly. The mention of her name was too much – I realised I hadn't said it or heard it in over a week and didn't want to hear it now, either. I stepped unconsciously away, backing into someone.

'Sorry,' I automatically apologised to the other student, who murmured the same though it wasn't her fault and circled widely around me to get into the dining room. I felt her suppressed irritation with me, and her fear. Of me? I pushed my hair back off my face with one hand as I moved to get the door at my back where I couldn't walk into anyone. My other hand brushed the door handle.

Fingers curling around the handle... Frustration... Dana, one of the staff, pulling the door shut...

I whipped my hand away. My wards were shaky today, my energy not steady enough to sustain them.

'Sorry,' I said again, this time to Addison, who was still watching me. I wanted him to stop, I wanted him to go away, but I couldn't say that. 'What were you saying?'

'Nothing.' He smiled. It looked genuine. He tilted his head aside at the doorway. 'You hungry?'

I shook my head, trying to smile, trying not to feel the concern emanating from him. Trying not to notice the way his voice was carefully modulated to sound gentle. Why?

'No, I'm... I'm...' I pointed directionlessly and started for the staircase, then stopped. What was upstairs? Classrooms. Empty rooms. My dorm, once shared with Hiroko and the other girls, but I hadn't been in there since... well. Since. Ana's bedroom, which Renatus had given me after I became his apprentice, which I'd slept in all this week to avoid going into my own.

I must have looked utterly lost as I stood there, undecided. Addison came up beside me, tall frame casting me in shadow from the open front doors, and touched my arm to get my attention.

Worry concern gentle does it what do I say what does she need she's going to lose her shit I know it–

I yanked violently away from him, shocked by the onslaught. '*Don't* touch me.' Addison raised both hands in a show of peace, eyes wide, while I rubbed my arm where he'd touched. My heart thudded wildly in my chest. 'What *was* that? What did you do?'

'I didn't...' He shook his head slowly, helplessly, and I had to consider the possibility that he hadn't done it on purpose. Somehow, instead of just picking up on his emotional energy in the air around him, I'd channelled it from skin contact, but more than that, carried on unfiltered emotion had come *thought*. Addison wasn't a Telepath and neither was I, but I'd experienced the phenomena with Renatus in our mental bond, and though scrambled, that's what this had felt like. Subconscious thought, cyclic and undirected.

'I don't know what you mean,' he said finally, trying again to sound honest and gentle, and I felt a flash of anger toward him. Toward what he'd just reminded me of. I was the unpredictable, unstable friend.

And I was confirming it. I tried to reel myself in, closing my eyes and counting to five.

'I'm sorry,' I said yet again. I breathed a forced laugh and opened my eyes. He was still standing there, painfully tall, dark hair gelled up into his trademark spikes, brows knitted together in genuine alarm. Still standing there. More than I deserved, with the way I'd been acting. 'I'm being a crazy person. I'm sorry.'

'Don't be sorry. You're our crazy person.'

It was sweet and I smiled and my smile seemed to relax him, but at the edge of my mind, kind of behind my ear, I felt a strange itch. An itch that persisted into a sharp scratch.

…ris…

It was strange, but the feeling again seemed to manifest as a sound. I blinked a few times. My vision wasn't one hundred percent, my stomach was knotted, my heart felt tight, and now I was hearing things. Hearing things from Addison, hearing senseless syllables. Near my temple, behind the scar along my eye, the scratch became a briefly piercing pain. My ear started to ring.

… ris… a… Ar…

'Ouch.' I rubbed my cheek and opened my jaw, trying to relieve the pressure. It helped a little.

'You okay?' Addison asked, watching me curiously. *Worry intrigue weird what's wrong should I even ask she'll say it's nothing.* His voice again, inside my head, this time without touch, I realised even as I started to step away. Thoughts riding into my head on the tail end of emotions. This had never happened before, and I couldn't convince myself it was deliberate on Addison's part. New powers often came on abruptly for me.

'It's…' not nothing, though that's what I wanted to say. I shook my head and made another stab at seeming normal. 'Earache, or something. It just started to hurt. But I haven't been sleeping,' I made myself admit when he frowned a little, worried again – *probably lying awake every night looks like shit needs a good night's sleep* – 'so maybe it's just that. So,' I redirected, determined to stop being a downer, 'what's new? What have I missed?'

He visibly brightened to hear me take an interest in something other than my miserable self, and distantly I felt the swell of his good vibes, but they didn't make it through my dark shell.

'Iseult was here all day yesterday,' he said, his voice

beating out the droning ring in my left ear, at least to begin with. 'She was sorry to miss you. She's going to come every Thursday to continue her lessons with Elijah, Qasim and Emmanuelle – they're the three she picked, since she can't fit everything into just one day. You'll see a bit of her, she said she's in two of those classes with you?' *Reluctant admiration level 3 for everything of course best at everything bet Byrne gives her a run for her money in their classes.*

'Aye, yeah,' I agreed vaguely, feeling around the edges of my aura for gaps in my warding. I did not want to hear the unfiltered private thoughts of people around me. 'But you've got her back for Displacement?'

'Ultimately my takeover is not panning out,' Addison conceded. He smirked playfully and went on, 'I mean, up until five minutes ago I thought I'd gotten rid of you, and with Hiroko gone…'

'Well, that part worked out for you,' I said without thinking, and his smile faltered.

'You know I was joking when I said I wanted her to leave, yeah?' he checked seriously, his words slipping beneath the drone in my ear *pity irony got nothing to do with me wonder if she knows.* '…didn't mean I wanted…'

'Knows what?' I interjected sharply. He frowned.

'What? I said I didn't want her to leave.' *Frustration she isn't even present isn't listening.* I rubbed my ear again.

'You know more about why she left?' I demanded, feeling my anger stirring again. He was keeping secrets from me now? He shrugged. *Discomfort irritation really not my place what's her problem it's hardly a state secret.*

'I guess.'

'Well? Are you going to tell me?' I snapped, and finally Addison's frown narrowed into real annoyance. *Her own damn fault.*

'You'd probably know more, too, if you'd bothered to ask,' he responded flatly. His irritation was lost amid my own surprised hurt as he continued. *Selfish didn't even notice didn't even ask didn't even say goodbye.* 'Or if, I don't know, you'd just plain paid attention to how she was handling what had

240

happened to you. You were in *hospital*. You were messed up. You're still messed up. It scared her.'

'Her dad wants her to go to university,' I insisted, less strongly than I would have liked. The ringing in my ear had expanded to both, the eyestrain headache throbbed, my heart ached and Addison's words were destabilising.

'You think anyone could make Sasaki do what she didn't want to?' he countered. *Annoyance does she even know us how could you miss that guess that's grief she's in a bad place.* Behind him, my blurry gaze caught briefly on someone coming down the staircase. Sterling, one of my roommates. She froze on the bottom step to stare at me, maybe having thought she and Xanthe were free of both Hiroko and me. I pulled my attention back to Addison, who was genuinely annoyed with me and trying valiantly not to be. *Frustrated pity you miss things when you're stressed meant to be best friends though.* He was still talking. 'I don't know what you guys talk about but she said to me you just weren't around to hear her. You weren't *here*,' he added irritably, tapping my forehead with a finger to emphasise his point, but with a hiss he pulled his hand away and touched his own temple in surprise. 'What is that? Static?'

'No, I don't...' I was making a mess. I should walk away. His thoughts were filling my head, his negativity fuelling mine, other disjointed voices from inside the dining room starting to seep in through some impossible holes in my shielding. *Uncertainty she just shocked me what is that some kind of magic spell I guess – peas again I hate peas maybe I – meant to be funny? Laugh anyway – Aristea? Can you hear me?*

Aristea? Renatus's voice, quite unlike that last unfamiliar one to address me. *What is it?*

Something's wrong, I told him wildly as I stepped quickly away from Addison.

'I have to go,' I claimed, starting for the staircase, surprised when Sterling hopped down into my path and smiled at me. Sterling *never* smiled at me.

Can you hear me now?

I stopped and had to blink. Was it me, or was that a flash

241

of green reflected in her eyes? *Sterling?*

And a welling of unthinkable bitterness and resentment rose from her, almost choking me in its intensity.

'Yeah, fine,' Addison snapped, misinterpreting my halt and following me. *Frustration now I get it she must have gotten this all the time.* 'Walk away.' *It's like dealing with a different person when she's like this no wonder Hiroko left.* 'It's not like we're friends or anything.'

My restraint, I think, came loose at the mention of her name, and everything behind it – my anger, his, Sterling's, the sensory overload that had been building up – rushed through me all at once. His hand landed on my shoulder and I turned tightly with my swing without even thinking. Like a stone on a string, my fist lashed out, and two explosions of shock, his and mine, hit me harder than the pain of the collision.

Something else to regret.

The voices had gone silent, the ringing in my ears mysteriously gone, and I was left standing in the entrance hall slowly shaking out my fist, feeling just as stunned as Addison looked. He straightened, rubbing his jaw.

'You throw a good punch,' he said lightly, his every emotion tightly tucked away from me. His eyes met mine – his were cool, exactly as I deserved.

I didn't have the energy to work out how I was going to fix this.

'Thanks,' I answered instead, numbness filling me where the anger had so quickly dissipated. I looked around. Sterling had almost reached me but stood frozen, her attention drawn like a deer to headlights by Renatus, who'd appeared in the doorway. Looking every bit as disappointed as he should. I turned back to Addison and gave him full eye contact, the least of what I owed him. 'My brother taught me. Today's the day he died.'

chapter seventeen

'You need to get her under control.'

'I know. It's been a difficult couple of weeks for her.'

'That's an explanation, not an excuse. Have you considered how this looks? You're the headmaster of this institution. Aristea represents our whole council, not just you.'

'Our whole nation knows who she is by now. Of all the students to be acting out…'

'I *know*. So does she. She's sorry.'

'Sorry doesn't cut it forever. She's getting stronger, and you're getting lax. What if she'd lashed out with magic instead of her fist?'

'She wouldn't–'

'She wouldn't what? Hurt anyone?'

The heated, "private" conversation in Renatus's office rang clear in my head the next morning after a much-needed sleep. The door was shut and soundproof and I wasn't technically present, halfway across the house in my own room, but Lord Gawain and Lady Miranda maybe weren't aware that mine and Renatus's bond now allowed us to listen through each other's ears. I felt so much more alert and awake today and it was shocking to think of how I'd behaved yesterday. There'd been no repeat of the weird telepathy, and my turbulent anger, along with my powers, felt more under my control.

'I've issued her with detention,' I heard Renatus tell his superiors. 'Fionnuala's given her a list of chores. Polishing antiques, I think.'

'Perhaps there's something gentler I can give her to do?' Fionnuala had asked anxiously when she'd hesitantly handed over the bucket of cleaning supplies I now had propped against the door. I'd gotten the distinct impression she expected me to stuff this up. Renatus had shrugged.

'She wasn't gentle when she punched another student in the face.'

He was livid, rightfully so. I felt no resentment, totally onboard with any measure that reduced my likelihood of interaction with Addison or the Prescotts. Even the thought of crossing paths with them and having to say or do something to bridge the inevitable awkwardness made me feel unwell with shame and put more effort behind my arm as I rubbed wax into the old grain of the little side table. Hopefully the list would take days.

'This house isn't lacking in those,' Lord Gawain agreed tiredly with Renatus, ending the conversation. 'Should keep her out of trouble for a while.'

Like anything in this house *wasn't* antique, come on. I wondered what made things qualify for the list as I finished with the table and got to my feet, tossing the polishing cloth into the bucket from six metres away. Score. I tugged the gloves off and idly plucked a fist-sized ruby from the dressing table as I consulted the list it was pinning down. Of everything in here, the stone felt the most like mine, Renatus having handed it to me and having said the words *it's yours*. Maybe it was an effect of having seen Angela and our house from a distance yesterday, or just the passing of the morbid anniversary, but today especially this room did not feel like mine. It did not feel like home. I missed my sunlit little bedroom at Ange's, the seashells on my white-washed bookshelves with my tatty childhood books. I didn't have a single seashell here.

Oversized and fit for a princess, all the carved timber furniture in here was designed to match, coloured with the same stain and wrought from the same kind of wood. Everything beautiful, everything ornate. Nothing much had been touched since the heiress died, and had been kept dust-free and pristine by Fionnuala and her staff. I'd come to terms with sleeping in here, mainly because it beat the room Hiroko had vacated, but there was an undeniable creep factor to the dead girl's room. So many secrets, so much buried in the layers of memory.

And so many antiques. I pocketed the ruby and got to work moving the first of many perfume bottles, lipsticks, glass trinket bowls and jewellery boxes from the dresser.

A spritz of perfume… particles landing on a bare neck… Three teenaged girls… two dark, one fair… Laughter, forced… Jealousy…

When I wasn't deliriously tired, I was getting better at handling these unexpected insights into the past, because I managed to not drop the beautiful glass bottle on the floor. Carefully I put it right back where I'd found it. Creepy antiques one, Aristea zero.

I felt Renatus before I saw him.

'I wish you'd said something.'

I shrugged and fitted the gloves back on, berating myself for my stupidity in taking them off. I'd been glad for the distraction from my problems but hadn't counted on reminders of my other ones. And this room promised countless reminders. Ana Morrissey's death had messed up her brother for life. *Everything* in here, minus my yesterday's clothes on the floor, had been hers and had the potential to carry intense energetic leftovers from the intense girl's final years. Now memories of Ana with the Shanahan girls, Caitlin and Keely, were finding me.

'Not really something I wanted to talk about,' I pointed out as I went back to shifting all the trinkets from the dresser to the bed, safely gloved. I looked back at him over my shoulder, pretending not to notice the haunted look in his eyes as he surveyed the room from the doorway. 'You couldn't have known; I don't have a disturbing telltale ritual to mark the anniversary.'

'Charming and tactful, as always.' But Renatus relaxed slightly at my jibe about finding him in here last month drowning in misery, lightly kicking my bucket of supplies aside so he could stand in its place and lean against the door.

'Normally I'd visit their gravesite with Angela,' I admitted, dumping more perfume bottles and things on the bed. 'You were right. I should have been less of an arse about it. I should have gone and seen her.' Instead I'd been selfish, afraid to face Angela because I didn't want to have to explain my scar and my tattoo, forgetting that *she* might have really loved to see *me*, tattooed and scarred or otherwise. Just to be with me on the anniversary of the day we lost everyone else. I cleared my throat. 'Well, it's her birthday in a couple of days. Maybe I'll see her for that, if I'm finished with this furniture.'

I overheard Renatus's musing about what terrible timing the deaths in my family had come at, right between our birthdays, a permanent black mark on the family calendar, but I couldn't feel that it was worse than the day Lisandro and chosen to exact the same fate on the Morrisseys: Ana Morrissey's twentieth birthday.

What a miserable pair we made.

'I'll take you,' he promised. 'Antiques done or not – which they won't be,' he advised, leaning forward to view the list I'd left on the dresser. I passed it to him on my way back to get another handful of jewel boxes. 'I need you to take a break after this one anyway.'

'A break?' I repeated, noting his old-style jacket with its high collar. He had a unique sense of fashion at the best of times, but honestly so did I, and I had come to associate some more distinct items of his wardrobe with more formal or social settings. This jacket was one of his impressing-people items. 'I just started. Where are we going?' I paused. 'Am I *allowed* to go?'

'You've got detention; you're not grounded,' he clarified, ever the one to pick holes, 'and antiques aren't going anywhere, so I don't care how long it takes you to get through this list. We're going to Shanahan's.'

'Is that safe?' I asked, dusting the emptied surface. We'd spent the last week compiling names from the Archives in the hope of matching them with Thomas Shanahan's clients so we could prove he was providing Lisandro with manpower, now Renatus was going to spend the day schmoozing and cultivating that friendship?

'Why would he suspect my motives?' my master countered. 'I'm a relative. He knows I'm White Elm and I'll occasionally come looking for information I can't get anywhere else. Valero hasn't cut us loose yet but the only contact they're accepting from us right now are visits to Glen.'

'And why do we want to talk to Valero?'

'We don't. We want to know what happened to you yesterday.' He stooped to hand me the bucket when I came over. 'Everyone knows who you are now. Someone singled out your sister, now your mind has come under attack. Some*one* did that. Speaking selfishly, if your mind is compromised by another attempt, *my* mind is compromised.'

And if his was broken into, what could that mean for the White Elm? Speaking selfishly, I cared more for him than his council. I oiled the cloth and got to work rubbing it into the beautiful wood of the dresser.

'And Shanahan might know who?' I asked uneasily. Did we want to deal with a man so dangerous? Unconvicted and uncharged he might be, evidence against him was piling up in the Archives. With discomfort, I thought of what I knew of his daughter Keely Shanahan – the woman I was fairly certain Renatus's cousin Keely Shanahan had become. Once Ana Morrissey's confidant, an admirable rebel resisting a restrictive society, I recalled her chasing me through a forest at night, my heart in my throat as her violent spells blasted trees apart whenever she missed me by a hairsbreadth. I recalled her looking glorious at Teagan's engagement party, Lisandro's date with a dress of butterflies. Lisandro's *wife*, masked to hide her face. This was not a family Renatus and I needed in our social circle.

'If anyone's paying for that information, he'll have heard about it,' Renatus assured me. 'My uncle does not miss a penny, even if it's not his.'

'You could ask Declan,' I suggested, though I wasn't sure how I felt about Renatus's roguish frenemy after my interaction with him at the Raymond house. Renatus snorted.

'I could *pay* Declan. We've got an appointment with Shanahan, and he deals in more than rumours and traded secrets. And Lord Gawain says that until a suspect is charged, he's a potential informant. Keep your enemies close, and all that.' Renatus shrugged, squashing an uncomfortable thought. I pretended not to overhear – we both knew the council leader loved Renatus, but I had to wonder whether the old Seer knew what Susannah had told me. Right at his side, Lord Gawain had the best chance of controlling him if he ever flew off the rails. 'I'll be fine. I'm told Teagan has invited you to tea.'

Stomach sinking, I knelt beside the dressing table and got into the side panelling. 'I find myself suddenly and unyieldingly busy.'

'Downstairs in twenty?'

'I shouldn't be going.' I slowed in my work, ashamed again. 'I shouldn't be getting a break. I hurt one of the nicest people I know and he's probably never going to speak to me again. I don't want you to be lenient.'

Renatus pushed forward off the door to press Fionnuala's chores list to the mirror, where it stuck without adhesive. Show off.

'I think you sell Mr James short if you believe he won't speak to you again,' he answered. 'It's not really a break. It's work, and you're welcome to carry on with this when you get back. Downstairs in twenty. Teagan's post script was quite insistent.'

He left the room. 'Quite insistent'. I wondered what heights of brattiness the youngest Shanahan had mastered to be able to manipulate Renatus into taking me off the estate an hour after issuing me detention with nothing more than a *post script* on her dad's correspondence. I was clearly an amateur.

I finished with the dresser and tossed the gloves into the bucket on my way out.

He probably won't say anything helpful with me around, I reminded Renatus in a last-ditch attempt to be let off the hook. His sexist contacts had made clear their understanding of me as some kind of consort or daughterly dependent.

You won't be around, my master replied. *I detect a strong chance of teacups in your future.*

I paused at the stairs, looking down at myself for a moment of reflection. Teacups. Lacy day dresses. Little sandwiches out on the balcony. Mindless gossip. *Not* my scene, especially in worn jeans and biker boots and my hair loose like it always was. I'd worried for days about fitting in at her ostentatious engagement party, and now I waited for the inevitable self-consciousness at the thought of their judgement, but it didn't come.

Well, really, what did I have to lose? I continued down the staircase, tossing my unbrushed hair over my shoulder and feeling surprisingly free about it. I couldn't find it in myself to *care* what spoiled Teagan and her dick of a dad thought of me. Thomas Shanahan was the prime suspect in a White Elm investigation into what could be described at best as obstruction of justice, at worst human trafficking. His opinion meant *zilch*. Teagan said in her letter she wanted to be friends, and while I was notably low on those at present, I had zero investment in conscripting her to those ranks. If she didn't like me in my natural state, her loss.

Besides, I wasn't going there to make friends. Teagan was the closest thing I had to an insider on Nastassja. Perhaps there was something I could learn about her from Lisandro's unknowing sister-in-law.

Renatus met me at the gate, and had it open for me when I reached it. He was squinting at the blue sky over the estate, feeling the shapes of the magic threaded and woven over it like a big upside-down energetic basket.

'Someone's had another try at unravelling the ward work,' he commented as I stepped through and he locked the gate behind me. He kept a hand on the wrought iron of the gate for a very long moment, channelling magic into it, manipulating. Even where I stood beside him, I could feel the pressure change exerted by the pulling and twisting of the fabric of the world over us. I shifted my focus to see the shimmer of the strands of the spells arching over the house and the grounds, to watch as they were tightened, pulled closer together.

Just, you know, casually.

'You still think someone's taking advantage of the time you're spending away from the house?' I asked when he finished the quick patch and started away from the fence line. He raised an uncertain hand in a sort of shrug.

'It seems that way. Like... someone's digging a fingernail into the little natural cracks of it and trying to spread them enough to get a finger or hand through.' He looked back at the gate suspiciously. 'It doesn't look like they've gotten that far yet.'

His lack of panic over the idea that someone was slowly trying to break into his sacred fortress made me laugh in disbelief. 'Have you considered... just staying home? So they can't?'

He ignored me, Displacing us both across the countryside. The truth was he'd go crazy if he felt he couldn't leave the estate.

Our destination was surprising. I turned suddenly at the sound of a fast-approaching car, but a perfectly pruned hedge separated this little courtyard from the road, which couldn't be more than a few paces behind me. I spun to take it all in. Renatus had brought us to a small hedged garden in the front yard of a huge Edwardian townhouse in the middle of some city. Time of day, climate and instinct said we hadn't gone far. The building's façade was very pretty, white-trimmed windows set into red brick, and the boutique-style sign above the front patio arch swung gently in the morning breeze. *Vacancy.*

'*This* is where they live?' I demanded. Renatus headed for the front steps and I followed, feeling unsettled. This was not what I pictured, vastly different from Sean Raymond's misty mansion where I'd met the Shanahans previously. 'In a hotel?'

'One of their hotels, yes. Uncle Thomas owns a small chain, but this is where he conducts the sort of business we're here for.' He waited for me atop the stairs, one hand on the classic front door's handle. 'The Displacement point in the garden has been made by hundreds, maybe thousands, of past arrivals and departures from that exact spot. That kind of gravity makes it a safer bet than any other location in Belfast – as you know, unless you're Elijah, Displacement isn't hard to get drastically wrong, so people appreciate an accurate option.'

I looked back at it as he pushed the door open. The courtyard was now out of sight thanks to some clever planting choices in the bordering garden, and the hedge blocked it from the road, too, making it ideal for receiving teleporting visitors straight into the middle of the city.

So... he just lets people use his garden? Like a public transport station?

One of many services, he would say, Renatus answered, leading me into the hotel's foyer, an over-the-top entrance hall lovingly updated and restored to balance its period beauty with its modern functionality. Electricity, the mandatory fire escape signs over the doors and a front counter complete with EFTPOS facilities settled somehow comfortably amidst a sweeping gallery staircase and plush armchairs arranged as a waiting area beside the window. It was like a brighter, smaller version of Renatus's place ran headlong into present day and this was the result.

Man of the people, I noted wryly, pushing out with my senses to get my bearings. A few non-magical guests staying on the first floor above me, surprisingly. Or maybe not so surprisingly. I'd never considered it before, but it was doubtless much easier to keep bad-guy business and the kind of money these people dealt with clean and unquestioned when you were running an honest enterprise. Like mobsters with their Italian restaurants. On the top two floors I detected a mess of magic – wards, traps, ongoing spells, some energy signatures I wasn't familiar with – too dense for my senses to penetrate, and I withdrew my attention, equal parts wary and intrigued. The nest. Renatus and I had been trawling through mountains of data looking for matches with Shanahan clients.

What was the bet that some kind of ledger or master list existed and was literally hanging over my head right now?

Doubtful. Who'd be silly enough to record that kind of wrongdoing?

Renatus cleared his throat, a reminder not to wonder, and I rolled my shoulders, fortifying my wards. He had nothing to worry about. After yesterday, after this morning's lapse with Ana's things, nothing was getting through to me.

'Right on time,' a man's voice commented from the doorway behind the counter. The speaker was overweight and well-dressed with fair hair that was going grey at the temples, but I didn't recognise his face at first. Green eyes, full lips... imagine the elaborate gold mask he'd worn at the party over the top of all his other features and...

'Mr Shanahan,' I realised as he entered the lobby with a clipboard and pen, filling in a form just like any normal business owner. No playful, reckless magic on show. No outrageous outfit to match his outrageous daughter's. I hadn't been prepared for such normality.

'Miss Byrne, such a pleasure to see you again.' He smiled his girls' smile at me as he switched the pen to his other hand to offer me a free hand. To shake. He didn't try to kiss my hand in this setting. I remembered being furious with Renatus for shaking hands with Lisandro at the party, for playing along in the game of fakeness, and tried not to dwell on my own slipping integrity as I smiled back. 'Teagan will be delighted you're here. Thank you for changing your plans to accommodate her eagerness.'

His eyes lingered on my scar, and I felt the quick sequence of emotions that passed through him. Curiosity, pity, then admiration. He thought I was brave for wearing the scar and making no attempt to disguise it. Extra points for me, I supposed.

'I... really didn't have any better plans,' I said. Thomas Shanahan released my hand and waited, still smiling, and I detected that though the setting had changed, the game had not. It was still my turn to offer pleasantries. 'Thank you for inviting me to your home. I was happy to rearrange my

252

schedule, Mr Shanahan.'

Yeah, of polishing furniture. The man beamed, so I knew I'd passed game level one.

'Please. You're family now. Call me Uncle Thomas.' Fat chance, but I smiled and nodded. 'Come along upstairs,' he urged us, leading us through the door behind the front desk to a small office that must have once been a service space even before this building was repurposed. A beautifully restored servants bell indicator box remained in pride of place on the wall above a work counter, clearly original to the house, and the wooden staircase in the corner was decidedly less grand than the one in the foyer, purely for servicing the upper floors. The room lent itself well to Shanahan's new use for it, storing ring binders neatly on the countertop and hanging jackets and umbrellas on the coat rack. 'Teagan could hardly contain herself when you confirmed you'd be bringing Aristea. She's making tea.'

Don't start, I warned Renatus when I felt the stirrings of amusement in him. He followed the hotel owner up the stairs but I paused, eyeing the handrail. A century of potential impressions. I should have worn gloves.

But we were here for information, so I bit the bullet and lowered my palm experimentally onto the smooth worn wood. Nothing. Yet. I started up after him.

'You said you had some business to discuss, Renatus?' the older sorcerer mentioned idly as we trekked upward. The stairs were narrow and steep, built to be discreet in the townhouse's design, and Shanahan was a tight fit, but he didn't pant or slow for breaks. He must do this a few times every day.

'More that I'm looking for someone and don't know who else to ask,' Renatus admitted, mindfully positioning his uncle as expert. The older man smiled back at him smugly, and I detected his sly pleasure at being thought of in such a way.

'The White Elm doesn't have its own resources to draw on in this area?' he asked, faux innocently. Digging for information.

There's some give and take in any relationship, Renatus

253

reminded me, and said aloud, 'We lost one of our chief Telepaths at Prague, and I'm afraid the fallout's got us considerably short-staffed.'

'I see.' Shanahan took us up another flight and smiled again. 'We'll get the girls settled in the parlour and you and I can discuss further in my library.'

Not all sorcerers were recluses in old country manors, apparently, but the inner-city life hadn't impacted on Thomas Shanahan the second's opinion on the place of girls and women in their world. Increasingly I was feeling a profound connection with his runaway daughter Keely. I couldn't approve of her choice in husband, but I also couldn't blame her for wanting out of this life.

I bit my tongue to keep my irritation to myself, a mature decision I felt, and stayed silent to the top floor. It was immediately apparent that this was a witch family's home. Dense magic lapped against the walls of my wards, the air full of it. Years, maybe generations, of rampant and carefree magic use had left layer upon layer of energy, some of it still live. The lobby, it seemed, had been 'cleaned up', probably to prevent the sort of eerie feelings intense magic generated in non-witches, but up here, based on what I'd been told about magic breeding more magic, the Shanahans were probably thriving on it.

Visually, the top floor was similar to the lobby. The furnishings and wall hangings indicated the same era of décor. Thomas Shanahan, chief suspect in our investigation, led us along a high-ceilinged line of closed doors, reminiscent of Renatus's except brighter with its white walls and a larger, windowed sitting room space at each end reflecting light down the hallway. But the house was much bigger than what I could see right now. I stretched out my senses but again could detect nothing of the physical space I was in. Sneaky spells at work. I imagined it reduced the chances of robbery.

I also imagined Shanahan – underworld king of disappearing people and cleaning up impossible messes – had a lot to protect, hidden somewhere in this house.

He stopped at one door indistinguishable from the others and knocked politely.

'You're all she's talked about since her party,' he intimated to me with an indulgent smile that, coupled with the feelings I got from him, seemed genuine. Teagan was his baby, that much was painfully obvious and, in his mind, I was essentially Renatus's. A dependent, a kid. A little doll.

Exactly as I'd let them think at the party.

Exactly what I hated them to think.

But a glance from Renatus kept me smiling, however falsely. There were advantages to being underestimated, he'd suggested, advantages he'd never been able to tap into as the White Elm's resident badass and the heir to a powerful line of sorcerers. Everyone expected him to be unbelievable. No one knew what to expect or believe of me. They'd never see me coming.

The door flew open, and I was greeted with a squeal and a flurry of yellow blonde hair as Teagan Shanahan threw herself at me in a tight hug.

'*You're here!*' She withdrew long enough to look me in the face, and I blinked, trying to get my bearings amidst the intensity of her emotional reaction to seeing me. Excitement, delight, curiosity, disappointment, hope, jealousy, desire, joy, all in the one person – whoa. Even before I'd really gotten a look at her she was hugging me again. 'I wasn't sure you'd gotten my letter. I've been so looking forward to seeing you again.'

I didn't know what to say. Renatus's amusement was a huge irritant at the edge of my awareness.

'Look after our guest, Teagan darling,' Shanahan said warmly, and his daughter released me to beam at her father. 'Renatus and I will be in my parlour. No interruptions please.'

'Of course, Daddy.' Impulsively and possessively Teagan grabbed my hand tightly. 'We'll be fine. Thank you, cousin, for bringing her.'

Yes, thank you, I added with an ironic smile. Thanks for bringing along your pet to share in all the cuddles and cooing.

'Not a problem,' my master answered smoothly. I could have kicked him. He looked meaningfully at me. 'It's only a short visit. This won't take long.'

Teagan stuck out her bottom lip theatrically. 'Fine. We'll make the most of it.' The last I saw of the hallway was the sparkle of entertainment in Renatus's eyes before the door was closed between us.

Teagan released me instantly and stalked away to get some distance between us before she turned back to face me.

'Thank goodness they're gone, stuffy boys.' She huffed excitedly, clenching her hands in front of her like she could barely contain herself, and judging from what I felt from her, that was perfectly true. 'Off to talk about boring stuff, no doubt. I've been waiting and waiting to meet you properly. Daddy said you were probably busy, but,' she shrugged, smiling cutely, a little deviously, 'I usually get what I want. And here you are! Gosh, your *face*.' She leaned closer when she noticed my scar, wonderstruck with curiosity. I couldn't help leaning instinctively away, repulsed by the unwanted attention. She seemed to get the hint. 'You're still very pretty, of course, though I didn't know what to expect you to look like, having only seen you in your mask. I heard all about Prague. Everyone says you're such a hero. I can't wait to tell them you were here. I bet none of them have seen a girl with a scar like yours.'

I brushed my hair behind my ear, still with no idea what to say. Shanahan's daughter was a mile-a-minute, a whirlwind of energy totally lacking the bait-and-switch intermittent tact of her father and his peers. I'd thought, after a few hours watching them, that I'd learned the ins and outs of their game, but dealing with Teagan would take a completely different skillset I wasn't sure I'd ever master.

She was still talking. 'I hope you like tea. Chai and ginger.' She gestured behind her at a steaming china tea set on a table beside the window. 'I made it myself, from a blend one of Daddy's clients gave me from his travels to India. Doesn't it smell incredible?' She turned back to me with her overexcited smile, but it faltered a little when I didn't react properly. 'Aren't you going to say anything?'

I blinked, incredulous. 'Am *I* going to say anything?' I repeated. The girl had barely stopped for a breath until right now. Her big green eyes widened uncertainly when I noted, 'I don't think I need to.'

Her truly adorable face scrunched in a pouty frown of concern. 'Don't you remember me?'

I almost choked on an unexpected laugh. 'Oh, definitely. You're exactly as I recall.' Talkative, self-absorbed, and with that distinctive curved mouth she shared with her sisters and with both Morrissey siblings.

Her worried expression and her spiralling nervousness suddenly relaxed.

'You're overwhelmed,' she realised calmly. I nodded, willing to accept that oversimplification. I took the brief gap in "conversation" to look around the room I'd come to. Décor in the same era as the rest of the place, but prettier. Distinctly feminised. A vase of white flowers and a lace table cloth across the dainty little table, needlework cushions on the high-backed chairs, gorgeous chaise lounge, white writing desk with more flowers. High ceiling, lace curtains, tall French doors leading out onto the balcony I'd seen in the vision I'd tapped from her letter. 'Do you like my parlour? It's pretty, isn't it? My Daddy gave it to me so I could receive my own guests like he does, but I haven't had anyone to receive before, except, you know, people I already knew.'

She shook her head and smiled, looking down. I stared at her, even more acutely aware of her *youngness* than I was at her engagement party. I looked at her left hand and saw her massive ring. I wasn't even sure if she was sixteen.

'It's... very pretty,' I said finally, and her face lit up at my meagre praise.

'Thank you,' she said graciously, and apparently because I'd now passed the threshold of saying more than twelve words to her, we were best friends and boundaries had dissolved because next she said, 'I'm glad you're my first guest, though you're not what I expected. Are those boy shoes?'

We couldn't have been from more different universes.

'You… haven't seen girls in boots before?' I asked slowly, feeling awkward. I glanced at the bright light streaming through the French doors and considered what the balcony must look down upon. 'You live in Belfast. It rains two hundred days of the year.'

Teagan smiled and nodded vacantly, giving me the distinct impression that she couldn't see the connection, and folded her soft, pale hands demurely in front of her. Her dainty satin sandals had clearly never seen a city street. I looked around the room again, starting to get a yucky feeling.

'They're comfortable,' I offered. 'Good for running down bad guys with Renatus.'

'Wow. And you do that?' Teagan visibly shivered, impressed.

'Not often.'

My short answer left the conversation hanging, and Teagan smiled uncertainly in the silence before regaining her puppy-like composure.

'Tea?' She led me to the table and started fussing over the teapot as I came slowly over to join her. 'Brigid was here last Tuesday and I told her I'd written you. She didn't think you'd come. Now I can–'

'*How* is that your view?' I demanded, looking over the table through the glass of the doors. The lacy curtains obscured only slightly the rolling green acreage, which didn't go away when I yanked the curtains aside. 'That is not where we are.'

'The proper view is quite awful,' Teagan explained as she poured. 'Rooves, gutters, alleys. Daddy fixed it.'

Fixed it. Because an eyesore of a view was just another broken toy, easily mended with over-the-top magic. I sat down. What I'd seen at Sean Raymond's mansion, what I had grown accustomed to at Morrissey House, that was just the tip of the iceberg with magic, it seemed.

'I'm so glad you're finally here,' Teagan gushed again,

beaming at me. I forced a return smile that I hoped was more convincing than it felt. 'I put on my new dress for you to see. What do you think?' She spun at the hips to make the skirt of the soft chiffon party dress swirl. While not as over-the-top as her engagement dress – nothing I'd seen outside of a Disney movie could match that – it was still several rungs higher on the formality meter than anything I owned, bar what I'd inherited from Ana.

'It's beautiful,' I said honestly, prompting a welling of delight and pride from inside Teagan.

'Thank you. I knew when I met you that we were going to become friends. I mean,' she said, thinking aloud, 'Renatus doesn't have any other family – you must have been glad to meet us, too.'

Vapid, pointless girl. 'I have my own family,' I said shortly before I could stop myself, immensely annoyed by her presumption that I was so eager to be part of her social circle. Teagan nodded quickly.

'Of course. You're Cassán Ó Gráidaigh's granddaughter. What?' she asked when I started abruptly, taken by surprise. She shrugged delicately and swept her skirt gracefully aside so she could sit. 'I hear things.'

'What things?' I pressed, wondering what Shanahan and his colleagues were careless enough to spill in front of a girl, thinking her too silly or distracted to absorb points of note.

'Boring things, mostly, while I do Daddy's books. But I want to talk about you. I want to know everything about you. I want us to be like sisters.'

'I don't need another sister.'

'But I do.'

I sat back slowly in my seat, dazed. This girl was *full on*. She watched me with bright, overeager eyes. I realised she was as fascinated with me as I was by her and her family's way of life. While pointless and weird, this tea party was her way of trying to connect with me and get to know me. Wasn't I here for the same reason? Didn't I have questions I hadn't yet thought to ask?

'Aye, alright,' I said finally, deciding to try and take some control of this ridiculous conversation. 'I'll tell you something about me if you tell me about your sister.'

'Caitlin?'

'No. Not Caitlin.'

Teagan's eyes widened and I felt her immediate discomfort.

'We don't... I'm not supposed to...' Flustered, she reached for her teacup. I mirrored her instinctively.

Man's hand taking a sip... nervousness... 'Has your father spoken to you about my visit?'... Teagan with hands folded in her lap... nervous smile...

I retracted my hand without comment on the awkward proposal I'd tapped into and cleared my throat.

'We don't really talk about her,' Teagan managed after her sip, calmer. I nodded.

'But you remember her, I suppose?' I prompted, letting her uncertainty roll off my wards. 'And Ana Morrissey?'

'My daddy doesn't like my second sister to be talked about much,' she insisted, a little panicky. She stared adamantly into her teacup, distressed. I let it go, rethinking my angle. Teagan was young but she was still a slave to this world of pomp and pretense.

'I didn't mean to pry,' I said finally. 'There's a lot about your world that's foreign to me.' I tilted my head toward the windows. 'Artificial balcony views, my grandfather's legacy... arranged marriages.'

All was immediately forgiven. Teagan laughed lightly and played with her ring.

'Daddy said Renatus has been turning down offers for you ever since you both appeared at my party. Robert Quinn's son?' She leaned conspiratorially across the table. 'Complete creep. You're lucky my cousin is so discerning.'

I smiled back at her. 'Not really. I'm lucky I live in a time and place that acknowledges my rights. That's about the extent to which I'm willing to label it *luck*.' She smiled in a way that said she had missed my point, and I took the breath of silence to properly look at her. 'You look like them. Your sisters.'

'*Them?*' she echoed, intrigued despite herself.

'Caitlin... and Keely,' I agreed, sitting forward again and chancing a second touch of my teacup. Nothing. As per usual, the impression had evaporated after the first contact, released back into the world after spending months or years trapped in the sticky web of emotion that bound them to physical objects. 'I saw them both in a vision this morning when I touched something of Ana Morrissey's. I want...' I considered the most persuasive way to word this. 'I want to know more about my new family.'

Teagan sipped her tea, conflicted but deeply curious.

'I remember Ana,' she said finally, choosing the safer topic. 'It's very sad, what happened.'

'Yes, it is. Can you tell me what you remember of her?'

'I wanted to be friends with her, but I was too young to be invited to play. Caitlin and Keely were friends with her. Keely especially. What did you see? In the vision?'

'Not much,' I admitted, strangely connected to the younger girl for a moment at her mention of being the uninvited little sister. I could relate. 'Just the three of them together, playing with Ana's perfumes and jewels and things in her bedroom.'

'Caitlin always said Ana Morrissey had beautiful things,' Teagan said enviously, and added conspiratorially, 'in her *bedroom*, and she could have them *whenever* she liked.'

I stared. 'Doesn't every girl keep their nice things in their bedrooms?'

'She also said Ana liked to practise spells whenever my sisters came over to play,' Teagan redirected in defence. She dropped her voice. 'Daddy doesn't like us messing with *that* kind of magic; you know, blood magic.'

'Blood magic – isn't that what you use?' I countered in challenge. She tilted her head in surprise; soft curls tumbled.

'Me? I don't do much magic, but there are scales to everything. Sacrifice magic, like when you kill something or someone, is a bit darker than nail clippings, no?'

'Why don't you do much magic?' I asked, shifting my focus to view her aura. Full, bold, similar in capacity to mine, but without the black sinkholes that characterised my energy field and with some weird silvery film around the edges I'd never seen before.

'Girls who do too much magic get into trouble. Like Ana.' She dropped her eyes to my cup and smiled again. 'How's your tea?'

'It's nice,' I said carelessly, thoughts trapped on the previous track. 'You think Ana–'

'Thank you, I made it myself,' Teagan said before I could ask my question, smiling proudly at her tea set. I frowned, incredulous.

'You mean you just poured it?'

'Oh, no,' she answered hurriedly. 'I prepared it all myself.'

I waited for the punchline, but there wasn't one. 'As opposed to…?'

'Daddy always has the hotel staff make his tea for his guests,' Teagan explained, and I nodded with a sarcastic 'Ahh…' of understanding. She seemed to miss it. 'I chose the set especially. It's my best set. Do you like it?'

'Aye, yeah, it's spectacular,' I said flatly. I did not have time for teapot discussions with a sheltered girl-child who thought making a pot of tea on her own was a real achievement. 'A fact about me: I'm impatient. We were talking about Ana Morrissey doing too much magic. What did you mean?'

'It's just what people say,' Teagan said, taken aback by my abruptness, tracing the porcelain rim of her teacup with a dainty fingertip. 'Girls shouldn't do too much magic.'

'*I'm* a girl,' I reminded her tediously. '*I* do my fair share of magic. How was Ana different?'

'I didn't know her well. I meant no offence. I'm sure she was lovely,' she added hurriedly, remembering her manners, 'just like you, and just like my dear cousin. I'm sure he misses her terribly.'

262

'He does.' I fidgeted with the delicate handle of the teacup, disappointment setting in. 'So you can't tell me much about either Ana or Keely?'

Teagan shrugged a little incredulously, the most attitude I'd seen from her since I arrived.

'Can't you just scry?'

'Scry…?' I was going to ask *scry what*, but it was suddenly obvious. I'd tapped into Ana's life by accident a thousand times just by touch, and though I'd never looked for her specifically, I'd proven myself even more capable of the craft using mediums like flame, or… Wow, Fate really knew what it was doing, huh? I slipped my hand into the pocket of my light jacket and withdrew the ruby I'd unknowingly brought with me. Teagan put her teacup down and leaned across the table to look curiously at the stone when I placed it in front of me.

'That's a nice rock,' she commented admiringly. 'I bet you could scry centuries back with that. Not literally, but you know what I mean.'

I flicked my gaze back up to her. 'I've never scried further than a few months except in dreams and impressions.'

'So?' Teagan laughed, a clear bell-like tinkle of a sound. 'You're practically a Morrissey, aren't you?' When I didn't respond, she quietened, scoffing lightly. 'Aren't you?'

'What's that meant to mean?'

'Oh, wow,' she said, truly surprised. 'There *is* a lot you don't know, isn't there?'

I had to bite my tongue to avoid snarling something incoherent and bitter at her, because her words immediately pissed me off but I didn't have anything specific or witty lined up. I really did *not* need the reminder of how much of a newbie I was to her world, and she was the last person I wanted to hear it from. I shouldn't have come along today. I should have known this was a bad idea.

'You know what?' I said irritably, patience running to its inevitable end, reaching out to snatch back my ruby. 'Whatever. I'm out of here.'

chapter eighteen

1962 – Morrissey Estate

You couldn't have asked for a more beautiful day. The bright sun shone in clear expansive skies and guests arrived to a surprisingly mild temperature for March, especially given that it was only snowing a week ago and the lush grounds were still spongy underfoot.

'Subtle, isn't she?' Mánus asked, mostly rhetorically. 'I'm sure she thinks she's being helpful.'

Beside him, face upturned to the first warm weather of the Irish calendar, soaking in the delight and good vibes of the other guests, Cassán opened an eye. He hadn't spoken, but his friend hadn't seemed to need him to since the events of that horrific night a year earlier, the night neither acknowledged.

'With any luck she'll overreach and get herself caught by the White Elm,' he replied lazily, not caring if it was apparent that this was a genuine wish, not just sarcasm. The charm of Moira Dawes had long worn off for him. Reckless, dramatic, increasingly daring, she was the little sister he was glad he'd never had. Pure trouble. Some consequences would not go amiss, he felt, sooner rather than later.

'Be careful what you wish for,' Mánus advised. 'You really want them questioning her? She's plenty likely to sell the rest of us out.'

Both men smiled and raised their glasses in greeting to the friendly waves of Seamus and Imogen Murphy as the aging couple crossed the sloped front lawn of the estate, heading for the main attraction past the little garden tables and the rest of the guests.

'Us, maybe. I don't think you've got much to worry about.'

Mánus snorted cynically. 'I'm surprised she didn't send a storm or something. Wash the whole thing out.'

'Ah, but the day's still young.'

Neither man harboured any real illusion that Moira would *ever* be caught by the wretched Elm. Since Cassán's invention of wards programmed to hide people, places and activity only from the White Elm, regardless of new initiates or changing council roles (the downside to previous attempts by other Crafters), none of his friends had much reason to fear the thirteen do-gooders. Nor did any of his wealthy clients, word of his much-coveted magical product spreading to all the right ears thanks to Mánus's network of connections.

Research and writing had never paid as well as helping criminals.

A burst of laughter drew their attention to the crowd that had gathered on Morrissey's lawn. Several of the younger consorts and wives, including Cassán's, had been sitting together at the edge of the party, a little separate from the mothers fussing over small children and the starstruck courting couples and the old people telling grand old tales. Apparently they'd been joined by Andrew Hawke, and from the wash of humour he felt from them, not to mention the number of gloved hands covering giggling mouths, he was on fire, in full entertaining form.

'Yes, I had to invite him,' Mánus said before Cassán could open his mouth to complain. He hadn't even finished that thought. 'Party like this, you think anyone doesn't know about it? I think everyone I've ever met is here.'

Cassán kept his gaze on the Scottish Seer and tried to keep himself open to the cheer and calm of the party, but he could feel his anger stirring, and magic building behind it. As an Empath, his emotions had always been more intense than those of others, his magic linked with how he felt. That's what he'd told himself when he'd noticed himself quickening to frustration and rage after... that night. But also since that night, his capacity for magic had exploded, and he was still exploring what his new limits were.

Best not to risk letting them out in public, a risk heightened by unstable emotions. Even if Hawke was leaning a little too close to Anthea as he told his polished jokes around the enthralled circle.

Mánus nudged him with his elbow, knocking Cassán from his dark pondering.

'I'm sure you already know she's not that impressed with him,' the younger Irish sorcerer pointed out, and Cassán tried again to swallow his irritation. Yes, he could feel his wife's polite interest in Hawke's story as she smiled with the other young women he'd seated her with, her big, dark eyes skimming the faces of her companions intermittently for cues of when to laugh, when to nod. Her English, though functional, was still slow, and her grasp of humour, irony and sarcasm were tenuous. Her disinterest wasn't what bothered him, however.

'If he tells her something about her future...'

Omnipotence had done nothing to improve Andrew Hawke's sense of morality, but his relationship with Fate had blurred. Cassán and the others no longer knew where the Seer stood on that front. At first, in the weeks after the ritual, Hawke had been panicky, disorientated, unable to feel his connection to Fate as he had before. He was no longer part of its web, after all; none of them were its puppets any longer. When he'd "found" it again, he'd been vague on what this meant, but it was clear from the occasional thing he said, especially to other people who still were part of Fate's plan, that he was very capable of viewing the futures. And sharing them.

'So don't give him the chance,' Mánus pointed out as Cassán irritably downed the last of his drink. 'Get her out of there. Come on,' he prompted patiently, taking Cassán's glass and starting across the lawn. 'I'll introduce her to Áine.'

Mumbling his thanks for the other's sensible thinking,

Cassán followed through the beautifully, warmly dressed crowd to the little group of young women and Hawke. Up closer, as the women around her laughed with increasing intensity at Hawke's escalating joke and wiped tears of mirth from their eyes with soft gloves, Thea's uncertainty in this situation hit Cassán harder, and his guilt pushed him past Mánus to reach her first. He laid a gentle hand on her shoulder and she turned, startled. As soon as she saw him, her eyes softened in relief, and he felt her immediate relaxation. He felt bad for having left her here with these strangers, where she'd been trying her best to keep up and understand.

'Cassán,' she said with a quick, hopeful smile, saying nothing else because part of his appeal, he was sure, was that he could read her complex emotions without her needing to articulate them. He'd been inattentive today, he knew; he could feel now that her discomfort when she'd first arrived had not abated as he'd hoped. This was not her crowd – nor was it his, truth be told – and she felt like an outsider. He took her hand affectionately, hoping to convey his support and understanding without words. He would try to be better for the rest of the afternoon.

'Mrs Ó Gráidaigh,' Mánus leaned past them both to put the two glasses down on the nearest tabletop, 'I apologise for keeping your husband from you. I hope you are enjoying the party.'

Thea blushed a little to be addressed directly, especially by the clearly powerful host she'd only met for the first time today and easily the handsomest man here, her hand tightening on Cassán's almost imperceptibly. She needed a moment to process his words, and he patiently waited her out.

'Uh, thank you, yes. I am enjoying the party,' she said finally with a shy smile. Lies told to yourself don't register with magic. She clutched her purse nervously like a shield before her chest.

'Let's go for a walk,' Cassán suggested, tugging her away, noting her mild flinch when the tight circle of giggling young wives burst into another fit of laughter around her.

'Cassán,' Hawke called, interrupting his own joke to make sure he caught the other before he moved too far away. Trying to keep his irritation to himself – this was a party, after all – Cassán looked back. The Seer was smiling easily, arm looped around a pretty heiress with thick, lush red hair, a hungry expression in her shapely eyes as she gazed at him, and an engagement ring sparkling on her finger. 'It's lovely to finally meet your wife. Where are you taking her? We're just getting to the best bit.'

Naturally. There was the painful chorus of agreement from his captive audience and Cassán smiled tightly. He felt his opinion of Hawke spread into his aura, beginning to affect the emotional atmosphere around him before he could rein it in, and he saw the enthralled expressions on the women's faces start to falter. This was always something he could do, but using it against people was a distasteful behaviour he associated with spoilt Moira, and he was somewhat dismayed to notice it happening increasingly without his intention.

Mánus, usually so together, suddenly took notice of the young woman hanging off Andrew, and Cassán registered his shock. '*Helen?*'

The group quietened further, sharing querying glances, and Mánus stepped closer to get a better look at the woman. She realised he was addressing her, and turned her face to look at him instead, surprised. His expression immediately shut down, realising his mistake.

'My apologies. You look… like someone…'

'Someone we knew in the States,' Cassán finished for him, working to shift the atmosphere from irritable to calm and to influence his friend with that same calm, not knowing what had just happened. The heiress was clearly not the woman they'd let die in their arms last year, burnt out and gasping for air. Hawke was watching Morrissey sharply. Cassán, eager to end this exchange, pushed Mánus away and followed with Thea. 'Sorry. We'll be back soon.'

Hawke tried to insist they stay and hear out his joke, to no avail, and Cassán ignored the depleted laughter behind him as the Seer dove back into his stupid story. Anthea shook off an involuntary shudder as she crossed the sloped sloshy lawn with the two men. Mánus glanced sidelong at her, physically shrugging off whatever ghosts had clutched him momentarily back there.

'Your wife has excellent instincts, my friend.'

Cassán could guess that the scrier's intuition was read directly from her thoughts, and that those thoughts were connected to the feeling of discomfort still radiating from her, which he knew he hadn't helped.

'I don't like Hawke either,' he told her, squeezing her hand as they walked. 'Did he... tell you anything?'

Thea looked confused by the admission. 'He told me he is your friend.'

'He says a lot of things.'

'Have you met my wife?' Mánus asked smoothly, redirecting, knowing full well that Anthea and Áine had not yet been introduced. When the young Greek witch shook her head, he elaborated, 'Would you like to see the baby?'

She visibly brightened and released Cassán's hand to fall into step with the host. 'Yes, the baby. Please.'

Mánus, for all his broodiness and dislike of attention, was well-accustomed to playing the role at the centre of it, and engaged Thea in conversation as they walked toward the main cluster of people. Cassán fell back a little, glad that she was feeling secure and had someone to talk to other than just him. This was so different from her life with him, her mostly absent writer husband in their modest little cottage up north, and even further removed from the remote, want-for-nothing little island home in the Mediterranean he'd whisked her from. He knew she felt out of place; he could see even as she got ready this morning that she wasn't confident that her dress was fancy enough, or that her hair was done in the appropriate style. But, he'd reasoned, Mánus Morrissey, for all his wealth and reputation, was not the pompous sort, and his baby son's christening was the least terrifying social event he could think of to bring Anthea to. Plus, Mánus had insisted.

'Cassán has told me,' she was saying, still shyly, 'that you are the friend who told him... he should marry me.'

She blushed furiously as both friends laughed in surprise. It felt good to laugh, Cassán reflected, and his wife was often funny, intentionally and otherwise.

'He needed a kick in the right direction,' Mánus confirmed. He glanced back at the fairer sorcerer. 'Sometimes he thinks he needs permission to go after what he knows is good for him. A character flaw I hope you don't pass onto your heirs.'

Cassán rolled his eyes and was saved from having to generate a witty response by their arrival at the hushed cluster of garden chairs, cakes and flowers that marked the site of most significance – the baby and its mother, seated primly with her lace-gowned son in her arms and surrounded by guests admiring the blinking infant. Nothing attracts a crowd quite like a new baby, and if you add more babies into the equation, the crowd just seems to intensify, though it might have been an illusion caused by the fancy baby carriages taking up all the space. Several other new mothers were sitting with Áine, cooing over each other's little ones while the bigger ones toddled or crawled around on blankets on the grass. Kathleen Franklin was there with her toddler, a blonde pig-tailed miniature version of herself. She looked away when Cassán made eye contact; he shared a knowing look with Mánus.

'Cass!' Moira Dawes was among the women sitting closest to Áine, dressed to the nines in the trendiest mod fashion in direct contrast to the very traditional, very demure attire of the other guests. She stood now, striking and bright dress catching the attention of anyone who hadn't yet noticed her, as she intended. She rushed over and made a show of embracing him and kissing both his cheeks, and he reluctantly hugged her back. She pulled away and beamed at him. She no longer looked like the baby of the coven, no longer the rebellious college girl who'd brought them together in the first place, but had grown into a woman exactly as beautiful as she thought. She'd cut her hair into a sleek pixie bob that looked even shorter than Cassán's fair hair, but controversy was Moira's best friend. 'I'm so glad you're here. And this,' she turned spiritedly to Thea, grasping both of his wife's hands in hers, 'must be your wife. Anthea. I'm *so* pleased to *finally* meet you. Cassán has kept you all to himself. Aren't you going to introduce us?' she added back to him with a sweet smile. He smiled back, a sarcastic mirror.

'It looks like you're doing just fine,' he sang back, but it was less work with her just to play along. 'Thea, darling, this is Moira Dawes, a colleague.'

'Oh, no, more than a colleague,' Moira insisted, swinging Thea's hands. 'A friend. Your husband has been such a wonderful friend to me. He's taught me so much about magic, about this world.'

His wife was overwhelmed by Moira's exuberance but Cassán was distracted by a distant and growing sense of mistrust, anger and determination. He let Mánus pry Moira off Thea and guide the Greek sorceress to his little family while Cassán took a few steps away to be able to see the gate at the bottom of the sloped lawn.

'What is it?' Moira asked him in a low voice as she sidled closer, dropping her act now that everyone was staring instead at the foreign wife of the millionaire host's eccentric writer friend. He squinted, then felt guilty. It was getting harder and harder to recognise him.

'It's Dubois.'

Eugene had gotten thin and sickly-looking since the ritual that had made the rest of them superhuman. His jacket was old and oversized, his sleeve hanging loose over his missing hand, and he seemed to move with a hunched posture now that he didn't have before; his confidence missing, his identity trimmed back. Two other men from the party headed down to meet him.

'Cassán?' It was Anthea, behind him, and he looked back to her. She was crouched at Áine's side, gazing at the new Morrissey baby. Cassán left Moira to return to his wife and to offer his congratulations again to the new mother. He'd seen the baby a few weeks ago after a very hushed transaction that Mánus, with his trustworthy surname, had brokered between Cassán and some frightening folks. The pair had come back here to drink their relief at surviving, as though they could die at all. It was easy to forget when faced with sorcerers like those. Thea looked up at him, eyes sparkling. 'Isn't he beautiful? His name is… is…' She'd lost it. Helplessly she looked back to Áine, evidently embarrassed to have forgotten the pronunciation already. Traditional Irish names did not come easily to her Greek tongue.

'Aindréas,' the mother repeated, patiently, and broke it down twice into syllables for Anthea to imitate. Not far away, Cassán could hear the sly giggles of onlookers, deriving shallow enjoyment from a foreigner's difficulties with accented English. A more mature person might have succeeded in ignoring it; another might have turned and told them to grow up and mind their business. An Empathic Crafter, though, channelled their spite alongside his own and sent it back to them as atmosphere. Their laughter died. Their moods dropped. Whatever dark and painful thoughts that sprung from that deep mood were their own problems.

'It was my father's name,' Áine explained. 'It was in our family, first born son after first born son, for six generations, before me. My poor father had only daughters.'

'He's a good mix of you both, isn't he?' Cassán offered to the new parents, because "beautiful" wasn't a word he associated with infants, nor was it one he thought these two would want to hear associated with their heir. He smiled at Thea's gasp of delight when the little boy wrapped delicate, pale fingers around hers. The baby blinked again, huge eyes already lightening to the same eerie violet-blue as his father's. 'It looks like he got his mother's nose – lucky little fellow.'

'Yes, I had hoped he would,' Áine agreed seriously, then shot a playful look at her husband when he feigned outrage. 'Well, he wouldn't want yours.'

'Ladies and gentlemen, my two best friends. You see how they treat me?' he said to Thea, who was able to follow the gist

272

of the teasing to find it amusing. 'So unkind.' He leant over to kiss the top of Áine's head and met Cassán's gaze discreetly, assessing what he already knew about Eugene's appearance. The former Telepath of their coven was spreading discontent with every person that intercepted him on his way up the hill. 'It looks as though Cassán and I are required elsewhere for a moment. Will you be alright?'

He asked it of Thea, the question Cassán should be asking if he was concentrating on being a proper husband, and she nodded vaguely, still holding the baby's fingers. Áine, though, nodded with more meaning in her gaze. He had wondered in the past how much the elegant, stately young woman knew about their dealings. More than Thea, evidently.

Moira fell automatically into step with them as they departed the group of mothers and baby-admirers. Just another way in which she set herself apart from the other women of this society, which Cassán begrudgingly admired of her, since this bubble of richness, inherited reputations and castles for homes was not his world, either. These people were his clients; he was a provider of magic they shouldn't have, Mánus his willing, native middleman. Eugene saw them coming and raised his one hand in weary greeting. He stood already with Lorcan O'Malley and Thomas Shanahan, and the three were having a very intense conversation.

'White Elm,' Mánus deduced from a distance. Cassán went wide to avoid a rabbit hole in the sloshy lawn, weathering the rush of negativity that rose from both Mánus and Moira at the mere mention of the governing council. He shared their feelings. 'Another raid. That's the third this month.'

Shanahan and O'Malley visibly deferred when the three came close enough to hear, gazes dropping, shifting to make space. Cassán had noticed this behaviour in the other men of the magical aristocracy increasingly over the past year, particularly toward Mánus but also toward himself, Hawke and even Moira. It felt like they'd cut the line in the pecking order. Eyes slanted to them when decisions needed making;

things he said seemed to hold more sway. He didn't pretend not to know why.

'Who did they hit this time?' Mánus asked before anyone could greet him. Cassán saw Shanahan glance expressionlessly at the air above Morrissey's head. The swollen, power-heavy auras of the four who'd successfully completed the ritual were as impossible to miss as they were to explain, given that, to the casual observer, they were moderates on the Trefzer scale one day and nines and tens the next. But the violet-eyed Irish millionaire was something else entirely, and those he kept company with treated his mysterious increase in magic and ability with wary respect.

Eugene Dubois looked at the same oversized aura with his now-usual melancholy, and Cassán, struck with the depth of his feeling, extended a welcoming hand. He felt the relief to Eugene's awkward sadness; he felt Mánus's regret for not thinking of that first.

'It's bad,' Eugene reported, shaking hands firmly, more confident. 'I don't know how they managed it, how they knew. They arrested Jack McKenna, seized everything.'

'They *what*?' Cassán stopped himself, thinking of the relatively harmless McKenna and his prattling about the wisdom of various historical figures – an interest supported by occasional dabbling in blood sacrifice séances. While communion with the dead and the use of blood in magical practice was on the White Elm's no-go list as of 1958, the funny little man was far from criminal mastermind, and would likely go free with a slap on the wrist, a mark against his name on council records and the confiscation of all illegal items from his home. 'He'll be alright.'

'He's already out. But it gets worse,' Eugene said grimly. 'Turns out McKenna *writes*. Keeps a ledger.'

'Nothing wrong with that,' Tom Shanahan said with a defensive frown. Moira gave him an exasperated look.

'Not if you keep it somewhere safe.' She turned back to the former Telepath. 'You didn't mention that for character-building.'

'They've got the ledger.' Eugene scratched his head,

worry rolling off him. 'It led them to the Tresaighs.'

There was a beat of concerned silence. Cassán thought of Tresaigh's abattoir, which all presented as perfectly legitimate. He thought of the old sheds, skins tanning, cuts of meat hanging. He thought of the brown paper bags Eoin Tresaigh always handed over when he came to collect an order, brown paper bags containing jars and bottles and paper-wrapped parcels of flesh he *shouldn't* have and which were procured from somewhere on the premises but Cassán was screwed if he thought he could guess where. The abattoir was layered in careful magic too deep and too elegant for any overlaps or seams to be detected – generations of Tresaighs had seen to that. It was a point of pride that no visitor to the family's old farm had ever found where they stored their *real* merchandise.

'They've been raided before,' Mánus dismissed. 'The White Elm isn't *that* good.'

'This time they were,' Eugene insisted. 'Check. Both of you,' he added to O'Malley, who'd been listening with his usual sceptical silence. The two scriers went quiet, eyes glazing over as they looked further afield. 'Eoin was hit hard by the restrictions but this time he's done.'

Cassán was starting to feel unsettled by this news.

'But they can't have gotten–'

'Everything,' Dubois confirmed. 'I don't know how, but they found the door to his storage room. One hundred and seventy-two years in the trade and no one's ever been able to find it, and suddenly these sons of bitches storm the place and walk straight to it? Rumour is old Eoin was using a *pocket universe* – I didn't even know that was possible, but that would explain a lot. So that's a top-level crime to start with, and then with what they seized? *Months* of orders, every jar, every pickling brain and dried skin. Not to mention the corpses. Poor bastard.'

'But...' Tom Shanahan rubbed his chin, shocked and angered. He dropped his voice. 'But I had *thousands*–'

'Not anymore, by the sounds,' Moira interrupted, silencing him. 'I imagine a lot of others will be out of pocket, too.'

The small group shook their heads in dismay. Few

serious sorcerers of their level could manage their practice without people like Eoin Tresaigh, willing to source and trade the less appealing ingredients of magic. Unless one was subscribing to the White Elm's new "clean" energy magic – as the weak-minded masses seemed to be falling into line with, disappointingly but unsurprisingly – a sorcerer needed to give something up every time they asked for Fate's favour. Better someone else's blood; better someone else's flakes of skin; better someone else's powdered bone. And better still if that someone else no longer had need of it. All of the Tresaighs' clients kept an unspoken solidarity, protecting the family with their silence and what occasional magical or financial misdirection they could offer, knowing that if their grave-robbing and morgue-visiting were to stop, so too would the already dwindling supply.

'It's true,' Mánus said suddenly, uncharacteristically spooked, coming out of his trance. His cousin Lorcan O'Malley needed a few extra seconds. The two scriers had been of comparable skill and strength up until a year ago. Along with the White Elm crackdown that had resulted in the closure of all seven of the O'Malley family's bookstores and the burning of most their stock – nothing short of a witch hunt, Cassán recalled with venom; his own books had been among the burned – Lorcan had to be feeling the reduction of business that came with being suddenly the "lesser" scrier to go to.

'They've got their Scrier there, looking for traces,' O'Malley confirmed uneasily. 'Lines and lines of jars out on the abattoir floor for cataloguing. Probably destruction.'

'That's my stock!' Shanahan fumed. '*Our* stock. They have no right…'

'Rumour is Eoin's going to Valero,' Eugene shared, further upsetting and shocking the group. 'He's the biggest fish they've yet had to fry.'

Cassán exhaled slowly, running his hands back through his hair. *Valero*. The mythical Russian prison no one came back from. The Tresaighs had dealt in dark and dangerous goods but so had the rest of them, as their clients, and he and his little book club had done even worse. If the White Elm was disappearing people who dug up graves and stole John Does from undertakers, how would they treat five people who'd killed five unwitting anchors and a small boy, disconnected themselves from Fate and granted themselves eternal life? Not to mention everything else they'd done, which easily met the severity of Eoin's rap sheet.

Mánus clapped a light hand on his shoulder, pulling Cassán out of his spiralling thoughts, and addressed the other men. 'Is this going to come back on the rest of us?'

'If it was, I think it would have by now,' Eugene advised, eliciting relief from Mánus and Tom, two of Tresaigh's biggest customers. 'Eoin wasn't stupid enough to write anything down.'

'The real question is how they knew where to look,' Moira pointed out. 'What did you say, hundred seventy years without anyone working it out? Then the White Elm turns up and finds it straightaway.'

'Johnny Donovan was working that day, and he says they went straight for the back wall. They knew what they were looking for.'

'Their Scrier?'

'Joseph? That traitor?' Eugene spat on the lawn, infuriated. 'Used to cross paths with him back home, when we were both PIs.' Back when he had two hands, but he didn't say. None but the four who were there that night knew how he'd lost it. 'Can't believe he sold us all out to go work for *them*.'

'He's good though, right?'

'It has to have been a scrier. Only way they could have seen Eoin opening his freaky little doorway.'

'Well, don't look at me.'

'No one is blaming you of all people, Mánus...'

Andrew Hawke arrived. 'Something's about to happen.'

'Something's *already* happened...'

Cassán had been listening to the tense conversation but his Empathic sense was always primary, and it was impossible to ignore the complex dread and delayed relief emanating

277

from Lorcan O'Malley. Dread was a fear of something still to come. As Tom Shanahan had just said, something had *already* happened, and everyone else's emotional reaction was matched to that – outrage, shock, dismay. So…?

Lorcan slid his carefully blank gaze to his and Cassán immediately knew. His stomach dropped and he swallowed, trying to maintain a likewise stoic face. He didn't advertise his Empathy; the bookseller mightn't even know what Cassán was capable of reading from him. It was unfair, really, to have this ability and then to have had it so enhanced by the ritual in Salem, and for no one around him to be aware.

Lorcan O'Malley had told the White Elm where to find the Tresaighs' incriminating merchandise. He'd scried Eoin accessing it – obviously not the lesser scrier in these circles after all – and shared the location and nature of it with the council that had shut down all his bookstores and burned all his books. Why? Aside from directly assisting an oppressive dictatorial regime he had no reason to be loyal to, his actions had condemned Eoin to life in an unthinkable prison, and destroyed the livelihood of his daughters and nephews.

Cassán turned back to the conversation, disturbed and conflicted, and tried to look like he was listening. Lorcan was a traitor to their kind, to their way of life, to the carefully held secrets that sustained their tenuous freedom from the White Elm's grip. But if he spoke up now, in this group, Lorcan would be even worse off than Eoin. The others were fired up with speculation and fury – there would be no forgiveness. Did Cassán need another death on his conscience? O'Malley was the first bookseller to agree to sell his book, back when he was a first-time, unknown author. Surely, the scrier must have had a reason for what he'd done…?

Thinking in questions is a bad idea when you're around Telepaths, and even though Cassán was not yet accustomed to thinking of Mánus as one, he'd learned to be careful around Eugene before the accident last year. So it was just distraction that left him open to Morrissey.

'You're sure?' he asked Cassán sharply, breaking the rest

of the conversations cleanly to make way to listen to them. Cassán didn't mean to but he looked automatically to Lorcan, guilt already flooding him, the scrier's nervousness curling at his edges, every feeling so much stronger than it was a year ago. He met the secret-seller's dark eyes and read the fear in them, wishing he'd not realised, wishing he wouldn't have to fall asleep tonight knowing he was responsible for this.

But he had, and he was, and there was nothing he could do. Mánus knew. Cassán couldn't take that back. Moira, Eugene, Andrew and Tom would back whatever ruling Mánus made on his cousin, and Lorcan would break. Fate had already planned it – Andrew had seen it. It was as good as done. And to stick up for a traitor against these others? Mánus? He could talk his friend around if he truly wanted to; he had the power to manipulate the opinions of all five of them in this moment, in this place. But later, when they walked away, the spell would wear thin. Mánus's decision would be questioned.

A man who saw ghosts *and* let traitors walk.

'I'm sure I'm not having any part in this,' Cassán responded, pretending that meant he wasn't choosing a side, and he turned away from Lorcan's silent, pleading eyes, and walked back up the hill to where his wife still waited before he could be violently sick with who he'd become.

While everyone else turned, seething, on O'Malley for an explanation they did not care for, Andrew Hawke watched the Crafter leave. His eyes narrowed against the watery sun, following the plaid back of the other man's jacket, and then, seeming to sense something the others did not, his gaze lifted suddenly to the sky to look directly at–

chapter nineteen

Me. Directly at me.

I yanked back from the ruby with so much force that I came off my chair and stumbled back into one of the bookcases against the wall. Teagan Shanahan's hand came loose from the back of mine and she held it against her chest like it was burned.

I'm sure I'm not having any part of this.

'What *the hell* was that?' I demanded, gasping unevenly for breath. Teagan's breathing matched mine. That'd never happened while I scried before. 'Did he *see* me? Was that...?' *Aindréas. It was my father's name.* This was *years* ago. 'I don't understand.'

'Wow,' Teagan murmured, cradling her hand and staring at my ruby with wide, amazed eyes. 'That was...'

'That was what?' My voice shook. That vision was unlike any other I'd tapped into, and I struggled to make sense of the spiral of faces and emotions from decades earlier. 'A man, I just saw a man in my vision. He looked at me.'

'Or maybe at me,' she offered helpfully, touching her temples lightly like they were troubling her, 'but probably just at you. You were the one scrying.'

You don't say? 'Why would he be looking at you?' I snapped, raising my hands incredulously, bumping books behind my shoulders. 'Did we share a vision?' I paused. She was breathing hard, like she'd experienced the same. 'Did we?'

A few times before we were bonded, I'd channelled

scried images through Renatus by touching his hand while he was scrying. Renatus had indicated it wasn't a common phenomenon. Now sometimes we did that without physical contact, our minds permanently connected, but it wasn't noticeably different from scrying independently. Maybe I'd done the same with Teagan. Maybe we had some unusual bond, too.

Actually, I didn't want to know. I'd sooner sort this out with Renatus than with his pointless cousin. I wanted out of this place. I wanted nothing in common with this girl, but the bead of shiny red that appeared under Teagan's nose caught my immediate attention.

'What's wrong?'

She raised her fingers to stem it, trying and failing to look unconcerned.

'Oh. Blood,' she said in uneasy explanation. Her bright eyes clung to the ruby, and I stared, trying to get my heart rate under control. 'I don't like blood, but that must have been fifty, sixty years. I–' She stopped when the blood tipped over her fingertips and spilled down her hand.

'Shit.' All my uncharitable thoughts about her evaporated. I reacted automatically, pushing off the bookshelf to go to her. She stood quickly, scooting her hips back to swish the skirt out of harm's way, and I reached into the air – I don't know how I did it, didn't even try – and closed my hand on a tissue from *somewhere*. A Renatus trick, no doubt captured from someplace in his head. I scrunched the tissue and pressed it above her lip to stem the nosebleed.

'Thank you.' Her voice was a little muffled. 'I'm being a terrible hostess.'

'Bleeding does not make you a bad host,' I pointed out. My voice wavered with borderline panic, the vision still swirling in my head along with, now, worry for Teagan. Was this a reaction to piggybacking into the past with me? Had I done this to her?

'I've never been back that far. And you…' She tried to pull away to look at me. Irritably I pushed her head forward again to keep draining her nose and shifted the scrunched tissue to catch more blood, which was not slowing. 'You're not affected at all. I bet Renatus is the same. Is he?'

'Back…? We didn't *go* anywhere. It was just a vision. A creepy weird vision.' Of people I wasn't even thinking about. Faces were burned into my mind's eye. Voices echoed in my ears. Fear and dread and regret lay like dust in my chest, irritating and threatening something worse.

Something's already happened.

'My grandfather was there, and I think my great-aunt and uncle,' she murmured, reverent. Her amazement was like a glow. 'I've seen them in pictures.'

'Which one? Which one was your grandfather?' I clarified. 'The guy who… looked at us?'

It was too weird, because in my experience with scrying, I was only ever a passive viewer on a present or long-ago scene. A cinemagoer separated from the action by a solid screen of distance and time. The idea of someone *looking at* me while I viewed them was ridiculous. Not possible. His time had already been and gone.

'No idea who that was,' Teagan dismissed, taking over holding the bloody tissue. She hovered bloody hands over the napkins on the table; I grabbed them for her so she wouldn't make a mess. 'Thank you. My grandfather was standing beside him. Thomas Shanahan the first.'

The faces flashed in my mind again and I saw the one she referred to – a thinner version of her father – but he wasn't the one I was worried about.

'How can he possibly have seen me?' I demanded. 'The Scot? It makes no sense.'

'Well…' She bunched up another napkin when the bleed seemed to get heavier. 'I suppose he sensed it? You know, when you feel the trace of another scrier, but they haven't caught up in real time yet…?' She paused to watch my reaction, to see if I understood, and I turned away slightly, a little embarrassed by my apparent ignorance of my own craft. I wiped my hands on the hips of my jeans though I hadn't

282

gotten any blood on them.

'Are you sure you're alright?' I asked awkwardly, gesturing at her bright red tissues. She nodded.

'I will be. My daddy always stops it. He knows so many things.'

'Should we...?'

'Oh, no.' She beamed through the blood. 'He'll be along.'

I nodded slowly. 'So... the guy who saw me...?'

'It's a loop. It has to happen because it's already happened. I can't remember the equations but my daddy did teach it to me.' My eyebrows went up and timeline paradoxes and boggling logic started to do unpleasant battle in my head; Teagan, lowering the tissue, laughed, but not at me. 'I've never explained that to anyone before,' she confessed, positively delighted to realise this. 'I never taught anyone anything.' She looked at me with great interest and warmth. 'You can scry *fifty years* into the past,' she noted with admiration, 'but it's like you don't know anything.'

'I'm learning as fast as I can,' I snapped, self-conscious and wishing now that I'd left already, not stopped to help her. 'Not everyone was *born* knowing this stuff, thanks very much.' I snatched my ruby back off the table. I should have stayed home and polished antiques. 'I'm out of here.'

'Those were your grandparents,' Teagan said as I walked toward the door. I paused with my hand on the doorknob, discomfort stirring. 'Ó Gráidaigh, and his wife. That's why you could connect with them so far back. You look a bit like her. In the cheeks, your hairline.' She hummed a laugh through the thick blood streaming from her nose. 'Funny, you'd just said the same about me and my sisters. Families are funny things.'

I looked over my shoulder at her. Beautiful little Teagan with her tumbling blonde curls and cupid's bow lips and bright eyes and the stain of red under her nose. Irritatingly knowledgeable about this world we both inhabited. I wanted to get as far away from her and this picture-perfect tea party setting as I could and back to the friendships I'd demolished. I didn't want to keep talking to her, but I'd come here for a

283

purpose I'd mostly forgotten about.

'They are,' I concurred, empathy sneaking through cracks in my resentment. I'd lost an older sibling to senseless circumstances, too. How much would it rock her world to be told that I was reasonably certain her sister was still alive, and had been almost close enough to touch at her engagement party? That her missing sister had *left* rather than face her and offer her congratulations?

I didn't think I could ever be cruel enough to tell her that.

The door handle turned in my hand.

'Teagan?' Thomas Shanahan the second was on the other side, a fatter version of his father in the 1960s, breathless and looking in with worry rolling off him in invisible waves. I tightened my wards. 'I felt... you're bleeding.'

He could tell when his children were injured, at least in his own house. It wasn't a power I'd encountered before, or perhaps not one that I'd been made aware of because I hadn't met many sorcerers with their parents. Teagan smiled benignly at her father.

'I'm fine, Daddy,' she insisted, still mopping blood with now-soaked tissue as he wavered in the doorway, suspicious and worried and not wanting to appear so. 'We were scrying.'

Renatus was behind Shanahan, and he met my gaze over his second cousin's shoulder. I didn't get to telling him that I wanted to leave; he must have read it on my face, in my chaotic undirected thoughts.

'We should go,' he said smoothly, gesturing for me, and I nodded, slipping past Teagan's father to reach my master. Renatus handled the goodbyes. 'Thank you for your help, Uncle. We hope you're alright, Teagan.'

Teagan stayed inside her parlour with her unfinished tea while goodbyes were exchanged, and though I said nothing to her – had nothing *to* say to her – I glanced back as Renatus led me away to see her being fussed over by her father. She raised a hand slightly in disappointed farewell.

That hadn't gone the way either of us had hoped.

Renatus leaned close to me as we started down the

narrow stairs. 'Tell me you didn't hit her, too.'

I couldn't tell if he was serious, but I gave him a suitably exasperated eyeroll all the same. He and I didn't say much else to each other until we were safely back at Morrissey House, where I froze at the gate.

'What is it?' Renatus asked, hand on the iron of the gate, pausing in his unlocking of it. I shook my head and came forward to cling to the wrought iron palings, staring through at the sloping green of Morrissey Estate's front lawn, with the winding path curving up its side. How little it had changed. I was *just* looking at this place from my mind's eye, channelled through time and the very stable medium of a large ruby. Easily I populated the large, flat area of grass off to the side with picnicking partygoers in my head, a few garden tables and chairs, some parasols and a cluster of old-style baby carriages. I could see the less even patch of slope on the other side of the path where Cassán had stood with Mánus Morrissey, drinking and keeping slightly away from the rest of the crowd. *Ladies and gentlemen, my two best friends.*

'When we'd just met,' I said slowly, pulling my attention from Cassán's memory to my own, recalling the conversation in question, 'you said our grandfathers ran in the same circles, had some of the same friends.'

'So my father used to boast,' Renatus replied. I turned my head to look at him. I could see Mánus in his face, in his eyes, the fall of his hair around his ears, his height. Not his nose, as his grandmother had predicted, and not his mouth, which must have come from his mother's side. Shanahan's side. But the aura I'd seen around his grandfather in today's vision was the same. The power. 'You were scrying with Teagan and that's who you saw? Your grandfather, again?'

I wasn't going to call them dreams anymore. The insights I'd gained into my mother's father's life through night-time scrying over the last few months were coming back to me in little smoggy snippets.

'It was an accident,' I admitted. Like usual. 'I tried to grab my stone and leave, but when I touched it…' I turned the ruby

285

over in my hands, remembering the vivid scene, the richness of the feelings. The fear and reverence of the other men. 'I think they might have been supervillains together,' I added worriedly. His eyebrow quirked, startled into amusement, and he released the gate to wait me out and humour me.

'Supervillains?' he repeated, folding his arms loosely and turning around to survey the dirt road and rolling moors opposite the gate. 'An ancestor of mine, probably. Yours?' He hesitated, seeming to think harder before outright dismissing it, and came to an uneasy conclusion. 'Maybe.'

'*Maybe*?' I don't know why it scared me so much for him to confirm the possibility. I mean, I'd just seen that the pair were much closer friends, at least at one point, than I'd suspected, and little details were solidifying from previous visions, too. Clouded pictures and impressions pushing at my subconscious. Yucky feelings.

'When are you going to read his books?'

'I'm getting there, alright?' I slid my hands through the gate to lean my elbows on two of the scrolls in the ironwork and examined my stone. 'It's weird that I see into his life, isn't it?'

'You are a scrier.'

'But it doesn't happen to you,' I pointed out. 'Or Qasim. No one else gets fifty-year-old visions of their grandparents they never even knew.'

'I imagine it's rare,' Renatus relented, leaning back beside me. 'A bit like your Empathy. It seems to influence your scrying gift. It lets you tap other scriers' channels, and I expect today it let you bring Teagan into your channel, much deeper through time than she was prepared for.'

Hence the nosebleed. 'Is she really alright?'

'I've never heard of death by scrying, except for Hauntings.'

'She said I was connecting with Cassán because he's family. But I don't know why she connected with me. I mean, she's *your* family, and maybe you're kind of mine... I don't know. I wasn't even thinking about them, I was asking about Keely.' And now that I'd been back to the day of the christening, other moments in my grandfather's life were sharpening and organising themselves into a distinct order. Things I'd forgotten I'd seen. A basement. Pages of an official letter thrown to the floor. A bar on New Years Eve. An uncomfortable agreement. A barren field with ten pairs of hands joined in a circle while a bloody pool stretched toward shoes... That scene made me feel especially nauseous, though I didn't recall much except for the sick feeling that soaked it, so I changed the subject forcibly. 'Your grandfather was there, and your father. I saw his christening.'

Renatus looked down, feigning disinterest, forgetting I felt everything he felt. 'A while ago, then.'

'There was a guy at the end. I think he saw me.'

His gaze came straight back to my face. He felt more worried than surprised so I knew that Teagan's time loop explanation wasn't as bullshit as it had sounded, and when he opened his mouth to ask for elaboration I tiredly gestured toward my head, inviting him to go ahead and look at what I'd seen. He slowly settled back against the gate while he tuned into my thoughts, and I felt his presence in my mind, accessing the recent memory like a video recording.

I lifted my own gaze from the ruby's sunlit facets to the grounds. I'd come here to learn from the White Elm, the only magical government I'd ever known, who my family and therefore I trusted completely. My sister had dropped me at these very gates. I'd fallen in with Renatus, a councillor, but I'd since learned he was from a community and family much less supportive of the White Elm than mine. I'd gotten a sense of quiet council resentment at Shanahan and Raymond's party, but the open anti-council attitude of the men and women in my vision was a bit startling. *Their Scrier, Joseph. That traitor.*

How would they react to knowing their grandchildren would fight for that same council, half a century later, against dissent like theirs?

Near the front steps of the house, three distant people had stepped out for a walk. I knew immediately from their familiar shapes that they were the Prescott twins and Addison, tall and lanky and obediently carrying a board game box under his arm. I flexed my right hand, regretful. If I kept sabotaging all my relationships, all I'd have left was Teagan.

I sighed exhaustedly. I'd probably blown it with her today, too, or should have – other than the blood, she'd seemed alright when I left, despite my coldness. Still, it was a good motivator for trying to fix things with my real friends, if I could work out how to revoke punching someone in the face.

Renatus came out of his trance; I heard him exhale slowly, processing what he'd seen. Thankfully, he could be trusted to be single-minded and focused only on the topic at hand, and despite the world-shaking secrets I kept from him, there was little risk of him tripping over that lockbox while he was inside my head.

'This just came to you?' he clarified. 'By accident, you said?'

'We were talking about Keely and when I touched the stone that's what came through,' I reported. 'A few characters of note.'

'More than you might know.' Renatus pushed off the gate and turned to lean his elbows through it like me. 'I've heard of this happening but I didn't realise it started off here, and I didn't know my ancestor – and yours – were there. It's a famous story, the kind no one talks about but everyone knows. Lorcan's betrayal and the fall of the O'Malleys.'

'Declan?' I guessed, thinking of Renatus's scruffy informant.

'His grandfather,' he confirmed, without venom for once. 'Cut a deal and sold out Eoin Tresaigh to the White Elm. In the official story, it was Joseph's first big break as Scrier – Joseph was Qasim's master,' he quickly backfilled for my benefit, and I blinked in surprise, thinking of the tattoo on the current Scrier's left wrist. 'It became part of Joseph's legend but in truth that was the council's attempt to protect their informer. Of course, the truth came out.'

'Courtesy of our grandfathers, I gather.'

'I gather yours was an Empath,' he inferred, 'and mine

had some telepathic ability. Lorcan must have been like Declan, slippery and clever, but obviously not clever enough.'

'What happened to him?' I asked, not sure I wanted to know. Renatus winced and took my crystal for something to fidget with.

'You *don't* want to know. Ana used to tell me the O'Malleys were beheaded in the moors behind us,' he said, keeping his voice light, 'but when I was about five, I tactlessly asked Declan and he said they were chained up in their library, with the last of their books and secrets, and cut up for parts, alive, to replace the merchandise the White Elm had burned. I don't know why a five-year-old knew that, or if it's even true.'

'O'Malleys, plural?' I asked, horrified.

'Ten of them. Lorcan's brother and sister, their parents, their cousins, his brother's wife. Everyone with the surname but Lorcan's pregnant wife – her father's family wouldn't have stood for it, I assume – and their toddler daughter. Plus, you don't kill children, not for anything. It's not worth the consequences. They were ostracised when it came out, of course, the name was poison overnight, but someone needed to inherit the family's estate, what was left of it.'

That unborn baby was Declan's father, presumably, or maybe his mother, but I was too distressed to ask. What an awful story. And my grandfather was one of the instigators of that brutal massacre. Even if he'd wanted no part in what came next, he'd also not done anything to prevent it. He'd turned and walked away. Somehow, I knew he'd known what was going to happen to Lorcan.

'That's… the most horrible story I've ever heard,' I said faintly. Renatus nodded, and I could tell he was as uncomfortable with his ancestor's part in it as I was with mine. He tossed the gemstone gently from one hand to the other.

'It's as close as anyone's come to ending a whole family in our world in a very long time. I suppose magical blood is too precious to waste, especially a line as long as theirs.'

A weird feeling of unease with his words brushed me, like it did in Germany at the allies' summit – something he'd said was wrong, and deserved closer inspection.

'It's not the closest anyone's come,' I said slowly, puzzle pieces shifting in my head, unnerved by the poetic injustice I was starting to see. 'Ten family members is a lot but they left two heirs.'

'They saw it as technically one, the boy,' Renatus corrected. 'But yes, their power and talent survived in the two children. Robert Quinn married Lorcan's daughter and–'

'No, I mean, it's more than Lisandro left in your family,' I cut in. I didn't need to indicate the apple orchard we could both see from where we stood; Renatus's eyes went there anyway. 'One survivor. Two in mine. Do you think...' I swallowed, already feeling my master's struggle against his emotion shutdown. I'd chosen the wrong opening to this discussion. 'When Lisandro said he left us alive on purpose, do you think that's why? To preserve the bloodlines?'

'I imagine so.'

He went quiet, and I let him. I hadn't come at that very sensitively. Still, I tried not to reflect that he and I maybe should consider ourselves fortunate that our families were murdered by a sorcerer with a preoccupation with weather magic and a preference for keeping his hands clean. At least, for the most part, our families weren't brutalised and carved up.

Except for Ana.

'What did Shanahan say?'

'Not much. He's going to do some digging and get back to me.'

Silence again.

'Who was the man who saw me, at the end?' I asked finally.

'They called him Hawke, earlier. I assume he's an ancestor of Kenneth Hawke, Ana's godfather.'

'Also the dad of Aubrey's fiancée, Shell,' I filled in. The names kept matching up. It was getting eerie. 'Is it bad that Hawke saw me? Can he... I don't know, do anything?'

'From fifty years in the past? Not really. I don't know much

290

about him. I expect he's long dead, along with the rest of your supervillains.'

'It was like a full cast of old-world *us*. Even Teagan's grandad was there. The same names, the same families, playing a part in a different chapter of the same story.' I extricated one hand from the bars of the gate to push my hair back from my face, those uneasy half-forgotten memories simmering to the surface. 'I never expected…'

That Cassán had enabled a savage multiple murder. That my grandfather had practiced dark magic – the sort with trafficked organs and grave-robbed bones. That the best-known sorcerer in my line had stood in a circle around a murdered little–

My sense of self-preservation clamped down on the thought before it could finish, before I could see the memory clearly, much to my relief.

'That one of your ancestors might have been just as bad as mine?' Renatus guessed, very seriously. 'Yes, I'm glad we found out now. This completely changes things.'

I smiled, grateful, and leaned aside to nudge him with my shoulder.

'You know, when Teagan's nose started bleeding, I did that thing you do, with the tissue,' I told him, more than a little proud. I twisted my fingers the way I'd seen him do before, the same way I did earlier. Nothing happened this time. 'I didn't even think about it.'

'The most useful spell I could ever have hoped to teach you.'

'It's a sign I'm getting more awesome, finally. And, since I used my powers for good, it's a sign of non-villainy,' I explained earnestly, accepting my stone back when Renatus offered it. We both straightened and he opened the gate.

'We're not our families.'

'Obviously,' I agreed, stepping through and into the grounds ahead of him. I gestured widely at the stately home, wild with magic. 'Why are you like *you* when your uncle has an EFTPOS machine?'

291

chapter twenty

Antiques have a habit of being big chunky pieces of furniture with lots of intricately carved crevices for collecting dust. Fionnuala tried to insist I'd done enough when she brought me dinner in my room two nights in a row, but I really didn't want to get off easy, nor did I want the free time to reflect on my friendlessness, my newfound villainous ancestry, or any of the other uncomfortable options I had waiting in the wings of my subconscious.

Hiroko. Angela's birthday on Tuesday. The classes I'd been missing. Renatus's fate. The void. Declan's massacred and harvested family. Oh, the choices.

One choice was made easy for me while I polished, however. I had just plonked my bucket down beside my last item late on Sunday, a pointless spindly table in the ballroom, and had not yet donned my gloves when I thoughtlessly wiped the dust from the surface.

Two hands, one large and one small… 'If you want her to hear it, you've got to touch it'… Small hand presses large hand to the tabletop… Butterflies, nervousness, attraction… 'How do you know Byrne will see this?'… Leafy green eyes…

I swallowed, butterflies of my own erupting in my stomach. Sophia and Addison, with Kendra standing nearby. They'd been here, recently, talking about me. Not that I didn't deserve it. But they'd *deliberately* touched the table while talking about me, and must have noticed or been made aware that I was on antiques duty this weekend for assaulting

Addison. They knew I was a scrier and this was one of the manifestations of my gift. What had they wanted me to hear?

I'd been a colossal jerk and I deserved whatever I got for that, but if I wanted to mend things with Addison and the twins, I needed to woman up and make that happen. The onus wasn't on them when the fault was all mine.

I roughly dusted off the table and pronounced it clean enough – no one used the ballroom anyway, not since the White Elm had used it for a funeral in our first month of school here, turning everyone off it completely – and ran the bucket and cleaning things back to the kitchens. The staff had finished for the night so I made sure to put everything away where I'd seen it all come from.

I headed up to the third floor and went to a door that wasn't mine, but on which I'd only ever knocked at night. Mind out of the gutter, thanks. I knocked before I could chicken out.

It was like déjà vu.

'This is familiar,' Jin commented dryly as he opened the door. Beyond him, the other two residents of the room leaned into view from atop their beds where they were sitting facing each other, notebooks open and biros in hand.

'Very,' I agreed in the same tone, though without the twisting in my stomach I'd felt last time I was greeted at this door by my American-born Korean classmate. These days, I could count on most of my peers being too scared of me to say the kinds of things he said to me then.

My pronouncement to Renatus that I wanted to be fearsome was working on some level, at least.

Jin seemed to be thinking along similar lines. He smiled thinly and said, 'I'll get him.'

Addison had already swung off his bed and come to switch places with his roommate. I swallowed nervous butterflies I'd inherited from the impression. His usually cheery face was impassive and his emotions were on shutdown. Closed off. Cold. I couldn't detect anything else from him.

I deserved this. I stiffly shoved my hands into my pockets, knowing it was my job to speak and say something to fix this but not knowing where to even begin. An apology seemed much too weak.

'If you're here for round two, you should know I've been taking lessons,' he said, not looking at me. He twirled his ballpoint pen in his fingers and I rocked back on my heels, trying to relax, ignoring the carefully averted eyes of our classmates behind him. I considered my words before I let them out, but they still came out wrong.

'I'm thinking I probably owe you a free one.'

Jin snorted and I cringed. Addison's eyebrow quirked.

'Free what? Lesson?'

'I–' I bit down on my tongue and looked down. Dumb, dumb... I couldn't get it right. 'A free hit. I won't even try to dodge.'

'Nah, you'd just use your wards,' he dismissed, flicking his pen lid off the end of his pen and catching it with his other hand. I shook my head and tapped my chest.

'Cross my heart.'

He eyed me then, sideways, suspicious. I straightened, wanting to see it coming even if he was going to throw one from that slouched stance – no strength in that, I could definitely take it.

He nudged himself upright and shifted his foot. That was a better stance. I made myself stand my ground, even though I was reminded now that Addison was much taller and bigger than I was. It would hurt, yeah, but not more than I'd hurt him. He'd always been a good friend to me. Sticking up for me when I was bullied. Running with me in the rain when I was trying to get fitter and stronger. Generally being lovely.

'In that case,' he said, flatly, rolling up his sleeve as I clenched my fists inside my pockets, trying to be ready, 'I'll take a raincheck.'

And he slumped back casually against the doorframe with a brief smile, and, just like that, our fight was over. I literally felt the tension between us fizzle away from the air, leaving us clean and clear and perfectly okay.

I felt the overwhelming urge to cry and hug him tightly for forgiving me so easily, but I swallowed it away and said instead, 'I'm really sorry.'

'Yeah? Well, then, don't do it again.'

'Never,' I promised. He winced and ran a hand along his jaw.

'Sophia healed it up good but there's only so much abuse a face this perfect can take. Come for a walk?'

He turned to throw the pen lid followed by the pen itself at Jin, then snatched up his shoes from beside the door and yanked the door shut, laughing as he shouldered me back out of the way of an airborne pillow. We heard it hit the other side of the door with force.

'Fuck it, I left my key in there,' Addison mourned, leaning back on the door to pull on his sneakers. 'You got my message, huh?'

'Aye. Very subtle.'

'Kendra's idea. I was at least eighteen percent worried you'd crack it again if I approached you directly, and she devised a means of reaching out to you while still facilitating my cowardice.'

I sighed, regretful. 'Addison, I'm really, really sorry. I can't believe what I did. It was so uncalled-for.' I covered the lower half of my face with my hand, humiliated at just the memory. 'I wouldn't blame you for being way madder than you are.'

'I'm guessing there was more to it than whatever I said to annoy you?' he supposed, tucking a loose shoelace into his sneaker and nodding for me to lead the way. I winced, heading for the stairs.

'You didn't annoy me. I was underslept. I had a migraine. And I was having a telepathy breakdown, hearing everyone's thoughts, including yours. And it was my family's death anniversary. Not that any of that is an excuse for hitting you,' I made sure to clarify as we started downstairs.

'Let's not belittle things,' he said mildly. 'You didn't just

295

hit me, you punched me in the face. Own it.' He paused to let me groan. 'No, I was out of line, too. I shouldn't have hassled you about Sasaki. I know you took it hard. And I didn't know that other stuff. Should have read your signals.'

I made myself smile. 'You didn't say – or think – anything that wasn't true. You were right, though. I nearly managed to get myself expelled, as you predicted.'

'My cunning plan in action at last.' He scratched his ear, intrigued. 'So you, uh, can hear thoughts now?'

'Not usually. Renatus and I still don't know what was up yesterday but he's chasing a lead.' I withheld Renatus's concern that it was some kind of attack. 'I'm hoping it was a one-off; it wasn't very pleasant.'

'Whose thoughts did you hear? Other than mine? Did you hear anything weird?'

'Lots,' I confirmed. 'Someone in our cohort hates peas and Sterling hates me. Alert the media.' I glanced at my companion out of the corner of my eye, weighing what to say next. 'I'm an Empath, so normally I can just feel other people's feelings.'

'Yeah?' Addison asked, deliberately lightly.

'Yeah. And while your message in a tabletop was a real stroke of genius, the only reason it worked was the emotional intensity of the moment.' I stopped on the landing and looked down the well of the next few flights, stalling for time while I tried to decide whether to go any further with this topic. It was none of my business, but I was desperately curious, and head-on had worked to repair the friendship itself. 'You... and Sophia?'

'Me... and no Sophia, sadly. I wish.' He shrugged easily, as if I hadn't just pried the deepest secret of his heart out by accident, though the electric terrified warmth I felt vibrating from him confirmed it. 'Don't tell anyone. A thousand hearts will break simultaneously.'

I couldn't help smiling, and continued down the stairs with him in step.

'I wouldn't want to be responsible for that kind of mass

anguish. Your secret's safe with me.'

'Also half the people here think I've got something going on with you, which makes me look pretty damn badass, thanks for that.' He grinned and offered me his fist to bump. 'So it'd be doubly in my interest for you to say nothing. None of them know I'd be too shit-scared to go there. Not that you're not awesome,' he hastened to add, 'you know, I love you, it's just that…'

'I'm a pale shadow of the angel that is Sophia Prescott?' I guessed, surprised to find myself unoffended. Even a casual platonic *I love you* has that effect. 'And sometimes kind of a moody bitch?'

'Yeah, that, but I was going to say you seem like a lot of hard work I don't need.'

'Oh. That's much nicer,' I said sardonically, running my hand down the banister. *Wrinkled hand leaning heavily...* '*…doesn't want to see it but she's…*' I jumped down the next two steps onto the landing to look back up at Addison. 'You know what, use that when you make your move with Soph. That's a killer pick-up line.'

'I thought so.' His little smile was warm and helped me forget completely that three minutes ago we weren't friends and our last interaction was an act of violence on my part. 'So, you know something, Empath Girl?'

'I know nothing,' I told him honestly, and he sighed dramatically. Nothing ever fazed him for long, but I could see now, when I shifted my focus to look, the changes in his aura. He had it bad. I wondered how long and whether either of the twins, especially sensitive Sophia, had cottoned on. None of the trio's interactions seemed to have changed, though I had admittedly not been around enough to be able to say for sure. 'You know,' I added lightly, 'a lesser man might have asked his Empathic friend to conduct underhanded emotional surveillance and provide him with intel on the object of his affection. But not you.'

'Madam, you insult me,' Addison claimed, clutching his chest as though pained. He broke character to flash me a smile.

'It hardly matters. It's too weird – I dated her sister.'

I scoffed. 'For five minutes. But, alright,' I relented. Sophia didn't have to be cool with that. 'Where are we going?' We were most of the way down the stairs, and the rest of the house was silent.

'Wherever we want. I'm guessing curfew doesn't apply for the lady of the manor?'

I shrugged noncommittally. Technically it applied to me in the same way it did everyone else boarding at Renatus's home, a means of minimising disruption and assisting with the management of timetables by enforcing a rest period. However, other responsibilities had taken me off-campus or at least elsewhere in the house after the official hours with some regularity, so I didn't pay much mind to the curfew except to go to bed when the house got quiet and boring.

'Enough about me and my hopeless infatuation,' Addison insisted brightly, stepping wide like he was going to miss a step and disappearing, Displacing, Skipping the distance to the bottom of the stairs, where he finished his stride gracefully. He looked up at me as I followed the traditional way. 'How many years? Your brother, you said, and… was it your parents, too?'

Other than with Hiroko and Renatus, I'd not discussed my family's circumstances with my friends at Morrissey House. They knew I lived with my sister; they knew I'd grown up with two big siblings. I hadn't said more. I faltered in my step at the change in topic and reached out to grasp the banister, but my foot landed safely and my other followed, keeping rhythm, and I realised I was actually fine. No balking, no panic. Addison's casual, curious tone made it feel like a safe topic.

I'd been insensitive to force the Keely thing with Teagan.

'Four years,' I answered, coming down to join him. He offered an apologetic smile.

'I'm sorry. Accident?'

People really didn't know – even my own friends. I'd been so insular, so caught up with my apprenticeship and all the dark and miserable stuff that went with it.

'Murder,' I said for the first time, instead of 'storm'. His shock couldn't be faked. 'Lisandro killed them.'

'Are you serious?' Addison stared at me, took in my calm and serious expression, and caught the door I opened to stop himself from walking into it. 'Holy shit. No wonder you're on this warpath.'

We headed outside into the starry dark. I didn't tell him everything, but I told him what I didn't mind everyone knowing. Like the day way back in March when I'd wandered these same grounds in the daylight with Hiroko, I was mildly surprised by the catharsis of opening up to someone I trusted. Of releasing a secret.

I carried enough of those.

We stopped at the place every mindless walk around this property seemed to end, at the mouth of the dirt path into the orchard, and we both shivered despite what I thought was quite a nice temperature. A breeze was stirring the wild twisting treetops of all the other densely planted old trees but the branches stretching over the path were creepily still, as always.

'Naturally the one time I take a late-night stroll, we end up at the spookiest spot in the whole place,' Addison noted. 'I swear it's haunted.'

It was, but not in the way he meant. 'Let's head back.'

Neither of us moved. The place where Renatus's whole family had died in terror and where he'd committed his very worst act had always attracted me, feeding me with power I didn't have anywhere else – except where Lisandro had drawn on that same power to cast the same fate on my family and Kenneth Hawke's. It creeped others out.

'What do you think's in there?' Addison asked conspiratorially. 'Constantine thinks it's a graveyard.'

'It is.' I looked over my shoulder at the lawn, lost in sudden thought. I hadn't yet considered why yesterday's vision had come to me. Why that specific moment? Fate, allegedly, pushed visions and intuitions onto scriers to prompt us to see things that had been overlooked – or so Qasim had argued at the summit. The scene had been uneventful relative to the brutality that had come of it later, but on reflection, the three families Lisandro had wiped almost clean off the table had all been represented in that last conversation. My grandfather, Renatus's and Shell Hawke's were all standing there, along with the first Thomas Shanahan and some striking American woman, when Lorcan O'Malley was outed. Coincidence? I knew better.

Renatus's attention was on other things but noticeably shied away from me when I reached out for him. He could feel the orchard's energy through our connection, and while it undoubtedly powered him up, too, it also repelled him with horrific memory.

Lisandro grew up with your father and Kenneth Hawke, you said, I sent to Renatus, taking Addison's arm wordlessly and walking him a few paces away from the orchard where the influence of its dark energy wasn't so prominent. *We've assumed that his motivation for killing them was the fallouts he had with both of his friends, but that never explained my mum and dad. What if there was a totally different reason for all three families he picked?*

Contacting Renatus from the orchard wasn't wise.

Obviously there's another reason for your family, he replied shortly, his irritation barely withheld over our connection. *Susannah told him about your brother and sister*.

I released Addison and sucked on my lip, trying not to feel that hurtful revelation over again. When Lisandro was still one of the good guys, Renatus a wildcard teenager from a bad family and both Aidan and Angela on a secret draft of potential council initiates, Susannah had learned that Renatus was destined to murder Lisandro – with the help of one of the Byrne siblings. And she'd told Lisandro, because he was her friend. The storm that killed Aidan also killed the pathway into the future that started with Renatus meeting my brother or sister before me.

But by attacking my family, Lisandro had cemented the

path that made *me* Renatus's accomplice. He'd stopped nothing.

I know that, I acknowledged with conscious patience, *but he only needed to target Aidan and Ange. Why my parents? Why not all of us? I've been thinking about the vision I got at Teagan's, all these interlinked families. What did he do to your dad to make him banish him from the estate and—*

We are not *discussing that tonight*, Renatus cut me off, anger and other ugly suppressed emotions slipping through his shaky defences. I stopped walking.

'I'm just checking in with Renatus,' I apologised to Addison by way of explanation for my silence, tapping the side of my head and forcing what I hoped was a natural smile. 'Work stuff.'

You don't have to tell me all the details, I said reasonably. *Just the basics.*

I don't have to tell you anything.

I almost laughed incredulously, and caught Addison's curious eye. 'He thinks he's funny.' Honestly, I was trying to be gentle, and maybe my timing wasn't great but I wasn't being hurtful, was I? I reached across the connection to bring my awareness to his, and for a moment the furniture and walls of his office swam before me, overlapping my own vision of the darkened grounds. His hand was outstretched to nudge his row of perfectly aligned fountain pens back into arrangement and there was a small unfolded note on the desktop, initialled *TS*. Correspondence from Shanahan? I released my hold and the dark hilly lawn came back into focus.

Alright, fine. How certain are we that whatever happened between them was a big enough deal to make Lisandro want to kill him?

Absolutely certain, was my master's staunch reply. I ran my fingers through the ends of my hair, frustrated by his dogged closedness. We'd been getting along so well lately that I'd forgotten I could catch him off-guard sometimes and stumble upon this side of his personality: the sharp, arrogant, bitter, insecure twenty-two-year-old. The least perfect foil for a sensitive, uncertain, stubborn and increasingly dark eighteen-year-old Empath.

How can you be absolutely certain? I challenged. *Lisandro had fights with heaps of people he never killed. Isn't he meant to hate Lord Gawain? And Declan told me Lisandro and Teagan's dad had a huge fight over your custody, too—*

Wrong move. *It wasn't his damn place to tell you that,* Renatus all but snarled. Anger came unfettered this time, no attempt to hold it back. I weathered it, determined not to get sucked into Renatus's bad mood, pretending it wasn't already happening. *And I really don't see the relevance. I'm busy. Are you done?*

I bit my tongue – it wouldn't do to shout back at him out here when the only person I'd startle was Addison – and bit down on my thoughts, which were heading in a *maybe if you'd just told me yourself* direction. I had secrets from him, too, and he was right, we both had the right to some privacy from each other. I took a breath.

At least four of the five people who were there when Lorcan O'Malley was caught out lost their descendants to Lisandro's storm fetish, I pointed out stiffly, *or their granddaughters have been collected into his cause. Maybe Lisandro's motive has something to do with this event.*

He wasn't even born yet, and why would he care about Declan's family? No one else does.

Nice. I rolled my eyes. *Well, maybe there's more there than what we're seeing. Or maybe it's not that event but those people. Something to do with our grandparents, not our parents.*

Like what. Renatus made the question sound flat even in my head, like he didn't care for the answer. I raised my eyes to the house. The light was on in the arched window at the top of the house.

'Everything okay?' Addison asked lightly. I nodded and smiled.

I don't know, Renatus. 'Oh, aye. Definitely.' Somewhere in the world. *That's why I'm trying to talk to you about it, my all-knowing master.*

The response I got was best described as the slamming of a door. *Very mature*, I shot at him, knowing it wouldn't reach him, that he'd shut himself off from me. I knew I was being rude. I didn't feel bad about it, though. He was being unreasonable and childish, and now I was fired up, too.

'Very convincing,' Addison told me good-naturedly, slinging his arm over my shoulders and getting me moving again toward the house. My gaze went automatically to Renatus's window, and I realised I was seething.

'Thanks. I've been taking lessons.'

Later, even after the entertainment of watching Addison quietly trying to get his roommates to let him back into his room, I couldn't fall asleep. Lying in bed in Ana's room, staring at the ceiling, the mismatched puzzle pieces continued shifting, almost but not quite clicking together. How was Lisandro's master plan of *almost* wiping out witch families connected to this vision Teagan and I had in her pretty parlour room? What about to the Shanahan family business of disappearing people, a skill inherited by their missing daughter Keely, now going by Nastassja? How did she fit into this? How did *I*?

I was annoyed with Renatus's reticence about his father's dispute with Lisandro. I knew it was deeply personal, but I was his apprentice, and what passed for family for him. If he couldn't trust me with his personal hurts, then who, and if he wouldn't let me in on historical facts pertinent to our investigations, how was I meant to be helpful?

How was I ever meant to save him from his own fate?

chapter twenty-one

Barcelona wasn't Emmanuelle's favourite city by any stretch but a request from an occupational therapist at the central hospital made it a late addition to her weekly rounds.

'No te hará *más* daño,' the tiny Spanish witch had explained to her patient, the teenage boy lying face-down on the specialised bed, held utterly still by straps and pins to take the pressure off his severed spine. Half of his long, rocker hair had been shaved off to dress head wounds, and skin was missing all up one side of his body. All expertly taken care of. Soft, clean dressings covered the middle of his back from recent, unsuccessful surgery. X-rays were up on the wall, showing a distinct crack through the T4 vertebra, below which he had no sensation. The image was as clear as the technology could provide but left the spinal cord itself blurred.

The patient was about the age of Aristea and the other students at the Academy – too young to be missing out on his future after a shocking car accident. Emmanuelle exhaled slowly. She'd reversed third-degree burns, closed countless cuts, repaired torn muscle, restitched fractured and broken bone, even treated a child's brain tumour, but a broken spine was a new one.

'We have only twenty minutes until the nurse's night rounds,' the therapist told the councillor. Emmanuelle extended her hands for the other woman's and grasped them over the patient's back.

'That's plenty of time for a first look,' she said softly,

304

closing her eyes and slipping straight into a well-practiced trance. With her consciousness, she gathered the therapist's anxious awareness with her own and guided her into the patient's body with her, showing her how she navigated the injury site. There was a fair level of inflammation from the recent surgery but that could be dealt with easily enough. Beneath that was the real issue, the torn and frayed spinal cord, disconnecting the lower half of the body from the brain's directions.

Far beyond Emmanuelle's level of experience, but she was here now, so she got to work, sending away the build-up that was causing the inflammation and treating the cord like she would any damaged nerve. She drew evenly on her own energy and the therapist's, feeling the other woman's rapt attention on her mental work.

'This is going to take weeks, probably months,' she said upfront when she withdrew and they were both looking at each other again. The Spanish therapist was wide-eyed and awed by the experience of delving so deep into a patient. 'Little by little, one strand at a time, every time you visit. And you,' she added, crouching down to be seen under the bed, prodding the boy's hip, 'more positive thought.'

He wasn't listening. His look of boredom was interrupted with a startled expression. 'Did you... I felt that. I felt something!'

In her bag, Emmanuelle heard her phone receive a message, and left the OT and the boy talking in rapid, excited Spanish to check it. Dr Lund, a medical examiner in Wisconsin.

I'm at a talk that I think you should hear.

'Have you got this?' Emmanuelle asked of the therapist, collecting up her things and checking the world clock application on her phone. It was still the middle of the afternoon in the States. Her designated Healer day each week messed with her sleep pattern regardless of where or what time she started, just from all the jumping between time zones for appointments. Morning sun, no sun, setting sun, full sun, rain storm, morning sun, home for bed. 'I'll leave you my

305

number and I'll be back to check progress in five or six weeks. But I think you will be fine, and I think you,' she bent over to smile at the boy hanging upside down, crying with disbelief, 'will be walking again soon.'

'*Grazias*, thank you so much,' the Spanish therapist gushed, wringing her hand and accepting the card Emmanuelle hurriedly wrote her number upon. 'I will tell everyone what you have done for us. My brother said you would not come. People are wrong about you.'

She beamed and went back to talk to her patient, and Emmanuelle smiled back uncertainly, slinging her backpack over her shoulder and walking out. Probably that was intended as a message of support for the whole council but it had also served as a reminder that for the first time in a long time, the White Elm did not have the full faith of their population.

She typed *Where?* as she walked the halls of the hospital, ignored by all staff as their gazes slid straight off the edges of her ward. She hadn't known Lund very long – the medical examiner had contacted her last month to help identify a John Doe who'd turned out to be a missing sorcerer, information that had assisted Renatus and Aristea in their increasingly convoluted investigation into Lisandro's more dangerous supporters. Emmanuelle had called on her for help with the victims in Prague, and she'd come through. A good contact to have. She liked the doctor, but she'd also liked Peter, her best friend who'd betrayed the council and stolen their weapon, and she'd liked Aubrey, her distant cousin who'd joined the White Elm in Peter's place and then betrayed the council, tried to fake his own death and kidnapped four of their students right off Morrissey Estate.

She'd liked Lisandro, charming and playful. She'd liked Jackson, friendly and a bit slow.

Emmanuelle was no longer in the habit of assuming people were on the right side because she found them likeable.

Any action in north-west United States I should be aware of? she asked of Renatus, someone she'd deeply disliked for years.

I'm following a lead to Wisconsin.

The address came through – a university campus – and she sent that through to the scrier for a thorough check before jumping into what could easily be a trap.

Nothing I can see, he answered, though he seemed wary. *Keep me in the loop?*

In an emergency, she knew both that she could count on him to be there to back her up and that she could hold her own until he did, so she wasn't too worried. It just didn't hurt to use the resources she had at her disposal.

As unlikeable as he might be, she wouldn't trade him for the world.

She'd gotten very adept at Displacement since joining the White Elm four years earlier, though wouldn't make bets on her accuracy. Her first jump to Wisconsin landed her in the huge walk-in freezer of a commercial kitchen; her second, a smaller distance, was closer, getting her into a parking lot on the campus. Quickly she glanced around to make sure she hadn't been seen. A young man in a car second-glanced her, rationalising her sudden appearance as his own inattention. Because she had to have come from somewhere, right?

Shaking off the freezer's cold and hitching her backpack more securely on her shoulders, Emmanuelle headed toward the Biomedical Sciences buildings in front of her, waving down some local students to point her on her way.

The hall she needed wasn't too far a walk away. A small lecture room in one of the Humanities buildings had been booked – a typed sign was taped to the door. *Folklore Club: Guest speaker 'Power imbalance in modern witchcraft' 2-4. All welcome.*

She was quite late to the party so she cautiously pushed the door, stretching her senses inside ahead of her own entry. Twenty-five or so people, most of them witches, none of much power, and, at the other end of the room… She frowned, feeling the energetic equivalent of a glassy orb. Black-out wards. Anti-council wards. Strictly illegal.

'… power in stories, isn't there? Like they say, history is

recorded by the victors.'

She entered the little lecture theatre from the rear, looking down the steeply tiered rows of seats peppered with listeners to the two men reclined comfortably in armchairs on the stage floor at the front. They were deep in animated discussion and her deflection wards were still up, allowing her to stand in the middle of the aisle and stare, unnoticed. The middle-aged gentleman with glasses was a stranger but the late-thirties African-American man he was addressing was shockingly familiar.

Nobody panic, she sent to the whole White Elm, *but I've found Jackson.*

Their former brother and Lisandro's biggest supporter listened to the other speaker without sparing any attention for the invisible Emmanuelle, though when the door shut behind her a little more loudly than she expected, a few students turned their heads to glance back disinterestedly. Their eyes slid straight past her, except one pair of eerie green in the front row. Emmanuelle ignored her, stepping slowly down the narrow aisle, assessing the situation tensely. The room had two exits. Jackson was encased in a ward intended to prevent him from being scried or sensed, which explained Renatus's ignorance of this event, and that ward expanded to include the first two rows of seating. No one inside that orb could be detected energetically, but now that she was here, she could see them perfectly.

Are you alright? Jadon demanded immediately.

At the university? Renatus was taken aback. *I'll be right there.*

No, hold off, Emmanuelle requested, spotting her contact on the right of the aisle and working toward her. *No one barge in. Let me hear them out.*

Jackson sat forward for a drink from the glass beside his chair, nodding in response to the other man's spiel. It seemed to be a kind of casual Q&A, led by the bespectacled man, perhaps a university staff member or a mature-aged student.

'That's right,' he agreed, putting his glass back down. 'It's difficult to argue against, how did you put it? The mainstream voice?'

'The dominant discourse,' the other confirmed patiently. Jackson nodded again, and Emmanuelle rolled her eyes. This ought to be good.

'Yes, that. The White Elm dominates our whole society. They control the stream of information; they decide what we're allowed to read; they decide who's good and bad and when they decide to paint you as an outlaw, it's very hard to challenge.'

Emmanuelle slid into the seat beside Dr Lund and made a small adjustment to her ward. The medical examiner noticed her and blinked in surprise.

'That was quick,' she whispered, putting her phone away. She nodded toward the front. 'What do you think?'

'I think I've been looking for this *fils de pute* for almost a year and you found 'im by accident,' Emmanuelle murmured back. She sent updates to her team, reassuring them that she had infiltrated the talk, unnoticed for now, and eyed Jackson critically. He'd changed his hair since last she saw him, a short afro top with immaculately styled fade that made him look younger and less dangerous than he was. He was still heavy and muscular, but he'd dressed in jeans and a loose button-up shirt, a disarmingly harmless façade.

A lie, because this was the man who'd imprisoned Teresa for a fortnight in a filthy basement and allowed her to be raped and humiliated by his crew of miscreants.

If you see a chance to make a safe arrest, call in Renatus and Jadon and take it, Lord Gawain instructed, and Emmanuelle confirmed without hesitation.

'What are *you* doing 'ere?' Emmanuelle asked her neighbour under her breath, eyes still on the front. Lund pushed her thick hair back with an awkward smile.

'Folklore club founding member,' she admitted. 'I dated the president in college. He never left.' She nodded at the professor-looking man leading Jackson's talk. 'He emailed me last week. Said he had a special event lined up and could I come? I wasn't doing anything else. And once it started, I thought it would be rude to stand up and leave.'

How many people, daily, endured uncomfortable or downright unpleasant situations in order to spare others from having to acknowledge their discomfort? Emmanuelle had always spoken her mind and done as she pleased, but knew that this wasn't the way most operated.

'You can leave whenever you like,' she told the other woman quietly, firmly. 'There are no rules around staying to listen to criminals, and no rules that oblige you make an ex-boyfriend feel like 'is *special event* is as interesting as 'e thinks it is.'

Lund smiled, and they both turned their attention back to the front of the theatre. The club president was speaking again.

'… think that's how you're being demonised? With the perpetration of this popular folk story, so to speak, of your villainy?'

Emmanuelle folded her arms and sat back, watching her former colleague's face as he nodded and considered his answer. When he, Lisandro and Peter had left the White Elm in a shock conflict in Susannah's backyard last year, Lisandro had caught her unawares with an illegal spell that had knocked her out cold. It had been an unwelcome surprise, when she'd come around, because *no one* got through her wards, and she'd learned an important lesson – the unexpected source, the unallowed attack, the safe place, these were where she was vulnerable.

Not anymore.

'I think a story is always going to be easier to swallow than a more complex truth,' Jackson replied, reclining to match the other speaker. Casual. As if he wasn't number two on the magical world's most wanted list. 'Unfortunately, it's the story that holds all the power, and the council gets to write the story. One which needs an antagonist, and there's really no way out of a power structure like that without positioning yourself as villain to their heroes.'

A few listeners nodded, and Emmanuelle reached the end of her patience. She raised her hand.

Don't, Renatus warned, but even as a voice in her head he sounded resigned.

'Excuse me,' she interrupted loudly, dropping the outer layer of her warding to make herself visible. Jackson and the president looked around in surprise. 'Could you elaborate on that more complex truth you mentioned? I'm sorry, I missed the beginning of your presentation.'

Jackson's wide-eyed expression of total shock and the way he sat bolt upright in his chair made exposure absolutely worthwhile.

Glad you think so, Qasim said sarcastically, apparently also keeping watch on her and what of the situation he could see.

'I didn't think the White Elm was invited.' Down the front, the green-eyed woman tilted her head to the side, enough that Emmanuelle knew she was being addressed but so that her wild dark hair still obscured her face. Jackson looked to the young woman as though for confirmation of something, and she nodded once, almost imperceptibly.

Emmanuelle deliberately relaxed back in her seat as all the bored eyes returned to her in force, people twisting in their seats to get a look, whispering. *White Elm?* She gestured back at the door she'd come through.

'The sign says *all welcome*,' she pointed out innocently. 'Please, continue. You're a riveting speaker, Jackson, truly.'

The president of the folklore club adjusted his glasses, looking like he didn't know what to do with this unexpected intrusion. The audience was looking between Jackson and Emmanuelle expectantly, aware of the tension.

'This doesn't seem wise,' Dr Lund breathed nervously, shrinking a bit in her seat in an attempt to deflect some of the attention.

Jackson started to recover some of his previous poise. Clearly he'd believed himself untouchable – invisible to the White Elm's scriers, unfindable by all – and her appearance in

311

the midst of his quiet audience without any indication of when she'd arrived was unsettling. Good. He exhaled one breath of bitter laughter.

'Emmanuelle,' he greeted, pressing his hands together as if in praise and offering her a mock bow from his armchair. Trying to reclaim his power here. He opened his hands helplessly and looked around at his tiny audience. 'See, this is exactly what I'm talking about. The White Elm, here to throw around their authority and crush free speech.'

'That's not what you were talking about,' Emmanuelle argued. 'You said we 'ave been making up stories about you. Which stories?'

'All of them,' the dark-haired woman in the front row snapped back, still not turning around fully. She had an unusual cadence to her voice in this room of midwestern accents, a rhythm Emmanuelle associated with Renatus and Aristea, both Irish. This had to be Nastassja, Lisandro's alleged new wife. Interesting. She turned the other way, letting the people on her left see her. 'Have you heard the one where a dozen White Elm fanatics dressed up as Magnus Moira went mental on a bunch of kids and tourists in central Europe, and the White Elm tried to cover it up as a gas leak?'

There was a soft hush of whispers at this; evidently, this story had gotten around, though how it got out of the safe house in Germany was a mystery.

Give us the word, Em, Jadon prompted.

I'm not sure it would work in our favour, Emmanuelle answered cautiously as she shot back at the woman, '*Oui*, I've 'eard it. Have *you* 'eard the one where fifty thousand or so of our people were executed in the Middle Ages? We in the White Elm like to find ways to avoid a repeat. Cover stories aren't only for the guilty.' *It's only a small audience but Jackson's been working on them for the last hour and it only takes a few to spread a catchy story.*

So don't storm in?

I think I've got this, Emmanuelle answered, hoping. *Give me one more minute.*

The dark-haired woman sat back in her seat, and Jackson took over, gesturing widely at Emmanuelle.

'Typical council move, deflecting the focus to maintain the story you want us to hear,' he said angrily. His temper had always been a challenge for him to control, not that anyone on the council had had to deal with it much back in the days of his membership. Before his and Lisandro's dramatic departure, the White Elm used to only meet monthly, and they had no real base of operations to continually run into each other like they did now with Renatus's house. She guessed that Jackson had practised this talk before coming, and her appearance had thrown him off. 'Here to bring me in, hmm? In front of witnesses, so you get to be the hero, and you can make an example out of me for daring to leave?' A handful of young people in the fourth row shared uncertain glances, Emmanuelle saw. Swaying loyalties, swaying opinions. A Crafter, Jackson had the ability to manipulate the emotional atmosphere of a space. Make people agreeable to him. How many of these little conscription talks had he presented to open ears in bars, clubs and schools like this one? Evidently this was the first that hadn't gone to plan, as his previously calm, collected, even articulate dialogue dissolved into spite-fuelled bravado. 'You know if she arrests me now, the timing's perfect. It's their MO – get you guys steaming mad with me, or some other supposed evil, to take the heat off their own mistakes. Prague, Anouk... the continuing fallout of the 1958 restrictions. They sell you this story of perfect, pure councillors but they're just like you and me. Flawed. And they'd hate for you to know that. Why don't you go ahead?' he demanded of her, the familiar manic gleam back in his eye and his grin. 'Arrest me. Prove me right.'

Pissed off but keeping her cool, determined to be better, confident now that she *was* better, Emmanuelle leaned forward in her seat. 'Drop the ward and ask me again.'

He can't have been silly enough to think she wouldn't have sensed it around him, but he *had* been silly enough to take his own attention off his shielding, giving her time to work at dismantling it. His eyes flashed with surprise and anger to realise what she'd done in the short time she'd been here.

'A trick I learned from you,' she said with a condescending smile. She stood up; taking it as a threat, Jackson did the same, and the folklore club president shrank down nervously in his seat.

'Cute,' Jackson snapped, working to rebuild before it could crumble, drawing the protected zone in closer to restabilise it. In the front row, apparently sensing that their safety net was about to blow over, Nastassja flicked her hair back and got up, too. The ward was thin enough now that, with the briefest shift of focus, Emmanuelle could see their auras. Jackson's was familiar. Nastassja's, surprisingly, was, too – huge, swollen with power, and pockmarked with the same black sinkholes as Renatus, Aristea and Lisandro – with a secondary welling of energy around her left hand.

Emmanuelle's heart skipped unexpectedly. *The Elm Stone*. She caught the swiftest of glimpses just before the woman stepped forward into the wormhole she generated in that moment, ignoring the resentful over-shoulder glance she was cast. Though it had been fashioned into a new setting, there was no mistaking the carved black gemstone that held centuries of White Elm magic, the stone Emmanuelle had worn last as its protector.

The stone Peter had left for her in a final act of defiance against Lisandro, too late to save himself.

Look at her face, Renatus urged, and Emmanuelle dragged her gaze up from the hand, but it was too late for that, too. The woman was gone, and most of the audience, lower level witches without access to those kinds of powers, gasped or jumped to their feet in shock.

Pardon, Emmanuelle apologised to Renatus. She knew he and his apprentice had had a few run-ins with Nastassja and were yet to get a good enough view of her face to positively identify her as the Shanahan family's runaway daughter.

'Let's skip ahead so these people can go 'ome,' she suggested to the club president, scooping up her backpack and rifling through the side pocket for the two blades she knew were inside. One was a medical scalpel, the other a Swiss army knife, because you just never know when you'll need one. She held the scalpel high, non-threatening, and tossed it to the front of the room. A few people cowered unnecessarily but it landed safely, just outside Jackson's shaky ward. 'Jackson, you are right, the timing is perfect. If I arrest you today, it won't be for leaving, or for speaking out against us. It'll be in relation to the charges we 'ave already brought against you, like your participation in the drowning murder of Peter Chisholm, the kidnapping and rape of a political prisoner, and your unlawful manipulation of the people in this room right now.'

Those fourth-row students shared looks again, this time with wide and startled eyes, and Emmanuelle saw Jackson's hold over the room crack in other faces, too. His brow grew heavy with dislike.

'She's lying,' he insisted. 'It's easy to paint a villain when you're the narrator–'

'Yes, yes, I 'eard the rhetoric. Luckily there are ways to be sure,' she went on, flicking open the Swiss knife. Beside her, Dr Lund looked up uncertainly. 'Such despicable, inhumane acts, or the use of dark magic, would inhibit a sorcerer's ability to do good, like healing. You don't mind proving to the room that this isn't a problem for you?'

She nodded to the scalpel near his feet, and everyone else looked to him, waiting. Jackson didn't move.

'If you're suggesting I–'

''ow about I go first?' she interrupted, dragging her own blade down the back of her forearm, drawing immediate blood but not striking any arteries. Controlling her nervous response to minimise the pain. She held her arm out for everyone to see, and offered it to her neighbour. 'Dr Lund, what is your assessment? An illusion?'

'Uh, a cut?' the medical examiner confirmed uneasily. 'A real cut? Do you want me to find a first aid kit...?'

The doctor's voice trailed off as Emmanuelle concentrated on closing the wound before enough blood could

315

gather on her skin to start dripping. A rolled-up bandage had fallen free of her bag onto the seat beside her, and she used it to mop up the blood that had escaped the cut. Beneath, she could see it was sealed, pink with newness. Slowly, Dr Lund stood, staring in amazement.

'It's... It's gone. It's healed.'

There were stares and impressed murmurs. Most of the people in this room wouldn't have seen or experienced healing at that speed before.

'It's alright not to want to, Jackson,' she reassured him, wiping her own blood away. 'You'll just be proving me right. The truth is always more compelling than a story of convenience, don't you think?'

He had to recognise a losing battle when he saw one. His audience was lost to her, his back-up had bailed, and his ward was about to cave under the pressure of her magic, now joined remotely by the two scriers, who'd identified the one little area of the room they could not access and were squeezing for gaps.

'Next time,' he sneered, hatefully, 'I'll give you something to heal.'

He Displaced before his ward could collapse, and the folklore club gasped again, turning to each other to mutter and discuss.

One less conversion on our plate, Emmanuelle reported back to Lord Gawain and the others as she headed down the aisle to collect her scalpel. Kneeling for it, she glanced up at the shell-shocked president.

'You need a better process for vetting guest speakers.'

Weakly, he smiled. 'Are you available?'

chapter twenty-two

I found out about Emmanuelle's university showdown with Jackson and Nastassja from Tian during my next lesson. Renatus wasn't talking to me, apparently. Not that I particularly blamed him, and when I did the time math I realised I'd been badgering him right as he was preparing to run to the aid of his friend, but it frustrated me all the same.

'I am surprised he did not tell you. Up high – one, two,' Tian coached, lifting his kali sticks for me to strike above our heads. Slowly, one, two. 'Again, one, two. We have suspected Lisandro's more convincing followers of conducting this kind of quiet recruitment for months. Now we have proof. Elbows in.' He lightly tapped my sticking-out elbow and returned to form. I obligingly tucked my arms in tighter and regrouped, then continued running through the move. Two slashes, the weighty silver shafts of my sai following each other's arc. One, two. Doubtless this would look more impressive with some speed, but I knew I still wasn't ready to put the moves together like in a fight.

'I suppose he's been busy,' I said evasively. One, two. 'So… they just left? Jackson and Nastassja?'

'That is Emmanuelle's report,' Tian confirmed. 'The woman was wearing the Elm Stone, as you described last time. I do not understand why she would be afraid to face us. She is very powerful.'

I recalled the intense energy of the woman who had attacked me in the forest, and in my unsettled distraction I missed my next strike. Patiently Tian waited for me to roll my shoulders and try again. I landed the two blows but my mind was drifting. Keely and Jackson were actively undermining the White Elm's reputation at these talks, putting an anti-authoritarian spin on Lisandro's attack on Prague. Using it against us.

'And where is Lisandro in all this?' I asked, repeating the exercise, feeling the strain in my shoulders but pushing through. Tian shrugged with one shoulder to keep the sticks in place for me.

'Usually when we see any of them, it is because Lisandro wills it. On this occasion, Emmanuelle found Jackson without intending it. She was given some dates of future lectures at different places. Hold,' he directed when I struck the stick exhaustedly. I kept my two blades against his, breathing a bit laboured. 'Your form is deteriorating. You are tired. Do not get lazy.' He straightened his back and shoulders to encourage me to do the same, but there was nothing wrong with his form; he had to slouch first to have anything to fix. I tensed my slackening arm muscles and tightened my core to strengthen my posture. 'Alright, again. One, two.'

Obediently I did as I was told. One, two. Metal struck wood.

'When's the next one? Lecture?' One, two.

'Soon, but perhaps now they will cancel, now that we know. Good. Last one,' Tian said with a knowing smile at my giveaway perk-up, 'but this time, when you make contact with the second blade, you will make a ward.'

'Channel a ward through the sai?' I checked, curious. I let my arms fall loosely to my sides and shook them out, giving them a moment to recover. Tian nodded. He shifted his feet fluidly to stand beside me where I could better see his example.

'The same motion,' he said, modelling with his two kali sticks slowly, left hand followed by a heavier right. When he hit the imaginary offending blade, I could picture how the first sai would meet it in a block, and the second would generate the push back. His second stick glowed briefly as he brought it behind the first, and I detected the snap of a small ward expelling forward. 'You channel with your hand. Then, your weapon is an extension. An extension of you.'

He'd covered this concept in his formal lessons, extending the path of our magic past our hand and into a tool better suited for directing it the way you intended. Daggers for taking magic apart, wands for precise or focused spells. I had been looking forward to applying it to my sai.

'Try,' he encouraged, running through the sequence slowly beside me so I could copy. I did, revitalised by the opportunity to add a new element. As I brought down the second blade I concentrated on pushing a ward through my right arm and out my hand.

My sword was shoved away from me forcibly, and I shied away from it clattering to the grass. Oops.

'If it is not part of you, it is not an extension,' Tian explained as I went to pick it up. 'It is outside your mind, it is outside your body, it is outside your ward.'

'So, be one with the sword?' I inferred, hefting them in my sweaty palms and repeating the double downward slice motion. One, two. One, two. Ward. Nope. Again. One, two. Getting faster. One-two. Shoulder muscles burning. Forget that, forget I'm even holding weapons. One-two-step-one-two. I stepped forward again, toward the house, drawing on my magic and channelling it down my arm.

I accidentally looked past my blades to the house in the background.

The ward fizzled to nothing.

'*Damn* it,' I growled, my patience finally snapping under the weight of my frustration. I threw both of my sai down on the lawn and turned away, running my hands back through my hair as though the pressure of my fingertips could keep the angry words and thoughts inside my skull. My scalp was damp with exertion. '*Stupid*.'

It was stupid to let my little dispute with Renatus interfere with my concentration. He was the reason I was doing these lessons. He'd given me the sai, he'd arranged for Tian to teach me, and he was going to go dark side after killing Lisandro unless I

319

could find a way to do it first.

The likelihood of which was looking increasingly low at this moment.

'No more today,' Tian said sagely, taking both sticks in one hand and regarding me as I paced back and forth, trying to get my breath back and my spiky, coiled emotions under my control. It was embarrassing to lose my temper in front of someone so calm and together.

'I'm sorry,' I said sincerely, realising who I was imitating in my pacing and stopping abruptly. My instructor smiled and shook his head, dismissing my apology.

'There is time,' he assured me. He picked up my discarded sai as he approached, and paused thoughtfully before offering them to me. I took them the proper way. 'More than you think.'

We both bowed, and I watched him go, disquieted by his parting words. Tian was a Seer, the class of sorcerer I understood the least clearly. Some, like Susannah, seemed to see extremely specific future events. Others, like Lord Gawain, seemed to sense much broader future themes and the steps required to ensure those, without knowing what that future actually looked like. All types seemed to still be able to be taken by surprise. I wasn't sure about Tian's gift, except what he'd told me about objects. Did he mean more than just teacherly encouragement? Did he know something?

I sighed heavily and shifted my sai into my two hands again. It wasn't like I could call after Tian and ask whether he'd divined a timeline for Renatus's unwilling downfall that I could work with.

'Never would be better,' I muttered, spinning my blades in my hands and slashing at the air. One, two. I looked up at the house. Renatus wasn't even here today, busy avoiding me at the Archives, working through our research without me. Nicely played. I turned away and slashed again, this time following with last week's spin and back-slash. I took a step, annoyed with having been left behind, and repeated the combination. My arms and shoulders protested; I pushed harder.

Maybe sooner would be better than later – that way I could quit keeping this stupid secret. Renatus could appreciate all my insensitivity and pigheadedness in trying so hard to understand his godfather, and he wouldn't be angry with me for digging. I swung again, stepped, again, ran forward, slashed again, improvising now. He would understand after. In the meantime, couldn't he just open up and *trust* me?

'I would tell you if I could,' I bit out frustratedly, attacking the empty air with ferocity. Swing, step, slash, thrust, block, *shove*... My ward finally burst from the shaft of the second sai, a forceful push of air that blew across the lawn and into the orchard. I'd battled invisible foes almost all the way to its edge. At least that ward would have definitely taken them down.

The branches of the first trees rustled as my ward pushed past and I rested my sai-wielding fists against my hips, breathing hard. I looked around. Tian was gone and no one else was in sight to witness me beat up ghosts like an idiot. Small mercies. Tentatively I broached the back of my mind where my connection to Renatus could be found. He was well and truly closed off, zero attention on me and where I was.

'I would tell you if I could,' I whispered again, gazing down the quiet dirt path I'd inevitably ended up in front of, to the rickety gate half-hidden by trees and the graveyard beyond it, a creepy shiver inching over the back of my neck. Was that how Renatus felt about the family secrets down here that he kept from me?

I didn't know how I was supposed to balance his need for secrets with my need to know anything that might help me save him, however maddening he could be sometimes.

A shadow passed my face as a cloud obscured the low sun. I twirled my sai one last time and turned to head back inside.

Don't.

I froze at the unexpectedly firm feeling from within. I didn't recognise the voice as anyone else's telepathic one and vaguely recognised the sense of certainty that accompanied it.

Fate? I looked back over my shoulder at the graveyard and took an experimental step down the path.

Yes.

Well, alright. Let's just pretend like it's normal to get instructions direct from the universe, shall we? Tightening my grip on my sai, I followed the path warily, acutely aware of the pure black energy saturating my aura and pumping me up, careful to skirt the epicentre of the power in the middle of the path. I'd felt the void now and knew that's what Renatus had opened here eight years ago, and I wanted exactly nothing to do with that.

I stood at the gate with my arms folded safely and gazed around. It was a quiet and peaceful place, not as morbid as you might expect, with the subdued sunlight warming the leaves overhead and the dimmed glow filtering through the canopy to brighten the old headstones. It was like an outdoor room for this family to enjoy together in their afterlife, though always with at least one missing, since Renatus wouldn't visit. His absence was noticeable, I thought, spotting the dull signs of neglect – chiselled names blurred by grime and moss, weeds going wild, stones tilting and tipping. But as annoyed as I'd been with him lately, I couldn't blame him. To keep my parents' and brother's gravesites tidy, my sister and I made regular trips up north to the cemetery together. I couldn't imagine the pain of having to go and do that alone, especially if the walk to the site meant walking through the place we'd found Aidan and had to kill somebody.

I would tell you if I could.

Hesitantly, I lowered my sai to the ground and nudged open the gate with my knee. It swung in with a soft creak. Epic creep factor, but somehow, I couldn't help myself. I'd felt pulled here since I first arrived at Morrissey House and had only stayed out that first day because Hiroko had caught my hand and pointed out how spooky and yucky it felt. To her. To everybody. Except me.

I fortified my wards, determined to not let myself connect with any of the grief or pain lingering here and approached the first grave. It was an old one, with a crumbling Celtic cross atop a box-like plinth as tall as me. I grasped a handful of vines covering the inscription and pulled. The vines did not come away easily, ripping strand by strand only as I pulled harder. It had been at least eight years since anyone had done this, and probably longer.

> *Here lies our Aoibhegréine Morrissey,*
> *wife of Muireadhach, mother of Lorcan*
> *December 31 1854 – November 12 1886*

I stood back. Just shy of her thirty-second birthday, Aoibhegréine had died young. Was that a common trend in the Morrissey family? I moved to the grave beside hers. Muireadhach had passed on ten years after his wife, hardly old, either. I read it again. The parents of another Lorcan. I did the math and wondered if this was the shared grandparent of Lorcan O'Malley and Mánus Morrissey, for them to be first cousins.

I began to wander, stepping softly. Aoibhegréine's wasn't even the oldest, though the more ancient ones were difficult to read. I brushed dirt from the headstone of her father-in-law, one Sárán Morrissey, born 1827. I found Sárán's stillborn daughters, and righted a worn statuette on the grave of his wife.

'Anastasia,' I wondered aloud, sitting down on my heels. The name was distinctly un-Irish, more of a Greek name, like mine and like Renatus's. It was also the name of Renatus's sister. I looked toward the opposite end of the plot and knew immediately which stone marked her place.

It made my stomach flip and I wanted to leave, but that feeling came back.

Don't.

I made my way slowly towards her, passing the graves of all her ancestors. Her grandmother, Áine, laid alone, the space beside her unoccupied. Áine's husband, Mánus Morrissey, was missing, though no comment of this was made on Áine's classical headstone. I thought of the stately woman I'd seen in the vision at Teagan's. Her face came immediately to mind as clearly as if I knew her myself, as did her patient voice as she kindly broke down her baby son's name for my foreign grandmother. It was a kindness she hadn't owed Thea, and other women at the party had sniggered at the unnecessary effort, but she'd been gracious about it. Hadn't minded, hadn't cared what anyone else thought.

I stopped to lovingly dust off her name, knowing where that heart had ended up, deep in the soul of her grandson.

I hadn't felt much since stepping through that gate, but looking now at the resting place of Aindréas Morrissey, I began to feel more and more intensely. These weren't distant ghosts of the past, but people I'd watched in visions. The body resting here was once the baby my grandmother had cooed over. He'd once walked, talked, felt, laughed... Although what I knew of him suggested he hadn't been the nicest of men, so maybe he hadn't laughed that much. His best friend was Lisandro, who had eventually betrayed him and later murdered him and his family. They'd fallen out in an undiscussable act that was *absolutely certainly* the cause of Lisandro's murder spree, apparently, because Renatus knew everything.

What would Aindréas think of current events, if he were alive? What would he think of me, his son's apprentice? Any chance of being welcomed as a second daughter, when my best guess was that he hadn't much liked his first one?

'Your wife would have liked me,' I informed the gravestone, nodding airily at the white marker for Renatus's mother. Why wouldn't she? On the whole, I was arguably good for him.

All that was left was Ana Morrissey. I reached to pull away the one vine wrapped around the plinth, and stopped, noticing a number of beautiful blossoming white flowers. I let my hand drop as I slowly looked over the impressive sight of her final marker.

What remained of Ana was a glorious stone angel atop an intricate pillar. Its carefully carved face was softened with a loving smile and its hands were folded gently. While vines had choked the graves of Ana's ancestors, the flowering ivy seemed only to add to the general beauty of hers, and so I couldn't bring myself to pull the plants away, and just sat down.

Anastasia Morrissey
June 9 1979 – June 9 1999

Renatus's sister had died young, much too young, like many Morrisseys before her. She'd been full of life, hope and power... She'd left impressions of her intense life all over this house. How quickly it could all be taken away; how quickly everything could be ripped from your hands.

'He gave me your room,' I said conversationally as I laid my hand on the soil above Ana. I didn't know what my connection to her was, exactly, but I reminded Renatus of her and I felt immensely intrigued by anything to do with her. It wasn't anything as silly as reincarnation or stuff like that, but somehow, some way, there was a connection. Like maybe I was meant to have known her, but now could not. 'I hope you don't mind. Thanks for all your stuff. Especially the ruby.'

She was a scrier, too. Maybe she would appreciate that I used her best gem for the same purpose. Renatus was meant to have known my brother and sister before he knew me, if Susannah hadn't ruined Fate's plan by telling Lisandro and giving him the chance to kill Aidan and traumatise my sister. Maybe Ana and I had missed a similar opportunity because of her untimely death.

That sense of niggling, uneasy certainty, of being watched expectantly, washed over me and I knew I was close to a powerful hidden truth, but missing something.

'Missing *what*?' I demanded of the empty air, of the silence. I stretched my senses out to catch anyone waiting in the shadows. 'The baiting and the mystery clues aren't cute.'

Emptiness and silence ensued, and I sighed. There was no one here.

My understanding of the spirit world, and also of my own gifts, was limited then.

I withdrew my senses like you cast your eyes down or put your hands into your pockets, and something unspeakable and yet also stupidly inevitable happened.

Images began to bombard me, blinding me.

Blood… incoherent mumbling… 'Wh…'… confusion, pain… heavy rain slashes at dazed eyes… darkness… broken ribs jar as the man carrying her stumbles… terror… blood runs from bruised and cut lips, down her throat…

I screamed and yanked my hand away from the hard-packed soil, scrambling to my feet, heart thudding. Breaking the physical connection that impressions relied on. But they kept coming, and I realised this wasn't a leftover impression.

This was a channel. Coming from deep underground.

Lightning, thunder, lightning, thunder… chaos, disorientation… wind whips leaves and sticks… water running over purpled skin, washing open wounds clean… thinned blood streaming over dangling broken fingers… distantly, a boy's frightened voice, words indistinguishable… hope… brief light illuminates an unrecognisable face against a stranger's broad shoulder… worry, fear…

I came back to myself long enough to retch and swallow forcefully, overwhelmed by the ugly horror and the sickly feelings of the people present for it. The victim's confused terror at her senseless agony, the stranger's unwillingness to be there in this petrifying storm. They were both dead but their intense emotions had waited eight years for an Empathic scrier to stumble in here. It seemed impatience was another trait I shared with the Morrissey heiress.

'No, Ana, stop it,' I begged breathlessly, grasping at the headstone to keep myself upright. I managed to sever my connection with the body in the ground, shutting off that stream of violent imagery, but now that my mind was open, I started picking up every single impression I'd avoided before.

Hired men in black shovel dirt over the glossy coffin… lace-gloved hands grasp for comfort in the small crowd… Teagan, in a bonnet, stares uncertainly into the hole… Fionnuala dries tears on a lace-trimmed handkerchief… a hand rested on the angel's foot… an envelope drops into the open grave… 'Ana'… Renatus's handwriting…

I pulled my hand away like I'd been burned and lost my balance. I threw out a hand to catch myself and as soon as my fingertips touched the grave's soil it began again.

A deep gash along her hairline… blood in bruised eyes… cracked open, pupils huge and stark with concussion… a boy blocks the path… horror, hope… the man drops her… an already-broken arm jolts… distantly, his voice… 'You're not supposed to be here'… darkness… life slips away…

'No!' I shouted, and saw that I was halfway to the gate. I almost ran into Áine Morrissey's headstone, and my hand brushed it as I passed.

Again, hired hands in black… rainy morning… four adults and a little girl look on… The woman holds a wide umbrella… black, water droplets… the man holding the toddler stands beside her to keep the child dry… another man tips his hat to let the water fall to the ground… red hair beneath… The third man stares blankly into the grave, one hand on the headstone… intense violet eyes, staring so blankly… hired hands finish and leave… The man in the hat touches his grieving friend's shoulder… 'I'm sorry, Aindréas. She was a classy lady'… 'Thanks, Kenneth. Thanks for coming'… The woman covers Kenneth with her umbrella… 'I'll show you back to the gate'… She is beautiful, with very long blonde hair… The man beside her – Lisandro, so young here, not yet an adult – immediately produces an identical umbrella from thin air to keep the dark-haired toddler dry… Kenneth and Luella leave the graveyard… 'He's right. She was so proud of you. And she adored your little princess,' Lisandro adds, kissing little Ana's hair… Aindréas speaks, voice harsh… 'She was just too kind to admit wanting an heir over any 'little princess''… Lisandro hoists Ana onto his shoulders and walks away…

I came to my senses with a cry of pain. My hand was covered in my blood. Apparently I'd reached the gate, focussed only on the visions I'd scried, and stabbed my hand down on a sharp iron spike. I'd cut a very impressive gash into the flesh of my palm. I bent to snatch up my sai and bolted blindly along the path, determined to get away.

'*Aristea!*'

I stopped when I heard Renatus's voice in my ears and in my head. Immediately before me, a mere arm's length away, was the epicentre of the path's darkness, invisible but almost painfully evident, the place where Renatus had found a man carrying his sister's broken body and killed him for it. This was where she was dropped. This was where she'd died. It was the darkest, scariest little spot in the world, and the overwhelming power of that moment in time had the power to knock me out cold.

And I'd nearly run straight into it.

I took a deep breath, feeling powerful and strong this close to Renatus's deepest regret, and as I exhaled I recalled what I'd seen and felt in the graveyard. I wanted to be sick.

Gingerly I edged around the danger zone and hurried out of the orchard. My heart thudded, seemingly in my throat, but I did relax somewhat with every step. Renatus was on the lawn at the mouth of the path, looking white and sickly like he always did when he pushed himself here. It was as close as he'd ever been, I knew. He watched me approach, eyes flicking between my expression and my bloody palm. I tucked both sai under my arm so I could cradle the injured hand in the other, and I stopped in front of him.

He looked like he wanted to say so many things. He must have been coming home from the Archives when he realised where I was, Displacing straight here from the gate. On instinct. Because he cared. His relief that I was okay was hard for him to hide from me, even tied up with his reluctance to be here and his helpless anger at my repeated insensitive visits to this place. He had to be so angry. He knew *I* knew how it affected him when I came here.

But he said nothing as we both stood there, our breathing the only sound. In my hand, my blood pooled and the skin tingled with discomfort. I waited for Renatus to get mad, to tell me to get away from here so we could talk properly, to ask why I'd gone into the graveyard, to break into a sudden articulate rant explaining why Lisandro had been banned from the estate until the day Aindréas died and why he'd sensibly chosen not to tell me before, to say *something*.

He seemed to have nothing to say, or didn't know what to say, which for some reason made me want to laugh bitterly. Of course. Even after my rudeness the other day he had no rebuttal to put me back in my place. Even as I stood here bleeding yet again because of my own stupid mistakes he had no 'I told you so'. Even after this latest transgression he had no words for me at all, except my name, called to stop me making things even worse for myself.

But still not the words I was waiting for.

I shook my head and muttered, 'Thanks for the warning,' and strode past him, back to the house to get treatment for my stinging palm.

I was halfway there when I realised my hand had healed on its own.

chapter twenty-three

As soon as I made my mind up I knew it was a bad idea but somehow that didn't stop me from swinging my legs out of bed, from redressing or from locking my key pendant around my neck. I shoved my birthday bracelet onto my wrist and felt reassured – a reservoir of Renatus's power for me to draw on, in case.

I opened and clenched my fist, eyeing the tender pink sore on my palm and then making the fading black cracks show up under my skin. Renatus cared about me, even if he was grumpy and distant sometimes. Hesitantly, tentatively, I reached for him. His mind was quiet, calm. Asleep. I felt my irritation soften.

He was going to be so mad.

Best get it over with.

I hadn't Displaced since the second Prague misadventure but I wasn't in the same panic as that day. Rather, I was entirely focused on my destination, and when I had locked the gate behind me and paced far enough away to see the whole estate over my shoulder, I found myself utterly composed, confident.

My Displacement was perfect. The void slid straight over me and then I was out, halfway across the country.

Doubt set in. Yep. Renatus was going to lose it.

I pulled my wards and jacket tighter, even though it wasn't cold, and started up the dusty path to the run-down mansion. It was the same era as Morrissey House but poorly preserved. Many windows were broken, the stone walls overtaken by creeping plants and the handrail of the cracked front steps long since collapsed. The newest and sturdiest piece of the entire structure seemed to be the door locks. I jumped over the caved-in steps to reach the top and knocked hard on the door.

I shivered. Locked in their library and gutted. This was the place.

There was a very long pause, designed to make me uncertain and wonder whether it was a good idea I even be here, but I ignored the homeowner's strategy and knocked again, harder and longer and more insistently. The door swung open.

'Miss Aristea! The legend in the flesh!'

Was it just the miserable story I'd learned of his family, or did Declan O'Malley look especially tragic tonight? His messy mop of dark brown hair looked scruffier than last time I'd seen him, with whole chunks chopped out so that the remaining few centimetres of those assaulted locks stuck up at odd angles. His clothes were rumpled, like he hadn't changed in days. His hands were covered in recent little cuts and he looked thinner, sharper. He desperately needed a shave, and his grin with the one tooth missing completed the dishevelled look.

'Declan – what happened to you?' I asked as he ushered me inside. I'd intended to come in demanding and strong, the way Renatus always treated our interactions with Declan, but I couldn't help feeling genuine concern for his deteriorated appearance. 'I mean, how did you get all... messy?'

'Back at you. Nice scar,' he added with a bright smile and no discernible judgement, shutting and locking the door behind me. I noticed new chains and bolts that hadn't been there before, all of which he carefully locked and spelled. 'Me, it's all self-inflicted. Keeping the baddies away. I actually don't mind the hair. I think I might keep it like this.'

'Keeping the baddies away?' I repeated, feeling unsettled, Lorcan O'Malley's fearful eyes coming to mind. What enemies did Declan inherit from his grandfather's mistake?

'Old magic lasts longer than new magic but at a price,' Declan explained, shifting so I could better see his hands. I noticed now that with every lock he slid shut, he scraped the edge of his hand across the top, leaving traces of his blood on every lock. Um, gross. 'Usually it's blood. Other times it's flesh, fingers or hair. You wouldn't have seen much of this, I suppose, having a barely functioning haemophobe for a master – no wonder he went clean. I avoid the fingery ones where I can, although once I run out of hair I might need to reassess.' He finished with the door and turned back to me. 'So, what can I do for you at this most obnoxious hour? Can I get you a drink?'

'No, thank you.' I followed Declan into a small dining hall. He didn't look like he'd been sleeping, and he didn't flinch like I did at the flare of candles he lit with his mind. He gestured for me to sit; I leaned against the table while he went about the room pulling the musty, ripped curtains shut against the darkness outside. He appeared his usual bright and cheery self but he seemed to feel that someone was after him. What other explanation for his primitive cloaking spells, awful appearance and avoidance of windows? I worked to maintain an impassive expression and shell of wards but I felt uneasy, simultaneously worried for him and worried by him.

'What's wrong, Declan?' I asked, watching him for clues. Was this one of his performative acts, or genuine paranoia? I clamped down on my mental questions and zipped my mind tight. 'Is someone coming after you?'

'I don't know.' He glanced back at me with a light smile, yanking another curtain closed. 'Is Renatus coming?'

I pressed my tongue against the back of my teeth, seeing how easily I'd walked into that and knowing there was no backing out. 'No.'

'Then nothing's wrong. You're not hungry?'

'No.'

'And it would be a stretch to wonder if you'd come to ask me on a date?'

'After last time?' I rolled my eyes, not sure if I'd forgiven him yet for hurting my feelings and then leaving me stranded at Teagan's party at the first sight of Lisandro. 'I was hoping you could help me.'

'Help you?' Declan stopped what he was doing and turned to face me. I swallowed. I mostly liked Declan, and Lorcan's story made me even more sympathetic towards him, but Renatus had told me many times that he was dangerous and not to be trusted. I'd taken a risk coming here without telling anyone, and not all risks paid off.

'I need… information,' I said. 'I need answers. I think you're the person who has them.'

'I think you're probably right,' Declan agreed, beginning to circle around the table so he was going to pass behind me. I turned slightly to be polite but when he moved out of my sight I stopped myself from twisting any further. I was at a disadvantage. I had to remember that. I'd already shared that I was here alone and no one was coming – information I hadn't been prepared to share. This was a game, his game. He got a kick out of his scary guy act and wanted to see me frightened, watching my back, and he wasn't getting anything else from me. I waited for him to reappear in my peripheral vision on the other side. 'What do you want to know?'

'I want you to tell me about Aindréas and Lisandro and what happened between them,' I said as he approached from my left, sensing him in my blind spot. 'I know you know what happened.'

'Yes, I do. But why that story? It's depressing and very messy.'

'Renatus won't tell me.'

'So I'll be in trouble with Renatus if I tell you?'

'Yes, probably,' I admitted as Declan came near. Too near. I held my ground and his gaze.

'Well, that does sweeten the pot, but aside from that…' He raised a hand as though to touch my face, but stopped millimetres short of my skin. 'You took my advice. Your wards are much better.'

'I learned from my mistakes,' I corrected, fighting my

instincts, self-preservation pushing me to shy away from this wolf I liked to pretend was a sheep. I stayed stock-still, refusing to shake, refusing to budge. My wards *were* better, and for the first time I utterly trusted that he would not be able to penetrate them. Not that he was trying. His fingertips hovered just beyond the shielding covering my skin, not pushing his luck. 'Trusting you to stay out of my head was one of them, but I learned.'

'You're welcome,' Declan replied sincerely, voice low. His eyes roamed my face, no subtlety, and inhaled slowly through his nose like he was breathing me in. This kind of objectification was unfamiliar to me and my sense of self-value, and I knew I would kick myself later for my hypocrisy. Renatus was getting the silent treatment for being cagey and cold, Addison had gotten a fist to the face for less, and I wanted almost nothing more than to shove Declan away and tell him to stop being a creep. But there was one thing I wanted more, and I needed him onside for that, so I kept my mouth shut, hoping I hadn't misjudged. He looked at my scar and traced long fingernails in the air above it, so close I could feel the warmth of his skin, but never quite touching. I didn't flinch. 'Old Lisandro certainly took a good shot at you, didn't he?' he asked softly, regretful. I said nothing, and he got back on topic. 'Aside from upsetting my dear cousin, what's in this for me?'

I hesitated for a very long time. I could think of a few things he wanted – information for one, sex for another – but it'd taken all of my self-control to let him rob me of my personal space, and I could think of nothing else I could bring myself to give.

'Nothing,' I said finally. 'Absolutely nothing.'

Declan slowly withdrew his wounded hand, all the while holding my gaze. I didn't blink. I didn't let myself think of what could happen now.

'Tempting,' he answered cautiously. 'Counter-offer: I tell you the story if you tell me why you want to know it. And don't say because Lisandro killed your family and you want to know why,' he cut me off as I opened my mouth to say just

334

that. I hurriedly ran a check of my wards, worried about telepathic gaps – he was slippery, after all. 'No, you're just predictable. Tell me, why now? What was the catalyst?'

'Take a step back,' I directed, 'and I'll tell you.'

His intense expression cracked a little, a smirk growing on his lips. 'Now we're negotiating. Alright – I'll move. In exchange for one strand of your hair.'

I slid my gaze from his to the ends of my long hair, hanging over my shoulder. I was quite precious about my hair, having grown it for most of my life. I hadn't even let Renatus cut it when he'd been trying to untangle me from a branch and save my life a few weeks ago. A single strand, though, would have been perfectly acceptable if Declan hadn't just told me hair was an ingredient for his kind of magic. Cue alarm bells.

'So you can do what?'

'What are you going to do with the story I give you?' Declan replied rhetorically. He placed his hands on the tabletop beside me, leaning in even closer to whisper in my ear. I couldn't help the unnerved shiver at the feeling of his breath on my skin. 'Commit murder?'

My stomach turned over and he withdrew a little, his intended effect clear in my discomfort. *No one* knew about that half-entertained notion I had of taking Renatus's cursed fate from him and making it my own. I had been so careful with that dangerous idea, and if Renatus hadn't found it in my labryrinthine mind, no one could have. So Declan didn't *know*; he was making another educated guess.

'It's not ideal to concern yourself with other people's intentions when conducting this sort of transaction,' Declan explained lightly, his point made. I frowned, irritated with myself for getting in this position, irritated with him for being right. For knowing me better than I knew him. 'But I don't judge. Do we have an arrangement?'

'No deal,' I retorted. 'Here's my counter: you move away from me. You tell me the story I came to hear. You don't ask me any more questions. In return I tell you what changed to make me desperate enough to come to you at all.'

He cocked his head curiously, his smile even more lopsided. 'That seems a peculiarly unbalanced deal.'

'Actually, I think you owe it to me.'

A long silence. Another exhalation on my cheek. Then that cheery, charming smile of Declan's returned with surprising suddenness, and he was immediately back at an appropriate distance.

'You drive a hard bargain,' he said. 'You're right, it was ungentlemanly of me to leave you with Lisandro at Raymond's. I do owe you a favour, but you can keep that for now. I expect with this new rebellious streak, you'll need it sooner rather than later anyway. So I'll take your story in exchange for mine, your personal space and a *decrease* in questions. It's reasonable for me to need a few; otherwise how would I ask you where I should start?'

I exhaled very slowly the breath I hadn't realised I'd been holding in. Apparently I'd passed some kind of test, or I'd won that round. I didn't know which.

'Deal,' I agreed, nodding with more relief than I hoped my face showed. 'I want to know everything – how they met, what drove them apart... everything in between that Renatus won't deal with and tell me.'

Declan dragged a worn-out chair from the dining set away so he could sit in front of me, still keeping that acquaintance-appropriate distance. It was amazing how quickly he could turn from predatorial creep to easygoing friend of the family, and how quickly I could forget that he was always both.

'I'm sure you know already that Aindréas and Lisandro met as children – their parents were supervillains together.' Declan turned his attention from me to his hands. Some of the cuts, though shallow, were still oozing blood. I tried not to wonder at his word choice. 'When Lisandro's mother disappeared, he went to live with Aindréas and his new wife. He was living there when Ana Morrissey was born and played such a huge part in her childhood that they made him godfather to Renatus. Lisandro and Aindréas were brothers in all the ways that matter.'

'So what happened?' I asked, pulling myself up to sit on the edge of the smooth wooden table, so much more at ease now. Declan was creating cloth bandages out of midair and gently wrapping them around his palms. 'How did Lisandro go from family to outcast?'

'Kenneth was disowned first – he was the third brother, the middle one. He was Ana's godfather but when he married a mortal his brothers shunned him. Marrying for love? The nerve of some people.' Declan spared me a quick grin, and I smiled back. 'Naturally, as the story of those who piss on Lisandro often goes, the Hawkes later found themselves utterly fucked up by a huge out-of-season storm... I think you know this bit so I might just skim over it.'

My smile was gone, and Declan cleared his throat, very aware that he'd offended his audience.

'Details are overrated. The basic story is that Lisandro hung around the Morrisseys for years and years until he committed the ultimate betrayal and got kicked off the estate and forbidden to ever return. The end.'

'But what *is* the ultimate betrayal?' I asked, frustrated. Declan tucked the end of the first bandage underneath itself to keep it tight, then began on the other hand. 'Lisandro doesn't murder *everyone* he hates with storms. You told me he had a big row with Shanahan over custody of Renatus, and everyone knows he hates the White Elm. What happened between him and Aindréas that was *so bad*?'

'You can't guess?' he asked ironically. 'This is really why you came all the way out here in the middle of the night? Oops, too many questions. But you're more than a pretty face – think. How did Kenneth Hawke lose his standing with the Morrisseys?'

'Something about mortals–'

'Love,' Declan interrupted me. He sat back a little. 'Lisandro fell in love. Nice in theory. Disastrous in reality.'

Little puzzle pieces quivered against each other in my head as the things I knew already came close to fitting together.

The imagined vibration set me on edge.

'With...?' I waited, and Declan's dark eyes flicked up to me briefly from his work on his hand. 'Aindréas? Luella?'

I searched my memory for clues to support either theory, but Declan laughed.

'Oh, unimaginative little lamb. This story is juicier than that. No.' His laughter died off while I tried to make sense of what he was saying. He fixed me with a serious look. 'You must know.'

No...

'Yes,' he confirmed as I struggled with the only remaining conclusion.

'I can't believe I'm entertaining this,' I said slowly, the enormity of Declan's story becoming suddenly apparent. 'But... she was so young.'

'Precisely,' Declan agreed, finishing his bandaging. 'You can imagine the scandal. Barely nineteen and banging her brother's godfather.'

Ana and Lisandro. Lisandro, the murderer of families and traitor of the White Elm, and Ana, the girl in the ground, whose loss had derailed years of Renatus's life. The man who'd nearly taken my eye out and the girl whose bed I slept in. I felt dizzy.

'You're making this up,' I claimed, but I already knew he wasn't. The ultimate betrayal, an act a father could never forgive of his friend. *Renatus knows this. This is why he hates Lisandro. This is why he won't talk about his sister.* 'You're trying to get a rise out of me by suggesting he... he seduced her,' I finished awkwardly. I didn't have a set of comfortable vocabulary for discussing this topic, least of all with a dangerous older guy who'd made his interest in me clear.

'If you say so,' my host said with a shrug. 'The way I heard it, it went the other way. And if you'd known Ana Morrissey, you'd know she always got what she wanted. Lisandro didn't stand a chance.'

'He murdered her!' I burst out, and Declan's expression and aura sobered slightly.

'So you said, yes. Definitely makes my story a touch darker. Obviously, the murdering came later, after all the sex and drama.'

'But... but why would she?' I asked, horrified as the ramifications crashed through my mind.

Declan's mouth quirked. 'I assume it's safe to say you've never been in love?'

I might have blushed if I weren't so shocked. In my months of fascination with Ana Morrissey's life, I had never seen or learned anything to make me suspect *this*.

'What's that got to do with anything?'

'Someone who had wouldn't need to ask. And if you had, you'd probably understand the compulsion to get intimate with the object of your forbidden desire–'

'Ugh, stop, stop. I've seen visions of Lisandro carrying Ana on his *shoulders* when she was like, two. Oh, God,' I groaned, leaning my head forward into my hands, my stomach twisting and my thoughts boggling. Ana and Lisandro. He helped raise her. 'I feel sick.'

'I told you it wasn't a nice story,' Declan reminded me delicately. I squeezed my eyes shut behind my fingers, wishing I'd never come here, wishing I'd left this alone like Renatus had warned me.

'No, it's...' I pushed my hands back through my hair, angry with my own insensitivity. 'I've been such an arse about this with Renatus. I had no idea.'

'Yes, this is one of his least favourite stories,' Declan agreed. He held his hand out to inspect his bandaging. 'I'm not surprised he didn't want to tell it to you.'

'How do you know it?'

'You knew I'd know it but didn't consider *how* I'd know? Your mind is a fascinating place, my sweet. Maybe Renatus talks in bed?'

I didn't hide my irritation. 'Don't. I know you're related, and I'm already at my limit with Ana and Lisandro.'

'Your limit is adorable,' Declan granted affectionately. 'We're not that closely related – I could tell you stories about the Chathams and the Murphies. But alright. You've probably noticed he rants. He ranted considerably about all this.'

'To you?' I asked sceptically.

'You think he's got a lot of other friends?'

I wasn't even sure Declan *was* one of Renatus's friends, but I reluctantly took his point.

'Okay. Okay.' I tried to pull myself together. It was difficult – I couldn't remember when I was last this grossed out. 'Ana… fell in love with…' I found I wasn't much more comfortable with this turn of phrase than I was with the explicit ones, 'Lisandro, and they acted on it, and her dad… flipped out. Understandably. What did he do? Do you know?'

'Well, I wasn't there, but an argument like that leaves an energetic aftermath, like, *everywhere*, so yeah, I know.' Declan rolled his eyes smugly. 'There was screaming, tears, a punch-up; all the theatre you'd expect. Aindréas didn't particularly *like* his daughter but if she didn't know after that how much he loved her, she wasn't paying attention. He beat Lisandro to within an inch of his life, and then he banished him from the estate and disowned him.'

'And Ana stayed with her family,' I guessed, trying to put the last few pieces together, 'so he came back and killed them all? Except Renatus?'

'Not quite. The storm didn't roll in and take them all out until, oh, nearly a year later. And Ana didn't stay by choice. She tried a few times to run away. The second time, she got as far as New York before Aindréas caught up with her and dragged her, kicking and screaming I imagine, back home. You don't want a young woman getting ideas about being independent, after all,' Declan added reasonably, flicking me a brief, wicked smile. 'She was… persuaded… to remain home after that.'

'Persuaded?' I repeated, another wave of yuckiness washing over me at the word. 'How?'

'Nope.' He locked his fingers together behind his head and leaned back in faux relaxation. 'Your turn. What made you desperate enough to come here? Obedient, sweet Aristea, sneaking out in the middle of the night to meet a dangerous, dark, older man her Morrissey master would never approve of. I feel like I've read this story before...' He wiggled his eyebrows suggestively.

'*How* are you single, Declan?' I asked with a roll of my eyes, and he shrugged emphatically.

'I *know*, right? Technically I'm still betrothed to my one true love Keely Shanahan, and no one's willing to make an offer if it means being the one to make old Thomas the second accept his daughter's probably dead.' He watched me idly. 'Unless you know something?'

I shook my head, not trusting myself to navigate that topic with him, but then I wasn't sure what else to say. I didn't want to tell him anything he could trade or use against me. I didn't want to tell him I'd seen what happened to Lorcan O'Malley, or about my sightings of Keely, now Nastassja, both of which I thought were insensitive subjects anyway. 'I... Do you... believe in ghosts, Declan?'

I hoped my voice came out steadier than it sounded in my ears. His eyes brightened in interest; I'd surprised him.

'Fate's, maybe,' he answered immediately. 'Why? Whose ghost have you seen?'

I shrugged. My experience in the graveyard was fresh and disturbing, and I didn't have words to describe it.

'I didn't *see* anything. Maybe you're right, and it was Fate? It wants me to know something, something about Lisandro's reasons for what he did to my family and the others, but I just don't have all the information. And I need to know.'

Declan watched me with intense curiosity for a long moment, like he was reading me, though there was no way he was in my head.

'Yes,' he agreed finally. 'You do. In that case, I'm so glad you asked.' He waved his hands around each other and caught the earthen bowl that materialised before him with a smile. 'Just one more question, and don't forget this one: there'll be a quiz. Would you miss what you don't remember?'

I stared at the empty bowl as he twirled bandaged fingers

to generate sprigs of herbs that he dropped in. 'A *memory spell*?'

'Your pure and beautiful heiress has done the deed with a family friend with no pedigree. Her potential for political marriage is threatened if that story gets out. So?'

'So you wipe your daughter's memory?' I demanded, sickened. This world Renatus and Ana had grown up in had a horrifying habit of treating their girls and women like property. Declan got to his feet and held the bowl out so I could see. He made a pestle appear and began to grind the mixture up.

'Cruel but clean. Everyone wins. Unless she realises what you've done, so you've got to do a tidy job. Hey,' he added, nodding at my wrist, 'what's the time, anyway?'

'Uh...' I checked my watch. Whoops. 'Three twenty-one. Renatus is going to kill me.'

'Unless you knew how to perform one of these babies,' Declan quipped, tearing a pinch of his scruffy hair out with a wince and adding it to the bowl. I watched in dark fascination.

'And... you *do* know how?' I checked. He nodded, continuing to stir what was becoming a paste, beginning to murmur unintelligible sounds or words. 'Can you make him not know I was ever here?'

'I could,' he confessed cautiously, 'but that would be, you know, illegal. Not to mention unethical. And I wouldn't want to lead a lovely, impressionable little thing like you astray. The White Elm frowns *very* heavily on memory tampering, however much they might use it themselves. What time did you say it was?'

'Three twenty-one,' I repeated, rubbing my scalp where it suddenly twinged. 'You think they use it?' He scoffed his agreement. 'On who?'

'The guy in my basement.' He flashed me that smile and I smiled back without meaning to. I hoped he was joking. 'Nobodies, not paranoid enough to suspect it. Commit a minor crime, not worth stripping their magic or throwing them to those savage Russians, just remove or rewrite the memory. Removal is easier than rewriting. And smooth down the edges, so to speak. It's important to join the new memory with their internal timeline. If they're eating dinner and you delete dessert and patch it to the washing up, they're going to know something's up. But if you seamlessly join the start of the conversation with the end, for instance, your subject is none the wiser. What's the time?'

Captivated with his free lesson, I glanced impatiently at my wristwatch again. 'It's three twen...'

Three thirty-seven.

I read it wrong before. Or I'm reading it wrong now. My brain kind of shorted out at the impossibility and logic tried to sort it out for me. Sixteen minutes. Sixteen minutes had *not* passed since I last looked.

'My watch...' I shook my wrist, worried it'd broken or run out of battery, but it was still ticking. Keeping time. Meanwhile, I seemed to have lost time. I looked back at Declan, who said nothing, only leaned to place the bowl on the tabletop beside me in my blind spot. I had to tilt my head to see.

There was paper inside, torn to little stained pieces, and everything from the paper to the herb paste to the bits of string and stone that I hadn't seen him add was blackened like it had been briefly burnt.

With a heart-stopping shock of realisation, I shoved myself off the tabletop and backed quickly away, knocking the bowl loudly as I tried to put as much distance as possible between myself and this wolf I'd stupidly delivered myself to. Stupid, stupid. I raised both hands warily, casting a solid ward with one and feeling a ball of black fire spark in the palm of the other one.

Declan stayed where he was.

'What did you do to me?' I demanded, furious with my stupid, *stupid* self for being so damn trusting, furious with him for taking advantage of my stupidity again, and feeling very, very vulnerable. As much as I didn't want him to see me scared or weak, I left my ward hanging between us and lowered my hand to pat myself over. Feeling for loose clothing. Feeling for anything missing from my pocket or necklace. Feeling, with petrified disgust, for foreign saliva on my lips, ew, *ew*. 'Did you... did you touch me?'

'Depends on your definition of *you*,' Declan considered calmly. 'I would say no. I showed you how to cast a memory spell.'

'By casting one on *me*?' I shouted, incredulous. I could feel nothing out of place, thank whatever gods were still with me after my epic failure with sense tonight. What had I been *thinking*? How did I *think* this was going to end? I'd walked straight into this trap, trying to punch well above my weight. 'Sixteen minutes. You stole *time* from me. What's wrong with you?'

Where are you?

Renatus's concerned voice cut sharply into my thoughts, and my spare hand went automatically to my ear as though to trap the sound of him, wanting to be back with him, wanting to forget I ever came here, wanting to wind time back and listen to his good advice.

I'm so sorry, I answered him, hoping he believed me. I felt him in my head, borrowing my eyes. *I'm coming back now*.

'It's not gone, sweetheart, and I made sure to do an uncharacteristically poor job of covering it up,' Declan insisted. 'It's important you understand the consequences of a bad spell.'

'This was supposed to be a *lesson*?'

Of course it was, one I refused to learn. Trust no one. Renatus recognised the scene immediately and I felt his stunned fear for me. *What are you doing there?!*

'Always. But don't worry, you don't owe me anything,' Declan assured me, still not moving, 'and your favour still stands.'

'I don't want anything from you!' I snapped. I went for the door and shoved it open with the force of my ward, Renatus's rage filling me and fuelling me. 'I shouldn't have come here at all. All you ever do is prove you can't be trusted.'

'No,' Declan agreed, 'but you knew that before you got here. And you're welcome,' he called after me as I stormed through the reception hall to the ultra-locked front door. *I'm sorry, I wasn't thinking.* As I watched, each lock unlatched and unbolted itself, and every chain fell away. The door swung open. The black spell in my hand faded away. I glanced behind me at the empty doorway and imagined – or scried – Declan still standing where I left him, smirking at his bandaged hand as he added, 'I'll see you soon.'

'Just stay away from me,' I snarled, shouldering my way out and leaping clear of the broken steps. I raced across the patchy dead field that passed for a front lawn, my heart in my throat, my skin crawling. I didn't know if anything had happened, whether he'd even touched me, but just the knowledge that he *could* have and I would have no memory of it made me want to be sick. I felt violated. My mind *had* been violated. I'd lost sixteen minutes of my life here and I didn't know how to get it back.

I didn't notice when my eyes filled with tears, blinding me in the dark; other senses that used to freak me out backfilled the gaps, including the area on my left I usually couldn't see, and I easily dodged the jagged tree stump that presented as an obstacle. When I approached the broken and nondescript wooden fence of the property at a run, my hands found the top beam without fumble. I vaulted over and landed like I knew what I was doing.

Which, according to all other evidence, I clearly did *not*.

I was four steps off the O'Malley property when Renatus appeared in front of me, catching my arm to slow me down, and in my immediate relief I lost control of all that extrasensory perception. The world went blurry and dark, his worry for me pushed my disappointment in myself over the edge into the realm of total humiliation, and I realised I was a sobbing mess. I let my head fall forward onto his shoulder. *I'm sorry, I'm sorry…*

'Aristea! What happened?' he demanded, maybe several times, trying to hold me at arm's length to look me over. I couldn't speak; I tried to hide my face when he turned me. 'Did he hurt you?'

Only my pride. I shook my head and felt rather than heard his sigh of relief, which thankfully in this moment was

345

more pronounced than his anger. He let me go and let me cry into his shoulder for half a minute, even stroking my hair once in a gesture of comfort I didn't deserve. I wondered what state he'd expected to find me in and shuddered to realise I had no idea of his informant's real capabilities or intentions.

'Did he touch you?' he asked firmly when I started gasping for more controlled breaths. I started to shake my head, then hesitated.

'I don't… I don't think so,' I managed. He pulled away, anger stirring back to the surface.

'You don't *think* so?'

'H-He said he didn't. I don't remember.'

Renatus stared at me, disbelieving. I was too wired and distressed to follow his speeding thoughts, but his intense emotions surrounded me.

'I'll kill him,' he decided, and turned away toward the rundown mansion. My heart skipped a beat in dread – I was meant to be saving him from committing murders, not pushing him to it.

'No, don't,' I tried to insist, hurrying after him and grabbing for his wrist. Spiky black magic was already building in his palm, much more potent than the imitation I'd generated a few minutes earlier. He shook me off. 'He won't let you in.'

I was right. Renatus blasted a hole in the fence I'd just leapt and strode to the door. He pounded his fist on the door.

'Declan!' he roared. 'Get out here!'

We got no response and when Renatus tried the door, it was locked again.

'*Declan!*'

'He's not coming,' I said tiredly, sniffing and blinking through tears. This was just the worst night in so long, and I wanted it to be over.

'Then I'll burn the whole goddamn house to the ground,' Renatus threatened loudly, twin balls of fire sparking and dying above his open hands. I blinked my tears away; his edges seemed to blur with unstable power. 'Get out here, Declan. I warned you.'

'Please, let's just go,' I begged, scared of what he might do. I tugged on his arm, trying to drag him down the broken steps. 'It's not him you should be angry with, it's me.'

He yanked away from me with enough force that I stumbled back down the last step onto the ground, where I stared up at him helplessly.

'I am *plenty* angry for you both,' he assured me, and I could feel that this was true. My wards protected me from most of it. 'What the hell are you doing here? Do you know what time it is?'

I winced at the second question. 'I…' I'd screwed up and I didn't know what I was meant to say in my defence. 'I'm sorry.'

'*Sorry?*' he spat back at me, more venomously than I'd ever heard. I flinched. 'You're sorry? What is going on with you? I told the council you were sorry for Addison James. You were sorry for running off to nearly lose yourself in the void. Now you're sorry for sneaking out of the house without telling me and coming *here*, of all places, putting yourself at unnecessary risk, having *whatever* happen to you…' He gestured helplessly at me, apparently referencing my visible distress. 'For what? For *what?*'

'I n-needed information,' I stammered, starting to cry again.

'Information?' Renatus echoed incredulously. 'You thought you'd come here? *Why?* You know what Declan's like. Nothing comes for free.'

'This is where *you* go when you need to know something no one else can tell you,' I said miserably, making him growl incoherently and claw at his scalp when I added, 'You didn't leave me with any other option and I thought I had it under control.'

'I'm *me!*' he shouted frustratedly. 'I know what I'm doing. *You* shouldn't be here. Anything could have happened.'

'I'm not a little kid!' I shouted back, not caring that Declan was hearing every word from the other side of his door. Anger at the unfairness rushed through me. 'It's always do as you say, not as you do. You can't treat me like your partner half the time and then push me back in the dark when it suits you. You can't protect me from everything.'

'Thanks for the reminder,' he sneered. 'You think I'm not working that out on my own?' He forcibly turned away, seething, but spun back almost straightaway and came at me down the uneven stairs. I backed up quickly. 'You could have died in Prague. Miles and miles away from home, leaving me to explain to this poor sister of yours I've never even met how this happened when you're meant to be safe on the estate and I'm supposed to be looking out for you.'

'But I didn't,' I reminded him, wiping my eyes. 'It didn't happen. I'm okay.'

'But you weren't, and I'm still not,' Renatus shot back. He towered over me. 'Whover this bastard is who keeps loosening the wards over the house, I'm going to kill him when I'm finished with Declan, because I'm dreaming again, and now when I close my eyes I'm back in that street finding you bleeding and screaming. And I can still do nothing. Do you have any idea what that did to me? Do you *care*?'

'Of course I care–'

'I had to carry you, bleeding *everywhere*, to London, not knowing if you'd live,' he went on, every word cutting. 'I had to knock you unconscious to stop you screaming because I couldn't do anything else. I had to pull a spell out of you and watch them operate on you. I had your blood all over my hands,' he spat, opening his hands as though to show me what was long since washed off. I felt awful, knowing his deep aversion to blood, and realising how my injury that day must have flashed him back to Ana's death in the orchard. He wasn't finished. 'You know I'd do it again if it meant you'd be safe, but you're *not*. All you've done since is push the boundaries; now you take off in the middle of the night for me to find you in tears outside Declan O'Malley's. I have a fortress, Aristea,' he reminded me desperately. 'Why can't you just stay in it?'

'I needed to know why your dad and Lisandro had their falling out,' I burst out. 'I knew you'd never tell me. I needed to know… if it's really why he killed them all.'

Even the crickets and other night-time bugs were quiet. Renatus was looking at me like he didn't know me. It hurt more than the anger.

'And?' he prompted finally, voice frozen. 'What's the verdict?'

'Declan told me. It... It wasn't the answer I was looking for,' I admitted. 'It makes no sense. If he loved her–'

'*Don't* say that!' Renatus screamed at me, and I covered my ears in fright. 'He never loved her! He didn't love any of us. If he did, he wouldn't have made her choose between him and her family. He wouldn't have *murdered* her and our parents or sent that stranger to our house to do his dirty work, and he wouldn't have married our runaway *cousin* and given her Ana's fucking *name*. I don't know what that is, but that better not be what love looks like.' He breathed heavily as he struggled to get it back under his control. I lowered my hands shakily, worried I'd broken him. His next words were calmer. 'So now you know.'

'Now I know,' I agreed softly, ashamed. His pain and anger started to retract from me as he reeled himself in with extreme effort. 'I'm so sorry I kept trying to bring it up. I had no idea.'

He nodded slowly. 'That much was obvious.'

'I wish I hadn't kept digging. I wish I hadn't come here and asked. It was horrible.'

'Our style of magic doesn't cover wishes.'

I bit the inside of my lip, not knowing how to fix this. This was worse than my spat with Addison or even the loss of Hiroko.

'I wish,' I said carefully, 'that you'd given me something to go off. Told me *something*.'

'I *did* tell you something,' Renatus snapped, getting angry again. 'I told you we weren't going to discuss it.'

'I know, and I'm sorry, but she keeps pushing me to find out,' I explained urgently. 'Ana. She wants–'

'No, stop.' He held up a hand as he loudly cut me off, squeezing his eyes shut as though to block me out. His hold on all his discomfort and hurt slipped and I felt it fall on me, soaking straight down to my vulnerable soul. 'I can't do this. Can you just respect one single thing I ask of you, and for once, shut up about my sister?'

It hurt to swallow and my face was hot and wet with embarrassed tears. He didn't deserve this searing and unexpected thrust into the worst moments of his memory, and he didn't deserve for it to come from me. I knew I'd hurt him, maybe hurt us. The consequences of my thoughtlessness were all around me, Renatus's intense emotional trauma spilled out where I couldn't escape it. I opened my mouth to say something to repair the harm, but he didn't want to hear it.

'Hurts, does it?' he asked, calming down. I looked up at him and he gestured vaguely at himself. 'Me?'

I nodded. I never felt as down and hopeless as when I came into contact with Renatus's deeply rooted and usually tightly managed depression. If I didn't feel worthless before, I did now.

'Sorry about that,' he said flatly, without meaning. 'I told you to leave it alone. I shouldn't have to spell out why.'

'Renatus–'

'This was none of your business,' he interrupted brutally. 'This is my family, and it's got *nothing* to do with you.' He shouldered past me roughly and I let the tears roll. Over his shoulder he yelled, 'I'll be back to deal with you, too, Declan.'

chapter twenty-four

In five hundred years of history, only once before had the White Elm council worked and lived in the tight, close conditions of today, and that was when they were first formed. The earliest version of the council had come together out of the witch residents of a single town, drawing on the authoritative magic of Fate to endorse their righteous claim to power against a dangerous enemy. That enemy had been defeated, but another had risen in their wake, and then another, and eventually one of the council's own original members had turned, too. And so the White Elm had remained relevant long past their intended reign, their power and usefulness spreading their influence further and further until they quite literally ruled the world – the largest recognised nation of magic users, anyway, with citizens all across the globe. Their reach had brought stability and that stability brought peace.

History shows that peace breeds poor soldiers.

Case in point, Qasim thought dryly, watching across the room as Aristea, his best student, gave up on her exercises and pinched out the candle wick in front of her. Over her shoulder, her friend Iseult Taylor glanced at her inconspicuously. It was difficult to miss the hopeless mood the apprentice had been in all week, but Iseult was only here now on Thursdays. Glad as she seemed to have her scrying partner back, the tiny elfin Crafter had quickly worked out to tread carefully.

Qasim kept his distance but flicked his attention briefly to the extinguished wick. Its flare back to life startled Aristea but the surprise in her eyes quickly died back to the same weariness she'd walked in with.

Don't bother coming to my class if you're not going to put in the work, he said flatly, directly into her head. He knew she heard; her brow furrowed in irritation and she sat up straighter. Good. Maybe now her compulsion to show him up would kick in.

'Extra challenge,' Qasim announced to his small class. He picked up the cardboard box on the central coffee table, distracting all six students, and shook it. Inside, they all heard the two internal boxes crashing about. Outside, they all groaned.

'But sir!'

'I was so close!'

'Well, speed it up,' he replied carelessly. 'How many high-stakes situations do you think you'll ever be asked to scry that will stay still for you for ten minutes?'

Idealists, all of them. Softened by a peace stretching back too far for living memory to properly appreciate. But Aristea knew better than the others what the world could look like without that peace, and that knowledge should be starting to toughen her.

Perhaps it was. She turned quietly to Iseult and compared notes. Each box inside the larger one had a word or phrase in Romanian, courtesy of Teresa and a permanent marker, handwritten on all six surfaces. The students' task, in their pairs, was to scry inside the sealed box clearly enough, with no provided light source, to read and transcribe all twelve passages. Khalida and Xanthe, despite never missing a lesson, were struggling. Dylan and Constantine were casting stealthy looks over at Iseult and Aristea's work to see how far ahead the dream team had gotten.

Qasim continued to pace the room slowly, watching each student's technique. Some had their eyes closed as they captured a vision of inside the box, their lips shifting as they tried to memorise the unfamiliar syllables before breaking their connection and scrawling them down. Others stared into their flames and wrote without looking at their page.

Only Aristea and Iseult broke the mould, competent enough to try multiple creative solutions. Seeing that she and her partner already had a good portion of the text transcribed, Aristea blew out her candle again and withdrew her ruby from her pocket. She was getting comfortable with the clarity and stability of the crystal medium, though she was strong enough that she really didn't need the external support anymore.

Across the room, comparing his own notes with Constantine's, Dylan started to wave his hand excitedly.

'I think we've got it. We've got it!'

Ultra-competitive Iseult slumped back in her seat dejectedly and Aristea put her ruby back in her pocket, interest in the lesson gone again. Other councillors had confided that she'd missed every one of her scheduled classes this week, initially explainable by some long days spent in the Archives, working on Anouk's research. But the Dark Keeper had been there for days without her, and he was about as mopey and useless as his apprentice whenever anyone happened to run into him.

Even Lord Gawain, who'd been too busy with international relations this week to even set foot on campus, had noticed Renatus's distance in their telepathic conversations, and had concernedly asked Qasim to see what he could find out. Like the Scrier had nothing better to do than run a mental health check on his least favourite upstart superior.

Though even Qasim could agree that an unfocused Renatus – the council's first and best line of defence in conflict – was not in anyone's interest while Lisandro remained in hiding with intentions unknown.

'Excellent work,' Qasim confirmed after a check of the boys' transcriptions. 'Personal exercises for all: find a non-English language book in the library downstairs and practise this skill. Leave the book open in another room, or facing away from you. Extension activities include turning the lights off, practising in a noisy or distracting environment, and trying to improve on your time.'

'Are there even any other-language books in the library?' Xanthe asked. Aristea, who hadn't spoken a direct word to her roommate in months as far as Qasim knew, answered without looking at her.

'Hiroko found a few. There's a small section near the back. Magical reference.'

'I saw those. They looked like originals,' Constantine commented, slanting his gaze to Aristea cautiously. 'Will the headmaster mind if we take them out of the library?'

'I don't think he'll care.'

The apprentice's deliberate nonchalance was not lost on either Qasim or Iseult, who met sceptical eyes across the room.

'Early mark today. You're all dismissed. Except you,' he said as he dismantled the cardboard. No point leaving it here for Renatus's poor overworked staff to deal with, and he wasn't sure they even received recycling services this far out. The class knew exactly who he was talking to and carried on grabbing their books, calling back their thanks and goodbyes to Qasim. Aristea, who likewise knew without even being looked at, sat back in her seat moodily and again withdrew her ruby to fidget with. She wasn't a fidgeter when he first met her.

Iseult offered to meet her for lunch, which boosted the apprentice's mood enough to make her smile, and then Qasim was alone with her.

'You're off your game,' he stated, opening the big box and tipping out the two small ones onto one of the chaise lounges nearby. 'I expect better.'

Aristea took a while to answer, her conflict evident in her face and the spikiness of her aura. She spun the crystal in her fingers, pretending to examine it from all sides.

'Maybe I'm not better,' she said finally. Qasim resisted the urge to roll his eyes at the childish self-esteem game.

'Then you might as well go home,' he responded flatly. He collapsed the big box loudly and she jumped a little. 'Give up now. I thought you wanted to join the White Elm?'

'One day,' she answered defensively. He tossed one of

the smaller cubes to her to pull apart and she raised an easy hand to catch it, her eyes on his wrist.

'I assume it's my job you want.'

Aristea turned the box over slowly in her hands, watching him. 'It's crossed my mind.'

'I've been the Scrier for more than half my life,' Qasim told her. 'And I've given it a lot. I'll do this job until Lord Gawain steps down, and then two things will happen. One, I'll ascend to High Priest of the White Elm, where I'll be back in a position to tell your master where to take his opinions,' and his short-sighted, self-indulgent arrogance, 'and two, I'll be in a position to approve the applicant who goes into my old role.' He collapsed the smaller box. 'I can tell you now, it won't be a lazy, self-absorbed child who skips classes offered to her at no cost from some of the foremost experts in the magical arts–'

'I turned up to yours!' Aristea argued, standing up. Qasim continued as if she hadn't cut in.

'–and tries to skate by on sixty percent effort when she *does* show, all because she's had some spat with her master she doesn't have the maturity to either deal with or shelve. Your apprenticeship comes with a guarantee of admission to the White Elm. It doesn't come with any such guarantee of *this* job.'

He flattened the two boxes he had with him and looked up at her to see her reaction. The girl was visibly upset as she frowned, tense, at the small cardboard box in her hand. She had the ruby in her other fist, clenched tight. He had strongly considered taking Aristea as his own apprentice, before Renatus had jumped the gun much too early. He was glad now he hadn't, because the girl aggravated him, even if she impressed him when she was switched on. She'd become increasingly unstable and rebellious as she came into her power and was exposed to the dangers of Renatus's role too soon. Still, looking at her now, seeing that pinkish scar she had not yet earned, Qasim had to remind himself that she was eighteen years old, older than his own children but a child still, with another child for a mentor and a lot of growing up yet to do.

'You saved seventy-two people's lives in Prague last month,' he reminded her, surprising her into looking up at him again. 'You're a hero to our whole nation. I know you don't get out much, but that's what they're saying. A hero doesn't put in sixty percent, Aristea, and I don't want someone beside me in a face-off with Lisandro or any of his supporters who blows out the candle when she's challenged. I need to see a hundred percent every time.'

Aristea looked down at her left hand. She tightened her already clenched grip on her stone and Qasim saw a web of smoky grey lines, like cracks, glow briefly under the skin of her hand and forearm.

'A hundred percent didn't save Anouk,' she said without emotion as the evidence of her near-burnout faded back to nothing. Qasim exhaled slowly, rethinking his angle. Pushing her further into her hopelessness wasn't his intention – where was the bite, the fieriness he usually got when he dangled his approval just out of her reach?

'My hundred percent wouldn't have, either. Not from that. Your hundred percent saved seventy-two other people, and that's a trade Anouk would have made in a heartbeat. That's a trade any of us would make, given the choice. She made it ten years ago when she left her home to join us. I made it when I followed my master onto his council. You made it in Prague, too,' he said, gentling his voice slightly when he saw that she had tears gathering unexpectedly in her eyes. 'You gave almost everything to save that crowd of innocent people. I know next time you'd like to be better. So, get better. Go to your classes. Put in the work. And work out what you'd give a hundred percent for.'

It didn't take a Telepath to know when that mile-a-minute brain of hers was in overdrive, too much going on in it, too much weighing on it. She frequently frustrated Qasim but he knew that most of what he disliked was Renatus's influence, and this dark mood was his doing, somehow or another.

He'd have the joy of yet another of these tiresome pep talks when he met up with the young scrier for their afternoon mission together.

Aristea pocketed her ruby to free up her hand, and began to open and flatten the cardboard cube.

'Your master was the Scrier, too,' she said finally, eyeing his wrist again. 'Joseph?'

Qasim nodded, surprised that she knew that. Perhaps she'd done her homework, so to speak, and read up or asked around about White Elm history. He shifted his sleeve and turned his wrist over so she could see the tattoo she was looking for. He'd always liked the unique symbol Fate had chosen to represent his apprenticeship to the calm, collected American private investigator who'd given him a job and a place to stay when he'd turned up in the country, a runaway, and later a lifetime of tutelage and mentorship, culminating in him joining his master on the White Elm. Before meeting Joseph by chance near the docks that rainy afternoon, Qasim hadn't even known that he was a sorcerer.

'I heard his name in a vision,' Aristea admitted. 'They said he was good.'

'He was better than good. He was everything I still aspire to one day be.' He paused to let this sink in, because there weren't words for the depth of his respect for his master. 'That's the legacy you're hoping to join. Luckily you've still got time to prove you're worthy.'

She swallowed with what looked like effort, handing back the unfolded box. 'I plan to.'

'And whatever this problem you have with Renatus–'

'I don't have a problem with Renatus,' she said instantly, irritating Qasim with her denial, but before he could snap at her, she finished, with a sigh, '*He's* mad with *me*. I... I screwed up.'

If it wasn't one it was the other, and Renatus was the council's most laden emotional baggage carrier. Couple that with an Empath for an apprentice... Qasim tilted his head in the direction of the door, dismissing Aristea, and she snatched up her notebook and pen and ran out. He scratched his temple, giving himself a minute before dealing with his next task. Who exactly had signed him up as the White Elm's junior scrier agony aunt?

Taking care of the recycling outside a shopping centre in the outskirts of Belfast took less than a minute, and another Skip later had Qasim walking into a wide field in the far west of England. The Stonehenge was out of sight, a few hundred metres over his shoulder, and though they all looked more or less the same, the hillock he wanted was right in front of him. He let the inhabitant know he had arrived, and waited.

'You're early,' Renatus noted grumpily a minute later when the Archive's portal door opened to let him out. His aura brimmed with his usual power but his strange eyes were dull with lack of sleep, underscored by the beginning of shadows beneath them.

'I'm allowing time,' Qasim corrected. The Archive sealed. 'We need to talk.'

The Dark Keeper scowled, not wasting time feigning misunderstanding, and turned to walk away.

'No, we don't.'

Qasim matched his pace, which was unnecessarily swift. 'She's a mess again. What have you done this time?'

'Me?' Renatus demanded before he could remember to be cold and dismissive. He pulled himself together somewhat. 'It's not your concern either way. Emmanuelle is Aristea's witness–'

'And Lord Gawain is yours, and he wants to know why his power team is on break,' Qasim interrupted. Renatus kept walking, focused with suppressed anger, as if he was going to walk to their destination. Qasim let him go for it; they had time. 'To be perfectly honest, I don't care what you're upset about, but when your mood interferes with me – with my lessons with Aristea, with our mission today – it becomes my concern. And given that you were *adamant* that you were ready for an apprentice when you took her on, I'm going with the assumption that you're in complete control of the situation and that you're going to fix it. Am I right?'

Renatus stopped abruptly and turned back so quickly

Qasim nearly ran into him.

'You want to know what you're missing out on?' he asked agitatedly, and the Scrier wondered how long it had actually been since the younger man had slept. 'Fine. She left the estate at three in the morning without telling me to visit Declan O'Malley to ask–'

'She *what*?' Qasim cut in, sideswiped both by the news and by Renatus's uncharacteristic forthrightness. A moment later the reality of that statement set in and he frowned, protective of the frustrating but sheltered little scrier. 'I *told* you not to introduce her to your scumbag friends. What did he do to her?'

'Nothing she remembers, which wouldn't normally fill me with confidence, but I actually don't think Declan would be that brave. He's a scrier – he knows you and I would find out sooner rather than later. But he's not my friend. And that's not the point,' Renatus fumed, getting back on track with his own anger. 'She went there to have him tell her why Lisandro and my father stopped speaking, after I'd already told her it had nothing to do with why he went after her family next, and now she knows.' He edgily wiped his hand across his mouth, eyes narrowed and glaring at the horizon without focus. 'I knew she wouldn't like it. I *told* her.'

Qasim exhaled exhaustedly. He hadn't signed up for an apprentice, let alone two. He was the only person on the White Elm who'd seen inside Renatus's whole mind, and it was a minefield of unaddressed fears, secrets and hurts, many of them tied up with his family, most of them tied to his dead sister. He'd watched her die in his arms as a boy, savagely beaten and bleeding profusely, and he'd learned the hard way to view himself as a failure for his unspoken inability to heal. He'd also killed someone, or close enough, in that moment, which he'd struggled to forgive himself for, and which must be eating him alive now that it had come out that Lisandro had been responsible, not the nameless henchman. Qasim had seen the recesses of Renatus's mind where Declan O'Malley's story about Lisandro and the Morrisseys resided, and didn't want to

359

even begin to unpack the complex layers of shame, disgust and betrayal that must be entwined with that. Yet here he was, about to turn his impatient floodlight directly onto it for Renatus to deal with.

Therapy took too long, and Qasim was no therapist.

'Why did she think she had to go to O'Malley?' he asked brusquely. 'Wouldn't it have been easier, and safer, to ask you?' He let the words hang for a moment, seeing in the younger scrier's face that he understood exactly where this was going. 'Unless she felt she couldn't.'

Renatus scowled again. 'I told her I didn't want to talk about it.'

'Excellent,' Qasim sneered, annoyed though he knew this would be the explanation. 'So our newest and most fragile asset hand-delivers herself to the wrong type of scrier because *your* precious ego must be preserved.'

'That's not–' Renatus bit down on his angry retort. He fumed silently for a moment, then tried again. 'I'm entitled to want to avoid–'

'Entitled, yes, that's *exactly* the word I was looking for.'

'I didn't want her to know,' the Dark Keeper snapped. He struggled visibly. 'What they did. I didn't want her to know that about Ana.'

'I don't know how many times we need to have this conversation,' Qasim said irritably. 'Aristea's apprenticeship isn't about what *you* want. If the truth is that your sibling was less of an angel than you like to remember, it's not Aristea's job to believe in a ghost *you* construct for her to help you sustain your illusion. Grow up.'

'They're connected.'

'Only by you.'

'No,' Renatus insisted, clearly upset by Qasim's brutal treatment of this very sensitive topic but trying to hold his ground. 'Aristea can't stay away from the graveyard in the orchard for more than a couple of weeks at a time. She taps into Ana's life constantly.'

Qasim wanted to groan loudly but held it in with effort

as he spelt out what should have been obvious. 'She's a scrier. She's an Empath. She's been blood-bonded to you. And you've got her living in your dead sister's *room*.'

'She said Ana *wants* her to know,' Renatus scoffed angrily. 'Like they talk.'

Qasim stared, waiting for the punchline. 'And?'

'And that's ridiculous. Dead people can't talk.'

'*You* are ridiculous,' the Scrier shot back, not caring how hurtful it might come out. 'Her interpretation might be imaginative but why would you assume she's wrong? How often is she wrong?' He waited for Renatus to click, but sleep-deprived Renatus wasn't as quick, and he stood glaring in silence. Qasim kept going, feeling like he was talking down to a child. 'Your sister was murdered. Violently. The memory of her held by the Fabric of the world wants it resolved. The same way you dreamed about the storm that killed your parents; the same way you both revisit Prague whenever you let yourselves dream. Can you really not believe a scrier as sensitive as your apprentice would feel the push you choose to ignore? It astounds me,' he added, frustratedly fixing his tie when a sharp wind cut across the plain, bringing the noise of the highway to disrupt the illusion of isolated wildness, 'how such an abstract thinker can become so narrow-minded as soon as it gets uncomfortable.'

Renatus's hair, perpetually overlong and in need of a cut, got caught up in the same noisy wind, and he turned away, seething quietly.

'Are we done?'

'Gladly. Just please, tell your apprentice she's forgiven, or whatever you've got to say to make at least *one* of you bearable again.'

Qasim folded his arms and waited out the younger scrier's internal tantrum, which took more than a minute of evident struggle and conflict. A lot of glaring at the hilly horizon in lieu of his usual window.

'Where are we going?' he asked finally, his voice more even than it had been since he stepped out of the Archive.

There. Back to his usual cold, professional self.

'Massachusetts, United States,' Qasim answered coolly, much preferring this version of Renatus he didn't have to feel responsible for. This version, he could deal with as a colleague and it didn't have to matter that they didn't like each other.

'Don't say Salem,' the younger scrier muttered, finally starting to push his windswept hair back into something resembling its 'place'.

'They're not hanging our kind there anymore,' Qasim said ironically, offering an arm. Renatus caught on, and they stepped through space and across an ocean. Instantly Qasim regretted the exit point.

'Is this the place?' Renatus asked curiously, looking around the small backyard they'd landed in. Qasim felt oddly unwell, a noxious and repellent energy permeating the very air he breathed, sapping his power when he reached for it.

Violent magical death left a stain deep in the Fabric of a place.

'I hope not,' Qasim answered. He withdrew the letter from his jacket's inner pocket to check the address. Over the flimsy fence he could hear children fighting and a baby crying while a parent called for them all to shut up. Lovely. He tried to shrug off the power drain and went for the tall side gate to get out the front of the property. Renatus trailed behind him, his aura overfull and swollen with magic.

The house number didn't match, and the dark energy followed them out to the street. What had happened here? While Renatus wandered to the nearby intersection to confirm the street name, Qasim looked around. The street they'd landed on was a narrow one, part of a larger housing estate that seemed to have been built all at once, in close quarters, about twenty, twenty-five years earlier. Some of the homes were tidy but most had too many cars parked on the driveway, uncut lawns, dead flower gardens and peeling paint.

Not sure he'd like what he'd see but determined after that confrontation with Renatus not to be an emotional hypocrite, Qasim knelt on the sidewalk and pressed his fingers to the cement. There were no impressions on the surface, obviously, and even deeper there were years and years of blockage between him and whatever had stained this place. But anything that dark couldn't be totally cleaned up, and he was the Scrier.

Screaming… darkened field… coven circle… knife into a soft, tensed throat… bodies as towers of flame…

He withdrew his hand, grimacing, and looked up as Renatus came back over.

'They built this estate over an old field,' he told the other. 'A spell went very wrong here, a long time ago. Mass burnout and a human sacrifice.'

Renatus looked appropriately disgusted – one of his few positive qualities, despite growing up in a blood magic tradition, was that he didn't practice any of its bloodier rituals. Probably he didn't need to.

'Sounds like they got what they deserved, then. Our street's that one,' he added, pointing at the quiet T-intersection. Qasim got to his feet.

'Why any of our kind would choose to live in a place that feels like this… unless they were you, of course,' he relented with a dark glance at Renatus's aura as they headed for the intersection. The Irish scrier was back in form, vague and cool, and let the swipe roll straight off him without bite.

'It doesn't feel good to me either,' he disagreed calmly, not paying much attention to their conversation. He was looking ahead. 'Who are we here to meet?'

Qasim offered the envelope; Renatus took it. They approached the corner.

'One of ours, a scrier called Freddie Poole,' Qasim said as his colleague unfolded the paper. 'Wanting to report seven missing sorcerers from his coven.'

'Seven? How did we lose seven sorcerers without noticing?' Renatus demanded. The pair of them passively monitored the White Elm nation, allowing important moments to cross their awareness throughout the day so that big things like murders and assaults didn't go unaddressed. Such moments, however, could be temporarily shielded from their notice, if the perpetrator knew how. 'Defection?'

'Poole thinks so. Apparently his coven meets once a month, and last week, without warning, seven of them didn't show up. Gone. When he's spoken to their friends or families, they've either been unwilling to talk or adamant that they're on holiday.'

'He thinks they've been paid off,' Renatus read as they walked. 'To what end?'

'To prevent them telling us their partners have gone to Lisandro, presumably. Luckily Poole wants to talk. He says there's more he can't put in a letter.'

The pair rounded the corner and stopped. The new street was flooded with red and blue flashing lights. An ambulance and police car were parked haphazardly outside a house halfway down the street, and emergency service personnel were standing around talking or making calls. No urgency. A stretcher bearing a black body bag was carried out. The large lettering on the open front door was just visible from this distance.

25.

Renatus turned the envelope over in his hand and they both checked the address they knew was written on it. How inconvenient.

'What do we know about the coven?' he asked, smoothing the now-useless letter distractedly in his hands. The fidgeter. Together they watched the paramedics load their informant into the back of the ambulance.

'Scriers. Salem descendants, some powerhouses among them. We had them on a watchlist a few years ago for some questionable practices. Attempting to learn to Active Scry. We sent them a warning, no further problems.'

'Until now.' Renatus looked down at the letter and envelope in his hands, eyes thoughtful. 'And here we are.'

'About a day too late, by the looks of it,' Qasim pointed out, but his colleague was on a new tangent, one of his annoying inspired spirals. He held out the folded letter suddenly.

'What organisation could get us in there right now?' he asked. In his hand, the folded paper transformed into a National Crime Agency ID badge with Qasim's photo on it. Before his current role, Renatus was the council's Illusionist. The Scrier snatched the fake identification away, affronted by the assumption that he would lie his way into a crime scene.

'NCA in Salem?' he asked scathingly, though considered that with the Dark Keeper's thick accent, it might be all he'd get away with. He eyed the other suspiciously. 'Why?'

'It's just a hunch. You might be as guilty as I am of ignoring imaginative explanations.'

Qasim scoffed with disdain. 'Right. Such as?'

'Missing scriers, Salem descendants, probably defectors, probably competent with Haunting by now if you slapped their wrist years ago,' Renatus spelt out, forgetting to sound condescending in his building certainty. 'Twelve killers, eleven who didn't want to be there. Now one unwitting whistleblower, dead. Why should we approach any investigation, let alone one connected to my godfather, as if everyone is playing by our rules?' He held up the envelope, now shifting between various authority ID formats he must have seen around the United Kingdom. Interpol. Border Agency. 'How do we get in?'

Starting to see the genius of the Dark Keeper's epiphany, Qasim shook out the letter, changing the fake badge to FBI.

'Try not to say much.'

chapter twenty-five

Oils soaking dry herbs, paper curling…

I migrated the bedclothes to the floor and slept restless nights staring at the ceiling of Ana's pretty princess bedroom, trying to remember what happened at Declan's, homesick for my simple single bed in Angela's house on Cairn Gardens. I'd never felt less like I belonged here. I might have packed up my things and finally gone back to my sister if not for Qasim telling me to do just that.

No way was he ever going to be right about me.

I tidied my little indoor campsite each morning to keep Fionnuala and any other household staff from worrying about me, and after Qasim's tough love yesterday I was back at my lessons, but my mind was still stuck on all my failures. Hurting Renatus. Letting Declan get the better of me. Not making the Ana-Lisandro connection myself earlier. And on top of it all, forgetting to ask Emmanuelle to let me call Angela for her birthday at the start of the week. I had made a hurried handcrafted card with the paper and scrapbooking stuff Fionnuala sometimes put out in the dining hall to occupy students throughout the day, and sent that, but I knew it would arrive late.

Salt ground into herbs…

My hand healed nicely, which only annoyed me further, because it was such a *giant freaking clue* and I'd ignored it. Another failure. Watching Declan wind bandages around small scrapes only hours after my own body had fixed a deep

366

gash in my hand, when only hours before *that* I'd heard the story of Emmanuelle demonstrating her goodness over Jackson's through healing… *Why* hadn't I questioned it?

'Everyone knows sorcerers heal unless there's bad magic involved,' Sophia said when she heard about Emmanuelle in Wisconsin. She tapped my palm twice after checking it for me, beaming. 'See? Because you're one of the good guys.'

I knew the equation was more complex than that, because it didn't allow for the Renatus variant, but I took it.

Words in ink…

I turned up early for Tian's mid-morning Friday sai lesson, determined to be better than last time, and sat on the grass waiting for him, half-heartedly stretching. I glanced warily in the direction of the orchard, harmless-looking in the bright sunlight. *I would tell you if I could.* Ana Morrissey had found a way to share her tragedy with me, how the man she'd loved her whole life had ended her, but rather than clarify our connection across time, my knowing had left us estranged. I used to think we were similar. Scriers. Overthinkers. Stubborn. Sisters for Renatus. Close in age. But there is so much more to a person, and so much I didn't know before. I'd thought it was a matter of pride to be reminiscent of Renatus's lost sister. Now I wasn't sure how I felt about any of it. A closet of ballgowns, twenty commissioned for her twentieth birthday, now seemed less like lavish spoiling and more like the guilt of regretful parents. Countless impressions I'd tapped of a vague and lost-looking heiress now seemed to speak less of childishness and more of a girl groping for stolen memories of her first love, out of reach but niggling at her consciousness the same way Monday night at Declan's niggled at mine.

Would you miss what you don't remember?

Barely nineteen, Declan had said about her affair with Lisandro. Only a year older than me. Old enough to know better, the cold sceptic in me claimed scathingly, but also young enough to be fooled and be foolish, my gentler side counselled. I'd told Renatus, stupidly, that I wasn't a kid, but I supposed in a lot of ways I was, even if Declan looked me up and down like I was an adult, even if the people we met on our missions eyed me like I might be a threat. Even if I told myself I'd be the one to take out Lisandro in the end.

What a weird age to be, caught in the middle, trying to be both.

Ana, it seemed, had believed herself grown up, though her parents and brother hadn't shared this perception. A whole family brought down, and piles of collateral damage done to other people's lives, because no one could agree when real adulthood – responsibility for one's own heart, body and choices – kicked in. Still, I couldn't comprehend Lisandro's appeal, and felt yucky at just the *thought* of anyone wanting him anything other than gone. I was definitely not ready for that part of adulthood.

'You are better today,' Tian acknowledged during our third set of exercises, lifting the kali sticks high for me to strike. One, two. I wasn't giving just sixty percent today. I wasn't going to mess up my footwork and I wasn't going to slacken my posture. The exertion of the lesson let me get my mind off all my failings and problems.

'Thank you,' I said between heavy breaths, opting against telling him I ran around after last week kinda practising, kinda fighting my demons. 'I wanted to be.'

'Good. I can see. Combination: one-two to the left, three-four high, ward. Yes?'

I nodded, shaking out my tension and preparing as Tian did exactly as he said he would. He brought the first stick toward me from my left where I couldn't see it, slowly enough that I could block with my first double slash, and then arced the second one down at me to catch with an overhead block. It meant that, unlike last week, my final contact came from the sword in my left hand, and that's where the ward would need to come from, too. I hadn't been casting with my left since Prague, not liking the tingle of the black cracks where the effort of my ward had almost broken me, but Tian's combination gave no choice.

On the third strike, I prepared the energy, and on contact

for four, I directed it through my arm.

The sai carried the ward right through, an extension of me, and a push of energy forced Tian's stick back and away. He took a step to keep his footing and grinned.

'*Shí*! Yes!' he exclaimed, lowering both kali sticks and coming back to me. I couldn't help smiling back, pleased to have finally impressed him. He opened his mouth to say something else, but a strange look passed over him, and he faltered. He looked down at the sticks in his hands, then quickly up at me with a brief smile. 'I think we are done today. Well done.'

He bowed his head to me in respectful dismissal and I copied, not sure what just happened. He dropped the sticks on the ground as he walked away. I went for my sai's box, bending to put one blade down and scoop up the polishing cloth.

'You're not done.'

I turned to see Renatus approach, and I felt equal parts hopeful and wary. Excited as I was by the prospect of being back on speaking terms, I also knew I'd done nothing to earn it, which meant either that some other catalyst had prompted Renatus to forgive me, or that he hadn't. His face gave nothing away, his mind was still shut off and he kept his emotions close and tight, which I took to mean the latter.

'Alright,' I said with a shrug, dropping the cloth back into the box and straightening with my one blade. I was still breathing a little heavily, but I had energy left for more sets. I eyed Renatus's unusually lightweight attire suspiciously. 'What do you have in mind?'

He stooped midstep for Tian's kali sticks. 'I was thinking you can show me what you've learned.'

I ran my tongue over my teeth. He hadn't been to any of my previous lessons, for which I'd been grateful. I was reasonably certain he had some training and though I failed at many tasks under his tutelage, to fail at a physical task seemed more embarrassing than failing a spell or other supernatural feat.

'Alright,' I said again, watching him heft the sticks in his hands, getting a feel for them, 'but it's not going to be very impressive. I've only learned a few blocks and parries. Footwork.'

'Alright,' he echoed. He nodded at my discarded second sword, a prompt to pick it up. 'Let's see all that in action.'

'As in…?' I bent to collect the sai from the box, taking my eyes off him for only a second. When I started to straighten, the end of a kali stick was in my face and he'd closed the space between us. I froze, caught out.

'As in, where's your guard?' he asked, lowering the stick to let me straighten. I rolled my eyes at myself and stepped away to get my distance back. Yeah, fine, one point to Renatus. I left myself open for that. I looked down to check my feet and raised my sai in preparation.

With a heavy sideways swipe he knocked both cleanly out of my hands.

'Hey! I wasn't ready!' I snapped, going after them as he circled away, but when he changed tack and came back toward me I leapt back, startled. 'What are you doing?!'

'I thought we were sparring,' he answered, backing down again and gesturing for me to collect my weapons. I kept my eyes on him this time, mistrustful. I'd never had much reason to fear him or question his intentions with me, and it felt alien to not know, to have him right in front of me and not hear his thoughts, feel his motives or have any real idea of what he wanted from me.

'I'm glad one of us knows what's going on,' I retorted, annoyed. I stood again with my sai, getting a better grip on them this time, watching my master uncertainly. I took a breath and a reality check. This was Renatus. Life on the line for me, carry me bleeding halfway across the continent to save my life, always there for me Renatus. It wasn't like he was going to hurt me. 'This isn't how Tian does it.'

'Do I look like Tian?' he asked rhetorically, moving the sticks in his hands, feeling out their weight. 'In a real fight, your opponent wouldn't wait until you were ready.'

'I wouldn't go head to head with you in a real fight,' I responded. I saw his feet move and tensed. 'I wouldn't win. You're fresher, bigger, stronger, more experienced, older.'

'That last one won't always be to my advantage.' He lashed out with his right hand and I only just reacted in time to block. One-two. The stick was rebounded and he circled with its momentum, moving back out of my range with thoughtless expertise that belied his next claim: 'I'm also years out of practice, and your weapons are sharpened. That evens the odds.'

'I think your calculations are flawed.' I caught the next slash with more confidence, and the next, recognising the same signs in my master's movement. The half-step forward, the pull of his shoulder. This was a more comfortable pace. More Tian-esque.

'*My* calculations?' he repeated, fluidly changing his stance. I quickly adjusted to match. 'Isn't that the same equation you used to work out that you could handle Declan on your own?' Too quick, he slashed one stick down and struck my elbow, which was admittedly sticking out too far after my change in stance. The whack was solid, and sent a wave of stunned pain up my arm. I yelped and backed off, no longer certain we were just playing.

'Ow,' I complained, rubbing my elbow with the heel of my other hand. I didn't protest that – I knew I'd deserved it, in both regards – but I protested when Renatus swung at me immediately, still coming after me when I hastily struck him away with my still-smarting arm. 'Give me a minute!'

'How about sixteen?' he shot back, mockery clear in his voice, but he did circle away from me. I flinched, breathing hard again. I wanted to drop my gaze from his but couldn't afford to, turning on the spot to keep him in my sights, not allowing him to get too far to my left where I couldn't see him. 'You wouldn't pick me for an opponent because you wouldn't win? Since when do you pick your battles that way?'

This. This was why we were here, having it out. He was still mad, perhaps rightfully so, but I didn't know how to fix it

371

and hoped that having my arse handed to me in full view of the whole house wasn't his idea of evening our score. Distantly, I could feel outside attention; classmates who'd been enjoying the sunshine had noticed us and were gathering on the steps and at the edge of the house where the view was best. I didn't dare look.

'I was wrong about Declan,' I offered, hoping to keep this conversation calmer than last time we'd had it. This time we were both armed. 'I was out of line going around you like that. I think I've paid for my mistakes.'

'Your memory hasn't come back?' he asked curiously, still circling, sticks held only loosely. I relaxed without meaning to.

'Not yet. Just parts.' I paused, drawn in by his interest in my wellbeing and the normalcy of the topic. 'Will it?'

He shrugged uncertainly. 'If you work at it. It helps that you know it's missing.' He stepped back in, and I tensed, ready. 'It would have helped more if you'd considered the danger before you went there.'

I sighed. 'I know, I—'

He pulled back his shoulder like he did before and I raised my guard toward the incoming heavy strike, but it didn't come. Instead the other stick brushed the outside of my sai and before I could do anything, struck the inside of my knee. I dropped my eyes to the site of pain, panicked. Renatus side-stepped as he circled the stick again, spinning it outside my range of view. Not that I noticed. The first stick came down on my lowered guard, sweeping both sai down. A whip of air against the left side of my face told me where the other one had ended up.

Dead.

'You should be able to see that,' he stated, reminding me subtly of the other senses I was failing to utilise. With a huff I yanked away and back-stepped in a hurry, deeply annoyed, cursing myself. How did I fall for that obvious fakeout?

He pulled back, too.

'It's not the feint that got you,' he corrected as I tried to regain my composure. I wanted to rub my knee, which was stinging, but didn't dare. 'It was going all in on it and blinding yourself to what else I might be doing. It was forgetting that my range is wider than yours.' He spun one of the sticks and I saw for the first time that they were longer than my sai. That, added with his extra height and longer limbs, added up to totally unfair. 'It was playing safe, to what I expected from you. Are you hearing what I'm saying?'

'I'm hearing you,' I assured him scathingly. The metaphor was far from hazy. 'Everyone's better than me, everyone's got an ace up their sleeve I can't see, I'm predictable. Is that the lesson?'

'Not quite.'

He went silent, staying back, pacing around me to keep me on my toes, and I glared at him, annoyed. I couldn't beat him – and I knew now we were playing to win – so what was he here for? To teach me a lesson, figuratively and literally?

Breathing hard, I looked at the wooden sticks he carried. As soon as I got close enough to get a strike in, he'd already be countering, and he could hit me from further back than I could hit him.

'Then what?' I demanded, getting frustrated with the futility of this exercise.

'You're overconfident,' Renatus replied flatly. I felt a pang in my chest at his critique, which I knew was intended exactly as personally as it felt. He continued. 'You're reckless and don't know when to bow out. You miss things you should see coming.'

Angry with the brutal honesty, I felt my restraint and fear of him snap. I charged forward two steps into his range, sai raised. He was ready for me, bringing both sticks at chest height to meet me. One – the left blades made contact. Two was meant to sweep them to the side. Instead I drove forward another step, forcing the blade and kali stick upward, and inverted the second sai in my palm. Closer to him than I'd been since the fight started, his second stick was too long and too far to stop me whipping the pommel of mine down on his forearm.

I had my own striking range, a ring inside his where he was undefended. I just had to break through to it.

He pulled away with a wince, shaking out his bruised arm, and I kept my distance, knowing I should be wary of him like I would be any wounded animal, but unable to help a moment of internal celebration.

'Yes,' I bit out, watching him as he seemed to recover, 'I'm all those things. If you don't like it, maybe you shouldn't have picked me.'

Renatus looked up at me, and for the first time in days I could read him, and I knew I'd impressed him by breaking my pattern and turning the tables to my own advantage. But his other hand, still on his elbow, gave me pause. I glanced at my sai as I flipped it back blade-forward. A steel post versus bone. Had I hurt him?

He knew me, and used my distraction against me. He came at me with both sticks pointed forward. I leapt back with fright – I hadn't learned a block for this attack – and threw my swords up to catch them. Both kali sticks clashed hard with the posts and stopped just as hard in the handguard when I shoved upwards.

It wasn't wise; I knew it immediately. All four weapons were locked in a tight cross above my face. I ran uncertain calculations through my head. There *had* to be a way out, but when I tried to dislodge one of the sai, I could see it would unlock one of his, too. Too risky. So, what? Stalemate? Renatus began to bear his weight down behind the kali sticks. My arms tensed with the effort of holding him back. Hastily I checked my stance. Pulled my elbows in tight. Shifted my back foot backward. Buying time.

I didn't have a strategy for getting out of this, so time was all I could ask for.

'I don't regret choosing you,' he said, pushing forward. I held strong, pushing too, trying to match him strength for strength. Against Tian's advice in my very first lesson. 'It's just... uncomfortable... looking in the mirror.'

My shoulders ached with the strain of maintaining the

hold. 'What mirror?'

'Mine.' He leaned to the right to shift the weight to my left. Mean. I tensed that arm further but didn't let it slip or give. 'Overconfident. Reckless. Arrogant. Ask Qasim, he'll give you a comprehensive list of bad traits we share.'

My chest was heaving with effort and in dismay I saw that, slowly, my stance was caving. The locked weapons were being driven closer and closer to me. My shaking arms were giving. The same truth still stood – Renatus was stronger. Maybe I could have thrown the attack aside earlier if I'd worked out how, but by now there was too much weight behind it and I was committed, if doomed.

'I've been thinking a lot about why you went,' he went on, and I felt a little validated to hear strain in his voice, too. 'You're right, I did back you into a corner by keeping secrets from you, and I should have known you'd find a way.' He leaned to the left, a welcome reprieve for my weaker left side, and seemed to wait for me to do something. I didn't know what, so I just held. 'If you and I only picked battles we could win, we wouldn't be ourselves. You wouldn't have tried your ward in Prague and saved all those people if you'd stopped to consider that you'd probably fail. You wouldn't have saved *me*. We'd both be dead.'

'But…' Breath, breath. '…we're not.'

'No. I don't think we're the only ones, either. Qasim and I have a new theory on the Prague attack.' His eyes flicked up at our crossed weapons, and he pressed harder with both sticks, forcing me to push back with all the remaining strength in my shaking arms and shoulders. I wanted to know more but I was puffing for air and all my concentration needed to be on holding him back. Forestalling the inevitable. 'Give up?'

I couldn't speak. About to break, I shook my head. Arrogance, overconfidence, I don't know. Qasim's harsh speech echoed in my master's words. I just had to hold out… until…

Renatus let off suddenly and I tipped forward in surprise, all my weight bearing forward into the defence. Destabilised.

375

Fluidly he swept our still-tangled weapons aside, out of our faces, and I tried to track them with my eyes to see where he'd come from next.

I wasn't watching his feet.

I'd landed heavily on my backside before I realised he'd planted his foot just below my bellybutton and pushed me over. My sai landed in a clatter beside me.

It was over.

'That wasn't fair,' I complained between exhausted breaths, rubbing my stomach where he'd kicked me. It hurt. I reasoned that it was probably the least painful place he could choose, low where I was tense, with minimal force, but it hurt. Added to that, I was aware of our distant audience, my classmates having called each other over to watch. My pride was at least a little bit injured. Renatus tossed the kali sticks aside and crouched in front of me.

'Why do we assume our opponents will play by *our* rules?' he asked, uncharacteristically animated. 'You wouldn't think to kick, so I wouldn't dare?'

I shrugged one shoulder in defeat. 'I guess?' I didn't know what he meant and my focus was still on my graceless fall. I gestured at the grass, at myself planted it in. 'Are you happy with the result?'

'Not as much as I thought,' he confessed, betraying what I'd suspected – he'd come here to best me. He got back on track easily. 'You've said that the men who attacked us in Prague didn't want to be there. You could sense it. Stay objective,' he warned, noticing my flinch as his words took me back to that frightful event. *Screams... two hands, slamming on impenetrable glass...* With effort I returned to the present moment. 'Don't think about Anouk. Think about the men. Twelve of them.'

He was back inside my head, and the barrier between us was gone. My next exhalation was heavy with relief. Okay. I nodded. I could remember them. *Crimson cloaks... shadowed faces... knives...disgust, fear, horror...*

'White Elm fanatics, trying to frame Magnus Moira,' I reminded him. 'They mustn't have been prepared for what they'd decided to do.' Slitting throats and creating terror, after all, was serious business.

'Maybe, but then why not stop? Why not back out? Why keep up the ruse and die for it? Is it possible,' Renatus broached, our whole fight apparently forgotten, 'that they were not in control of their own bodies?'

I considered it. 'Can that happen?' I watched as he dug in a pocket of his loose trousers for something, and then dangled a pendant on a chain. I stared, recognising it as the charm he'd loaned me the first time I'd accidentally Haunted, to lock my wandering soul inside my own body. Literally. 'Scriers?'

'The only ones who can scry at that level, and only when we're very skilled. If you'd touched Emmanuelle or I while Active Scrying us,' making out, he didn't say, and I made sure not to think, 'you would have possessed us. Taken over the body, controlled it like a puppet. We would have been powerless to stop you.'

'But would you have been aware of it?' I asked, adjusting my position. My arms, when I tried to lever my weight with them, quivered. I decided to stay down for now. Renatus swung the pendant, contemplating.

'I've never experienced it either way, but what I've read suggests yes, provided the person is awake when they're taken over. If they're asleep they stay asleep. I think our fanatics were aware.'

'But helpless, in their own bodies.' I pressed the back of my hand to my mouth, disturbed by the prospect. Made to commit crimes and used against your will to misrepresent what you love and believe in. I thought of their despair and horror at their own actions and felt awful for not realising sooner. 'It explains why none of their families believed them capable, and why the bomb took them out. They were prisoners.'

And we didn't save them.

'We couldn't have known, and if we did, I don't know what we could have done for them,' Renatus said firmly. He swung the chain around his hand and put it back in his pocket.

'We know *now*, and we need to prove it before Valero pulls the alliance.'

'How?' I leaned forward, attention captured.

'We've got the Archives, and everything we've put together in Anouk's old room. We need to find twelve dead or missing scriers who are neither dead, nor missing. Qasim and I think we found a few.' He pushed down on his knees to get back to his feet; I was quietly satisfied to see that our fight had taken it out of my ever-poised master, too. 'We'd better get started.'

He offered his hand and I took it, but hesitated before pulling myself up.

'I'm sorry for all this,' I said sincerely. His gaze dropped from mine. I kept going, making sure I was heard. 'I'm sorry for going to Declan's without telling you, and I'm sorry for going behind your back to dig into your history with Lisandro. It was out of line and unfair. You're in charge. For a reason, apparently.'

'Mostly because I'm older, I think,' Renatus relented after a moment, tugging on my hand to get me up. 'You don't have to say anything else. We agreed at the beginning that *sorry* has too much meaning to throw around unless it's earned. I'm undermining it if I won't accept it when you really mean it. I accept your apology.'

I straightened, wary of his weird formality. 'Okay. Thanks.'

'I'm still angry,' he made sure to tell me, stooping to collect my sai for me. 'But I'll get over it. Just…' He frowned at the sai in his hand, struggling to not get annoyed again. I could feel his emotions again. He thrust them at me in mild disgust. '*Declan*, really?'

'Oh, please. Give me some credit,' I insisted as I accepted them, but it became a wince when my back twinged at the motion. Renatus asked, 'Did I hurt you?'

'You've effectively knocked me down about three pegs, but other than that, no. I've been sleeping on the floor,' I admitted, rubbing the tight spot beside my spine. 'Too creeped out to sleep in the bed now.'

Renatus winced too, taking my meaning, and I thought I'd turned him off talking to me, but after a pause he spoke.

'Her bedroom door was spelled not to admit men or boys, even me,' he said. 'The bed's safe.'

I groaned. 'Wish you'd told me that earlier.'

chapter twenty-six

By the end of the next day, with less than twenty-four hours left before our deadline, we had nine of our suspects nailed. The seven missing from Salem only became dirtier the deeper Susannah and Tian dug, and two more names joined theirs after revisiting the work Renatus and I had been doing with Anouk's investigation.

'Suspicious deaths, unexplained disappearances, anti-council sentiments, reasons for wanting to get away, and scriers,' Renatus summarised each list to anyone who came to help. 'Looking for correlations.'

We hit a wall with the last two or three. To be honest, we weren't sure whether the Irish ringleader *was* possessed, being the only one to have spoken or otherwise indicated a personality during the Prague attack, so we scoured the photographs of every discarded file just in case he was there of his own volition.

'There aren't a lot of scriers in 'ere,' Emmanuelle noted about half an hour after we conscripted her to our task. She flicked through the pages of the file in front of her, bored already. 'Many do not 'ave their class mentioned.'

'Most witches don't know what type of sorcerer they are, and their surviving family are even less likely to know,' Qasim answered, not lifting his attention from the file he was reading. He'd been here at the Archives with us all day and remained the picture of discipline, posture straight and proper, methodically working through box after box. He was his usual unpleasant self but he was a great help, tapping into impressions the same way Renatus and I did. He'd also filled in a lot of these files himself as the White Elm's lead investigator for the past thirty-two years, and remembered details we couldn't have gotten otherwise.

We should have gotten him onboard earlier.

'Next box,' Jadon announced, pushing an empty one aside for Teresa to move to the floor, the pair exchanging quick smiles. She still wasn't fully back onboard with White Elm work but he seemed to be helping to ease her back into it. Plus, well. I *am* an Empath, people seem to frequently forget.

'Council proceedings 1994-1996,' Qasim answered flatly as he worked through another file. Flicked to the photo. Threw it aside. Renatus's next one followed, keeping pace. Oneida plonked the offending box on the table beside Teresa, having already retrieved it before Qasim spoke. Seers.

'And if there is nothing about their type?' Emmanuelle checked, waving her file. Renatus, opposite, took it without looking at her and threw it into the "no" pile for Oneida to reorganise. He had been intensely focused all day, a competitive response, I suspected, to Qasim's machine-like composure. They sped through the documents and updated the lists much more frequently than the rest of us. Determined to out-study the other.

Nothing alike.

At least it kept the attention off my own uncharacteristic slowness, the memory spell in my head crumbling slowly into nonsense flashes of ingredients going into a bowl and out-of-sequence conversation. Declan hadn't lied; I could *feel* the poorly patched sixteen minutes now, and bits were coming back. They were niggly and annoying, but preferable to the chill of recalling the graveyard, or the sinking feeling of wondering whether Renatus was still upset when he was silent for a long time.

'No one at the level we're looking for is unaware of their classification,' Renatus said. He flipped pages to the photograph stapled at the back, immediately wrote it off, and tossed it down the table to Oneida. The new Scribe had just finished gathering what was there into a neat pile, and it was sent into disarray. She lifted her eyes to him in veiled irritation but he'd already reached for the next file. I shot her an apologetic smile. 'They're high-level scriers with control of their gift. They're in covens with other scriers to practise together. Their next of kin knows they're scriers, or at the very least knows what kind of magic they're playing with – enough to make an educated guess.'

A noise upstairs alerted us when someone else entered the Archives, provoking a heavy exhalation from Renatus and a momentary pause from Qasim, their shared frustration at the prospect of explaining the task to yet another kind helper painfully clear. The magic guarding the place was only meant to admit White Elm or associated good guys, but I was learning that even magic could be tricked. For their sake, I hoped the entrant was one of ours, because if I were a bad guy, I would not like to walk in on a study group of White Elm like this one. Their displeasure quickly cleared, however, and they glanced at each other in surprise as they turned in their seats to see the new arrivals.

'Lord Gawain? What are you doing here?' Qasim asked as the council's leader descended the stairs, grasping the handrail for support. He was followed by Elijah, who was in turn followed by another pair of legs.

'Here to help,' the old Seer said with a cryptic look upward at the men behind him. Renatus recognised the third pair of legs, or more probably their owner's energy, before his face came into view.

'What's *he* doing here?' he asked in tactless disgust. I sat up straighter beside him, the immensity of his dislike for the newcomer streaming across our connection.

'I *am* the help,' Gabriel Winter drawled pleasantly. Ahead of him, Elijah stepped off the staircase to join Lord Gawain on the Archive's hard-packed floor. 'Lord Gawain explained the Scrier's theory to the Steward and we both agree that it makes considerably more sense than the White Elm orchestrating an attack on their own people to undermine a political adversary.'

Renatus scoffed in disbelief; Jadon and Teresa shared a dubious glance; Qasim narrowed his eyes in mockery.

'I'm glad to hear it,' he said. 'You didn't seem so convinced last time we saw you.'

'Well, regardless, I'm not the one who needs convincing,' Winter replied smoothly. 'This looks productive. Where are you up to?'

Qasim turned back to his files with a silenced flicker of irritation I felt mirrored in my master.

'If you're here to help, sit down and work it out,' Qasim said in exasperation. 'It's not hard.'

Renatus nodded tightly as he turned away as well. 'Even if we've explained the process on repeat for the last thirty minutes.'

It was a dig at Emmanuelle, who surged with aggravation and snatched the pen out of his hand. She snapped something angry in fast French, and he flared in response, her anger always driving his like in any healthy friendship.

'Renatus, Emmanuelle,' Lord Gawain chastised. 'You can explain it again.'

My master cast a moody look at Qasim, who had completed another file and was now ahead in their unspoken count. Teresa, timidly, spoke up.

'Scriers, either reported for illegal activity or experiencing something terrible in their life that might make them choose to fake their deaths,' she explained quickly. 'We've found two we think, uh...'

'Likely suspects?' the detective asked kindly. He came over to the table, cradling a leather-wrapped bundle in his arms, eyeing our spread of papers. 'It's a fascinating theory. Even in Avalon there are very few scriers with the ability you're looking for, but of course they are in every population.'

'The world felt safer when I didn't know about them,' Jadon admitted.

Tell me about it. The realisation that magic was not all fun and wonder, but enabled some sorcerers to take others prisoner and control them to commit acts of terror, was still not sitting well with me, and I knew that there was plenty more about the darker side of sorcery that I was yet to learn.

'… *funny.' My voice, sarcastic. Declan's playful smile, eyes angled up from his bowl as he answers, 'So check for yourself. You're a scrier, aren't you?'*

Go away, Monday night.

Qasim scratched his ear with his pen. 'Scriers are relatively rare. Not like Displacers, but much fewer than Seers, Telepaths or Healers. And most of us don't Haunt.' He didn't forget to look up and meet my gaze. I caught it by accident and went back to my reading with deliberate nonchalance. Winter nodded.

'Small mercies. Tell me: what do you most need to complete this investigation and prove your innocence to the Valeroans?'

No one spoke. Lord Gawain sighed.

'Renatus? Answer him, please.'

My master put his page down and took a few breaths.

'Our challenge is proving our suspects aren't dead,' he said reluctantly. He absent-mindedly pushed his sleeves up to his elbows and in the light of Teresa's spelled lantern dangling above us, I saw a shadow of bruising on his forearm. Oops. 'That they're clients of Shanahan's, a man we've linked to other Magnus Moira members. There has to be a way.'

Emmanuelle had been feeling cold toward him since his unnecessary rudeness before, but I felt her soften when she spotted the same thing. She reached across like she was taking a folder and brushed his arm; he noticed and drew his sleeve down, hiding the sign of weakness, however slight.

'There is,' Oneida said vaguely as she came back over to organise the latest discarded files back into their Russian-labelled boxes. There was a silence in which everyone stopped reading and looked up at her. Confirmation from a Seer – there *was* a way. But in typical Seer fashion she seemed uncompelled to go into detail.

'You are right, of course,' Winter agreed with her,

bowing politely. 'Perhaps Avalon can assist.'

He laid the leather-wrapped package in front of me. It was held together with a darker leather belt around its middle, yellowy paper visible between gaps in the wrapping. Rough, maybe handmade, probably old. I clasped my hands in my lap, torn between wanting to touch it to experience the rich-looking textures and wanting to avoid the impressions I knew would be embedded within.

Winter started to uncinch the ancient-looking belt buckle, and I don't know whether I was the only one who noticed the swift prick of his finger on the sharpened prong or if the others chose not to acknowledge the use of illegal blood magic in their sacred Archive. It hadn't occurred to me until now that Avalon must use a similar style of magic to the old Pagan traditions of the United Kingdom, like Shanahan and co, and Declan. They were neighbours and had probably intermixed considerably before the island had cut themselves off.

'What is it?' I asked when he revealed a pile of loose papers, handwritten notes inside hand-ruled columns to look like forms. He smiled at me, that strange bland smile of his. I still didn't like him even one bit. I suspected he knew it.

'Avalon and the White Elm have a complex relationship,' he answered cagily. 'Your nation is very open while our borders are tightly controlled. While this is Avalon's choice and ensures the continuation of our way of life, an unfortunate downside to this arrangement is a dangerous lack of genetic diversity.'

'No new blood introduced to a small population for hundreds of years,' Lord Gawain filled in, carefully avoiding looking at Renatus, who was tense with displeasure beside me. 'Everyone ends up sharing a majority of their genes. A single virus could have wiped out one of the world's oldest magical societies.'

'So we provide them with fresh blood – misfits, outcasts and orphans,' Qasim said flatly, not caring how insensitive it might be to say beside one of them. 'I'm aware. What does that have to do with our investigation?'

'It's important you appreciate the olive branch this gesture represents,' Winter said firmly, a hand on the stack of parchment. 'Most of our ruling class would have fought the Steward on this decision if they knew what I'm bringing you. Understand that he has risked his standing with his own people, and with you, to ensure the White Elm and Valero alliance is preserved.' He lifted his hand away and resumed his smooth, detached way of speaking. 'Avalon vets your offerings.'

Renatus and I glanced at each other, not catching the significance.

'At the Schwarzwald cottage,' Renatus finished, coldly. 'This isn't news, nor helpful.'

'*Before* the Schwarzwald cottage,' Winter corrected, licking his fingertip and leafing through the topmost pages, 'and sometimes, *instead*. Some may be threats.' He counted out five very old-looking sheets of parchment and tossed them in front of Renatus. 'That's the file on you. And this one,' he kept flicking through, drawing out the next couple, 'is what the Steward's scriers had on me before I was invited to join Avalon.'

He offered those pages diligently to Lord Gawain, but they were snatched halfway there by an irate Qasim, who'd stood abruptly. Renatus had lifted his hands away from the scrappy-edged papers that fanned out before him, reluctant for once to access any of its secrets. Immediately protective – a file on Renatus? – I reached past him to spread them out where everyone could see. The pages felt rough and crunchy to my fingertips, and the penmanship on each one was different, indicating numerous writers, all of them near-illegible. Old-timey script, oddly formed letters. Only the dates at the top of each page were clear to me.

'What are we looking at?' Emmanuelle asked impatiently. I shifted one sheet closer to me to check. Twenty-one years before I was born; eight; forty-two; a more recent one, the last digit smudged. A page every ten years, give or take.

'They look like observation reports,' I said. 'Dating back decades.'

'Observations on bloodlines in your nation already not complying with White Elm magic restrictions,' Winter confirmed. 'Individuals likely to be caught and be singled out for transfer to Avalon.'

Qasim looked up disbelievingly from what he was reading. 'Avalon is *spying* on our citizens? In direct violation with the conditions of our treaty?'

'It's not my doing,' the detective replied coolly. 'I'm just the messenger.'

My brain was playing catch-up. 'Did you say *you* were invited to join Avalon? Meaning… you used to live here? Out here, with the rest of the world?'

'Gabriel Winter is the poster child for the Avalon breeding program,' Renatus answered scathingly before the white-haired detective could say a word. 'He's the one they bring along to meet new conscripts to convince us to go with them.'

He'd started to stand, bitter anger surging through him, and I quickly laid a hand on his arm, imploring him to stay put, to relax. No one missed it, though, and Lord Gawain pushed forward with a sigh.

'This is getting us nowhere,' he said. Winter nodded.

'I agree. We are wasting time. You can make your opinions of me known later.' He leafed through the stack still before him and began divvying out handfuls of parchment to the councillors around the table. Renatus and Qasim watched him with silent but tangible dislike. 'While it might violate the terms of your arrangement with Avalon, today you may be grateful for it.'

'And why is that?' Renatus bit out. Winter smiled at him with that bland patience.

'Because if you were as advanced a scrier as you like everyone to think, you would know already that you cannot hide from those you don't know are watching,' he said, and I tightened my hand on my master's arm at the open insult.

'Avalon keeps intermittent watch on what you deem illegal magic. Magic use masked from you,' Winter nodded respectfully to Qasim, 'is not masked from us. When we heard your theory on the Prague attack, we realised that *we* have records that may prove helpful.'

'Because you're checking up on the same individuals every few years,' Jadon noted, rearranging the pages he'd been handed into a row before him. 'You don't know to stop looking for them if we have recorded them as dead or missing. If they're still alive, you'll have a dated observation.'

That's exactly what we need. Renatus finally sat back and beneath my hand, his arm untensed. *If we can match any of those records with the names on our list...*

'Turning up with evidence of your people's betrayal of our trust is a bold and unusual way of honouring international goodwill,' Lord Gawain said cynically. Winter smiled at him.

'The Steward came into new information from the Fates,' he explained cryptically, though the council leader did not seem put off. 'The breakdown of the alliance of White Elm and Valero would have dangerous consequences for Avalon. He decided it would be worth the risk of offending you to prevent that. Besides,' he added casually, looking around the table at councillors who were already poring over their handwritten files, interest in his dialogue lost, 'in the end, what harm is truly done? Our records are, of course, open to you.'

I met Renatus's eye as I tidied up the observations on his family and as the older councillors spoke in low, unhappy tones with Detective Winter. How *convenient* that Avalon was suddenly so helpful once they realised that it was in their direct interest instead of just the right thing to do.

'Got one,' Jadon announced, pulling the master list closer to compare with the record he'd just pulled off the pile. 'Two months ago, Marek Vernadsky sighted casting protective spells in far-eastern Europe. Ingredients: caraway, dried blood flakes...' His eyebrows lifted in bemusement. 'There's an extensive list. But *we* have him recorded dead. Workplace accident.'

'Why do we have records of workplace accidents?' Emmanuelle asked, leaning over to look. Qasim heard and glanced over from his irritable discussion with Avalon's detective.

'Follow-up to watch-listed cases, so we can close them and stop checking in on their activities. Though apparently,' he growled, angling his glare back to Winter, 'our *allies* have neglected to tell us until now that some of them are still worth watching.'

Emmanuelle took charge, pulling the Avalon documents to her side of the table.

'We will decode these,' she said briskly, distributing the loose pages like playing cards between Jadon and Teresa either side of her and dumping the rest in front of herself. She met Renatus's eye coolly. 'You can carry on with what you were doing, since you've got a system.'

He nodded his agreement and went back to reading. I waited for Qasim to extract his hand from the box before following suit, my eyes drifting over the loose pile of parchment in front of Jadon. *If it's so damaging to their alliance with us, why would they share this?*

Avalon has several bloodlines of historically powerful Seers, Renatus admitted. *It's helped them stay isolated and independent for fifteen hundred years, always knowing the best course of action. Sharing isn't their style, so the alternative must be bad.* He threw his file to Oneida and went for a new one. *I'll hope they're right and this helps us with Valero, because we can't afford to break ties with both of them.*

Trying to ignore the intensifying but mostly one-sided argument behind me, I brought my attention back to my task. File in hand. Job to carry on with. Let's go. I read the basic details on the front but most of it filtered through my brain, irrelevant. Name, date of birth, date of death, cause of death. Seer. Strike out. I flipped to the very back page where Anouk always stapled the subject's photograph.

The face stared straight through time, straight through memory, but not mine.

It was *him*.

The sounds in the subterranean chamber seemed to dull, like I'd been submerged in water. I ran my fingers over the photo to confirm it was real. Weeks, months of searching these boxes for *this face*, and now I was looking at it. Sick feelings of loss and horror swarmed inside me to see him, though for me it was the first time; I felt towards him the same way I would if it were *my* sister he carried, bloodied and beaten beyond recognition, in the moments after the deaths of both my parents. As if it were *my* sister he dropped in a graceless heap to free up his hands to attack me. As if it were *my* instinctual reaction that ripped a hole in the Fabric of space and cast him into the void.

For a moment of choked silence, it was as though Ana's ghost reached for me again from the orchard's soil and grabbed the sides of my face and screamed *look. Look at him. Look at me. See what happened*.

Renatus couldn't miss my short-circuiting thoughts.

'What?' he asked, tossing his second file across the table and reaching for another, speeding through them again. The others' eyes lifted in mild interest but dropped away again when all I did, unable to say a word anyway, was offer the file I held to Renatus for inspection. He hardly looked, stuck in his new momentum, already leafing through the next one. Then his hands froze, and disbelief flooded him, and he looked again.

There were really no words. He took the roughly folded-back stapled pages from me to stare openly at the face of the man he'd thought *for years* had murdered his family, until we'd learned Lisandro was responsible. He'd essentially killed this man for that crime, though Qasim and I both argued that it didn't count as murder, and he'd struggled these past few months to come to terms with the realisation that his rage had been wrongly directed.

Now we could find out who the stranger was. Now we could find out what he was doing there and clear Renatus's conscience.

One demon down, fifty million to go, yes, but it was still a step in the right direction.

'Who is it?' Teresa queried when we both stared for what must have been an inappropriate amount of time. I blinked, feeling immediately guilty – I shouldn't have brought this up in front of other councillors. This was our private little side quest and a very dangerous secret of my master's. Renatus didn't seem to hear her; he finally broke eye contact with the stranger who dropped his sister in the mud and flipped back to the front page.

'A suspect in another case,' Qasim said smoothly from behind us, making me jump. I hadn't realised he'd come back over to the table. He read the personal details over Renatus's shoulder. 'One of Jackson's investigations – explains why I didn't make the connection.'

I pushed my hair back, overwhelmed by what we'd just stumbled across. The stranger. We hadn't even been looking for him.

'Recorded dead four months beforehand. Watchlisted for suspected illegal magic use in a number of violent altercations, including...' Qasim reached between us to turn the page, holding the stapled cover up to read what was beneath. My breath felt tight with suspense; beside me, Renatus's whole being radiated with the same. 'Sought by mortal authorities to face charges of burglary, aggravated breaking and entering and aggravated assault resulting in a man's death. Among other unanswered crimes.' My scrying teacher flicked through the following pages to indicate the stranger's many misdeeds, then let the front page fall back so we could see the cover details again. 'Sean Glassner. First class scum.'

In a subtle but still unusual show of support, Qasim clapped his hand on Renatus's shoulder briefly. No one else thought anything of it as the older scrier simply sat back down and returned to work, but I saw, or rather felt, the weight that came away with his hand. The relief at the unspoken clemency. Renatus stared at the closed file he held. *Sean Glassner*. The stranger finally had a name, and a history to go with it, and after all this time we knew what, really, we'd both known from the outset – the victim of Renatus's first magical outburst was no innocent. He hadn't been there by accident. He'd faked his own death to escape the consequences of previous violence, and he'd been perfectly capable of hurting the teenage boy he came across, as well as the girl he dropped.

First class scum, Renatus repeated, perhaps an affirmation to himself – I didn't know if he knew I overheard the thought. He returned to the photo and looked for a very, very long moment. His thoughts and feelings around it were too complex to unpack, and I watched his face as he struggled. I could hardly breathe; I wished there was something I could say or do to help move him through the moment into the next one.

But in the end he came through on his own. He loosened his hold on the file so that the top pages rolled back into place, and after an extended painful second of residual guilt staring at the name, he finally, *finally* tossed the file down the table onto the pile Oneida was gathering up for reboxing.

'I'm glad you found what you were looking for,' she said diplomatically. It sounded nonchalant, but Renatus glanced up at her as he reached for a new file, and from her loaded look I knew she somehow knew the significance of that tossed-away document.

'Me too,' he said, scanning the cover of his new file. He turned it over to access the photo at the back, but spared me a quick look. 'Thank you.'

There was so much in that. I knew I was finally forgiven for my recent stupidity and that in this moment, we were all good, because the immense weight of his self-blame had just been lightened, if only by as much as a feather. It made a difference. I smiled.

'Keep up,' Qasim snipped from the other end of the table, powering through files, and we both hurriedly grabbed a new one each.

chapter twenty-seven

It's a strange feeling the first time you find yourself with nothing to be mad at yourself about. Sean Glassner. If Renatus tried, he would be able to find other things to blame himself for – he'd made plenty of mistakes in his short years of life – but weirdly, nothing came forward on its own to plague him in the wake of Aristea finding that improperly closed case.

He looked past his raised hands at the distant night sky, unfamiliar with the feeling of lightness that seemed to have replaced the dead weight of revulsion built up over eight years. It was hard to explain, because nothing had really changed. His actions weren't retracted. A man's life was still ended and thrown irrevocably into the void between spaces and that was still Renatus's doing. The only thing that was different, and probably it shouldn't have changed things, was that he no longer felt bad about it.

Did that make him a bad person? Perhaps, but what did it matter if the only two people who truly knew it didn't seem to think it? Sean Glassner. The stranger had a name, and Renatus had confirmation that Glassner was the kind of waste of space the world was better off without. Not worth the years of angst and remorse. Maybe better people would possess the moral integrity to feel equally guilty for their wrongdoings regardless of their victim's shortfalls, but two of the *best* people he knew had made it clear that, to them, he was not a murderer, and that Sean Glassner's death was justified. *First class scum*, Qasim had confirmed, and Renatus's shame fell away. It was really all he'd been wanting to believe all these years, what he'd tried unconvincingly to tell himself, what Aristea had insisted when she first saw this memory. The stranger – Glassner – deserved it. *It was him or me.* The words felt true now. He wouldn't have hesitated to hurt Renatus; he wouldn't have carried eight years of guilt over it, either. And knowing all this for sure, Renatus found he'd spent enough energy hating himself to last a lifetime, and he was done.

He was done with a lot of things, strangely.

His hands kept working at the spellwork woven over the estate, working fast so as not to lose his nerve, but his gaze drifted down from the stars to the darkened windows of the house. His apprentice was sleeping, but her mind was not as quiet as his. Since Anouk she'd been plagued with guilt; but even before that, before he'd met her, she'd dreamed nightly of her family's tragedy in their own storm – a scrier's natural means of processing unnoticed truths from the past, Qasim kept reminding him. Renatus had woven magic into the protective webbing of wards over the estate to prevent dreaming, and he'd been glad for the years of respite from those persistent nightmares. He knew she'd appreciated it, too.

But for the first time, his mind was quiet enough to see, in the frustrated cycling of his apprentice's brain, what this suppression was doing to them both. In fascination he watched recent mysteries turn over and over – Declan, the missing memory, whatever happened to her at Ana's grave, those moments of her grandfather's long-ago life she kept tapping into, the hours they'd spent in the Archives with the files – processing on endless repeat without her knowing.

Any conclusions she might have come to would be forgotten by morning, all flying beneath the radar of her conscious mind. Was this happening every single night she didn't dream? Was it happening to *him* every night?

Qasim was right. He was selfish.

He'd been afraid. No longer. Sean Glassner had been released; so too could this spell. A refocusing of his eyes and the shimmery weave of spellwork doming over the estate

394

wavered into visibility. Spider silk. Much of it wasn't his work but the newer magic was. Whoever had been messing with his warding had taken a few days off, apparently, because it was as tight as he'd last left it, and was difficult to unthread.

Feeling like he had when he'd thrown Glassner's file across the table, he grasped the central thread and yanked downward. The dream spell came loose, the web twisting and warping in response. With both hands he worked to shift, reshape and reposition the other spells tied so tightly together, steadily unpicking the offending one from its taut weave. He would not like the result of this choice, but it was the right thing to do. The smart thing. How much had he avoided knowing because he couldn't bear the process of working through it? How much was Aristea's brain struggling to show her *right now* that she simply couldn't see because he'd cast this spell? He hated to consider her layered grief and guilt and secrets and confusion from all the things that had happened to her since she met him, unable to settle, unable to resolve.

It was slow – he wasn't a Crafter – but after ten or so minutes the whole spell was dismantled, and the warding protecting the property was tightened to fill the gaps he left. He dropped his arms tiredly and looked back up at the house behind him. Everyone asleep within could now dream again, including Aristea.

Including himself, when he dared go back to bed.

But more importantly, when he stood again at the edge of her awareness, he could already see that her subconscious thought patterns had changed. No more pointless circles. Intense focus on one thing at a time – she was dreaming.

Hopefully he hadn't just returned her nightmares to her for no gain; but even if he had, he was quietly convinced she was much more capable of handling it than he was.

Renatus continued out onto the lawn, taking advantage of the late hour to enjoy his own property without the concern of crossing paths with anyone else. A lifelong introvert, he needed copious time alone with his thoughts, time that he didn't usually get until he was lying awake at night berating himself for all the reasons he wasn't good enough to manage all the ambitious tasks he'd set himself.

The flat area where Aristea had her lessons with Tian had a good view of the orchard without being close enough to feel its sickening magnetic pull, and Renatus sat down, resting his elbows on his knees.

'Sean Glassner,' he said aloud for the first time, the sound of his voice indecently voluminous in the night stillness. He looked around; there was no one to hear him. In that orchard he'd lost both his parents, and on the path through the middle, he'd come across Glassner carrying his near-death sister. The minutes that followed were a blur he couldn't forget. Ana on the ground. Glassner raising his hands. Renatus, quicker, and Glassner, gone. Ana bleeding. Renatus, useless to stop it. Ana, gone. Rain, rain, how long? Then another stranger at his side, invisible behind his own tears, dragging him to his feet and promising things would be alright.

Lord Gawain may have suspected that Renatus had done something untoward in the minutes before they met, but he'd never said, never asked. He'd done nothing but love him and guide him since, his unconditional faith only shaken once or twice. He'd given the last Morrissey unspoken hope that he could one day make amends for that mistake, and the whole and simple truth was that he was on the White Elm today – on a council his family would have been ashamed to see him on, serving a purpose none of their society believed in – because of what happened in that orchard, in those blurry minutes after he ran into Sean Glassner.

You aren't supposed to be here.

Sean Glassner wasn't responsible for the storm, but he'd unknowingly put Renatus on the path to finding out who was, putting him in a position of power to go after Lisandro. And to win.

Even amidst all the other problems circulating Renatus on this night, from the disintegrating political alliances with the White Elm's most powerful neighbours to the list of not-dead scriers still out there somewhere to his own lurking fear of sleep tonight, he felt contentedly confident. He had everything he needed going forward. He and Aristea were talking again after their spat literally came to push and shove, and his stranger had a name, and he was going to take Lisandro down. Give it time.

Everything was under control.

Distantly, at the edge of his awareness, he sensed the flurry of mental activity as Aristea woke up, rattled. He glanced back at the house, relatively unconcerned, forgetting he'd essentially flipped a switch for her, giving back her access to her dreams. Which, he began to remember with a cringe, were as exclusively nightmarish as his own.

Where are you? she asked sharply, uncharacteristically alert upon waking. *Where... you're here.*

Renatus felt the soft brush of her attention as she swiftly scried him. Good, she was getting better at automatically reaching for those higher-level skills. He avoided scrying her at night, feeling it was an invasion of her privacy, though he'd broken that rule when he'd woken a few nights ago to realise she wasn't *anywhere* on the premises.

His heart had nearly stopped. How exactly does one *misplace* a girl of Aristea's age? His only experience of such a thing was his own sister running away, chasing the spectre of her first, and only, forbidden love.

So to find Aristea halfway across the country with *Declan O'Malley* was a kick he didn't need. His hands clenched. He was still going to kill Declan, honestly, if his lowlife childhood associate didn't have the sense to stay underground for at least the next ten years...

He fell forward in shock as Aristea collided with his back, grabbing his shoulders to keep them both from toppling.

'Whoa, I'm sorry!' she gasped out, collapsing onto the lawn beside him. She was out of breath, like she'd been running, but she'd also just clearly Displaced, using his position in space as an anchor. Getting a little close there, but still, another pleasing automation. She swallowed, trying to catch her breath, and when he looked at her he saw that her eyes were gleaming to match her manic, racing mind. 'I dreamed.'

Renatus nodded, shifting to get comfortable again now that he'd been almost knocked over. 'I know. I took down the spell.' He indicated the invisible-again webbing over their heads with a glance upward. Aristea stared at him, her breath beginning to even out.

'Wow. Okay, we'll talk about what a significant move that is for your personal growth in a second,' she said, a little stunned. Her hand was still on his shoulder, and her fingers jigged with unexpected energy as she brought her focus back to what she'd come here to say. 'I get it now. I get... In the dream,' she said hurriedly, gesturing back at the house, 'I saw it. I know why.'

'Why you can't find your nouns?' Renatus asked rhetorically, interested despite himself. She exhaled deliberately, working to slow herself down.

'Why that vision came to me at Teagan's,' she explained, more clearly. 'About my grandfather, and yours, at the christening, and what happened to Declan's ancestor. I've been wondering, why that moment? I've tapped into other things from his life, but I never remember it well. I think that's probably for the best,' she added grimly, indistinct impressions of dark and distressing scenes flashing through her head before she could stop them. 'But the christening... it doesn't seem that big of a moment for Cassán, so why was I taken there? And now I know.'

She was fervent, inspired, and Renatus tried not to look as sceptical as he felt. He'd suspected the dream spell was preventing her from processing things only her subconscious knew, maybe something like this, but so quickly? It had been less than an hour.

'And?' he pressed, waiting for the reveal.

'Oneida said there's a way to prove which of our not-dead, not-missing scriers are alive and working for Lisandro,' Aristea reminded him, not that he usually put much stock in what Seers said. 'That's why the vision came to me. I just hadn't realised.' She shrugged excitedly. 'Shanahan's client list. Details of every business dealing, services rendered and payment taken. It's all the proof we need.'

Renatus nodded again, stroking the grass. 'That would be perfect, if such a thing existed.'

'It does,' Aristea insisted. 'Shanahan keeps a ledger.'

'He doesn't keep a ledger, he wouldn't be that stupid.'

'He *does*.' His apprentice was adamant. She tapped her forehead. 'His father kept one, and your uncle doesn't strike me as any different. Penny-pinching accountant type, every laundered coin accounted for, that hotel running like clockwork. Those folders in the room behind reception, remember? Everything. Written. Down.'

The family tree papers he'd turned up with after Aindréas and Luella died, Renatus recalled uncomfortably. Uncle Thomas had records of everything else; perhaps Aristea's claim wasn't so far-fetched.

'It's not,' she replied to his thoughts, and tapped her forehead again. 'Look. It's coming back. Not the whole thing, God knows what else he said,' she admitted with an embarrassed roll of her eyes. Renatus realised what she was talking about and turned to her, her hand finally falling from his shoulder. The buried memory. If he hadn't known it could do drastic harm to the stability of her mind, he would have dug for its frayed edges days ago and torn it out himself to find what Declan had hidden beneath it. Sixteen minutes. The friendship their parents insisted the boys develop – Declan's because they needed the connection, his own because an O'Malley in the pocket could only be a benefit – had always been fraught, swaying from close to hateful to begrudging on repeat for twenty years. Right now it was at the hateful end of its swing.

Still, Renatus tried to push that aside to focus on what was in his apprentice's head. Her attention was on a roughly rendered area of her labyrinthine mental space, a vaguely camouflaged patch he wouldn't have noticed except that she'd drawn him to it, and now he saw its hewn edges, gelling poorly with the landscape around it.

With a smile Declan scatters the dried petals into the bowl in his other hand. It's through Aristea's eyes, not as tall as the other, the angle slightly upward.

Blank.

Stirring.

Blank. The majority of the sixteen minutes were still hidden beneath the memory spell, but it appeared that to begin with, Declan really had been showing her how to build the spell. Little pieces of time were rising back to the surface, broken up but still in sequence. Eventually, hopefully, the parts in between would follow.

'Keep watching,' Aristea instructed aloud. She brushed a stray leaf away from her bare foot, eyes unfocused as she concentrated on the partial memory. Renatus followed her attention back to it.

Shanahan's business card held between bandaged fingers. 'I want that ledger…'

Blank.

Dark. Man tied to a chair in the dark, head down. Declan's basement.

Blank.

Declan has the bowl, Aristea holds the card. He pinches the top of the card so they are both touching it, but not each other. 'This wasn't part of our initial negotiation, and I'm afraid it'll cost you extra.' Aristea scoffs in amused disbelief. 'Naturally.' He plucks the card back from her, smiling sweetly, and says, 'I want that ledger, sweetheart.'

Blank. Renatus blinked, his eyes having been opened and unfocussed for too long.

'There really is a ledger,' he supposed, since Declan was a scumbag but not one to ask for anything he didn't know for sure he wanted. 'How fast did you put this together?' He reached for Aristea's wrist, turning it to see her watch, but it was dark and he realised he hadn't taken note of when he'd gotten out of bed or undone the spell. Twenty-five, thirty minutes?

Taking down the spell was obviously the right move, whatever his own personal reservations.

'I don't know. There was nothing, like every night when I sleep, and then the dreams started, but it was just the end of that vision from the christening, the whole crew down by the gate.' She nodded in that direction, and Renatus recalled the scene she'd shared with him the last time they left Shanahan's. 'And I kept hearing the same bit over and over, Teagan's grandad and that woman Moira, talking about someone else's ledger, and I kept feeling his shock and discomfort to hear it got someone else in trouble. And then, I don't know.' She looked annoyed and embarrassed. 'Declan's voice sort of started bleeding through, talking about the ledger, too.'

'And the memory started surfacing,' Renatus finished for her. Aristea nodded, pulling her knees against her chest. The memory was not what he'd expected Declan to have buried, but inspired in Renatus a similar manic fervor as it did in his apprentice. A ledger, proving Shanahan's dealing with Lisandro and who knew who else, possibly providing the White Elm with dozens of Magnus Moira names. With their names he and Qasim stood a better chance of scrying them; with their names they knew who to look for, who to watch, and could potentially start to get ahead of Lisandro's movements. Get those four boys back. Undermine Magnus Moira's next otherwise unpredictable move.

A game-changer.

'Declan literally has a guy tied up in his basement,' his apprentice added, having apparently thought that was a joke up until the dream helped her chip away at some of the covering of that memory. 'Who was that?'

For Renatus this was the least of the questions raised by her dream. 'I didn't see his face.'

'Neither did I. You're not even surprised.' She rubbed her temple like she was trying to recover more of Monday night. 'I think he *told me* to scry his basement. Why would he want me to know?'

'Because he likes playing with you.' And you let him, he

401

almost thought, but managed to squash it before it could form. She didn't look at him or react, so he figured he'd been successful. 'This ledger, or ledgers – this record must be real and it must be valuable if Declan wants it. It could prove our case to Valero tomorrow. We've only got a few hours left – that's why Fate pushed this realisation on you *now*.' Why it pushed him to dismantle the spellwork by sending him Sean Glassner's name. Nothing left to chance. A thought occurred to Aristea, and Renatus heard it before she voiced it, immediately knowing the answer. 'I know exactly where he'd keep it.'

He felt her attention in his mind as he revisited memories of Shanahan's place, an ever-closed door barred with rusted chains and a heavy padlock and a whole lot of magic, the stereotypical lair except it was on the top floor of a Belfast hotel and directly opposite the parlour where the patriarch met all his visitors. Hardly secret. Overconfidence was an inherited trait, apparently. Aristea viewed the details of the memory with interest.

'Could you dismantle that?' she asked curiously, mirroring his thoughts.

'Let's hope so,' he suggested, and reached with his mind for Lord Gawain and Lady Miranda, knowing they were asleep but feeling that this couldn't really wait. If they were asleep, so too probably was Shanahan himself. They could storm the hotel and take him by surprise before he had the chance to hide any evidence – there were no scriers in the household to give them the heads up. Between Renatus and some of the other councillors, Qasim and maybe Oneida, that door shouldn't present too great a problem.

And then they'd have it: proof to back up their scrier theory, proof to Valero that what happened to Anouk was not their fault, proof that Shanahan was in league, somehow, with Lisandro and Magnus Moira.

But before he woke the council leaders, Renatus hesitated. Lord Gawain and Lady Miranda were gentle moderates – they would not support the sort of raid he was envisioning. Miranda often criticised previous councils for the reputation they'd bestowed upon future iterations through this unseemly behaviour, and they had both expressed their wish for Renatus to develop a relationship with Shanahan and his other associates, to use them as informants. Arresting Shanahan and plundering his vault would cut Renatus from that world forever, proving him the White Elm scum they all quietly suspected him of being.

Not to mention, the source was shaky. Aristea's visions had been a keen edge to the White Elm's pool of talents since her arrival on the team, an Empath and a scrier who could not be blocked with blanket anti-White Elm wards, but her increasing erraticism had left the senior councillors somewhat wary of her input, even if they wouldn't say it. Admitting she'd been told of the ledger's existence by Declan O'Malley would require admitting that she'd gone there without his knowledge or approval and fallen victim to an illegal memory spell, which Renatus had managed to avoid telling anyone but Qasim, and would do little to advance his argument.

'We can't take the ledger,' he said finally. He couldn't arrest his uncle. He couldn't do anything to upset the fragile relationship he was building with that community. 'We won't be granted permission to seize something when *Declan* is our only proof it exists.'

'Do we need *the* ledger?' Aristea asked. Her thoughts were fast but he caught a few of them – Sean Glassner, Teagan, the ledger, himself. She locked them away when she noticed his attention and turned back to him, an idea taking shape. Her idea, if it could be called that in this indistinct and incomplete form, was hard to get a read on, a knot of unfinished thoughts and impulsively thrown-in assumptions. The starter pack for any bad idea. 'Or will a look do?'

He considered, ideas flying, enthusiasm building. 'If I got into the vault, and I got a look…' He could stream everything he saw to her and to other councillors. The collective memory could be shared with Zarubin and Vasiliev and their other Telepaths, proof enough to them. But there were lots of problems with this hazy plan. 'I'd need to know what I was looking for.'

'Teagan,' Aristea said promptly. 'She told me she sits with her dad when he does his bookkeeping.' Surprising. 'If I get her talking about it, can you see into her thoughts?'

Telepathy without digging wasn't illegal, but Renatus pictured his distant cousin, the protective spellwork bound tightly to her aura, and shook his head.

'Shanahan's got her spelled to the hilt. She's a vault all on her own. Her thoughts locked away, her every heart fluctuation on his radar in case she's attacked.'

'And I thought *you* were paranoid.'

'I know. He doesn't want to lose another daughter. But,' he conceded, thinking of the structure of that spellwork, 'she's the one powering it. She could, hypothetically, dismantle it herself, if you could find a way to convince her.'

'Done.' Assumptions connected with their most natural conclusions, and what was going to pass for a plan in the context of this conversation suddenly materialised at the front of Aristea's brain. A very bad plan. 'What else?'

'You know, it doesn't matter,' Renatus answered after a moment's hesitation. He brushed himself off and got to his feet. 'It isn't going to work. I'll never get a moment to myself in Shanahan's house, certainly not the *minimum* twenty minutes it will take for me to break into that vault on my own.' He paused, hearing her erratic thoughts. 'But he left you alone with Teagan.'

Because a girl was not to be perceived as a threat. Maybe that was something they could use. Aristea's wards were near faultless by now. She could make herself impossible to scry, impossible to see, and their bond could allow her to follow his instructions at the door while he looked through her eyes from another room, or even for him to control and guide her magic to unravel the spellwork... Visions and their timing were Fate's language for communicating with scriers, so he couldn't ignore the coincidence of Aristea's multiple insights, all indicating the same easily overlooked detail.

'It will work,' Aristea insisted, jumping up beside him. 'Once we get into the vault, no one has to know we were in there. You know how to remove magic traces. Shanahan taught you. Plus we've got everything else you can do. You're *you*,' she reminded him, and he winced, recalling his arrogance on Monday night, yelling at her outside Declan's. 'And I'm me. I can go unnoticed. We can work with my limitations, especially my being a useless little girl.'

They were going to get caught. They were going to disgrace the council and be strung up for misconduct. This was all going to blow up in their faces.

But her confidence was infectious, and he was looking in the mirror again. Overconfident, reckless. It had worked for them this far.

'It can't leave the vault,' Renatus warned. 'Not only would we be stealing – and my superiors would be *furious* – but Shanahan will have safeguards to prevent it. Taking that book could kill us.'

'It might be too big to take,' Aristea said reasonably. 'It might be the same old book Shanahan senior used, or it could be a huge set, or it could be chained down, like in those old libraries. But I get it. Leave it be.'

Renatus ran both hands back through his hair, torn by opposing logic. This could go spectacularly badly, he knew it, but going against the current of the White Elm was his job as the Dark Keeper, and Lord Gawain had overlooked worse transgressions than a little breaking and entering. Nothing was being taken, and everything was being gained. This ledger could change everything. Imagine keeping a written record of a lifetime of illegal activity? Renatus and Aristea had been through boxes and folders and desk drawers full of old paperwork of his father's and found nothing of interest, certainly nothing incriminating. There was less use for records of transactions when you were in the practice of expecting payment on delivery, instead of whatever debt system Shanahan was using.

'This is a very dangerous idea,' Renatus mentioned,

looking back at his apprentice. He was having trouble accepting it, but really, this heist was *her* idea. She smiled, not the smile of the girl he'd first met but the forlorn expression of an adult carrying adult troubles. It wasn't comfortable to see, another crack in the childlike exterior she'd come with. That was the problem with young people – nothing could be done to keep them from growing up.

He hadn't realised when he chose her that his own urgent need for her to become quickly competent and capable came at such a cost, or that once paid, he'd regret the price.

'When is it not?' she replied rhetorically, and he had to nod ruefully. Two superpowered White Elm scriers in pyjamas and bare feet in the middle of the night and yet another high stakes showdown to attend. 'We'll have to go first thing in the morning to give ourselves enough time. Are you going to tell Lord Gawain?'

'Better to beg forgiveness,' Renatus said, 'as per my usual style.'

But not alone, unfortunately. Irritably he snatched at the air, manifesting with a small targeted pulse of energy, and grabbed the pen with his other hand. He felt his apprentice's eyes on him, curious, as he dragged the nib on his forearm. He winced when it stung; paper would have been preferable, but this was more direct. In the dark he didn't doubt his penmanship suffered. At least the message would get through.

We need Shanahan out tomorrow morning.

Magic is always open to new paths, new ways of existing, but often "new" spells are only reinvented old ones. As children they'd found this one in a book and used it the same way non-witch children used telephones. Fingertips glowing, focus on the recipient, Renatus wiped the ink left to right. All trace disappeared. Aristea was fascinated.

'Are you calling in who I think you're calling in?'

He hated to confirm her suspicions, and hated that Declan O'Malley was the only person he had to call on who fell anywhere within the vicinity of trustworthy, especially after what he'd done to Aristea. He would have liked to discount that dirty little snake from all future schemes and keep her as far from him as possible, but he knew already that he was more upset about Declan's transgression than Aristea was. She'd gotten her distress out as frustrated tears on that first night and had mostly moved on; Renatus was better at holding grudges.

'If he comes through, I'll reconsider finishing what my grandfather started,' he muttered, pocketing the pen. 'We won't even see him. All he's got to do is lure Shanahan out of the house. First sign that things aren't going to plan, we abort,' he warned her seriously, and she nodded automatically.

'You're in charge,' she said, but he wasn't so sure.

chapter twenty-eight

'What are you *doing* here?!'

The morning was already off-track, but not yet in a way that compromised our plot. Renatus and I had only just stepped into the elegant foyer of Shanahan's hotel first thing the next morning when our names were shrieked. We both shrank down instinctively like we'd been caught doing something wrong, when in fact we hadn't yet gotten to that point.

And our intended crime was relatively small, right, next to the crimes of the people we were imposing on?

Teagan Shanahan was sitting behind the reception desk, though now she dropped the pen into the open spine of the huge book she was writing in and leapt off her seat. Eyes wide, her aura almost vibrating with surprised delight, she swept around the desk to meet us, throwing herself at Renatus first for her customary bear hug.

'We were in the neighbourhood,' Renatus invented weakly, patting her back uncertainly until she let go and beamed up at him.

'Working?' she asked, but turned to me excitedly before he could respond. 'You're here too.'

I made myself smile, and though it was so fallacious, I opened my hands in offer. 'Aye. I didn't like how I ended things with you last– oof.' She'd already barrelled into my arms and was hugging me tightly around the neck. I went through the motions, hugged her in return. She pulled away and grasped both my hands.

'I didn't think you'd come back,' she admitted, 'but I'm so glad you have. No one could believe it when I told them you had visited, and then I thought maybe you didn't enjoy yourself last time you were here. That maybe you were mad with me. But you weren't, were you?' She waited exactly as long as it took for me to blink numbly and start to shake my head before breaking into an even brighter smile and swinging my hands joyfully. 'I knew it. I *told* those girls you and I were friends now. Brigid's so jealous, as you can imagine, and Stacey wants to invite you to her high tea party next month.' Teagan rolled her eyes and sniffed, the very picture of spoiled dramatic, with her rosied cheeks and adorable peasant dress and victory rolls – all at eight in the morning, mind.

'Right,' I said when she left a breath in conversation that I gathered was my turn. I tried to catch Renatus's eye for aid but he artfully avoided my gaze, admiring the décor. *Very helpful, thank you.* 'But… it would be so much better if *you* threw a tea party, and invited Stacey and Brigid, and…' and whoever, since I couldn't remember any of her other girlfriends' names from her engagement ball. 'And all the rest, and I could come to that and be *your* guest. Since… I'm your friend.'

It was a stab in the dark at the right thing to say and seemed to hit the mark. Teagan gasped in excitement – the little things in life, honestly – and bounced a little in her kitten heels.

'*Yes*. Oh, good idea. Everyone would be so impressed. Oh,' she said suddenly, recalling that Renatus was with us, 'silly me, I completely forgot to ask: do you have time to stay for a bit? Or are you only passing through? I'm sorry, I'm hardly dressed for receiving visitors,' she apologised, gesturing sadly at her picture-perfect vintage look.

Renatus's turn for the green puppy eyes. 'We thought we'd stay a while, if it's not an imposition?'

'Oh, no, never. You're family,' she added proudly, sparing him an extra adoring smile before looking around for someone. I took back one of my hands to gesture at the abandoned front desk.

'... so specific?' I ask. Declan half-shrugs idly, circling his hand over the bowl and counting under his breath. 'The brain is quite incredible. It autofills a lot of details to a very convincing degree but...'

'Umm... Are you sure we're not intruding?' I asked, blinking away the shard of surfacing memory and ignoring Renatus's sharp look. I smiled at Teagan. 'You looked busy.'

'Did I really?' she asked, sounding pleased to hear it. 'I was doing the books for Daddy's business. You inspired me, actually. Paisley!' she called out to someone, while Renatus and I looked in disbelief at the big book laying out in the open. Could *that* be...?

Renatus's senses were quicker than mine. *Hotel accounts only.* A slender woman swathed in apathy appeared from the back room to take over the quiet reception.

'Thank you, Paisley, I'm done for now. Come,' Teagan added to Renatus and me, tugging me along behind her toward the door Paisley had come from. 'Normally Daddy and I do the books together at night but I said I bet Aristea Byrne doesn't still need help with *her* accounting. I bet she does everything herself. So he said *I* can keep the books *all by myself*, as well as still work in reception on weekday mornings.'

'I didn't know you were a budding accountant,' I confessed, feeling like this skill required acknowledgement, even if it sounded like it was a skill her father had fostered because he found it useful. Teagan positively glowed when I added, 'I'm terrible with money. You could teach me.'

We stepped through the door and I glanced back at Renatus while Teagan wasn't looking. *Easy as pie.* With Shanahan not at home, I'd not been sure how easy it would be to get his daughter to let us into the family's protected space or to talk about his accounts. Not an issue, it turned out.

'Where's your father this morning, Teagan?' Renatus asked innocently, knowing already what the answer would be. She grasped the handrail of the staircase and paused when the receptionist, Paisley, called out her name.

'He's upstairs. Yes?' she called back, while my stomach

twisted and Renatus's tension spiked at this unexpected development. That was *not* the answer we came here to hear.

Declan was meant to take care of that, he said furiously. I knew his belief in our plan hinged on Shanahan being out of the house, and this meant things were off. Teagan brushed between us to return to the foyer and our gazes met over her head.

Did you give him a time? I asked, reflecting on what I'd deciphered from his scrawled message in the dark last night. Renatus glared.

Don't stick up for him. He knows what morning looks like.

I hadn't needed another lesson in not trusting Declan so soon. I'd actually been surprised when Renatus opted to include him. His least favourite informant was further down his list of frenemies than ever, and he'd dropped a few rungs in my regard, too.

From the foyer, Teagan squealed and I was hit by her shock in the same instant Renatus and I bounded into action, racing back through the door. He caught himself abruptly on the doorframe and I crashed into him, leaning past him and his immediate disdain to see.

'*Declan!*' Teagan exclaimed in her trademark delight. Her heels clicked swiftly on the floor as she ran at the newcomer, colliding with him forcefully.

'Speak of the devil,' Renatus muttered to me as Declan caught the bubbly heiress with a lighthearted laugh and swung her around. When he set her back on the ground and adjusted the strap of his satchel, I noticed the improved state of his hands, the scabs and bandages absent. His hair, too, was full-looking and all the chopped-off bits seemed regrown, so that if he still appeared thin, it was less noticeable.

Declan keeps stirring. 'In the basement,' he prompts me, casting his gaze downward to direct my attention to, and through, the floor. 'Take a look.'

'Bigger every time I see you, kid,' I heard him say when I tuned back in. He affectionately patted her pinned hair, making her smile even brighter. How many levels of

411

luminence does the average person have? Teagan had double. 'Quit growing. Nice dress. And did you do this yourself?' He withdrew his hand from her hair to make a quick show of admiring the style from multiple angles, clearly practiced in all the right things to say with her. I could take a lesson, if I could trust him to conduct a lesson without casting an illegal spell on me. With Teagan Shanahan totally eating out of his hand, Declan pretended to suddenly notice us. 'Renatus, Aristea. Fancy seeing you here.'

'The coincidence astounds me,' Renatus replied flatly, which was a huge effort because he would rather hurl insults and strangle the other man with his tightly clenched hands. 'I'm surprised to see you *here*.'

The slightest inflection. Declan was supposed to have drawn Shanahan away from here for us to enact our plan. He smiled, that missing tooth obvious in an otherwise charming expression. I wanted to throw something at him, and not just because Renatus's sour mood was poisoning mine.

'I'm here to see your father,' he told Teagan, though I couldn't guess what the point was now, since our plan was already off thanks to his misinterpretation of our instructions. 'I know it's early, and I don't have an appointment…'

'Oh, don't worry,' she insisted, starting back toward us and the staircase up to the family's penthouse abode. 'Daddy said no visitors this morning but I don't think he meant that to include all of you.' She passed between Renatus and I in the doorway with Declan in tow. He met Renatus's glare with a bold salute that I thought was terribly brave considering the Dark Keeper had threatened to burn his house down less than a week ago. 'I'll tell him he simply *has* to see you. It's *you*, after all.'

It's me, Declan mouthed to me in mock sincerity as he passed with a falsely humble shrug, which I would have found funny in any other circumstance. Teagan stopped on the first stair to turn and survey us proudly.

We should go, I said to Renatus, and I felt his agreement. There was no way we were getting into that vault now. I opened my mouth to make our excuses.

'All my favourite people here at once,' Teagan announced with satisfaction, and I shut my mouth quickly. I could feel that she really meant that. It made me unexpectedly sad – what kind of people were her regular friends if her favourite people were a distant infamous cousin she'd only recently gotten to know, his disinterested grouch of an apprentice she'd met twice, and the outcast creep who was meant to have been her brother-in-law? She beamed at Renatus. 'It's like a family reunion for you, isn't it?'

My master never smiled but through his intense resentment and the restraint it was taking not to knock Declan to the floor, he made a pretty good approximation. 'That's exactly what it's like.'

The bowl is on the tabletop beside my hip and there's a business card in Declan's hand, outstretched in offer. My fingers are dangling above it, not sure whether to take it. 'What's wrong? Scared to see the name of who's taken such an interest in you and yours?'

Standing between Renatus and Declan at the foot of the staircase, the buried memory seemed determined to surface at this hugely inopportune time, perhaps reacting to being back in the spellcaster's presence. I forced a smile as Declan reached past me to clap Renatus's shoulder, quickly squeezing out from between them to jump up onto the steps and loop my arm through Teagan's.

'Let's go upstairs,' I suggested firmly, beginning to walk with her and casting a quick look back to see Renatus shove Declan's hand off and deliberately shouldering him into the balustrade post to get ahead of him. *Mature*, I thought, and he ignored me. I heard the two whispering crossly to each other like squabbling children as Teagan and I moved further ahead, and I tightened my grip on my host's arm to keep her attention with me instead. 'Boys, right?'

'They're just like my brothers,' she agreed fondly, smiling down at them before bringing her gaze back to the steps, taking care in her heels. I wondered how often she came downstairs. Just once a day, to work that front counter, before going back to her pampered life in the penthouse?

'Do your brothers still live here? I don't think I've met them,' I said, though my focus was split. Through Renatus's ears I could hear the irritable conversation taking place behind me, a summary of which would be that Renatus was pissed, Declan wasn't in a position to expect Thomas Shanahan to come running when he requested it, Renatus still intended to kill him, and Declan would believe it when he saw it and had everything under control. Even I rolled my eyes at that, glaring down at the informant as the staircase wound up another flight and Teagan babbled happily about her brothers' own hotel homes. Declan was already smiling at me, like he knew I was listening in. Jerk. 'Everything under control', like he was going to be the least bit of help when he'd already derailed the plan.

'It's a joy to see you again so soon, Miss Aristea,' he made sure to say when Teagan left a gap big enough for more than a breath. Renatus's pulse of dislike was impossible to miss, and I was sure we shot twin looks of contempt down at him. I swallowed the scorn, though, for Teagan's benefit and tried to moderate my voice to one of deliberate carelessness.

'Has it been so soon?' I wondered aloud, bitterness still seeping in to the practiced ear. 'I'm afraid our last encounter was less than memorable.'

'I'm sorry to hear that,' Declan lamented. For a moment our footsteps were the only sound in the stairwell, and I waited for the inevitable inappropriate line. 'Perhaps next time I can think of a way–'

'Okay, you know what–' I began to interrupt before more of the sixteen minutes he hid crumbled free.

Declan delicately tips a little glass bottle of essential oil over the mix.

'We can try another of my tea blends,' Teagan realised, oblivious to the tension, and I bit down on my retort, seething, 'and we can get down another of my tea sets. I think you're tall enough,' she added, leaning away to critically assess me. She nodded, satisfied. I didn't bother to enquire.

'Miss Teagan, have you had a chance to taste the Turkish

rose tea?' Declan asked, unable to help himself from being centre of attention. I was growing more supportive of Renatus's desire to stab him. 'I've been meaning to ask whether it was as nice as it smelled.'

'Oh, yes, thank you,' Teagan confirmed with a warm smile down at him. She brought her smile to me excitedly. 'Declan found me tea that turns *pink*, and smells *exactly* like Turkish delight. Let's have that one today.'

'Oh, let's,' I agreed with cheer I hoped sounded close to genuine. No *way* was I drinking something Declan provided. 'Or better yet, let's save it for your tea party next month.'

She stopped midstep and almost tripped us both over; I had to grab the handrail I'd been so careful not to touch previously.

Heavy hand, thick fingers... suspicion... '...will make a lovely couple'... Sean Raymond and Thomas Shanahan...

Cringing at the reminder of Teagan's arranged marriage, I ripped my hand away and the younger girl grasped it.

'That's genius,' she said, which should have been sarcastic except she was perfectly serious. 'I wonder if the other girls have ever had pink tea...'

'I bet they'll be jealous,' I offered, the right thing to say, apparently, because it got her moving again. But again I felt sad for her, realising things I'd overlooked in my initial encounters. She had no real friends, only rivals in the daughters of other rich underworld kings like her own dad, competitors for social standing. Was that the real reason she wanted so badly to get to know me? Not only because I was a great bragging card, but because I wasn't in that game? Cautiously I looked once more back at the two men following me, catching Declan, the bloody chancer, demurely brushing his hand over the wooden rail where my hand had just touched. Renatus, the outcast by choice, and Declan, the outcast by circumstance. When Declan said her dress was nice, Teagan could believe he meant it. When Renatus and I came to visit, she could believe we really wanted to see her. Look how quickly she'd overstepped her father's no-visitors rule for the three of us.

At that moment the door at the top swung open and Shanahan himself, portly and immaculate in his pinstripe vest and fedora, the perfect gangster, leaned over the top rail.

'Visitors, Teagan?' he asked airily, a gentle but pointed reminder of his earlier request. She smiled knowingly up at him.

'Not *real* visitors, Daddy,' she dismissed as she and I climbed the final flight. She released me when we got to the top and kissed his cheek, melting his reservations immediately. 'Just the best people. Declan and Renatus are here to see you, and Aristea is back to see me.'

I smiled as sincerely as I could at the man I'd been investigating as a criminal, a man I had almost no respect for, and said, 'Thanks for having me back, Uncle Thomas.'

Integrity? What integrity?

For a crime lord he had a deep mushy paternal streak. He immediately warmed at my greeting and took my offered hand to shake just once.

'What a surprise,' he said, smiling at each of us, shaking both Renatus and Declan's hands with more vigour than mine. If he found it odd to see the pair of them together, he didn't show it. He gestured us welcomingly through the open door into the penthouse. 'Please. To what do we owe the pleasure?'

And just like that, we were in, the thick magic pressing on my skin, sunlight streaming into the high-ceilinged space. I felt glad now that we weren't going to try and carry out our plan, intensely aware of the layers and layers of different kinds of live spellwork woven into this place. I'd forgotten to factor this in – no wonder Renatus had initially insisted this wouldn't work.

'Aristea was eager to see Teagan,' Renatus said, looking to me for inspiration because we hadn't planned for having to explain his presence, 'and I wanted to check in with you about our last discussion.' He turned expectantly to Declan, who was meant to have saved us from this part. Standing together, similarly built and with the same colouring, they did look a bit like brothers, with Shanahan regarding them both with geniality like favoured nephews. Declan smiled brightly.

'Just business,' he confirmed, patting the satchel at his side. My eyes followed his hand and for the first time noticed the thin layer of magic coating his skin. Illusion, hiding the inconvenient marks of his craft. The regrown patches in his hair were the same.

'Ah,' Shanahan answered in recognition, like he knew what to expect from the contents of the bag, and he waved the two of them toward his receiving room. Toward the vault I'd seen in Renatus's memory. He smiled again at Teagan. 'Do you have everything you need?'

'We're going to make tea,' his daughter said sunnily. 'Perhaps we'll bring you some?'

Shanahan laughed. 'You spoil me. Maybe later? But no scrying today, hmm?' He included me in his fatherly gentle authoritarian gaze. No making my girl bleed. I got the message. Teagan sighed good-naturedly.

'No scrying, Daddy, we promise.'

He turned away with Renatus and Declan, who shot a quick playful wink at Teagan over his shoulder. My host practically glowed at the small show of attention, and grabbed my hand to drag me off in the other direction.

Alone. No adult chaperone. Shanahan had the real threats under close surveillance. What harm could two unattended teenage girls possibly manage on their own? I twisted my bangle on my arm and sped up to Teagan.

'No scrying doesn't mean no magic at all, though?' I murmured, and she giggled.

Since we're here we can at least make a start on the first stage, I suggested to Renatus as Teagan started telling me about her most recently acquired tea set.

Be careful, he warned in response. *No unnecessary risks*.

The youngest Shanahan let me into a room a few identical doors down from her parlour. The walls were lined with fancy glass-doored cabinets. Teagan went straight to the first one and swung open the doors, revealing a dozen exquisite teapots and their accompanying cups, saucers and milk jugs. I stared at the variety of prettiness.

'This is your collection?' I asked, looking around and realising there were five other such display cases, as well as two large apothecary cabinets for storing all her exotic teas. 'It's so beautiful.'

And it was. Every porcelain set was gorgeously detailed in different styles and colours, some quite modern and others exceptionally old. No girl could possibly drink enough tea to warrant this many teapots, but I realised from the careful arrangement that this was not the intention. Despite my initial misgivings of Shanahan's daughter, I was coming to appreciate her over-the-top sweetness as genuine, and her wholesome hobbies – antiques collecting, vintage clothing and even bookkeeping – as harmless manifestations of a sheltered, extended childhood being prepared for an adulthood as a kept trophy wife.

'Thank you,' she said graciously, admiring the cabinet's contents with me. 'These are my favourite ones.'

I nodded at a familiar set on a mid-level shelf. 'That's the one you served me last time. Your best set.' She beamed at my recognition. I raised my gaze; she'd made a point to assess my superior height. 'But you have all these pretty ones up high.'

'Oh, well, they're very old, so they're up high so I don't knock them or break them,' she explained hurriedly. It was easy to guess whose idea that was. 'I have to ask someone to get them down for me.'

I frowned. 'You shouldn't have to ask someone to use your own things, and I doubt you're anything short of entirely careful. Here.' I extended my hands to show her I could reach the top shelf easily. 'Which one do you want?'

'Oh, any,' she said, pleased excitement surrounding her at the incredible emancipation of a taller friend willing to bend rules with her. Oh, sweetie, I thought, and I'm hardly a rebel. I looked thoroughly at the three top-shelf options and picked a pumpkin-shaped silver-and-white teapot, taking it in both hands and passing it to its owner. The delight in her face when its weight settled in her palms gave me the courage to push forward with my agenda, feeling now like it was less for my own selfish gain.

'Your dad has a lot of rules for you, hmm?' I prompted, reaching back to the shelf for teacups and saucers. The question gave rise to the slightest discomfort in my host.

'He just wants to look after me, and help me look after my things,' she said reasonably. I positioned the teacups on a lower shelf to free up my hands to stretch for the saucers. My fingers brushed the fine cool china.

Delicate fingers arranging saucers on a table… Bell-like laughter… Dainty brunette woman with rosy cheeks…

'These were your mother's?' I asked as I stacked the saucers together and picked the teacups back up, looping my fingers through the handles. Teagan looked taken aback but nodded, gently elbowing the cabinet closed.

'My sisters didn't want them,' she said, starting for the exit. I knew better than to question notably absent parents but had long guessed that there was no longer a Mrs Shanahan. She glanced around at the other cabinets. 'I'm glad, because I always loved her collection, and now I have my own sets to keep them company. Oh, silly me,' she cursed herself, stopping when she realised she'd let the door close behind us and both our hands were full of priceless antique china. She looked around for somewhere to place the teapot.

'Stop saying that,' I scolded, jerking my head. A small ward grew and quickly popped in the narrow doorway, pushing the door open again. 'You're not silly, you're a clever and powerful sorceress. Why don't you just use magic?' I led the way out. 'You could use magic to get the teapots down whenever you wanted. Or would your dad not like it?'

She trailed behind me down the hall to her parlour, awkwardly shrugging. 'He doesn't mind me doing magic, I'm just… not very good at it.'

'Why, because no one taught you?' I replied rhetorically. We stopped outside her special receiving room, the door of which was also closed. 'You've got as much power as I do, and you've got a lifetime of exposure to magic I don't have. Plus you're a *Crafter*; you can do any magic you damn well want.' She giggled nervously, clutching her mother's silver pumpkin teapot close. 'Go on. Open the door. Unless your dad will know about it, like he knew about us scrying last time.'

I looked further up the hall for eavesdroppers, trying to extend my other senses but again finding them useless here. Teagan squared her shoulders and fixed her eyes on the doorknob.

'He doesn't know when I do magic,' she told me. 'He only knows when I'm hurt or when I have an extreme emotional… Oh!' The door flew open and she nearly dropped the teapot in excitement. It slipped from her fingers and we both reacted simultaneously to freeze its fall, me with a soft ward and her with… something else. Time dilation? She grabbed the teapot securely out of the air and we both released the magic we'd so swiftly gathered, sharing a relieved grin.

'See? You're amazing,' I reminded the other girl as we went into the sunny tea room. She smiled humbly, hurrying to place the teapot safely on the table. I put the cups and saucers beside it, and followed her when she headed back out. Of course – we hadn't yet selected a tea flavour.

'Well, of course I know I have a lot of magic,' she admitted. It gave her a small flutter of pride to close the door behind us without touching it. 'It makes our family very important. That's why Geroid wants to marry me, because my children can make the magic in their family line even stronger.'

And my voice, reluctant. 'No. I… just never know whether to trust you, in honesty.' Declan laughs and twirls the card to reveal the business name. 'Oh, definitely don't trust me. But don't trust them *either.' My hand takes the card and the logo of Shanahan's hotel chain is clearly visible. I ask, 'This was in his pocket?' and he replies, 'I thought you should know who your friends are.'*

I eyed her sidelong, ignoring the stupid memory still slowly expanding in the back of my head. 'And you're okay with that being his chief reason for wanting to marry you? Not because you're beautiful, or because you're kind and generous, or because you're clever with figures and numbers? You're a lot more than your bloodline, Teagan.'

I could feel that she struggled with that concept, which was maybe too big to lump her with all at once, but rather than brush it off she responded with mild frustration.

'Obviously I would *prefer* if he liked me best for those things, but he'll grow to see what I'm like, and he'll love me for it.' She pushed down her unladylike reaction and smiled at me, trying to shift the locus of attention. 'At least you know Renatus will let you marry whoever you want.'

'There is no *let*,' I corrected. 'Renatus doesn't get a say. Besides, my life's too complicated for a boyfriend, let alone a wedding. But hey,' I redirected, turning to walk backwards to face her, 'you said your dad knows when you're hurt or when you're extremely emotional. Is that for when you're scared?'

'That's right,' she agreed, looking at her arms, at the magic there. 'Even if I was on the other side of the world. It's like an alarm. A lot of parents cast it on their children,' she added, slightly defensively. I nodded, backing into the teapot room, squeezing my eyes shut against another unwelcome push of the buried memory.

'… *very interested to know whatever he learned, of course,*' Declan explains as he continues to stir his ingredients, '*but even more interested to know* who *is paying for it.*'

Piss off, Declan.

'It sounds useful,' I admitted. I stood with her at the first medicine chest, idling while she picked through the small square drawers filled with tea leaves, wondering whether to broach the topic that came to mind. 'But now that you're practically an adult… What if you were to have an extreme emotional reaction, say, while you were with Geroid?' Teagan snorted, and I thought of her glowing in the hall. 'Or someone else?' I nudged her softly. She pursed her lips together and nudged me back, blushing furiously and smiling despite herself. Oh, wow. 'What if you fell wildly in love, or felt an unexpected rush of attraction?'

'I'm engaged to Geroid,' she reminded me primly.

'But everyone's got a secret childhood crush,' I said,

trying not to smirk because *wow*, that was a bad one. 'Mine's Orlando Bloom.' She blinked at me, trying to place the name and what family he came from. 'Never mind. Yours is embarrassing.'

'I am not confirming anything,' she replied with a helpless giggle, grasping my hand playfully. 'My father would have a fit if I even *thought* about it.' She suddenly sobered. 'The spell might let him *know* if I thought about it.' Her hands fluttered to her warm cheeks and to her chest over her heartbeat, perhaps considering the biological indicators of attraction akin to stress and fear. 'Oh. It's got to go. He'd just die.'

'Not that I recommend thinking any harder about Declan O'Malley, but–'

'It's gone.' Teagan's skin lit up with a spider web-like blue weave. As I watched the threads disintegrated, and within four or five seconds it was totally dismantled. With her mind to it, Teagan Shanahan was a force to be reckoned with. She shook out her arms like shaking off the last of her father's spell. Then, good-naturedly, she fixed me with an accusing finger. 'And not another word about Declan. He's lovely, he's always been lovely, and that's all.'

'I thought you should know who your friends are.'

I scoffed, hating the sound of his voice still buried under that memory spell. 'Lovely?'

You got her to take the spell down? Renatus asked in surprise. *I can see into her head. Can you get her to think about the ledger?*

I cleared my throat apologetically when Teagan pouted.

'Sorry,' I said. 'He and I had a disagreement. Let's change the topic,' I suggested, pushing shut the open drawer where I saw the pink rose buds, 'and let's not drink his tea. You said you do your dad's accounting for the hotel? That must be so much work.'

I could tell she was desperately intrigued by my dispute with Declan but too well-mannered to ask. She chose another drawer and leaned forward to get a better sniff of the perfume.

'It is, but as I know you think already, I don't have a lot else to do.' She smiled wryly at me, and it was my turn to blush abashedly. 'I mostly keep track of the hotel accounts. Payments, invoices, refunds. It's not every day, and you get quicker at it.'

'And what about personal accounts?' I asked, knowing that despite suggesting she had a crush on Declan and bringing up her dead mother, it was only now that I was really on dangerous ground. 'Your dad handles all that himself, I suppose? Renatus handles all his money stuff himself,' I added for personalisation. Teagan looked only briefly and mildly suspicious, and the look vanished when I added, 'I guess important men like to know who owes them what and where all their money is, but it means it's a skill I haven't learned. You're lucky.'

I can see it, Renatus said, sounding honestly surprised by how easy that was. *It looks like…* He stopped trying to describe and simply visualised what he saw in his cousin's head. A battered old brown leather book appeared in the front of mine. *Next time we'll get a look at the real thing.*

'Yes, Daddy keeps track of all that himself, but he wanted me to be able to handle finances as well as he does. I don't think he thinks Geroid is very good with money,' my host mentioned in a low voice. 'Daddy knows lots of things about lots of people.'

Teagan was still talking but that pesky memory was pushing at its seal, and suddenly the last of it spilled out, the final pieces filling the gaps all out of sequence but coalescing quickly into something I realised I remembered.

'*…but even more interested to know* who *is paying for it.' The logo of Shanahan's hotel chain on the card…* '*This was in his pocket?'* *and he replies,* '*I thought you should know who your friends are.'*

Stirring.

It's a sparse cold space, poorly lit for the scare factor – Declan's basement, after he invited me to scry into it *– and there's a chair in the middle with an unconscious man strapped to it. His head tips back, revealing smears of herb mixtures and painted-on symbols and* *lettering across his temples and jawline, hallmarks of blood magic telepathy. But his face is familiar.*

I inhaled suddenly, struck with horrific realisation. I had seen that face before, though only in a vision. Shanahan's business card. Shanahan *hired* him.

'I thought you should know who your friends are,' Declan had said, a connection I would never have guessed without his roundabout help, and I reached now for Renatus as blind, reckless rage filled me and made my hands shake.

Renatus, we need to–

chapter twenty-nine

I coughed violently trying to exhale that last breath when what I needed was an inhale. That came quickly as a startled gasp.

I was outside.

I tried to take a step back.

But I was sitting. My head knocked back against something hard. I twisted; a tree trunk. *What the…?* Heart thudding, I looked around for Teagan and her teapot display room but somehow, in a split second, I'd been transported far away. Details struck my disorientated awareness all at once. Trees. Sky. Sunlight. A bad smell. I was sweating, and cold. Dirt. No leaves. A shell of magic. Power, throbbing power, and a deep sense of unease.

My stomach flipped. I was in the orchard at Morrissey House, on the path to the graveyard. How *the hell* had I gotten here? Displacement? No – the Shanahan penthouse couldn't be Displaced in or out of, just like the Morrissey Estate. And I always knew when I teleported. This… I couldn't explain this. I was sitting in the dirt inside a dome of my own magic, a ward I knew *I* must have created. Feeling its parameters, I recognised it made me invisible and unscryable. Why would I want that? When did I build it? I was at a loss. And it was about to get worse.

'Oh, no.'

I drew a series of shallow, shaky breaths as my gaze zeroed in on the most sickening features of this already unsettling scene. In my lap, a copper bowl, its mixed and singed contents of plant matter, paper, oils and what looked like a thick lock of hair all smoking slightly and giving off that terrible smell. And my hands, unsteadily quivering with shock, swam red before my unbelieving eyes, unchanging even as I turned them and blinked hard. *No, no, no…* They were tacky with drying blood, thick between my fingers and smeared down my wrists. My tattoo, a black symbol kind of like an A and an R entwined, was obscured by the rusty scarlet of whatever horror I'd been party to, looking like I, or someone, had tried to rub it clean. Unsuccessfully. A bloody scrap of paper was stuck to my palm, crinkled like I'd been holding it tight.

My handwriting. *Whatever it takes.*

'What happened?' I looked myself over in growing panic, seeing the stain of blood spatter on my clothing and even on my collarbone, but unable to see or feel any obvious injury to my own body. Which only made me feel more terrified. How much time had passed in that not-even-a-blink in Teagan's display room? Where was Teagan? What had I done and how did I get here? Staring at my bloodied hands, at the note I didn't recall writing, it wasn't hard to imagine I'd screwed up, even if I couldn't understand how. *Oh, god, oh god…* Disgusted and scared almost to tears, I hastily wiped my hands on my legs, but little was fresh enough to come off. Yuck, yuck…

I needed to get out of here. Back to the house, get help, get answers. Giving up on my hands, I gingerly pushed the bowl off my legs and two things happened.

Bloody hand on the bowl… other hand throws in petals… my hand… utter panic… string of curse words… me, scar visible, blood down my neck, sitting right here, battered brown book beside my knee in the dirt…

The bowl landed on something softer than the ground and rolled into something wooden, then something metal; detecting the difference in sounds, my organs in knots, I ripped my gaze from my horror-movie hands to follow the bowl.

'No, no…' It wasn't even possible. Beside me, just like in the impression, Shanahan's legendary ledger lay inanimate and waiting, beside my still-sealed blood-smeared puzzle box from Ange and a fucking *knife*. I raised my right hand to dazedly stare at my watch. Ten-ninteen. *Ten-ninteen*. 'Two hours?!' I shoved the bowl aside and twisted over onto my hands and knees, letting its very telling ingredients spill on the packed soil of the path, refusing to accept the obvious conclusion this all suggested. 'No. Renatus? Declan? Ren...'

My voice died in my throat. From my new position on all fours, I could see around the tree I had been leaning on, and a familiar black combat boot was sticking out into the path from the other side. Petrified, I scrambled over the book, the weapon, the bowl and an exposed tree root that almost saw me flat on my face, to reach my unmoving master.

'Renatus?' I breathed in terror, grabbing his leg and shaking it. He was propped up against the tree like I had been, eyes closed, head lowered to his chest. I crawled closer on limbs wobbly with the shock of something I couldn't recall, collapsing beside him and grabbing the collar of his jacket. I expected him to wake up when I yanked, but instead he tipped, dead weight, toward me, and I had to catch him against my chest. No, no, no... 'Renatus. Wake up.' I shook him once more, getting no response, and pressed my bloody fingers to his neck to feel for a pulse. There was a smear of blood in the same place, and no discernible injury, and though I couldn't believe it, I knew this meant I'd already done exactly this. When? How? *What the actual hell happened to us?* I held my breath but my hand still quaked too much to be able to tell if I was feeling his pulse. His skin was cool, which made me want to be sick, but I had the presence of mind to remember it always was. Not conclusive.

I reached for him with my extra senses and was stunned to find his aura empty, or diminished, just *grey*. Renatus could *not* be dead, and certainly not *here*, the exact place the other Morrisseys met their end, his least favourite place in the world, and I couldn't have lost him, not when the last thing I remembered doing was helping his cousin choose a flavour of tea. I just couldn't have lost him, end of story. My vision began to thin, and I made myself start breathing again before I could pass out.

'Renatus? Please, wake up. Please, please.' I tilted his head back in my hand, his hair falling back from his face. His eyes stayed shut. There was some blood on his mouth and quite a bit more in his hairline. I swallowed but my throat was dry. *Get a goddamn grip, Aristea,* I berated myself. Either he was dead and my world was demolished again, or he was in a bad way and he needed my help. There was no one else, no one better coming to fix this. Not knowing if I could handle the answer, I laid trembling fingertips over his mouth and nose.

Nothing.

Nothing.

A soft exhalation warmed the dried blood on my skin and I almost burst into tears.

'Oh, thank you, thank you,' I whispered, choking back a sob and letting my forehead fall exhaustedly to the crown of his head. I didn't know why I was so tired; I hugged him protectively close to me, not caring that he was heavy and squashed me a bit, just holding him as close as I could while I worked not to cry. 'Don't scare me like that.' I thought of all the times I'd given him the same scare, disappearing to Declan's in the middle of the night, being captured by Lisandro the night he took the Elm Stone, but especially just weeks ago in Prague, and considered it was probably fair that this time the tables were reversed, but I didn't much appreciate the justice. Renatus was the strength of our partnership, in every sense of the word, and I didn't know what I was meant to do if I lost him.

I drew a deep, deliberate breath to steel myself, steadied by the familiar scent of *my* favourite person outside of my sister and sat up. Time to take stock. Time to act like a White Elm apprentice instead of a scared kid.

Alright. Renatus was unconscious, a state I'd never known him to be in despite our many escapades. Now that I wasn't freaking out, I could see Renatus's chest rising and falling shallowly, but this defencelessness scared me. The blood by his mouth could have been another previous check of mine, but the dark stickiness in his hairline looked like an injury. I looked around cautiously. Had someone done this to us, or was this me? *Whatever it takes.* My eyes strayed back to the knife beside the stupid ledger. Clean blade, thank *heavens*. But still, blood on my hands, blood on his head...? Gods, I hoped not. We'd sparred with the sai but I couldn't imagine a scenario in which I'd want to truly hurt him.

I extended my senses into our surroundings and came up with nothing. We were alone in the bubble of my ward. Gently I brushed his hair back to check his scalp. It was bloodied, concerningly so, but I could find no wound.

'What happened to you?' I asked softly, feeling around the back of his head for unseen injuries, looking over him for any cuts to his clothing or any bloody patches. I touched his cold cheek and tried to channel my attention into his body to detect any other damage, but whipped my hand back with shock when my tiny injection of energy was met with black cracks under his skin. 'Jesus...' The webbed pattern started to fade immediately, until I touched him again and pushed more power from me to him, watching in repulsed fascination as the cracks spread across his porcelain face, down his neck... I moved my gaze to my hand, seeing the same pattern, though mine was much less pronounced. Burnout. A lock of my hair fell into my eyes and I shoved it away, freezing when I noticed how short it was compared with the rest. Missing hair. A knife with no blood on its blade. Hair in the bowl with ingredients I couldn't explain but could only be for one spell, the only way I knew to lose two hours off the clock, but what in two hours could cause such damage to Renatus was beyond even my wild imagination. 'I'm sorry, whatever I did, I'm so sorry.'

Distantly I heard a shout. I tried to see over my shoulder but couldn't move without dislodging my master. Innately I extended my awareness, and found my focus shift to the property's gate.

The gate clicking shut... Elijah gesturing at something in the air he was squinting at while Lord Gawain hurries down the sloped lawn... frightened, hopeful... Elijah steps forward and disappears...

'Renatus?' I heard my Displacement teacher's voice nearby, and my breath caught to see him walk straight past me, not six metres away, picking his way between the trees and looking all around without seeing us. The ward. I opened my mouth to answer.

I closed it again quickly. Why had I built that ward? Who was I hiding from? I looked down at Renatus cradled in my arms and tried to put the pieces together. Whatever had happened, it was clearly bad. We stole the ledger. He'd gotten hurt and I'd, I didn't even know, maybe done something terrible. On Renatus's other side, I saw new evidence I didn't notice before: Declan's satchel, a pen, and a damp grotty pile of herbs and hair and paper that had to be the discarded remains of another memory spell.

Whatever it takes. I'd wiped *both* our memories. Me. I'd done this, and left myself an unhelpful message in explanation. I had absolutely no recollection of leaving Shanahan's, getting into the vault, taking the book or getting back here, but Elijah had just traced my Displacement from the gate to here. He was getting further away now, calling out for us, looking behind trees, expecting the worst. I could feel his deep apprehension, his anxiety over what he'd find of us. I looked again at Declan's bag. He'd brought the ingredients for a memory spell to Shanahan's? He *had* said he had everything under control, but this felt anything but.

I looked again at Renatus and knew it didn't matter why I'd made the ward or who I was hiding from or how much trouble I was about to be in. He needed help. His energy was depleted and he'd clearly come close to burning to death. I knew that had to be why I'd brought him here, to the orchard path where the dark energy of Sean Glassner's not-death and the Morrissey triple murder fuelled both our auras, hoping to hasten his recovery.

It wasn't fast enough.

I dropped the ward, prepared to accept any consequences. Whatever it took.

'Elijah!' I shouted, feeling the energetic attentions of all the White Elm, especially Qasim's scrying, and for a single second I felt shaky with relief to know that they were on their way to take responsibility and to make everything right.

Then nothing was right.

Lord Gawain appeared at my shoulder, looking stricken, and as his horror washed over me I saw the scene twice over through his eyes – Renatus cradling bloodied and unmoving Ana, his hands incriminatingly red, and me holding the younger Morrissey, him likewise still, me likewise redhanded, in the very same place eight years later.

His reaction was not the same. Disjointedly I processed the scene out of sequence. Yelling. Marching me away, only a few steps but too far. Pain in my shoulder. Me, begging to stay, begging for help, panic flooding me again. A hand on my elbow yanking me so hard I was immediately on my feet. Elijah and Emmanuelle crouching over Renatus's slumped form.

'What are they doing? What's wrong with him?' I kept asking, not paying attention to the accusations and demands being flung my way from the indistinct faces hovering in mine. 'He won't wake up. Is he going to be okay?'

'You tell me!' Lord Gawain ordered, grasping my shoulders roughly, his distress bleeding straight through me. Sorry, mate, I'm already filled up with that stuff. 'What happened? What have you done?' When I couldn't answer and kept leaning aside to see past him, he gave up and called back to the rescue team. 'Emmanuelle?'

'He's alive,' she reported, relieving the council leader more than it did me. Alive I knew, but alive is not necessarily okay. She pressed practiced fingertips to Renatus's sternum, preparing to run her usual energetic diagnostic, what I'd tried to copy, and she got the same result, black cracks spidering out from her touch. Lord Gawain let me go, horrified. Emmanuelle glanced up grimly. 'Burnout.' She looked at me, at my arm hanging by my side, the only other place either of us had seen the phenomenon. 'What kind of spell would it take to burn *'im* out?'

'But it didn't, did it?' I pleaded with her as if she had a say. She went back to work on him as the black marks faded away.

'No, but 'e was close. It drained 'im, that's why 'e won't wake up.' She placed her other palm across his forehead, both hands glowing subtly and those awful cracks showing up all over Renatus's exposed fair skin, the enviably symmetrical features that made everyone second-glance him appreciatively marred like the china face of a shattered doll. Gods, what did we do?! 'No other injuries.'

'The blood?' Elijah asked, as unable to help glancing between my master's clearly matted hair and my hands as I was unable to help detecting his wariness of me. Emmanuelle waved me closer, patience never her chief demeanour, and I staggered forward, hovering at her side. She ran a quick finger across the back of my hand, through the dirt-speckled blood.

'Not 'is,' she said automatically, straight back to the business of assessing and healing her friend while I felt dizzy at the simple proclamation. *Not his*. Then whose? 'Not 'ers, either. She's uninjured.' Not that anyone seemed to care. Lightly she touched the corner of his mouth where the blood still stained him, and his temple just below his hair. 'He's been recently 'ealed.' She was looking at me again, waiting for my confirmation. I didn't know what to say. I wasn't great at healing, so it didn't seem likely, but I'd also never been pushed to desperation like this before today. Surely I would have *tried* healing him before wiping both our memories? Emmanuelle gave up waiting for me and said, 'It's your energy signature. Can we get 'im out of 'ere? This place makes me sick, I can't 'elp 'im 'ere,' she told Elijah, and the pair of them awkwardly pulled Renatus upright. In a blink they were gone, Displaced by Elijah, and I made a strangled noise of protest that was supposed to be a 'No' except that they immediately reappeared on my energetic scope inside the house.

I wasted no time. I stooped to snatch up the ledger that had caused all this trouble and gathered my magic and concentration close. I stepped out of my hasty wormhole, shrugging off the pull of the void and catching the edge of the grand piano I walked straight into. We were in the ballroom, which students never used, though I could feel the presence of some of my classmates in the reception hall and dining room nearby. The Displacer and the Healer dropped Renatus onto one of the soft couches against the far wall beside the tall bay windows and I jogged to meet them.

Qasim stepped into my path, pulling me up short, and Lord Gawain appeared right beside him.

'I suggest you get talking,' Qasim said, not a suggestion at all. I hugged the book against my chest, no idea where to start. 'Oneida and Teresa are in Belfast with a *furious* Mr Shanahan demanding your *organs* in compensation for burglary and a violent attack on himself and his daughter.'

I stared at the Scrier, his words fuzzy in my ears. Violent attack? Us? Me? 'My organs?' I repeated faintly. Then the words started making sense. 'Teagan? Is she alright?'

'She's in hospital,' Qasim replied coldly, eyeing my hands. My stomach flipped over again. What was that look supposed to mean? 'Luckily Teresa is experienced with healing around curses.'

'*Curses?*' I echoed, horrified. I grasped at this morning's events but there was nothing along those lines. 'We... we were at Shanahan's. But I did *not* curse anyone.' I had no proof but I wouldn't know where to begin with cursing someone, even with two hours up my sleeve.

'Then what *did* you do?' Lord Gawain pushed. I shook my head, unable to explain, and opened the ledger. At that moment, behind the two men, Renatus suddenly awoke with a violent gasp. Everyone's attention was arrested as the Dark Keeper sat bolt upright, shoving Emmanuelle's hands off his chest and blasting her with an innate defensive ward. Powered down as he was, it did little against the wards she already had up, and she grasped at his hands as he struck out, disorientated.

'Arist... Em?' he mumbled, eyes struggling to focus, thoughts wild. I'd clearly done a terrible job of matching the before and after in the mental timeline, freaking us both right out with the impossible transitions. Still, I felt my arms and legs weaken with relief to see him awake and responsive, and when his wide, distinctive eyes flickered around the room, taking in sparing details the way I had when I first came to in the orchard, and caught mine, I smiled so hard I almost started crying again.

'Renatus,' Lord Gawain said, as relieved as I was, going to him. 'What–'

'What happened?' my master asked thickly, noticing my bloody hands and leaning back. Frightened. 'How did… How did we get here? Are you alright?'

For him no time had passed since he was with Shanahan and Declan, and I understood the disorientation, except he didn't have the context of the memory spell bowl to wake up to. I heard the others trying to calm him, explaining where they'd found him and in what state, promising him I was unharmed, asking him to describe the events of this morning. Wary. Unsure of his part. Assuming if I'd managed to bloody myself up, he must have done even worse.

'We were just trying to get a look at the…' He frowned, recognising what I held. 'At the ledger…' I looked down at the open pages in my arms. Divided into columns, dates and names and amounts and shorthand descriptions of services written in small, sloped calligraphy made up the entries. I tried to read the one at the top of the page but Qasim yanked the big book out of my grip. Renatus struggled to get to his feet but wasn't strong enough, and Emmanuelle tugged him back down. 'We didn't take that. We only just got there. I was with…' He looked again at me, confused. *What happened?*

'This?' Qasim flipped through the pages with disdain. 'Did you steal this?'

I swallowed. 'It's Shanahan's ledger. It proves that our attackers in Prague were possessed by scriers who were clients of his, and he helped them fake their deaths so they could join Magnus Moira without suspicion.'

'And this was worth hospitalising a girl, hurting her

father and trespassing upon a very dangerous family's private property?' Lord Gawain demanded of me, shaming me, before turning on his favourite. 'We've discussed this. I don't like surprises.'

'I didn't do anything,' Renatus defended. 'All I did was see what it looked like in Teagan's head. She's in hospital?'

'Yes, after the two of you allegedly led an assault on their household to steal a book, without council support, in broad daylight.' Lord Gawain stared at him, disbelieving, and I felt his confidence in Renatus shaking. I saw in Renatus's eyes that he could sense it, too. 'You're *White Elm*. You just conducted an illegal search and attacked civilians. What were you thinking? *What* were you *thinking*?'

Jadon and Susannah arrived simultaneously, looking like they'd just woken up on the other side of the Atlantic, and Susannah caught my eye meaningfully. By this point she had to be my least favourite councillor for the part she'd inadvertently played in the murders of my parents and brother, but her words from earlier in the year had haunted me ever since she uttered them. She'd told me Renatus would be the one to kill Lisandro, and that it would start him down a path to becoming someone we couldn't salvage.

'I… We didn't,' Renatus insisted, unable to explain further. He gestured at me helplessly, trying to appeal to his mentor. Anxiously I fidgeted with the little silver ring on my pinky finger, the one Hiroko made me, seeking comfort. 'We were just there. We just got there…'

It made no sense, and Lord Gawain couldn't string it together.

'We're meeting Valero in *hours*, Renatus, to convince them we're not what Lisandro's been painting us as, and you do *this*? You've threatened our most important alliance, not to mention put yourself and your apprentice offside with your uncle. He's making wild demands that we hand you both over, presumably for some brutal, old-world justice involving bleeding you both dry. What did you *do*? And *why*? When you *know* better?'

It wasn't often that I saw Renatus as young, but I did in this moment, too weak to stand up for himself and without a reasonable explanation to offer to wash away the heavy disappointment in Lord Gawain's gaze. He looked hopelessly lost. And it was my fault. But chances were, if I'd felt compelled to wipe his memory, he wouldn't *want* to remember what he'd done.

'I don't know what to tell you,' he said finally, a pang of hurt passing from him straight to me when Lord Gawain pulled away from him, shaking his head. Let down. Trust trembling.

That trust was half of what kept Renatus together. Without it, what chance did I have of redirecting his fate, regardless of who pulled the trigger on his godfather?

Whatever it takes. Cryptic, but I understood.

'He can't tell you what he doesn't know,' I spoke up, drawing the room's attention. 'He doesn't know.'

Qasim cottoned on first. 'What time is it?' he barked at Renatus. My master looked taken aback.

'Eight, eight-thirty?'

All the other adults shared uncomfortable looks. Elijah disappeared. I swallowed, terrified, preparing myself for what was going to be an ugly scene.

'I… I took his memory away,' I stammered, the only thing I knew for certain. 'Of what happened this morning. At Shanahan's.'

'You *what?*' Renatus questioned incredulously, shock radiating from him. Elijah returned, holding the copper bowl for confirmation. He hadn't been gone long enough to collect or take note of the discarded second spell. I saw my chance, knowing already it was a godawful idea but that it must have been my plan. Next time I'd leave myself clearer instructions.

'Get talking,' Qasim instructed in a low voice. I nodded, twisting the ring harder, gathering what remained of my wits, too panicked to think this through clearly.

'We went to Shanahan's,' I recited, thinking through what I honestly remembered, determined not to get caught in a lie. The remaining councillors were showing up, eyes wide with what their counterparts had been telling them. 'I... I realised he was the one who sent the scout to Angela's. Dan O'Conner.' And that was the last thing I recalled before missing a breath in the orchard, that memory of who Declan was keeping in his basement. That thick hair, the same nose, the creep who'd manipulated his way into my sister's house to spy on us. Rage filled me again. The rest? Obviously a bad time for everybody, and not one I remembered, but I was going to need to come up with something feasible. 'I wasn't thinking.' A safe inference, not a lie. 'I decided to try and get to the ledger.' Clearly, since I'd gotten hold of it. 'Renatus got hurt. I brought him back here. I did the memory spell.'

'The *highly illegal* memory spell,' Lady Miranda pointed out, circling around to stand with the others. 'You could have done irreparable damage to Renatus's brain if you'd mishandled it.'

'I didn't hurt him,' I defended myself adamantly. I couldn't remember a thing but about that I was feeling increasingly confident. I would never, so I hadn't.

'Tell us exactly what happened,' Lord Gawain ordered angrily. 'The blood on your hands, what happened to the Shanahans, what happened to Renatus. Every detail. Now.'

Every detail. I didn't have them. Slowly I shook my head. 'I can't.'

'What do you mean?' Emmanuelle asked, watching me suspiciously. 'Of course you can. Explain. This is a mistake,' she assured Renatus, who was visibly stressing. He was staring at me like he wasn't sure who I was, and that hurt, but I withheld the very important fact that could save me and pushed on with my fabrication.

'I can't say,' I repeated softly, staring back at him. *I'm sorry.* 'I didn't want Renatus to know what I did. That's why...' I inhaled a painful breath and looked to the bowl in Elijah's hand, thinking this was a safe enough guess not to be a lie. 'That's why I spelled him.'

No flicker. I'd become an adept little liar.

'That's not…' Renatus ran his hands back through his hair, looking between his leaders, whose faces were set with displeasure. 'That's not what happened. She didn't do anything.'

'His memory's blank,' Jadon reported quietly, undermining the other with an apologetic glance his way. 'There's nothing for the past two hours. It might come back, weeks or months, maybe.'

Lady Miranda stepped forward to take my shoulders in her hands, trying to see dishonesty in my eyes, but she wouldn't find it. My wards were clamped tight over my mind, my expression determinedly slack. Some things meant more than the truth.

'Aristea,' she said carefully, clearly, 'that spell was a terrible thing to do to another person, especially a friend. It's the sort of thing we bind magic for. We would have to charge you, if you can't explain to us why you felt it was warranted. And the robbery, and whatever happened to Mr and Miss Shanahan. Please. Think this through,' she added when I shook my head childishly. 'You're threatening your future.'

I wanted to cry. Deceit wasn't my default mode, and this didn't feel good. The consequences were stacking up and I didn't even know if I deserved them. I could just admit I didn't know. I could confess I'd spelled myself too. They would lay off and go investigate, and discover that of course I didn't hurt anyone.

But if I didn't… I tugged my gaze from Lady Miranda's to Renatus's. I heard his voice in my head and I still couldn't answer him. *What are you doing?*

'I've got nothing to say,' I confessed in honesty. 'Do what you need to. You won't get through my wards,' I added when I felt pressure at the edges of my mind, Jadon and others digging to see my memory. 'Try if you want.'

They all dropped away, seeing my point. Lord Gawain turned to the Scrier.

'Qasim?'

'The whole time period is blocked, for both of them,' he

answered irritably. 'The hotel is unscryable, and she must have continued to shield herself from being scried when she left and came back here. I can't see any of it.' He snapped the ledger shut and raised it at me, unconvinced. 'You expect me to believe you were stupid enough to take on two Shanahans on their own turf for a blank book?'

'She didn't,' Renatus insisted, getting to his feet with effort. Slowly his aura was refilling now that he was awake. 'It was me. It was my idea, I did it. Whatever it was, I told her–'

'No, you were unconscious,' I argued. I turned to Lord Gawain determinedly. 'He did nothing. He was out the whole time.'

The council leader looked dubiously at Emmanuelle, who was still seated on the plush sofa, looking distraught. She pursed her lips.

'Whatever caused the burnout is mostly out of 'is nerves,' she confirmed uncomfortably. 'Roughly two hours. It adds up.'

'The blood's about two hours old,' Lady Miranda agreed, looking down at my filthy hands. She sighed slowly, hands dropping from my shoulders. My heart thudded in my chest like it did when I found Renatus unmoving in the orchard. She'd saved my life only a few weeks ago. I had so much respect for this woman, and I had to disappoint her. 'Aristea, help us out here. This isn't you. You're on the verge of losing your apprenticeship if you don't talk.'

'No.' Renatus shoved through the wall of his colleagues to reach me, taking my face in his hands and staring down at me from up close like he'd see something different. *Stop! Aren't you hearing what they're saying?!* 'What are you doing?' He looked back at the surgeon. 'You can't separate us. You've said before it could kill us. Tell her,' he snapped at Emmanuelle, who uncertainly got to her feet.

'We're not making any decisions about that today,' Lord Gawain said, a small mercy before the other shoe fell, 'but a criminal isn't a White Elm apprentice. Even if you stay bonded,' he told me, 'you're losing your guaranteed position with us if you can't justify your actions or provide an explanation.'

439

My chest felt tight and I clasped Renatus's hands over my cheeks, petrified. *A criminal isn't a White Elm apprentice*. I'd thought I'd screwed up when I went to Declan's without asking but I'd really done it this time. I was about to lose the very thing I came here for on the first day of March, not even half a year ago, when my sister dropped me off at the gates with my handstitched rabbit hidden in my bag for comfort and a tidy selection of interview-style blouses to help me make the right impression.

I looked down at my funky skirt and fishnets and boots, the stains of what I had to assume was Teagan's blood. Where was that girl Angela left here? I couldn't see her. That girl hadn't been chosen. She wasn't scarred. I thought of everything Renatus and I had been through since then. Everything we'd achieved, and how. My talents were a help, of course, but it was his instinct for magic, his experience, his contacts, his reputation, his power, his reach as a White Elm councillor that had gotten us where we were.

To finish what we started, getting justice for our families, we needed him, not my idealised future. *Whatever it takes*. He could not go down for this.

'The alternative's worse,' I said finally, pulling Renatus's hands away from my face and closing my eyes as he tried to argue with Lord Gawain, as Lady Miranda tried to reason with us both, as Qasim cursed and Emmanuelle insisted something was amiss and beyond the door, half the student population had gathered, drawn by the yelling to eavesdrop. I tried to keep the tears in, but by the time the arguing was done and Lord Gawain had decided they would still go to meet Valero, bringing Renatus along to see if the Telepaths could do anything about the memory spell, my master's dismay had fully soaked me through. When my name was said sternly and I opened my eyes, there were tracks down both my cheeks and everyone was blurry.

'You're not to leave this house,' Lady Miranda told me, and I nodded automatically. 'We'll talk more when we get back, and arrange a trial if necessary.'

She looked down at me with such disappointment and swept away, unable to look at me. The others – Jadon who'd taught me how to channel my magic, Elijah who'd taught me to Displace, Tian who'd trained me with my sai, Emmanuelle who perfected my wards, Susannah who'd armed me with the warning about Renatus's fate, Lord Gawain who voted yes to break the tie when Renatus chose me, Qasim who taught me to scry and who I so badly wanted to please – stared at me with disbelief, unable to understand my behaviour, and slowly filtered out.

Renatus was the only one left, at a total loss.

'You're a liar,' he murmured, shrugging helplessly, because he had no evidence to back that up. I'd performed perfectly. 'We're not done.'

I forced a smile. 'Never.'

With nothing left to say, the council's decision made, he stepped around me and fell into step with Qasim, who handed him the ledger. I watched them over my shoulder, and saw as Renatus flicked the cover open and leafed through. Every page was blank.

At the door they paused, exchanged words with somebody briefly, and Qasim held it open for someone else to squeeze inside. I don't know what magic she put into that ring when she made it or how it worked, but I was a heap of exhausted emotions on the floor before Hiroko Sasaki settled wordlessly beside me and pulled me into the tightest, warmest hug.

chapter thirty

1963

The flames devoured another book, pages curling, glue crackling, and Cassán pretended not to see ghosts in the fire. Hear screams. He would have done anything, given almost anything, by this point to be able to reverse time and take back a few choices, starting with the one in Moira's basement. He should have walked out on all four of them. But there was no greater proof of time's relentless forward march than the curve of his sleeping wife's belly, more pronounced every week.

Thea was pregnant, and Cassán had never been so terrified to be happy.

He'd known before she did, though he'd tried to convince himself he was wrong. It was a trick. An anomaly in her energy field, put there by some clever spellwork since he couldn't decipher it. Moira, maybe, spiteful as she was. It couldn't be what it seemed, because he'd done nothing to deserve that kind of unadulterated bliss.

Probably why his bliss, when proven true, was far from unadulterated.

Anthea shifted in her sleep, her head in his lap, their small fireplace casting a warm glow on the swell of their growing baby. A perfect spark of magic in a world Cassán himself had helped to darken. Sitting here with a pile of his own books and original writings, feeding them steadily into the fireplace to burn up, watching the brief flare of paper first catching, he had to believe the darkness was his own, and something he could shield his child from. Some of his work, though underground, had sold well enough that he had no way of ever taking that back, but what he'd managed to get hold of was curling with the heat, leaving the world forever so they could do no more harm.

The story of the sleeping beauty itched at his subconscious. Though the princess's father had burned every spinning wheel in his kingdom, he still hadn't been able to protect his daughter. But Cassán was no king. Amidst the ash of other books and papers was the very worst spell he'd ever written, stained deep with blood and guilt, the only copy now destroyed but the memory seared too deep in him to really be gone, no matter how many other books he threw in on top. The cheery flickers of the hungry household fire were reminders of the five towers of human flame in Salem; the glowing embers of book covers reminders of Helen Flanagan's black, cracked skin, her body burnt from the inside out. It was inescapable. The screams. The searing in his hands. The little boy bleeding out to die in that field, scarring that land with memory... Blood spreading...

Cassán carefully got to his feet to leave the fireside, minding not to jostle Thea, but as he gently laid her head on the loveseat cushion, her flecked hazel eyes opened.

Reflecting towers of human flame. He smiled as the vision receded, but it was becoming more frequent, and he didn't have an explanation for it. Guilt? The mortal medical profession was only beginning to understand the impacts of distressing experiences on the mind, and even if he'd been following those developments closely enough to recognise it in himself, he'd have been just as certain that this was a symptom of magical ailment.

It was a spell that started all this, after all.

'I didn't mean to wake you,' he whispered. 'I'm going to see Mánus.'

His wife shook wild dark hair out of her eyes and sat up. 'This late?'

'It's not that late,' he teased. 'He'll be up. I won't be long.'

'Shall I dress?' Thea asked, a simmering of hope beneath her stillness. She made no move to stand, knowing already what his answer would be.

'No, it's fine, just rest,' he assured her, and she nodded. The resentment might have been hidden in her smile but she couldn't keep him from feeling it. She and Morrissey's wife had gotten along unexpectedly well after their first meeting at the christening, happily spending time together on the lawn or in the drawing room with Áine's baby while their husbands talked increasingly frustrating business with an increasingly paranoid and underground magical community. But Cassán hadn't taken her there in five months now, and she had noticed. How was she supposed to believe him when he said he didn't want his friends to know he'd fathered a child when he still regularly spent time with them himself? It was impossible to explain.

She didn't understand what Andrew Hawke and Moira Dawes were, or how tightly bound he and Mánus were to them, or how desperately he wanted to protect their little family from that influence.

Thea looked around at the piles of books remaining for the fire.

'Are you burning that one too?'

He knew immediately what she was referring to without her needing to point. He shrugged and went over to pick up the manuscript of his very first book.

'I haven't decided,' he admitted. It was the only piece of writing he was still proud of, and he felt like, of all his work, this was what should be remembered, though it was one of his least-read works. The interrelationships of love, choice and destiny, and how magic and human life danced between the three. He brought it over to the loveseat, a hand on the warmed cover. Inspiration struck him. 'Do you remember when we met, and–'

'You read to me from this book,' Thea finished, a little more abruptly than she meant. He felt her soften with effort.

444

'On the beach. Every day until you left the island.' She lowered her eyes from his to the book's spine, sadness and memory and half-forgotten hopes surrounding her like a cloud. 'I don't want you to burn it.'

Cassán made himself smile. She never asked for anything. He set the book down in her lap.

'Then I won't. In fact, it's yours.' He gestured at the piles in front of the hearth. 'If it gets cold, use any of that. I don't want any of it. Love you both,' he added, and he meant it every time even if it sounded automatic, taking a second to kiss her hair and then her belly. The smile he got back was like a real one, the kind he'd fallen in love with and made him imagine, as he made his way across country, that maybe things could be fine.

Maybe for others, they could be, but if his friends were anything to go by, Cassán could more realistically expect a steady descent into some very dark places.

'Don't make excuses.'

He heard Áine first, her voice strong and carrying through the halls of Morrissey House as he was led through by a member of staff. Everyone he passed felt harried, strung out, though they made the effort to appear calm as they went about evening chores. A nanny, bouncing the screaming two-year-old Aindréas in her arms on her way downstairs, was trying unsuccessfully to cast silencing wards around herself. The boy flung his head back, and Cassán saw the bloody slash carved by Moira, except this boy was untouched. He blinked the sight away, hard, and the child was fine. The kitchen maid escorting him offered an apologetic half-smile, and said, 'I'm very sorry for the noise, sir.'

They both paused awkwardly to hear Mánus yell back at his wife that she was being ridiculous, and Cassán waved the nanny over.

'I'm sorry–'

'Don't be,' he interrupted, dismantling her shaky spellwork and casting a new one. 'Like that. Take it down with this,' he added, lighting up a loose thread of magic hanging over her, a seam to pull once she tired of silence and had learned what she could from the ward. He took the boy from her arms while she looked around in wonder. 'It won't hurt them to hear him.'

The nanny mouthed her thanks but no sound came out. She grinned, the spell proving effective. The kitchen maid spoke up over the softening screams of the distracted Aindréas.

'The master and mistress of the house are just through that door,' she said, nodding ahead to one of the mansion's many sitting rooms. Probably the proper thing for her to do was seat Cassán elsewhere and go fetch the Morrisseys, giving them time to regain their poise before facing a visitor, but perhaps even servants get sick of that charade.

'Thank you,' he replied, shifting his friends' son to his hip. His baby would be much smaller, though he or she would grow to this size soon enough. He locked those thoughts away fast and knocked heavily on the door to the sitting room. If they were paying any attention at all they should both already know he was here, an energetic anomaly right outside. 'Mánus?'

He pushed the door cautiously, discreet wards already coating him and extending now to shield the boy he held in case anything was thrown awry. The child went oddly quiet.

'Oh, good, someone who can give me a straight answer,' Áine snarled at her husband, gesturing angrily at Cassán as he slunk inside. The room was aching with negativity, storms of it, and Aindréas, though far from an Empath, shrank against the Crafter's shoulder in response. Áine, always beautiful and dressed to perfection, stood at one end of the room with her hands on her slender hips, dark hair spilling from her upstyle. A letter was scrunched in one of her hands. Opposite her, leaning more heavily than he ought to be on the back of an armchair, Mánus took an angry swig from a bottle of spirits, his normally elegantly lacquered hair dishevelled, its clean part not even visible tonight. Other victims of their wrath included broken glasses and lamps scattered against skirting boards. Áine turned on Cassán. 'Don't lie for him, I'll know. Who is he sending money to? Is it Helen?'

Cassán looked between them, mystified. Mánus waved the bottle at his wife irritably.

'I told you, it's nothing,' he said with only the slightest angry slur, keeping one hand out of sight, 'so mind your goddamn business.'

'Mánus,' Cassán warned, feeling the wave of hurt and anger from Mrs Morrissey, but the lady of the house needed no one to stand up for her.

'It's my business when it's our household's money, which you can't be bothered handling,' she sneered, scrunching the letter tighter. 'I can't count the times you've called me Helen. If you've got another child somewhere–'

Mánus lost his temper and shoved a chair over. The air shimmered, atoms stretching. Aindréas started to shake. Cassán worked on the feel of the small room, starting over the little boy, bringing unnatural calm.

'Her child's dead!' the scrier shouted at his wife. Magic vibrated in the room, too much magic for one person. 'He wasn't mine, I never even met her.'

'Then why send her money? Oh, don't tell me this has something to do with Moira–'

'Okay, okay, stop,' Cassán demanded, stepping between them before his friend could explode the whole floor. He'd never seen it done but neither had he known a sorcerer with two people's worth of magic to lose control. 'Calm down. Your son's watching. Here,' he gestured impatiently with his free hand to Áine for the letter. She reluctantly held it out and he leaned closer to look. It was from Tom Shanahan, asking for confirmation that Mánus was sure he wanted his share sent to an unnamed mortal woman in the States.

Cassán exhaled slowly, realisation setting in. He had books to burn; Mánus had money to throw at his demons.

'It's not Helen, and neither of us are talking to Moira,' he told Áine reassuringly. She seethed but his effect on the atmosphere of the room was already setting in. 'Helen was a coven mate from years ago.'

'It's none of her business, Cass,' Morrissey said loudly and approached, knocking over furniture, bottle raised threateningly. Cassán blocked his way with a ward, and he visibly bounced off like walking into a window.

'Put that bottle down,' the Crafter snapped, losing patience with his friend. The younger Irishman scowled but listened, backing off with angry mutters, spare hand deep in his pocket. 'You'll thank me later.' Cassán tried to smile calmly at Áine, who was much less agitated already. 'Helen and this little boy died. A tragedy. Mánus and I couldn't stop it.'

The first flicker of a lie. He could have stopped it. He could have never written the blasted spell. He could have backed out at any time. He could have called Moira back when she raised that knife to that boy's throat. Áine felt it, knew it, he could see it in her eyes. He tried to rephrase.

'We didn't do enough to stop it,' he said, this time ringing true, and her eyes softened, 'and we've both suffered for it. It's not something we talk about. Even Thea doesn't know. Don't worry about this,' he advised his friend's wife, gesturing at the letter. She nodded amiably, easily manipulated despite a strong mind simply because she wanted to be. 'It really is nothing. It's not money you'll miss.'

'You're right. It's just what Lorcan owed us,' she agreed, screwing up the paper and throwing it down on a chair, not sensitive enough to notice Cassán's flinch. 'Mánus tried to forfeit the debt. But you know Tom, every coin accounted for, it probably physically pains him not to be able to complete a transaction.' She reached up to fix her hair. 'You look good with a baby.'

It was something she'd said before, a playful jibe, and he smiled easily even when she watched him hopefully for clues in his response.

'I look even better handing them back,' he replied, and she smiled wryly, accepting her contented child from him. Bouncing Aindréas lightly, she tilted her head at her husband.

'He's lucky to have you,' she said, intimating that she

448

knew what impact he was having by being here, and headed for the door. 'Sort him out, will you? And please give my regards to Thea.'

Cassán promised he would and wished her goodnight. The silence in the sitting room was swollen and unpleasant in the wake of the closing door.

'Thank you for cleaning up my mess, as usual,' Mánus muttered over the mouth of the bottle before taking another drink. With a sigh Cassán marched over and wrenched it from his hand, eliciting a noise of protest but no fight. The scrier's magic was back under control, the air and walls no longer shaking with the potential of his rage. What would happen the day he, his son or any other descendant to inherit this unnatural power finally went over the edge? Cassán's best guess was a tear in the Fabric, an unrestrained wormhole to nowhere consuming anyone in the path of his blind fury.

'I shouldn't have to,' Cassán snapped, slamming the bottle down on a table recently relieved of its lamp. His friend didn't even flinch at the noise, still swallowing that last burning mouthful, the back of his hand pressed against his lips. 'This isn't you. The booze, the temper, scaring your boy…'

'Scaring you?' Mánus asked the question like a light joke, but Cassán could feel the genuine curiosity and the tendril of angst wrapped around it. He knew the millionaire no longer socialised like he once did, skipping card games and race days and parties wherever he thought he could get away with it, eager to avoid relaxed encounters with the people he used to call his friends. Cassán knew he preferred now to engage with other society sorcerers one-on-one in business settings here at the house, or if he visited others for work, he liked to have Cassán with him. He wouldn't say it, but the Empath had seen the change in behaviour, felt the new anxieties grow inside his friend, and he knew about the hallucinations. Mánus Morrissey had become a recluse, and Cassán Ó Gráidaigh was his only real friend.

'I'm not afraid of you, Mánus,' the Crafter muttered, waving a hand in the direction of the shattered lamp. The

449

shards rose from the floor and began piecing themselves back together. If only every mistake was as easy to undo as broken things and ruined toys. 'Sick of your bullshit, maybe. Is this yours?' A piece of the frosted glass lampshade caught his attention, its edges red with blood, and he reached for it. It came with only the faintest prompt of energy, landing neatly in his fingers; Mánus instinctively turned his shoulder away to better hide that left hand.

'It's nothing. Already healed,' he insisted, his mouth tightening in frustration when the lie flicked between them. Cassán rolled his eyes. Like he didn't know. Mánus overheard the thought and looked away, sulkily withdrawing his bloody hand from his jacket. The lamp seemed to have smashed against his hand and sliced along the back from the thumb almost to the wrist. Cassán let the half-fixed lamp settle back on the floor and instead materialised a handkerchief from the air to offer his friend. Mánus took it, tipsily impressed, and he was already in Cassán's head, examining the electrical pathways through his brain to complete the same skill as he absently dabbed at his dripping hand. Eyes clouding.

'Focus,' Cassán instructed, seeing the temptation to collect more magic to his already advanced spell vocabulary take priority over self-care and irritably taking the handkerchief back to just do it himself. The blood flow was slow, sluggish, seeping through the thin layer of illusion wrapping the deeply scarred skin. Cassán made no comment; his ugly hands were marred with the same burns beneath similar magic, his fingers less dextrous than they were before.

Mánus, in now-typical delayed fashion, came out of his mental cataloguing and pulled his hand back moodily. Cassán narrowed his eyes. Heal it yourself, then, he thought, knowing it would be heard, and the injured hand came back reluctantly while Mánus distracted himself with his other hand, the only good hand left in the coven, practising twirling his fingers to generate his own handkerchief.

'What's going on with the money, Mánus?'

A cut that small took very little energy to close, and a

sorcerer as powerful as Morrissey, even before he absorbed Eugene Dubois's power into his own, shouldn't have had an issue with it. Cassán wasn't a Healer but he had it shut before his friend had even answered the question.

'Goddamn Shanahan,' the scrier replied vaguely, nodding in grateful acknowledgement at his mended hand. 'Couldn't just send the money. Got Áine thinking all sorts of nonsense. I'll curse him,' he decided, rage building again, and Cassán blinked in response to the unexpected escalation. 'I'll curse his whole family.'

'Or not,' the Crafter asserted, working again on the room's atmosphere. Morrisseys had such strong temperaments; all of them very hard work.

'It's not worse than what he did to Lorcan.' Mánus concentrated wholly on cleaning the blood from his hand for a long moment, and Cassán let him, silent, glad to see him present and not angry. He came back to the conversation eventually. 'She's fundraising. The mortal police have given up looking but the mother won't, and she's spent all her own money, her house, everything, on search efforts. She thinks he's still alive.'

The little boy. Bunny. Cassán disintegrated the bloody handkerchief into the air around them, his mood darkening, in no small part a response to his friend's. He'd shared what little he had with Áine in the hopes it would stimulate some sympathy in her expectant treatment of her deteriorating husband, but it was true that this wasn't something they talked about. It was too dark, too terrible, too guilt-laden.

'And you know all this,' Cassán realised slowly, 'because you're a scrier with too much time on his hands. We killed her son,' he stated flatly, the words vibrating with the same intensity as the power build-up of a few minutes ago, making them both flinch to hear it aloud. It didn't matter who wielded the blade on the night. They were all guilty. 'We can't take it back, we can't fix it. This fixation isn't healthy.'

'Tom keeps writing, wanting to balance out his books. He set aside my "share" of what he made off the O'Malleys. I told

451

him I didn't want it. Just another mistake I can't take back. I don't need the money. So, I said, send it to this woman. She needs it.'

'Nothing suspicious about that,' Cassán scolded, but he felt a twinge in his chest. The good in Mánus, the part of him that tried to revive Helen Flanagan, the part that tried desperately to heal Eugene's hand after it was blasted off in that aborted ritual, was trying so hard to redeem itself, only to be slapped down for its efforts. 'And you couldn't know what Shanahan was going to do to Lorcan. To any of them.'

'Stop making excuses for me. Of course I knew, or knew enough. We both did. You're right to keep your child far away from me.'

Cassán swallowed, careful to keep his thoughts immobile. 'I don't have a child.'

It wasn't a lie, but this was the only person he felt any guilt about misleading. It was not remotely a matter of trust. He'd committed the most atrocious of acts with his four coven mates, and there was nobody he could be as honest with as he was with Mánus. But Mánus was embedded in a world of the same magic that had gotten them into this mess of a life, a life he didn't want for his unborn heir, and sharing his joy even with his best friend felt like an irrevocable blurring of realities.

'Of course not,' Mánus agreed smoothly, too smoothly for a drunk Telepath who always knew more than he should. 'If you did, you'd tell me.'

'That's right,' Cassán said cautiously, shutting down as many of his thoughts as possible, reining in his emotions even though his friend couldn't read those. 'I'll leave parenting to you for now.'

Mánus scoffed. 'Because I'm doing such a stellar job.'

'Mostly, you are. He'll be a fine man one day – he has you for a father.'

'No chance, then. Listen to you,' Mánus said now, reaching for the bottle again, frowning when Cassán moved it away, 'still looking for righteousness in me. You'll find it sooner in the mirror.' He gazed at the floor for a moment, conflicted emotions swimming through his alcohol-fuelled haze. 'Quinn's claimed Lorcan's daughter for his boy Robert, did you hear?'

'And you think that makes him a better father than you?' Cassán checked behind him for the nearest seat, and sat down heavily. 'Choosing Robert a wife while he's still a toddler? Even classier, he helped Tom orphan that poor girl. All the best marriages are built on murder and resentment, I hear.'

Mánus leaned on the back of one of the armchairs he'd displaced in his earlier rage.

'Áine thinks we should be thinking of it. We've had offers, but she's holding out.'

'She's got her dream match for your boy, I imagine.'

'She does,' Mánus agreed delicately, watching his friend closely. 'Her ideal match would be a daughter from your line.' Cassán worked hard to think cyclic pointless thoughts, hiding images and impressions of Thea's growing body at the back of his mind. 'If you had one, of course.'

'Which I don't,' Cassán said carefully, hoping to sound casual. Mánus was harder to fool than his wife, and he nodded with an unconvinced smile.

'Of course,' he said slickly. He picked at a stitch in the upholstery of the armchair. 'But you should know, Andrew told her you would. Due in autumn.' Eerie violet eyes flickered up when Cassán couldn't help thinking uncharitable things about the unethical Seer. 'Fucking Hawke, I know. I have to keep reminding her, unfortunately, that's not the case. Thea isn't pregnant, and there's no baby Ó Gráidaigh for any of us to get excited about.'

Exhaling slowly, Cassán reclined into the seat. He felt… okay. Relieved. He hadn't wanted to share his terrifying joy with anybody at all from this part of his life, but if one was to know, he would prefer it be the scrier. A thousand times over. The release of the secret felt like a weight lifted free of his shoulders.

'You always have my back, Mánus.'

'Of course,' the other agreed without hesitation. He raised his freshly healed hand in silent acknowledgement, and

Cassán nodded reluctantly at the reminder. Their trust was already sealed. It wasn't just the book club, the anti-council spells they'd sold, the ritual they shouldn't have done. He was the only person who knew the extent of the spell he'd just burned tonight. Absorbing Eugene's magic and skills in the explosion, sacrificing his ability to heal when he tried to save him, Mánus Morrissey had become the most powerful and most vulnerable sorcerer alive and neither condition had equalised even after all this time, both passing down his bloodline to Aindréas.

Friends keep each other's secrets, even when they're world-ending.

'Well,' Cassán said finally, reaching forward for the bottle, ignoring the reflection of towering human flames he imagined in the amber glass, 'if I did have a daughter, my friend, your boy wouldn't be getting near her. A girl of mine throwing away her future to clean up after a Morrissey?' He pushed his fair bangs out of his eyes and sipped the drink; it was stronger than he expected. 'Ugh. You'll give me nightmares.'

Mánus snorted, amused, and rounded the armchair to sit down opposite, motioning with his fingers for the bottle. Cassán leaned forward to hand it over, and his scrier friend grasped the neck. Froze, concern flushing through him.

'Cass,' he said, very seriously, the both of them holding the bottle in limbo between them, 'when did the hallucinations start?'

chapter thirty-one

'And you still do not remember *any* of this?'

Hiroko's echoey voice as she returned to the bathroom broke me out of the vision. My freshly dried hand was still on the lamp I'd been turning off on my way into the dormitory we used to share. Her voice indicated there'd been no break in conversation so the rush of images that began with this lamp once being smashed against a wall in what was now Susannah's classroom must have just downloaded into my head instantaneously. While it had felt real-time, I was already having trouble recalling details and sequencing them. I shook my head to clear it, disturbed. Disorientated. Time was not playing by the rules today.

'Nothing at all,' I answered honestly. I was showered, my hands and fingers pink from scrubbing, and redressed. 'I was standing in the room with Teagan one second, I breathed in, and when I went to breathe *out* I was actually up to an *in* again and I was in the orchard with *this*.' I grabbed the lock of offending hair hanging in my face, even more obvious now that it was all wet and clean. 'Whatever went down, it was bad enough to make me want to cut my own hair off.'

Scrunching her nose in sympathy, my friend took the lock in her fingers and tugged lightly to get it to straighten to its new length.

'At least the cut is neat,' she offered, leaning in to eye the hack job closely. 'You said you used a knife?'

'I *think* I used a knife,' I corrected. I angled my gaze up at the chopped lock sadly as she dropped it back onto my forehead. 'It was beside me, along with a gross bowl of herbs and this creepy diary I apparently stole, and my hands straight out of a horror film.'

Tossing her own shiny hair over her shoulder, Hiroko sighed and sat down on the bed that used to be hers. She'd Displaced here from Japan when she'd sensed my distress through her ring, bless her, but being with her in this room felt like she'd never left and no time had passed. Her presence today was the best temporary memory spell I could have asked for.

'I cannot believe you lied to them,' she said in a low voice. It was unnecessary; I had our interaction protected by wards that made us inaudible and unscryable. Thank you, Emmanuelle, for your brilliant and diverse instruction. 'I do not understand. Why did you not explain that you do not remember, either?'

I chewed the inside of my lip, smiling but unable to meet her eyes. I'd told her everything that happened today, insofar as I recalled, and the basic precursors that created the conditions for whatever disaster I was part of, but left out the same detail I'd been keeping from her for months – what Susannah told me about Renatus's destiny.

'I figured, if my hands were bloody, his must be even worse,' I reasoned, though of course my justification ran deeper than this. Hiroko looked sceptical. 'I mean, he doesn't need to get his hands dirty to do damage, and whatever we did, it almost killed him. I thought he really was dead.' An ill feeling washed through me at the recent memory of his stillness, my inability to sense a pulse, his cold skin, and I shivered, taking comfort in the subdued presence at the back of my head. 'I don't know what he did any more than I know what I did, but I can guess it was at least as bad. Why else would I wipe both our memories, except to protect us from anyone finding out?'

She shrugged uncomfortably, fidgeting with the string around her neck. I felt bad for her. She'd come here to offer me support, sensing I needed it, but had arrived to find her friend was now literally a red-handed criminal, booted from the White Elm. She was treating me graciously despite that, but was struggling to understand why I'd dug my hole even deeper by lying to paint myself as the sole wrongdoer.

'I do not think… Renatus would want you to protect him,' she said eventually, tugging the misshapen origami crane out from under her shirt to pinch its folds by force of habit, keeping it in shape. 'This is a very great cost.'

'Aye, he's not happy,' I agreed. Distantly I felt his sudden nearness and knew he was back from meeting with Valero. 'I might regret it more tomorrow, but I think it was the right thing to do.'

We fell into silence for a minute or so, but though it was weighty with everything unexplained that had just happened to me and my inexplicable behaviour, it was companionable, warm, and I realised something.

'I've really missed you,' I told her, and she looked up, surprised. 'I was awful to you when you left. I didn't even say goodbye, and maybe it looked like I didn't care, but that's not it. I didn't want you to go, and I didn't know how to be happy for you, following other opportunities. And I'm sorry you had to come back to more of my drama,' I added, gesturing helplessly at my now-clean self, 'but I've wondered every day what you're doing and I really want to know how great your life is now that you're back home with your father.'

She had the best smile, the warm, best-friend smile only best friends have. She pulled her legs up onto her bed to cross them, and leaned forward on her knees to take my hand.

'I miss you, too,' she said. 'I was not surprised you did not want me to leave, and I was sorry to leave you. I know you have a challenging life here.'

'And I was really selfish not to acknowledge how much that must have been impacting you,' I rushed to add, though she shrugged more amiably, a gentle dismissal.

'You have enough to worry about,' she insisted, making excuses for me I would never make for myself. 'Beside –

besides? – I do not hate your drama. It is more interesting than anything that has happened to me since I left here.' She couldn't help a laugh, startling one out of me, too. 'Preparing for the semester, study, going to shops, talking to my father. Practising magic at home so my skills do not suffer.'

'I've been lost without you,' I confessed, our hands swinging over the gap between our beds. I covered my eyes with the other hand. 'I alienated the twins, punched Addison, and maybe hospitalised this poor girl, Teagan. I think I even accidentally spoke to Xanthe when she asked a question in class.'

'Oh, then something is definitely wrong with you,' Hiroko confirmed seriously. She cast me a quick smirk before glancing over her shoulder at "their" side of the room, though since neither of us stayed in here anymore I supposed it was now all 'theirs'. 'How is Sterling? Does she still sleepwalk?'

I frowned. I hadn't been in here at night since she left, so I couldn't say, but I'd mostly forgotten the strange experience of our bounciest roommate getting out of bed one night and leading me around the house, only to "wake" standing up, disorientated, with no memory of leaving the dorm.

I now knew the feeling.

'I thought it was just that one time,' I said. Hiroko shook her head.

'She started to do it more and more until I left. Every night when you were in hospital, and then some other nights. She got up in the dark, did not answer Xanthe or me, and walked out.' She turned my wrist to admire my bracelet from my sister. 'She was always back in bed when I woke up in the morning, and she never seemed injured.'

The door to the bedroom opened without even the sound of the key turning, and we dropped our hands so I could twist toward the newcomer. Renatus stood in the doorway, the blood cleaned off his face and hair, energy field more than halfway refilled. It was so wonderful to see him standing on his feet unsupported when ninety minutes ago I couldn't wake him up.

458

'Hiroko,' he greeted my friend warmly. 'Thank you for coming all this way for Aristea.'

'It's okay. Thank you for not cancelling my key,' she answered, removing it from the pocket of her skirt. The tiny part of me that wasn't preoccupied with all my more pressing dramas was totally envious of her new outfit. Living at Morrissey House for so many months meant a lot of recycling of the same combination of clothes, and I'd become used to seeing Hiroko, like my other classmates, in a set wardrobe.

'I'm glad you kept it,' the headmaster replied. 'You're welcome here any time. Can we talk?' he asked of me. 'I'm assuming Miss Sasaki already knows everything I'm yet to hear?'

Hiroko and I exchanged a mildly guilty look, but I knew he meant Hiroko wasn't being sent away. I nodded and patted the bed beside me.

'I don't think so. There are enough rumours.' Renatus jerked his head authoritatively in a clear message of "out" and stepped back into the hall. I tried not to roll my eyes at his rejuvenated sass and to remember that I was grateful for him, regardless, as I dragged myself to my feet and followed the spritelier Hiroko out of the bedroom. It was bedtime in her timezone and midday for me, but you wouldn't know it.

'We're not at war with Valero, I thought you'd be glad to know,' Renatus told me as I pulled the door shut. I looked over with interest. He and Hiroko headed for the stairs. His emotions were tightly controlled, tucked away from me, making him appear cool and calm but really making him impossible for me to read. 'Qasim presented our scrier case but I think only Vasiliev was particularly interested to hear it. Winter's apparently been there already, advocating for us, and I think he had them convinced to give us the benefit of the doubt.'

'Wonders never cease,' I noted. 'Did you see Glen?'

Renatus nodded, stopping at the banister. 'He isn't ready to rejoin the council's circle of minds – he can only take one at a time for now, and he still isn't speaking aloud – but Jadon communicated to him that we needed someone to take a look inside my head.' He leaned his elbows on the handrail. Hiroko and I joined him, looking down over the staircase and the lower two floors. 'He was in there for a while. He sounded well, all things considered.'

Considering his mind was ripped in two. *Two hands...* I rolled my head away from the memory, reminding myself that's all it was now – a memory, which apparently wasn't that fixed a thing, since I'd managed to lose my whole morning.

'And your memory?' He was in my blind spot. I turned my head to look up at him nervously. The rest of the council leadership hadn't arrived with him calling me out for my bizarre dishonesty, so there was that, but Lady Miranda's suggestion that my spell could have hurt him had stung. 'What did Glen say?'

'Apparently you did an excellent job,' Renatus answered without looking at me. I released my held breath heavily, dropping my forehead onto my arms. Below us, voices echoed from the entrance hall as students came inside for lunch. 'Even more shocking, it seems Declan is a good teacher, because you remembered the steps perfectly – ironic, really.'

'I guess Declan has to be good at something, since he totally lacks other redeeming qualities,' I muttered. I half-blamed him for what I couldn't remember, given that he'd derailed our initial plan, hidden a secret about Shanahan in my head that changed my feelings toward that family, and of course because he was the one who'd put the memory spell in my repertoire to begin with and that was *definitely* his bag of tricks I used in the orchard.

'Where did he go?' Renatus asked, and I scratched the back of my neck to buy myself time to think. I hadn't needed to explain his presence or his disappearance to the White Elm because hello, it was Declan and they didn't need to know we were consorting with him, but Renatus was with Declan and Shanahan one second, waking up in the ballroom the next. 'I stopped at his place on the way back here but it's quiet. Is he alright?'

'I'm going to say hi to the twins and Addison,' Hiroko piped up, recognising their voices downstairs and pushing away from the handrail. 'I'll see you before I go home.'

I smiled as she diplomatically took her leave from us, and waited in silence until she was two flights away before turning to Renatus, putting him in the middle of my field of vision and prepared to take whatever he'd saved up for me.

'Aristea.' He finally looked right at me, and I saw he was too hopelessly confused to be mad. 'This is all wrong. Tell me what really happened.' At his edges, despite his careful control, I felt what could only be described as devastation. The consequence I'd brought down on myself in the ballroom with his leaders was a steeper price than he'd been willing to pay, and he couldn't understand what I'd spent it on. 'Did Declan spell me? Did he hurt you, threaten you?'

I pressed my clasped hands to my lips, watching Hiroko get further away. 'He didn't spell you.' I parted my hands, gathering the energy for yet another ward, letting it expand like a bubble just big enough for him and I. Soundproofing us and protecting us from being scried. 'But that's all I can tell you. *Because*,' I emphasised when he muttered a frustrated curse, more natural emotion slipping through his controls, 'I don't know. There were two bowls' worth of all the crap from Declan's spell, and I don't remember a thing after Teagan's teapot room.'

Renatus stared at me, and I could almost hear the conclusions stacking up in his head.

'You spelled *yourself*?!' he demanded in a sudden hiss, leaning close to look into my eyes like he might see a symptom of insanity in them. 'No one spells themselves. You could have removed whole episodes of your life or corrupted your consciousness. What were you *thinking*?'

'Redundant question, don't you think?' I countered dourly. 'How should I know what I was thinking? Best guess, I was thinking our actions this morning were appalling, already hidden behind Shanahan's wards, and better off without anyone able to dig the truth out of us.'

'And what you told Gawain and Miranda?' He never forgot their titles, so I knew he was bewildered. 'More guesses?' I nodded, and he jumped on it. 'Well, that's good, isn't it? We can tell them, we can explain. They'll have to see that this was all a mistake.'

'I didn't make a mistake,' I disagreed. I hesitated, recalling the blood on my hands. 'I mean, *that* wasn't a mistake. I'm not telling them, and neither are you.'

'Why not?' Renatus asked incredulously. 'Whatever we did, it was obviously not *your* idea. You wouldn't hurt anyone.'

I shrugged, uneasy. 'Maybe I would. Maybe I hurt Teagan, used her trust against her. Maybe I'm not who either of us would like me to be.' But he was already shaking his head in complete denial.

'No. Whatever you did, it was either because I okayed it, or you were manipulated by my dirty cad of a friend. I should have left as soon as he arrived.'

'Never thought I'd hear you call Declan your friend.'

'*Why* would you take this fall when it's so obviously mine?' he asked desperately, grasping the front of his shirt.

'Because if I didn't, everything we've already done and given up would have been for nothing.' I twisted my sister's bracelet off my wrist and offered it to him. 'I powered it up for you,' I said, stalling. He looked down at it for a long moment before accepting reluctantly. *I don't need your energy. This is why you look even more tired than when I left?* I nodded. 'I know, you don't like taking from me. And you're going to like this even less, but...' I dug my ruby out of my pocket. 'When you gave me this you said I have to get used to accepting from you. It was yours to give.'

'I already like this less. What are you misinterpreting me as saying this time?'

I turned the stone over in my fingers. 'I didn't have a lot of time to think, alright? But they were about to fire you. Lord Gawain, Lady Miranda.' Renatus frowned at the bracelet, mimicking my fidgeting subconsciously, and I knew he'd detected the same thing. 'I had blood on my hands and that stupid ledger – no offence, Renatus, but if I went that far, what did *you* do? I was scared when I found you like that in the orchard. You were nearly dead.'

'I'm assuming if you took it upon yourself to relieve me of the whole episode, it's not something I want to remember,' he admitted, slipping his four fingers through the bangle and closing his thumb over it. Briefly, the black cracks shone through the very fair skin on the back of his hand. Conflict and worry twisted around him until he turned to me again, frustrated and upset, 'But that's not your problem–'

'Of course it is,' I interrupted. 'Are we partners or not?'

The question blindsided him. 'Of course we are.' He went back to playing with the bangle, deeply disturbed. I could tell he wanted to pull away from this difficult conversation and pace out his frustration, but he stayed there and fidgeted instead. He went through a cycle of different feelings, landing squarely on *sad* when he looked up at me again. 'But your whole future with the council, Aristea. Everything you came here for.'

'If you were taken off the council, I'd be in the same position,' I reasoned. 'And I know you get a power boost from being part of the council, however strong you might be on your own… and that extends to me. Listen,' I insisted when he shook his head in distress and pressed his fingers into his temples. 'It's a simple equation. If you're not on the White Elm, we won't get to finish things with Lisandro. That's it. That's why.'

He lowered his hands slowly from his face. 'Power and revenge. When did you turn into me?'

'What was it you said?'

'Don't you dare quote me again.'

'You said it's not nice looking in the mirror. And no, it's not what I came here for,' I admitted, gesturing at the stairs, the hall we stood in, the house in general, 'but I didn't know back then that my family was murdered, and yours, and I didn't know this work we do would mean so much to me. It does.' I checked the ward protecting our conversation's privacy. Still good. 'I'm not the same. Today I thought you were dead. Now I know how you must have felt when I took that hit in Prague.'

'Not nice, is it?'

'It must have killed you to see me bleeding like that,' I said, knowing this conversation was overdue. He stared hard at the stones in my bangle. 'To have to leave Anouk, and all those people defenceless, and to have to help Lady Miranda heal me. I know there's not much you wouldn't do for me, and not just because you're in charge, or you're older and you're meant to be responsible for me.' I hooked my finger through the bangle, detecting that he hadn't yet accepted the energy stores in it. I channelled some magic down that arm, letting the now-grey cracks flare under my skin. 'I wasn't going to let you die in that street, even if it meant burning all the way through to extend that ward, and I wasn't going to let you lose your position with the White Elm when it's half the reason you're sane.'

There – the closest I was going to get to admitting the most fundamental reason for my fall today. I could never come out and tell him what I knew, and it felt like flirting the line. He didn't fixate on it, luckily.

'When I woke up in the orchard, I had a note in my hand,' I admitted. 'My writing: *Whatever it takes*.'

'That's what you left yourself to explain the memory lapse?'

'I know, right? But maybe I didn't want anything more specific found by anyone else. I want exactly what you want: I want us to show everyone what Lisandro is and what he's done, and we can't do that if you're some criminal deadbeat who was kicked off the council. Whatever you did today, you don't deserve that when we're so close. We're *so close*,' I reiterated.

Renatus dropped his head back to stare at the underside of the stairs coming down above us from the top floor.

'I love that you think there's anything I don't deserve,' he commented finally. 'What are you going to tell your family?'

'The same thing I told them about my tattoo and what happened in Prague.'

'There'll be a trial. I expect it'll be a quiet thing – no one will know but us.' He paused. 'I don't care what you say, I'm going to fight for you.'

'I know,' I said. 'They wouldn't expect anything less.'

'You know I didn't want any of this for you. That I would never ask you to go down for me like this.'

'I know.'

We stood in companionable silence for a long time, turning priceless rubies over and over like the thoughts in our heads.

'Thank you,' he said finally as I dropped the wards around us, 'but don't do it again. *I* look out for *you*, not the other way around. You'll hurt my ego.' He gave me back my bracelet, unused. 'I'm going to get some things and see what I can find out about what happened at Shanahan's.'

'Be careful,' I cautioned, pushing away from the banister and starting down the stairs to find Hiroko and the others. 'I'd come along, obviously…'

'If you weren't grounded,' he agreed. He'd started up toward his office but slowed, distracted. I felt his refreshed mood take on an edge. 'We'll… see what we can do about that… later. Can I have that, actually?' He snapped back to reality, turning on his heel and coming after me. I stopped halfway down the flight, uncertain. He plucked the bangle out of my hand and carried on past me. 'Thanks. Tian and Emmanuelle are checking on one of those lectures Lisandro's followers were holding and I can't reach either of them.' He Displaced midstep and I felt him reappear downstairs. *Everyone else is on damage control with Shanahan and Teagan or still in talks with Valero. I'll be in touch.*

I told him to call on me if he needed me, but I knew it was more than my life was worth to push Lord Gawain and Lady Miranda's patience with me right now by insisting. Even hours after being almost evaporated by magical overdose, Renatus was still incredibly capable, and the energy in the bracelet would give him a small boost, maybe enough to either fake his usual aura with an illusion or to protect himself if it came to that. At a lecture. I rolled my eyes and carried on downstairs. I was being dramatic. Our day had been dramatic enough already without my imagination getting involved.

I had just reached the dining hall and swung through the doors when I started to feel strange. It had nothing to do with the nostalgic warmth of seeing my four friends sitting together again eating like nothing had changed, or the hushed slip of everyone else's gazes gravitating to me, the fact that I was in trouble having already reached every ear.

It was… Well, strange. A funny little flutter of energy was vibrating on my skin, all over. When I tried to tune into it, I had difficulty getting a fix on its source. Strange.

It was lunchtime, and Fionnuala softly excused herself to squeeze past where I'd stopped in the doorway, carrying a heavy-looking tray. Automatically I took it from her, our fingers brushing on the handles. She looked up at me in surprise.

'That's the house, dear,' she told me as I carried the tray over to the lunch table. When it was set down she caught my elbow. Beneath her hand, the flutter seemed to buzz more intensely. 'It's like a silent alarm. Something's not right.'

'Something like what?' I asked, wary. I knew Morrissey House had its own magic, wormholes for Renatus's bloodline and a web of wards and protective spells, but I'd never had much interaction with it except to step out of its vicinity to Displace away, and it had never interacted with *me*.

'I can't find anything wrong,' the housekeeper admitted, eyes cast down as she ran other senses through the different levels of the house. I followed suit, touching on familiar life signs, the normal sites of magic and memory. The gate was shut. 'If it's the gate or the door, it prompts me. This must be something it thinks you're best suited to handle. Tell you what, it's probably a glitch,' she said with a quick smile that didn't hide her discomfort with the situation. 'I'll do a sweep.'

'No, no, I'll help,' I insisted, giving my friends a quick

466

wave to let them know I'd be right back as I accompanied Fionnuala back out into the entrance hall. 'If you start at the bottom of the house, I'll check the top. What am I looking for?'

She shrugged. 'My best guess would be one of the structural spells corrupting or being circumvented.'

I nodded slowly as though this meant anything to me and said, 'Right. So something out of the ordinary.' I imagined a wall bursting with purple-pink sparks, magic going all wrong. 'I'll have a look.'

I jogged back up the stairs, reaching for Renatus. *What would make a magical alarm go off at your place?* By the second floor I dropped back to a walk, and by the time I reached the top I was puffing, wishing I'd been less noble. The energetic flutter was stronger on my skin, more insistent, and I ran my hands along the walls, over the doorknobs, across paintings, opening myself to unusual energies and impressions.

Fionnuala dusting…

A fist through the wall… Anger, no way out… Renatus, younger..

Hand on door handle… Me, yesterday, head full of worries…

I slowed down when I saw what the house must have been trying to tell me, though why it opted for me instead of Renatus or Fionnuala I still didn't get. The door of Renatus's office, the only door in the house with no handle and no way in without Renatus himself, was ajar.

It was never ajar.

'Not a good sign,' I uttered aloud before considering that it wasn't wise to make noise.

Did you leave your office open? I asked, extending my senses to the open door tentatively. The magic there felt… Look, I'm far from the expert, but normally it felt *smooth*, like you wouldn't even know it was there, and right now it felt *exposed*, raw and confused. Not broken, just… confused. A bit like me, when Renatus didn't reply. I hadn't heard back from him before, either. *Renatus? Your office is open. Did you forget to shut it?*

Still nothing. It was the same dead silence as this morning

when I found him in the orchard, his mind switched off, and when I felt for him at the back of my head I found only a closed door.

Quite unlike this one. Really unnerved now, I checked my wards, realising I was still inaudible, unscryable and energetically invisible – nice one, Aristea – and inched forward. If there was someone inside, their energy signature was likewise shielded, but when I changed my focus, I detected feelings of curiosity.

And those feelings were a direct gateway to a familiar aura of incredible, terrifying power.

Renatus, get back here, I pleaded to the void. That much power in one person, with Renatus not here, could only be one culprit, though I couldn't guess how she got onto the property without anyone noticing, or how she'd broken into the vault-like office.

So I was not ready, when I pushed the door open, for what I saw inside.

chapter thirty-two

'Sterling?'

My former roommate was visibly startled, her hands whipping out of the desk drawer like she'd been burned. I'd caught her offguard, my wards better than hers, and she looked up at me with wide sparkling brown eyes that quickly narrowed through overgrown strawberry bangs Xanthe had cut for her when we first moved here.

'Aristea,' she said breathlessly, quickly scanning the desktop for inspiration to explain herself. Her emotions – mostly fear and intense dislike – were unpractised, easy to read, but complicated. 'I was just…'

I came closer, wary but less afraid to find my impressionable classmate instead of Lisandro's psycho wife. The house's alarm on my nerves didn't let me relax completely, and what I saw on the desk only made me more dubious.

'What are you doing in Renatus's office?' I asked. The locked drawers had been emptied and recognisable items of note had been singled out. The dirty paper list of names Peter Chisholm wrapped around the Elm Stone ring when he tried to rectify his defection. The ledger. The pendant Renatus loaned both Sterling and me to counter scrying-related sleep problems, though it was half-covered with a handkerchief. And an open stapled document that looked like something I signed a few weeks ago. Sterling Adams, feelings still see-sawing, slowly placed her hands on the edge of the desk, more fixated on the document in front of her than on the consequences of being caught here.

'He made you his heir?' she said, staring at the photocopied words. Without her moving, the top page flicked over, showing her the next one, and then the next, and the next. I'd never seen Sterling exhibit this kind of flashy Renatus-like magic, and I looked around the office for anything out of place to explain how she got in or how she had powered herself up. With only a flash of violent rage for warning, she suddenly snatched up the contract Renatus's banker had had me sign on my birthday and brandished it at me. 'The house, the accounts, everything. If anything happens to him, you get everything.'

I met her disbelieving gaze with my own. I hadn't known that was what I was signing, but wasn't that surprised. Renatus knew I would refuse if he told me, and given that his own uncle had made attempts on his fortune before, he must have decided to secure it from squabbling extended family through me as soon as I hit eighteen.

'Not sure how it's your business,' I admitted, still coming closer, still trying to work her out. I nodded at the desk. 'Not sure how *anything* in this room is your business. How did you get in?'

'You don't know the first thing about this house,' she hissed with absolute contempt, tossing the contract at me. I caught it with my free hand and tucked it under my arm to keep the hand available. 'It shouldn't go to you.'

'Well, it won't,' I said, watching her cautiously as she cast a dark look at the desk, the cabinets, the arched window. 'It's only if he dies, and I'd rather that didn't happen.' Sterling folded her arms tightly, childishly, resentment circling her like snakes. *All the other girls will be so jealous*, I heard Teagan's voice bubbling in my recent memory, and I recognised this bizarre behaviour. Regardless, I didn't have time for it. 'Look, this crush of yours stopped being cute *so* long ago. Get out. You're not supposed to be here.'

She looked back at me with venom in her eyes, a half-imagined shine of bright green that would have been easier to pass off as a trick of the light if I hadn't seen it before.

'You can't tell me what to do, little girl,' she sneered, and I raised my eyebrow. This was not Sterling – who knew my birthday was before hers – but the face was hers, the freckled ski-jump nose... I glanced once more around the room for clues to what should already have been obvious as she continued speaking. 'I tried to get to know you; I thought I wanted to be your friend. But you're not what I thought.'

'Aye, sorry about that,' I said vaguely, my gaze catching on the forgotten box of Archive files beside Renatus's desk. Our research. Scriers. 'You're not the first person I've disappointed today, Nastassja.'

The green eyes of Lisandro's wife glittered behind my former friend's fringe and I felt her dual reaction of bitter amusement and helpless relief. Sterling was *awake* inside her body as it was puppeteered by an advanced scrier and used to break into Renatus's office, and when I focused I could see the shimmer of a second aura behind hers. Bigger, bolder, fuller, and totally in control. Nastassja was *here*. In her own body she'd chased me down and tried to kill me before confronting me at Teagan's party and trying to chat. In Sterling's, what was she capable of, and maybe more importantly, what was she inclined to try? Her erraticism made my recent behaviour look comparatively stable. I didn't know her tells, her motives or her limits.

Renatus? Now would be good, I tried, but I knew he wasn't hearing me. Wherever he went, wherever his colleagues were checking out this lecture, it was bad, just a typical Lisandro move of making noise over here while making a quiet move over there. Except that for once I was present at the *there* option, and I was alone. I needed an escape plan.

'Not too quick, are we?' Nastassja goaded in Sterling's voice. I was increasingly aware of the division between the two personalities in front of me and could hardly believe I hadn't noticed this about the attackers in Prague, their feelings mismatched from their actions. Sterling was afraid and desperate to be recognised; Nastassja was a welling of unstable power tied tightly to even less stable emotions. How many times had she possessed the American Seer? I thought of the times either Hiroko or I witnessed her sleepwalking, and of the loosened protective spells over the house. The timing lined up exactly.

'I learn,' I argued, taking in my situation once more. I'd come too far into the office to make a clean break for the door, and now that I knew my roommate was a literal hostage right in front of me, I couldn't just bail. The abandonment of the White Elm fan coven to the fear bomb's devastation made me reasonably sure that Haunting scriers could survive a host's death. Sterling was a pain but I wasn't adding her name to my list of failures, not after the day I'd already had.

'Oh, I see that,' Nastassja mocked, placing a hand on Sterling's round hip and gesturing elegantly at me with the other. I couldn't let those hands touch me. She'd gotten hold of Sterling from a distance but now her real soul was inside my old friend, and physical contact was all she'd need to body swap. 'Coming to face me at half power. An educated move.'

'To be fair, I wasn't coming here to face you,' I said, deciding to work with what I had to my advantage, which was little more than nothing. She was emotional, I knew, and I could read that. 'I wanted to see why the house was sending me weird chills. Renatus must have lined me up as his heir in more ways than just writing.'

It was fortunate my wards were always up. She snatched a handful of Renatus's neatly arranged pens from the desktop and hurled them at me, her anger snapping long before I would have estimated. They bounced off harmlessly but her mood pushed straight through.

'You're nobody,' she snarled. 'It doesn't matter who your grandfather was, you're *nobody*.'

'Maybe,' I offered evasively, edging closer, a reckless idea forming, 'but maybe so was Keely Shanahan.'

My words had the opposite effect from what I expected. She shut right down, anger simmering to almost nothing, a whiplash effect as bewildering as Teagan's mood shifts at the opposite end of the angst spectrum. She stared at me with what I thought to be honest surprise and a complicated mess of emotions. Contrition. Shame.

'Don't say that name,' she said resentfully. 'You don't know anything.'

'I know she was supposed to get married and didn't want to play her father's stupid political game. And I empathise, believe me,' I insisted, taking the contract from under my arm and rolling it with my fingers into a tight tube that might make a mini kali stick. My ruby was still enclosed in my palm. Could I utilise that? What had she come here for? 'I'd probably run away, too, but what did she really gain when she ran from one villain straight to another? I mean,' reckless, arrogant, wild assumptions, don't know when to quit, yes, I hear you, Qasim, '*Lisandro?*'

I instinctively ducked when her fury struck me only just ahead of a blast of flame from each of her hands. The wards took the brunt but I still felt the heat. Apparently she could use her own power through Sterling.

'Keely meant *nothing* to him,' Nastassja screamed, clenching her fists and cutting off the stream of fire. I stuffed the contract in my jeans pocket, seeing the error of that poorly considered idea. Dumb, anyway, considering I had real sai just a few rooms away. I went to tuck the ruby into the pocket with the paper roll to free up my palms, but Nastassja's brown-emerald eyes caught upon the motion and her rage froze again. 'Where did you get that?'

'Where do you think?' I sured up my wards before sinking my teeth in, patting the will in my pocket. 'Everything in this house is mine if I want it. Ana's stuff's no exception.'

I predicted her correctly this time; she launched at me with a noise like a snarl. I threw up a new ward between us as I leapt out of the way, deflecting her off to my left while I scampered around the desk, putting it between us. My heart thudded to feel the room literally quiver with her anger as she turned to track me, vague flashbacks of the vision in the bathroom peppering my already wild thoughts. She was so powerful; I was well out of my depth. I would never have picked her for an opponent, but I had her, regardless.

'I can see why you were drawn to Sterling as a host,' I taunted, mentally apologising to the prisoner in front of me, edging back and forth as Nastassja tried to decide which side of the desk to come at me from. 'Between you both, you're obsessed with the whole family. It must kill you that I'm here when you've worked so hard to become her. Taking her name; taking her boyfriend.'

Her rage and her spell came simultaneously this time, a crackly black ball of certain death accompanied by a wordless scream. I threw my hands up automatically and it ricocheted from too close to my face, blasting into the ceiling behind me. The collision was deafening, and I ducked in terror – *tree branches crash through, pieces of ceiling and upstairs collapse inward, two girls scream* – as burning shards of plaster rained down on my shields.

'He didn't love her!' Nastassja shouted, a deep, old hurt ripped freshly open by my words, anger a thin disguise. I flexed my sweating hands, gathering my courage. I let my eyes drop briefly to the disorganised desktop. 'He loved me. He proved it. No!' I had feinted left, getting her moving, then bolted right, sticking tight to the outside of Renatus's chair to prevent myself going too wide and losing even a split second of time. Right in the middle of the mess she'd made was what I had to assume she'd come for, her timing too precise to be connected to anything else. She'd already switched directions and was coming around the desk to meet me, her attention where I'd steered it. I extended my left hand for the ledger, knowing innately she'd do the same. Knowing she was closer, knowing she wanted it more, knowing she would blast me back into the wall the instant she had it, knowing I couldn't win.

But why play by her rules?

One – her hand landed first on Shanahan's book and mine diverted out of the way – two – my right hand followed, one of my sai Displacing perfectly into my open palm, blade down, and I slammed it down on her wrist. She yelled in startled shock as the guard dug into the timber, pinning her

474

hand to the edge of the desktop, and with her own metaphorical guard down, she reacted without thought when I snatched up the real prize and tossed it at her chest.

She caught the black pendant on the full.

She gasped like she'd just surfaced from the ocean, and the terrible quiver in the room ceased. The alarm in my nerves let up. The second aura disappeared and the turbulent rage evaporated, leaving only Sterling Adams' distress as the girl in front of me visibly came back to herself, overconfident posture dropping, brown-again eyes filling with tears.

'A-Aristea?' she said, lip trembling, yanking on her trapped hand as I backed up just in case, my second sai coming to my other hand at my urging. She waved the pendant at me, terrified, looking from me to the burning ceiling. 'Please don't, don't hurt me, i-it's me! It's me, it's Sterling!'

'I know.' I nodded at the pendant. 'Put that on. I don't know her capabilities and we don't want her coming back.'

Sterling shook her head in relieved agreement, the tears starting to fall, her shoulders quaking with the shock of the experience. Awkwardly with only one hand, she looped the long chain over her head and when the pendant fell against her chest, I came back to her. The sai was embedded in the timber and needed a good wrench to come free. Sorry, Renatus. Sterling rubbed her wrist, clutching it against herself.

'Th-thank you,' she whispered, almost lost under the loud cracking sound of part of the still-burning ceiling coming away. We both shrieked in fright as the ashy plaster fell; I grabbed her and pulled her close. The chunk of plaster shattered into bright embers on the invisible umbrella of my wards, raining black and white and orange around us. Sterling cowered against me and hurriedly I shoved the sai at her to hold while I brushed the little bright potential fires off Renatus's desk. There were important things here, things Nastassja couldn't get hold of if she took another host and came back.

Strewn on Renatus's chair, perhaps discarded there by Nastassja in her search, were the artefacts collected from the orchard. The bowl, the knife, the puzzle box. Declan's satchel.

Inspired, I grabbed it and threw the bowl and knife back in, then dumped the ledger and Peter's list and anything else that looked important in with them. I slung the bag over my shoulder and pushed Sterling to get moving, but then froze, spotting something I didn't expect in the still-open drawer. *No…* I shoved it into the bag too and got out from under the smouldering ceiling.

'Is the house going to burn down?' Sterling asked in a shuddery voice when I got us to the middle of the office to get a safer look. A good square metre of ceiling was gone and more was damaged, sprinkling sparks down on the delicious kindling that was a timber desk covered in paperwork. I cupped my hands like Renatus had taught me for fun when I was first initiated, trying to recall the chain of synapses and brain pathways it took to make my hands fill with water.

An upward rush of steam that had nothing to do with me swiftly dampened the worst of the blackened and exposed rafters, reducing the danger to glowing plaster, and I turned toward the newcomer in relief.

'Are you alright, Miss Aristea? Miss Sterling?' Fionnuala asked worriedly, gentle hands on our shoulders, checking us over. I started to nod, then shook my head. Nastassja was gone from *here*, which meant she and the focus of strife was now *there*. I took my swords back from Sterling.

'Renatus is in trouble,' I said with certainty. I rushed from the office, colliding with my friends at the door. Hiroko caught my wrist and I shifted the sai into the one hand.

'Are you alright?' she asked, looking past me with wide eyes at the small-scale destruction of my confrontation with Nastassja. 'We heard screaming.'

'And crashing,' Sophia added. Her aura and those of the others were as always, if a little frayed from concern. Not possessed. I gestured back at the office.

'One of Lisandro's big-name followers possessed Sterling to get in here,' I explained quickly. 'I have to go, but she might come back. She could come back as anyone.' I turned desperately to Hiroko. 'Can you get me to Renatus?'

She was Elijah's best student, a Displacer of immense talent, and we both knew she could, but she eyed my depleted aura with reluctance, seeing that I didn't have the power to do it myself safely and that I probably couldn't do much for him once I got there.

'If you think it is wise,' she said doubtfully with a glance at Addison. He looked again into the office, where Fionnuala was getting the story from a sobbing Sterling.

'We can guard this place but how do we tell if she's possessing someone?'

'She'll be real angry, and she'll be even stronger than Renatus. Don't get in her way,' I warned. Hurriedly they built and checked their wards. Hiroko smiled at me wryly.

'You've armed us well.'

'Aye. All we need are some pillows to throw.'

'Go,' Kendra urged, blinking rapidly. I didn't often see her getting information from Fate but I wasn't going to wait around staring. I twisted my hand to take Hiroko's and ran at the wall opposite the office door. I felt her strain against my pull, but I had faith.

'Wait! Aristea, that's–' We should have struck the wall but we slid straight through, the wormhole transporting us to the bottom of the house, skipping the stairs and arriving in the dim kitchens. 'A wall.' Hiroko only had a moment to orient herself before I tugged her up the steps and out into the brighter entrance hall. 'We went through a wall!'

'It's never worked for me before!' I called back to her as we ran for the front door. More accurately, I'd never tried it on my own. Maybe the house had adopted me when Renatus signed it over to me in his will, or maybe I'd become part of its bloodline at my initiation when our blood was mixed in a very icky ritualistic pact.

'Permanent wormholes,' she said in wonder. 'I felt them here before but I did not know…' We shoved through the doors and into the afternoon sun and she seemed to realise how much time we were wasting. Her hand tightened on mine and the Fabric moved over me and on my next step we were at the gate. She pulled up and I crashed into it, breathing hard. Declan's satchel of oddities clattered against the wrought iron posts.

'Do you know where he is?' she asked, fumbling for her key in her pocket. I shook my head and pressed my palm against the lock. Magically, literally, the mechanism responded and it swung open. We both slipped out and slammed it shut behind us.

'I can't hear him, and I don't think he can hear me,' I explained restlessly. 'He went to check on some other councillors when they stopped answering, too. They were at a lecture run by Lisandro, or his followers, or something. He's just gone from my head. And he doesn't know anything that's just happened here. It's like he's dead.'

'But he is not,' Hiroko said firmly, her certainty calming my spiralling fears. 'He is cut off from your thoughts. This has happened to you before. Do you have another way of contacting him, of sensing him?'

I nodded and closed my eyes, concentrating on slowing my breathing, finding my centre, and finding Renatus. She was right – she remembered my adventures better than I did. I returned to that closed door at the back of my head. No words or thoughts came through. It was locked tight. But, faintly, through the unsealed cracks around its hinges and bolts, sensations sneaked through. *Foreboding... unease...* I opened my eyes.

'I found him,' I breathed, relieved to find proof of his aliveness for the second time today, 'but I don't know *where–*'

'I can handle where,' Hiroko interrupted briskly, turning my hand over to show my tattoo. She covered it with her hand and glanced up at me apprehensively. 'Are you ready?'

I had time to fortify my wards as space pressed in on me, then we were standing together somewhere else.

My initial sense was of being dunked underwater, or perhaps yanked out of it without warning. The pressure in my ears seemed to change, the sounds dulling or thinning or something, the world taking on a surreal quality I couldn't better describe. The lights were low but I could see that we were in a dingy theatre, at least half of its seating full. We'd landed in the front row of the balcony level to the muted gasps of the strangers whose view we blocked, and Hiroko wasted no time leaning over the handrail to get a look. I too grabbed the rail, feeling oddly weightless, floaty, breaking my own rule about unacquainted handrails while distracted.

No impressions came to me.

A man's voice was filling the old theatre, its fabulous acoustics ensuring it surrounded me like water, but I only tuned into it when I heard my name echoing off the ripped velvet seats and cracked domed ceiling. Hiroko hastily shoved me toward the aisle, fear flashing through her, and I chanced a look over the handrail.

'It's a treat to have you join us,' Lisandro said from the centre of the stage below us. Equal parts terror and shock made me freeze at the aisle, my attention fixed on the bronze-brown gaze of the man who'd killed my parents and brother. How hadn't I recognised his energy the instant I arrived? He was smiling calmly up at me, his incredibly long black hair loose over the tailored shoulders of his grey blazer, his hands casual in the pockets of slim dark jeans, a long silhouette cast back behind him by a warm spotlight. Everything about him was lengthened, and he looked tall and imposing but also youthful and ultra-normal.

I shifted my sai into separate hands, cold hatred flooding me. I was still going to kill him, provided Renatus didn't get there first.

'Looking for someone?' Lisandro asked, and four more spotlights suddenly illuminated patches of crowd. My eyes flitted from one to the next, taking in the intended focus of each bright circle. Tian. Emmanuelle. Qasim. Renatus, closest to the stage. I hadn't sensed any of them. They all froze when they were lit up, shading their eyes. Renatus looked up in my direction, searching for me. *Top balcony*, I said urgently, reaching for him, but I still couldn't find our connection, and when I tried to tune into my extended senses, I felt nothing.

No energies. No auras. No magic. No life forces. I looked around warily. Surrounded by people and I couldn't feel a single one?

'Ladies and gentlemen, the White Elm *are* among us, as we predicted; but we'll get to them in a minute,' Lisandro dismissed, taking a hand out of his pocket to gesture up at me. Hiroko pressed closer, protective and afraid. 'Many of you know Aristea Byrne as the hero of Prague, saving several dozen lives in that tragic attack last month. I know her as my godson's apprentice.' An extra spotlight landed on Renatus, as bright as shame. I bit my lip, waiting for him to Displace out of the limelight or launch an attack on Lisandro. But nothing. His secret out on display, and nothing. Murmurs of interest erupted all around. 'There's a misconception that I hate the White Elm, and I know I've spoken strongly in the past, but I want to make it clear to you all now, that's not true. My family are on that council, people I love. *I* started my career with the White Elm. I know the people on it genuinely want to action good deeds.'

A rebranding, then. Lisandro had initially tried to distance himself from association with his White Elm past, but my popularity thanks to Marcy and Jaroslav's blogs must have been enough to change his tune. Around me, I felt a soft sea of casual interest and mellow agreement. Looking at the faces closest to me, I saw no one I recognised, but saw a too-willing audience. No scepticism. No uncertainty.

'This is creepy,' Hiroko whispered in my ear. She paused. 'Something is wrong with your magic.'

'Aristea is a stellar example of what the White Elm tries to stand for,' Lisandro went on, beginning to pace the width of the dusty stage. 'She put her life on the line to save those people, mortals and sorcerers alike, including her master, my godson Renatus. She used her gifts, her *magic*, to do what needed to be done. I'm so grateful to you,' he added with a heartfelt clap of his hand to his breast, eliciting an equally heartfelt applause that began as a scattershot and warmed to something bigger. I slunk back from the handrail, deeply uncomfortable. This was not what I expected when I came here. I looked down at Renatus. I needed to get to him. 'Yes, we're all immensely proud of her. Just a girl, but such courage. Her actions reminded me that the problem with the White Elm isn't the virtue of its members. It's their policy, their control, their authoritarianism. Their *monopoly* on magic.'

The crowd's idle levels of agreement swelled to more enthusiastic heights, his words striking something more fundamental to them, and calls of concurrence came from all around the theatre. I heard Magnus Moira's catchphrase 'Free magic for all!' more than once.

'Come on,' I whispered to Hiroko, avoiding the avid gazes of the people we passed on our way to the stairs. Lisandro's voice still carried.

'See, Aristea's actions in Prague might have broken White Elm law about exposing mortals to magic, but no one can deny it was the right thing to do. And besides, she used *their* magic. She applied her good judgement, her goodness of character, to weigh up the best use of her talents. So I expect that many of you here would be as disappointed as I was to learn that the White Elm has charged Aristea Byrne with illegal magic use and removed her from their admissions waiting list.'

I tripped on the last step of the stairwell and Hiroko caught my arm so I didn't impale myself on a sai. We stood in the corridor with wide eyes. *How* did he know that? The crowd's enthusiasm turned to stark disapproval and a few people booed.

'I know, I know. And it's not regarding the same event, I should point out. Aristea, an *apprentice* in magic, experimented for the first time with blood magic, writing a memory spell to protect someone she loves from further trauma. Maybe there are other factors that led to their decision, I don't know, but why isn't her good judgement enough this time if her intention was still the same? She's broken laws before. She's Haunted. Overstepped with some telepathy. But without malice, just learning. This is the problem with the White Elm. They're not about law; they're about controlling our magic. So I'm running a little experiment. Come up and join me, White Elm friends. Come on, Renatus.'

Filled with dread, I raced through a door to the first-floor balcony and skidded to a stop at the handrail, ignoring whispers of 'That's her!' The four spot-lit councillors glanced around as people approached, encircling, gently reaching for them. Two heavyset men closed in on Renatus, who should have taken care of them by now. One opened his hand to clasp his shoulder, which my master twisted to evade. My stomach twisted in response to seeing him not – not able to? – defend himself. He had my bracelet, and he wasn't totally flat when he left the house. Something was so very wrong. I pointed the pommel of my sai at them.

'Don't you touch him!' I shouted, my voice echoing with the same quality as Lisandro's around the decrepit theatre. Everything else fell silent, and the men intent on capturing my master stilled. Renatus looked up, finally catching sight of me. I waited to hear him in my head giving me instructions or reassurance, but I got neither. Was it just the overbright light on his face, a distortion of the distance, or did he look genuinely afraid?

'No one's hurting him, I promise,' Lisandro said silkily. 'Just a little demonstration, and I'm afraid you're a part of it, too, for illustrative purposes.'

'Your magic is blocked,' Hiroko murmured. 'All of you. It is the place; a spell.'

'My magic,' I repeated at the same volume, realisation setting in. No energies. No power. No Displacement or fighting back. 'But not yours?'

'No one else but White Elm.' She looked around uneasily. 'They are all witches.'

'And they're all lapping this up.' I raised my voice again. 'Step away from him.'

The men, both of them bearded and even dressed similarly in perfect henchmen attire, looked from me to their boss.

'You heard the lady,' he said smoothly, and they

immediately gave Renatus back his personal space. Lisandro smiled up at me. 'You inspired me today, Aristea, putting my boy ahead of your duty to uphold the council's laws,' and even from that distance, he must have seen my eyes narrow at his facetious claim of ownership of my master, 'but I wanted to give the rest of the White Elm this chance to show how equally pure and *righteous* they are. They restrict and monitor magic for pure and righteous reasons. They fired you today, presumably for pure and righteous reasons. But after all this restricting and monitoring and prohibiting, the only ones left in the world with any degree of real power... is them. Relieved of their magic, of their stranglehold on power, how does their integrity hold up? Who are you without your magic,' he asked, deliberately, roving his gaze from one illuminated councillor to the next, ending on Renatus, his expression glittering with cunning but an undercurrent of malice reaching only me, 'and how does it feel to be mortal in a world full of gods?'

An approving mumble vibrated out of the crowd, growing to a loud cheer. This was not a mixed crowd. This was a theatre full of Magnus Moira supporters and anti-council citizens, maybe some fence-sitters who'd just been tipped by the realisation that this was a lesson wrapped up inside a practical joke, and the joke was on the White Elm. Down on the lower floor, someone shoved Emmanuelle. Her usual wards not functioning, she fell into the crowd, only to be righted by a familiar bouncer, who kept other people back lazily. Forever fierce, Emmanuelle went for the woman who'd knocked her, again blocked by her half-hearted protector. She only now looked at him, unable to sense his energy, and backed up in disgust, recognising Jackson. But excitement spread around her, and to anyone who saw that, the message was clear – the normally untouchable White Elm were fair game.

All of them.

'Renatus,' I whispered, turning to run back for the stairs. He'd never known anything but a life fuelled on unbelievable magic. This block on his powers was worse for him than for anyone else. If I could just get to him, I could at least give him one of my sai. He knew what to do with them. I'd taken three steps before I was stopped by the arrival of Elijah right in front of me. He swore immediately.

'He warped the Fabric,' he complained, seeing where he'd landed. Lisandro was talking, encouraging a show of magic. 'I tried for outside but it funnelled me in. There's…' He trailed off, eyes widening when he couldn't Displace back out.

'No magic, yes,' I confirmed impatiently as Hiroko squeezed past me. Behind me, contradicting me, a firework exploded over the audience, a flashy spell that made everyone clap or duck or both. 'Lisandro's teaching us what it feels like to have our magic taken away, and he's got this crowd eating out of his hand.' I looked around uneasily at the people seated nearest to us. Spells of every kind were being cast – little lights captured inside hands, flyers levitating, illusions of bats, plus probably plenty we couldn't sense – and their casters were enraptured by their own freedom to play in full view of their world's police. 'I think soon they'll be eating us. We have to get out.'

'The exits are locked,' Hiroko reported, coming back from the corridor. An overeager teenager's attempt at casting fire resulted in a brief flare that made her lean well away. 'I think he intends to trap you inside. But I can take you out.'

Her magic was still operational – Lisandro and Jackson didn't know her, didn't know to craft their spell to account for her. She was our ace. Elijah shook his head.

'You go,' he urged his favourite student. 'The others, they're going to keep turning up.' With all their scriers here, the only way to investigate what was happening inside this black hole of telepathic silence was to get close, and any White Elm teleporting anywhere nearby would be sucked inside this theatre for what could very quickly become a slaughter. 'Teresa and Oneida are on the second floor of that big hospital in Belfast. Can you get there?'

'I can, but I will take you both with me,' Hiroko tried to insist, but just then a new spotlight beam fell on Elijah. She and I quickly backed out of its glare. Our always-cheerful teacher gave us a wry look of apology.

484

'He knows I'm here so he'll notice if I leave,' he said. 'Aristea too. Just go.'

Hiroko looked between us doubtfully, worry tight around her. 'Be careful.'

She Displaced and I drew a deep, guilty breath. She'd crossed the world to comfort a friend in need and ended up in the middle of *this*. At least she could get out.

I hoped she had the sense to stay away.

'Can you get down there?' Elijah asked me, stress tightening his voice as he nodded to the increasing jostling around his colleagues, especially Emmanuelle, as the crowd jeered and made plays at throwing magic at the councillors. One or two Magnus Moira sorcerers guarded each one but I could see even from up here the burns on Qasim's arm. 'Even with no magic, those might scare some of them off.'

He looked meaningfully at my sai and I nodded, racing back to the outer corridor in search of the stairs down to the ground floor.

'You know what I see?' Lisandro was saying, his voice rising even above the crackle of magic and the crowd's gasps and yells. I swung into the stairway and flew down. 'I see a room full of magic out of control, but no one getting hurt. I see magic the way it's supposed to be – wild, with the White Elm doing nothing to prevent it, and I see it equalising. Fate gave us these gifts. Everyone knows their own limits, or they'll learn them. By being *trusted* to experiment.' I burst through the doors into the more packed rows of the ground floor. 'The White Elm hasn't trusted its people. They've controlled you with policy, but you're proving right now you don't need policy, you don't need rules to manage yourselves.'

'Excuse me,' I muttered, trying to shoulder politely through the tightly grouped people standing in the aisle to get a better view of Lisandro and the pockets of violence surrounding the councillors. A few people budged but some just turned to stare at me with brainwashed interest. 'Excuse me.' I pushed between two older women. They weren't even appropriately annoyed, too taken in with Lisandro's control of the room's atmosphere. What was it Renatus said about Crafters? More trouble than they were worth. 'Please let me through.' I had my swords tucked close to my sides where they couldn't hurt anyone, but small-scale magic was still happening around me, uncontrolled and poorly considered, and I had no wards. I nudged the man in front of me. 'Excuse me.' He glanced at me and did not move. His apathy made me furious. 'What do I have to say to make you get the hell out of my way?'

I jabbed the pommel of my sai into his fleshy side and he cried out, stepping automatically away. A few others did the same, unnerved, and in the space they created I swung one of the swords in my hand to point blade-first. That made others move back, too, and I was able to push forward, peering over shoulders to check how far I was from Renatus or other councillors.

'When your magic was taken from you by *their* rules, how did you react? Were you even alive to protest, or were you born into this prison?'

I reached Qasim first. He was locked in a scuffle with a man of the same size trying to pull him to the ground. Luckily most of the crowd wasn't of a level of awareness of their magic to know how to use skin contact to hurt someone. I stepped up close and drove the hilt of a sai into the other man's ribs, winding him and giving Qasim the chance to bring his head down to meet his upcoming knee. Anyone else getting ideas about having a go at him backed off at the crack of the nose and the man's graceless crumple to his filthy seat.

'Now, when we take *their* magic from them, what do we see?'

'Thought you were grounded,' the Scrier said gruffly, shifting to guard my back. I pointed my weapons threateningly at the people in my way and they slunk away. We pushed forward, though the emotions in the room buffeted me as they began to rise, became more volatile. Lisandro was releasing control, or some other influence had entered the

486

space. Either way, mob mentality was gaining quick traction.

'Thought that was our little secret,' I called back to Qasim, 'but Lisandro knows what I did, and he knows about the ledger. Nastassja just broke into Renatus's office. As Sterling. Move it,' I firmly instructed a pair of sorcerers who stood between me and Renatus. I swiped at them when they delayed, and they moved quickly, spooked by the sharpened points of my weapons.

'Not sure why she'd want it,' Qasim said. 'It was empty, a decoy, maybe.'

'I'll tell you what we see,' Lisandro went on, voice climbing in conjunction with the emotions in the room. 'We see good people who don't know how to lead without magic, who can't conduct themselves non-violently when they're not the most powerful beings in the room. When they're not in *control*.'

'Hardly a fair experiment,' Qasim muttered, thudding someone on the back of the head to clear the way to Renatus, who was shoving against his pair of captors trying to drag him to the stage. My sai were as good a deterrent as Elijah had predicted, the crowd seeming reluctant to try me after Lisandro's apparent endorsement, but I ended up alone when Qasim stepped over the two rows separating us from my master. I climbed onto the grubby seat beside me and called out to Renatus. Qasim disentangled him from his Magnus Moira guards and they both looked over to me as I tossed one of the blades.

Renatus always had good reflexes and caught it with ease. I didn't watch to see what kind of damage he did, instead shouting for Lisandro's attention. I don't know how he heard me over the increasing noise but he did, raising a hand to quieten whoever was still watching him. I dug in Declan's satchel.

'Speaking of control,' I shouted, feeling the attention of more and more people as I withdrew the strapped-shut ledger and held it up high, 'did you think you had this?'

Lisandro had control of his face but my interpretation of even guarded emotion felt heightened by the blinding of my

487

other senses. My Empathy was not tied to my magic, it turned out. He was unhappy to see me with the book, though he made a show of pushing his long hair behind his shoulder carelessly.

'You might have control of this crowd – and he does,' I added, looking around at the balconies quickly quietening to listen to me, 'he's controlling everything you think and feel – you might have control of them, for now, but I have control of *this*.' Time to bluff. Lisandro didn't know it was empty. 'Proof that I shouldn't have needed my hero moment because *you* were behind the attack in Prague.'

'Get *down*,' Renatus hissed, shoving his way back toward me using the length of the sai as a battering ram. I tried not to notice the blood on its tip. 'What are you doing?'

I ignored him, though his words brought back memories of climbing onto a car at a rally much less ominous than this one. I'd come out of that with bloody hands, too. I stayed where I was, book in full view.

'Aristea, your tenacity continues to impress me,' Lisandro said fondly, choosing his best course of action. 'As of today, I'm making you an honourary member of Magnus Moira. I think there's a lot we can learn from you.'

The crowd cheered, my power over the situation slipping. I looked around urgently. Not far away from me, sitting in a row together, were four familiar faces looking over the back of their seats. My heart leapt with unexpected hope to see them alive – the four boys Aubrey had tricked into leaving the Academy, months and months ago, my friends Joshua and Garrett among them. I tried once more for the crowd's attention.

'This is Thomas Shanahan's ledger, of all his dealings, and it proves that Lisandro is working with misusers of magic, people who push their limits past not only policy but also morality–'

I'd said the magic word, and it wasn't *prove*. Hungry attention was totally on me. Most people in the room weren't from the elite world that Shanahan occupied but those who did knew what I was holding.

Lisandro smiled. 'I think it's best if you give that to me.'

A few things happened at once. The crowd came at me, and I had to slash at the people closest to keep them at bay. Renatus jumped onto the seat in front of him and reached out, grabbing my wrist and giving me enough of a pull that I could step onto the seat backs and come across. And Hiroko returned, appearing centre stage, right behind Lisandro. She had a small glass ball in her hand, but by the time I processed that she'd already thrown it at his feet and Displaced away.

An enormous ghostly bird erupted from the shattered ball with an eerie song, shooting for the ceiling, unfurling dead and sparse wings to fill the theatre, and even those whose magic was still with them, who could have sensed it was an illusion, screamed and scattered. Renatus and I stood still on our creaky seat, stunned, as the audience flashed to their feet and ran for their lives. The bird, some combination of Oneida's and Teresa's traditional magics, grew and grew, its song deepening thanks to the theatre's awesome acoustics. The terror it inspired broke Lisandro's spell on his audience's mood.

'We need to leave,' Hiroko said, appearing on the seat beside mine. She grabbed my hand for balance when it groaned under her sudden weight. 'Come, you both.'

'Not without Emmanuelle,' Renatus argued, letting me go and stepping down into the crush of people. 'But you go; he's going to be coming for that book.'

'No.' I looked up at the stage and saw Lisandro conferring with a new arrival with coiled dark hair and a really foul mood. My stomach turned over when bright green eyes met mine. I tugged my hand free of Hiroko's and told her, 'Go help Elijah and come back for me. Renatus, wait.' I shoved the book back in the satchel and ran along the unstable row of seats to keep pace with him as he fought the push of people running for the exits. Above us, the giant bird was thinning to smoke, its song softening. 'Nastassja's here. And there's something you need to know.'

'She's coming towards you!' Qasim shouted across to Renatus from further along the row. From my higher vantage point I could see that Emmanuelle was sidling through the tide of panicked people in our direction. And behind her I saw another figure following.

'So's Jackson!' I yelled back. I glanced again at the stage. Lisandro was stepping down the steps on the far side, and Nastassja was gone. I focused on her immense volatility; she was striding straight for us. Renatus was getting away from me, shoving people out of his way without hesitation. 'Wait, look! I think I was wrong. She got into your office. This whole time, I was wrong.'

'As soon as we have Emmanuelle, the four of us make straight for the door,' Renatus ordered over his shoulder. 'Can Hiroko take four at once?'

'I don't know.' I tripped on the armrest of a seat and dropped my sai. I had to jump down and wait for a gap in the now-thin crowd to duck and snatch it up. When I righted myself I felt once more inside the satchel for the last item I'd thrown in, hurrying to catch up with my master. He was running entirely on determination, determination I understood. His best friend was hurt and he wasn't leaving her behind any sooner than I'd leave Hiroko. But there was something else. I looked back. Nastassja was in view, her path easier than ours, and my heart leapt to see her face properly for the first time. I put on a burst of speed to reach Renatus just as he got to the aisle. 'Listen to me.' I grabbed his hand, the ribbon pressing between our palms, and I pulled him to a stop. 'I don't think she's Keely.'

Renatus took his hand from mine, staring at the red satin ribbon I'd found in his desk. Emmanuelle stumbled out of her row and into our aisle, with Jackson following at a distance. Too calm, too satisfied.

'Where are *your* wards now?' he called, a taunt. My wards teacher didn't glance back, just ran for Renatus and Qasim, desperate, bleeding, hopeful. Renatus forgot about the ribbon. Stepped toward her.

Jackson grinned and clicked his fingers. Like a mistreated doll, her head twisted to the side with unnatural speed and force. At once her desperation went silent, and her feet tangled in her dress as she went down hard.

Two hands… No, no…

Beside me, Renatus blanched at the sight of her falling, and Qasim dropped down to crawl to her, calling her name. My ears weren't processing sounds properly and my eyes felt delayed, too. Emmanuelle didn't respond to any of Qasim's attempts to rouse her, eyes shut, and Jackson looked too pleased with himself as he caught up to them.

'Heal that, bitch.' He turned his smile on the rest of us, high on power. 'Who's next?'

Emmanuelle wouldn't wake. We had no wards. We had no powers. This was it. Surging with blind fury, Renatus spun the blade.

'Renatus?'

My master and I both turned our blades to the new voice. In our efforts to reach the centre of the theatre floor we'd not noticed the few people not trying to escape with the masses, and now they encircled us, scattered through each row, staying at a distance. Magnus Moira. And closest to us, stepping tentatively closer, tense with uncharacteristic uncertainty, was Nastassja.

There was a loaded and heavy second of silence.

Renatus lowered his sai and took a step back into line with me. His breath out was shaky.

'That's not Keely.'

Her wide-eyed nervousness was briefly broken by an irked twitch of her shoulder, and she paused in her approach.

'No, I'm not.' Her accent was as I recalled when I'd met her at Teagan's party, an exotic mix of north American and eastern European over the rhythmic base of hard-to-shake Irish, but this time her face wasn't covered with a butterfly mask. I'd seen her face in a dozen visions, any time I touched anything in her old room. 'Renatus…'

She came another step closer, equal parts unsure and fascinated, and he backed up again, his emotions too complex to make sense.

'How?' was all he could ask. She shook her head helplessly, reminding me of myself just a few hours ago. *I can't tell you*. She advanced a step while Renatus stared, and I pushed him back. 'Aristea,' he said weakly. 'It's... Who's in the orchard?'

'It doesn't matter now,' I snapped. Hiroko flashed into existence beside Qasim, who was gathering Emmanuelle's limp form up, and the three of them disappeared before Jackson could get back to them. 'Better question: how'd she know about the ledger? About my charges?'

Nastassja addressed Renatus, not me. 'Scrier, Telepath, it's a very special mix. Sharing a mind. Sharing eyes.' She stepped into the aisle with us, unnatural green eyes that should have been brown holding his violet gaze. I tugged his arm to bring him back to the reality of the moment – that we were alone and surrounded and in a lot of danger without our magic – but he only vaguely handed me my other sai. 'I've wanted to see you for so long... to tell you everything. I've missed you... little brother.'

The former Ana Morrissey admitted this with a shaky smile, genuinely terrified of Renatus's reaction. Afraid of his rejection. For his part, I couldn't predict what he might do. He was stunned, overwhelmed. Lost. The last eight years, his whole vendetta, his *identity* was in sudden chaos, and with those powerful words of hers he was transported back a decade to when he had a big sister who meant the world to him.

Well, now he had a little one.

'Renatus,' I whispered, shifting my swords to a single hand and taking his again. The pressure went mostly unnoticed. I squeezed his fingers. 'We're in danger. I think they killed Emmanuelle. Get me out of here.'

His eye contact broke away from his not-dead sister's to look down at me. I didn't need to tell him I was afraid. Even dazed with shock, he should be able to read it in my face.

'Stay,' Nastassja urged. 'Both of you. Lisandro's gone, but we can go meet him. We can talk. We can be a family. There's so much to tell.'

Hiroko reappeared at our side, back for her last pick-up. Jackson was ready for her this time, firing an orangey ball of magic at her that ate straight into her ward. She back-stepped away from us, trying to escape the quickly burning spell that would soon break through her shielding. I cried out, casting a ward that didn't materialise, and the orange glow dissolved through.

It struck another ward and fizzled to nothing. But it wasn't my doing. Hiroko could sense its origin, and along with all the Magnus Moira members standing around, she looked up in the direction I'd come from.

Standing on a seat, staring at her, was Garrett Fischer. His hand was still extended. Hiroko straightened breathlessly, subconsciously touching the paper crane that had slipped out, hanging in full view. Garrett must have been able to see it from where he stood. Must have recognised it.

He Displaced, no real coming back to Magnus Moira's ranks after rescuing his sweetheart. Standing in his shadow, the other three boys looked at each other. Aubrey and Lisandro's spell on them seemed to have been shaken, but Josh was the only one I saw copy Garrett's example, taking advantage of this unguarded chance to disappear.

The violence and confusion seemed to wake Renatus up. He tightened his hand on mine and ran to close the few paces of distance between us and Hiroko.

'Don't!' Nastassja pleaded, at the same time Jackson pointed at me and exclaimed, 'The ledger!' The men and women around us moved in.

But Hiroko caught onto Renatus's elbow and then there was the void and then we were stumbling across the hill opposite Morrissey House. I tried to run toward it, magic flooding me again. Energies. Auras. But Renatus caught my shoulders.

'Get out of here!' he ordered me. Behind him, Qasim had almost reached the gate, carrying Emmanuelle like a ragdoll. No energy came off her at all, and she didn't move. Around us, sorcerers stepped out of nowhere, their auras fuller than ours, their magic ready. Any assaults bounced off wards I had built before I left here. Hiroko clung closer to me. Renatus shook me. 'You have to go. The house isn't safe. My mind isn't safe. Everyone is coming for that book.'

I understood, but also on another level, I didn't. I tried to hold onto him as he pushed me away.

'Where do I go?' I asked desperately, following when he turned on the two men closest to him, blasting them back with crackling red magic drawn from my bracelet. It was still on his wrist. He glanced back at me apologetically.

'Somewhere I wouldn't guess. Go. Please.' He looked to the side as Nastassja made her appearance, her aura swollen with power, the Elm Stone dense with magic on her left hand. Renatus started backing toward the gate where Qasim was holding it open with his foot, yelling for him to hurry. 'We're not done.'

I nodded, relieved and scared. 'Never.'

Nastassja looked between us and seemed to decide to deal with me first. Heart in my throat, magic pressing on my shaking wards, terror emanating in thick waves from beside me, Hiroko grabbed my wrist.

And we were gone.

epilogue

1998

Once the storm struck, it wasn't hard to disappear. Her mother wasted precious time trying to pack up the remnants of their picnic while her father turned his attention to dispelling the bad weather, frustrated when it didn't work. Renatus was the only one who seemed to recognise the danger they were in, and perhaps that was because he was closer to childhood and had not yet learned the arrogance of their father.

'Let's just go,' he called, his voice torn away by rising winds and then the roar of heavy rain coming at them with the speed of the stormfront. He started automatically for the house, raising a hand and a small ward to shield himself from the first rainfall, but it came down too hard to bother with. Water soaked his dark hair and leaves whipped from apple trees fluttered past his face.

'Run!' Ana shouted, pushing him between his shoulders when he slowed to look around for their parents. 'Go, across the lawn, go! They can take care of themselves.'

He broke into a run, aiming for the pathway out of the treeline, and his sister kept pace for a few steps before pulling up. He was fast, beating her at races by the time he was six. He would be alright. He could Displace back to the safety of the house. Snatching one last look at the only person here she cared about, her heart hurting with guilt at what she was about to put him through and missing him already, Ana activated the series of wards her cousin Keely had taught her. Invisible, inaudible, unscryable, untraceable. She turned away too soon to see that he looked back to check she was behind him.

The storm was as violent as Lisandro had promised. The winds bent unnaturally to his will, tearing branches from the fruit trees. She ran back the way she came, skirting past the abandoned picnic site and driving deeper into the darkening grove. She passed her mother, cowering beside a tree, shouting for Aindréas as sticks and water as heavy as stones thrashed her. Ana paused to kneel unsteadily, the majority of the storm's wrath flowing around her but not all, and swallowed her guilt. The gemstones she'd slipped into Luella Morrissey's pockets that morning were blockers, preventing her from casting any magic to defend herself.

'You're supposed to be my mother,' Ana said, surprised to find her own voice so thick and broken when she'd thought she'd come to terms with this betrayal. Brown eyes Ana herself had inherited squinted against the sharp rain, seeing nothing, unable to detect her own daughter right before her. 'You shouldn't have let him do this to me.'

'Ana! Ren!' Luella screamed, looking around wildly for her children and pushing fearfully away from the cover of the tree to go in search of them. Like she cared. Ana roughly shoved her back against the tree trunk, her ever-shallow anger surfacing without much prompt.

'After what you did to me, did you think I'd leave him alone with you?' she demanded of her helpless mother, holding tight against her blind struggles. Ever cool, ever distant, this was a desperation she'd never seen in the woman whose face her own had been modelled on. 'You don't deserve him. He's better off without any of us.'

A heavy branch carried by insane winds narrowly missed Ana's shoulder and slammed side-on into Luella. Her head snapped to the side and Ana threw herself back in horror, clutching her chest where a jagged rip tore at her soul. Lisandro had warned her it would feel like this, but she hadn't expected to be watching when it happened. Her mother slumped in the exposed roots of the apple tree, eyes open and unseeing, aura immediately extinguished.

Somewhere behind her, her little brother must have felt that same horrific tear. Ana hurriedly dug the spelled gemstones out of Luella's dress pockets and leapt to her feet. It felt beyond wrong to leave her here like this but it was what she'd asked for. She thought of what waited for her beyond the estate's back wall and it gave her the strength to hold her stomach contents down and get moving, fast.

Morrissey House had a special magic, woven by generations of the same family living here year after year, and one feature built in by some long-ago ancestor was a series of escape passages atuned to the bloodline. Some were invisible portals in walls and cupboards around the mansion itself, allowing the family to escape to and from any of the floors without needing to cast magic, so that even at death's door, unable to Displace or run, they still stood a chance. Thank you, paranoid ancestors. But the one Ana had found to be of most use was a door embedded into the wall at the very furthest corner of the estate, deep in the orchard. She and her cousins Caitlin and Keely had come across it while exploring as little girls, but only Ana had been able to see it. The Shanahan sisters had been insistent that there was nothing there but more stone wall. Sensitive to the bloodline, it could only be opened from the inside, leading straight out to the dense grove of trees behind the estate.

She'd thought she was the only one who knew about it.

'I thought this must be how you got out,' Aindréas said, his voice a shout to be heard. He stood opposite her, the door between them, and he held the nearest tree to keep from being blown off his feet. Ana frowned, checking her wards. 'I can't see you but I can hear you, thinking. You're my daughter. Of course I can hear you.'

Her father was cradling what looked like a broken arm and his face was bloody from a harsh graze. Lisandro's storm hadn't finished its job, obviously, if her least favourite person in the world was still standing.

497

'You didn't have to do this,' he told her, knocking a leafy branch aside when it flew at his face. 'We were sorry. Your mother…' He'd felt it too. 'No one's perfect, Anastasia, and children don't come with a guidebook. We made mistakes. We were trying to protect you.'

Renatus had mostly taken after their mother, cool and detached with little to say, but it was from their father's side that Ana had inherited her volatility. Her anger woke immediately; normally his rose to meet her, but now Aindréas seemed run dry. His wife dead. His daughter leaving.

'You don't take someone's memory if you love them!' she screamed, loosening her ward, wanting him to hear her. She wasn't sure how much carried through the crashing of thunder. 'You don't protect someone by hiding them from their past. You don't meddle with their minds and make them forget what they want, what they did, what they felt.'

'Of course you do,' Aindréas argued, bewildered. The most adult conversation they would ever have. 'If you don't know that, you haven't loved like we love you.'

He had good instincts and jumped back from his tree just before a dazzling bolt of lightning struck the topmost branch, illuminating the cracks in the bark. Breathing fast, Ana edged toward the door in the wall, but her father for once had no interest in fighting to keep her.

'I'm going back for your brother,' he called, grasping one tree then the next on his way back. Letting her go. Ana ran for the door.

'You won't have him for long,' she muttered, wiping her eyes, surprised to find them teary, and pressing her hands where a doorknob would be on any other door. It popped open and she spilled out into the mushy grass on the other side.

'Where have you been?' Jackson helped her up and drew her away from the open door, holding her upright in the wild winds. Their ring-in, Glassner, knelt beside the doorway to pick up his bloody bundle. 'The council is already on their way – Lord Gawain had some kind of watch on your estate we didn't know about. Lisandro's coming with him. You've got about sixty seconds,' he added to Glassner. The shaggy degenerate hoisted the dying teenager up in his arms and straightened.

'And after this, I'm in the clear?' he checked firmly, looking suspiciously between the rogue councillor and the bedraggled heiress. Ana's sickened gaze clung to the unrecognisable form of her dying cousin. Every inch of exposed skin bruised or slashed or just wet with the mixture of blood and rain, a shattered face that used to look like her own. Broken fingers flexed like they were trying to reach for her.

'I'm sorry, Keels,' she whispered while Jackson irritably reassured their henchman that they'd hold the door for him. Lightning flashed close by and thunder smashed and Ana's soul bled when, on the other side of the wall, Aindréas's life was cut short. It wasn't the last of today's tragedies. 'You should have remembered what happens when you take my things.'

Sean Glassner shouldered through the narrow doorway into the orchard, Keely's hand dropping unheld, her limp legs dangling in the saturated skirts of a dress identical to Ana's, and Ana stepped after him to watch him stagger through the trees.

'Lisandro just got to the gate,' Jackson reported to her, looking away as he listened. He frowned. 'He says what's your brother doing in the orchard?' He paused again. 'He's been hurt. We can't wait.'

Ana's chest tightened. This wasn't part of the plan; Renatus was supposed to be safe inside the house. She leaned through the door.

'Don't hurt my brother!' she shouted after Glassner, but he was out of sight. Jackson drew her away again, rubbing his hands together and preparing for the spell they'd worked on perfecting for the last three weeks.

'Ready?' he asked nervously. He didn't want to be here, she could tell, but he was doing this for Lisandro, out of loyalty. If anyone connected him to this storm, or to her disappearance, he'd be in Valero's prison with no magic by the end of the week, and his and Lisandro's quietly stirring underground movement toward freeing magic would be exposed and ended. He was taking a massive risk by being here, but Lisandro stood to lose even more, and had still ensured his friend was here to meet her.

Lisandro always came through for her. It was a universal constant.

'I'm ready,' Ana agreed, just as nervous but finding calm in the thought of the man she loved just a few hundred metres away, keeping the rest of the White Elm distracted and solidifying his alibi while Jackson's hands began to glow golden. 'Time to kill Ana Morrissey.'

The wind and rain buffeted them and some terrible draw on magic not far over the wall warped the world around them briefly, and because there was no time to run through and check what had happened, she dropped her hands into his.

Then everything went wrong.

THE END

Acknowledgements

First things first:

1. Thanks to you, reader, for making it to yet another cliffhanger ending after waiting so long.

2. Yes, I have started book 5.

While this was the longest wait for readers between Elm Stone Saga books, once I was on a roll with Haunted it was in fact the fastest to write. And once it was written, the processes that follow were smoothed along by the wonderful people in my life, and these pages are for them.

Thank you as always to Sabrina, fairy godmother of editing, formatting, design and publishing dreams. You go eternally above and beyond for me at every unreasonable turn I present you with, and I am grateful for your hard work, your talent and your friendship. Thank you for your beautiful work on the cover, building on the elements you and Laura-Jane have developed so perfectly across the series to make my books look so professional and gorgeous. Laura-Jane Kemp, who created the first three covers, was unavailable during cover development as she's enjoying her new life as a wonderful mum! The talent and vision of you two amazing ladies have helped my books find their way into hundreds of hands around the world and I'm so grateful to you both.

It's not just printing and design, though, that help books get into hands. Thank you immensely to the booksellers at the wonderful, generous stores who have supported me in my journey. Thank you to the team at Ouroborus Books who help sell my series at Supanova Brisbane and Gold Coast each year. Thank you to my fanfiction friends for not hating me when I take too long to update fics (I swear I haven't forgotten you!) and for continuing to cheerlead and support my book writing career. Thank you to the Bookstagram community for getting behind me and helping to spread my posts around. Thank you to every reader who has left a review online or recommended my books to someone else. Every bit helps and none of it goes unnoticed.

Making a book worthy of your recommendations and support isn't a one-person show, either. Thank you to my beta readers Brigid Kudzius and Dad for your input during the rewriting stage. Thank you to my enviably multilingual friends Jaroslav Košut and Katie English for help with translations, and thanks to Kirsten Lund for your ongoing friendship and support of this series. Thanks Kirsten and Jaroslav for letting me continue to drag your namesakes through my increasingly dark narrative.

Balancing life against writing a book of this size is no easy feat, but it's made possible by the people inside that life. Thanks to my supervisor Dallas Baker for everything you do to help keep writing on the table as I navigate academic life. Thanks to my teacher friends tribe at KP, especially Jenny, for encouraging me to take the leap out of the classroom, for believing in me and for so proudly supporting my writing. I wouldn't trade any of you for the world. Thanks to the seriously cool kids I have taught who still want to discuss books and writing with me, reminding me to keep my eyes on the prize. You guys inspire me endlessly. Thanks to your equally cool parents who are still following my writing and believing in you, too.

Becoming someone who wants to write, and who can, takes a village, and I don't think there will ever be an acknowledgements page where I don't make explicit thanks to my own teachers. Thanks for giving me the language to talk about my own writing and to critique it so I can keep making it better.

A book's themes are fuelled by the life and circumstances surrounding its production, and that has never been truer than it is for me with Haunted. Aristea interacts with a wider range of men in this story than ever before, and during the writing of this book, gender imbalance and negative male influences were a common media conversation. I wrote my way through those ideas, exploring Aristea's relationships with different male influences, and came to the conclusion that I owe thanks to the many upstanding, generous, strong, compassionate, thoughtful and hard-working men I have known in my life. Because of my dad, my brother, my husband, my grandfathers, my uncles, my male friends, my teachers and my colleagues, I have been freer than many others to believe myself equally capable of any ambition. Thanks to all the great men out there making the world awesome.

This has been a hard year for me and the deepest thanks go to those who have kept me loved and grounded through the tears that might have otherwise derailed important projects like this book. Thank you to all my beautiful friends, to Mum and Dad, to my grandparents and to my husband Matt. Thank you for believing in me always and for having a hug and a warm word ready whenever I need the extra love. These books happen because of you.

About the Author

Photo by Alena Gurenchuk   @alenagurenchuk

Shayla Morgansen is a whimsical language enthusiast and chronic daydreamer trapped in the body of a perfectionist control freak. She tries to divide her time between her lives as a writer, editor and academic, and spends any spare hours watching reruns of classic science fiction or working on her PhD. Shayla lives in Brisbane with her ever-patient husband and even more unread books than she had in the last bio she wrote.

You can follow Shayla on Instagram, Twitter and Facebook.